W9-AAT-281

THE DEVIL'S LIGHT

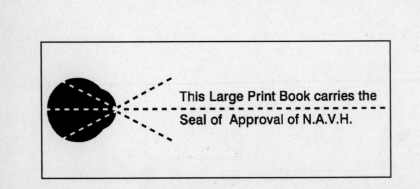

This Large Print Book carries the
Seal of Approval of N.A.V.H.

THE DEVIL'S LIGHT

RICHARD NORTH PATTERSON

THORNDIKE PRESS
A part of Gale, Cengage Learning

Detroit • New York • San Francisco • New Haven, Conn • Waterville, Maine • London

LIBRARY OF CONGRESS CATALOGING-IN-PUBLICATION DATA

Patterson, Richard North.
    The devil's light : a novel / by Richard North Patterson.
        p. cm. — (Thorndike Press large print basic)
    ISBN-13: 978-1-4104-3835-5 (hardcover)
    ISBN-10: 1-4104-3835-X (hardcover)
    1. Qaida (Organization)—Fiction. 2. Nuclear terrorism—Fiction.
    3. Pakistan—Fiction. 4. Large type books. I. Title.
PS3566.A8242D48 2011b
813'.54—dc22   2011012849

Published in 2011 by arrangement with Scribner, a division of Simon & Schuster, Inc.

Printed in the United States of America
1 2 3 4 5 6 7 15 14 13 12 11

For David Lewis

At ten o'clock on a night in late summer, a private aircraft ends a vertiginous upward climb by releasing a nuclear bomb over the city.

Seconds later, a missile turns the invader into an orange fireball against the night sky. As the bomb detonates in midair, a brilliant yellow light obliterates the darkness like a sheet of sun. After a last instant of silence there is a terrible explosion.

At the epicenter of the blast, the temperature is one million degrees Fahrenheit. Men and women on the sidewalks or in cars become ash; homes and apartments collapse into dust indistinguishable from their occupants; a massive wave sweeps the ocean, swamping boats and drowning anyone in them. For miles from its center the city is a radioactive scar without features. Farther out there are the photographic prints of buildings that no longer exist, imposed like shadows on the husks of ruined structures and charred bodies by the stunning light of the blast.

At its edge, walls of fire rise from nothing. On the highways ringing the city, cars collide, the eyeballs of their drivers and passengers turned to fluid. Others, also blinded, are buried in collapsing concrete or eviscerated by spears of falling glass. Birds ignite in midflight; a thick cloud of dust obscures the moon; airborne poisons fall like black rain; skin slides off the bodies of victims crying out in torment. The city itself is silent, the only movement ashes stirring in a nuclear wind. Two hundred thousand people no longer exist.

The slow death of a nation has begun.

Osama Bin Laden listened in silence, his long legs folded in front of him, his vitality drained by kidney disease, his liquid eyes still in a face so pale it seemed to match his whitening beard. When the narrator had finished, he said, "All this with a single bomb."

Sitting at the edge of the carpet, Ayman Al Zawahiri looked from Bin Laden to the narrator, his eyes darting and suspicious behind steel-framed glasses. With a voice thickened by emotion, Amer Al Zaroor replied, "I believe so, yes. If we use it well."

The words echoed in the stone cave, the Renewer's last refuge, concealed in the harsh mountains of western Pakistan. Its only comfort was the carpet on which they sat, light spawned by generators that, in the recesses beyond, powered the computers and cell phones that linked them to the world outside. Dressed in robes and turbans, the three men were alone and, for a moment, wordless. To Al Zaroor it felt as though Bin Laden's deep contemplation had rendered the others mute — the strange power, he supposed, of a man who faces death by holding fiercely to his vision. At last Bin Laden said, "A seductive dream, Amer. In which everything depends on our choice of targets."

Amer Al Zaroor nodded. "I understand this, Renewer."

"Do you?" Zawahiri cut in harshly. "Then surely you have weighed the consequences if such a dream becomes reality. You ask us to risk all."

Al Zaroor faced him, aware of the magnetism that his lean, handsome face and reasoned manner exerted on others — even Osama Bin Laden. "Our situation is bleak," he said. "We are inferior to the crusaders and Jews in knowledge, technology, resources, finance, and military training. Across the Muslim world we are betrayed by corrupt Saudi princes who have sold their souls to the Americans, the lackeys of the West in Egypt and Jordan, the infidels and compromisers in Pakistan, the apostates in Iran who posture as revolutionaries while siphoning their people's wealth." He turned to Bin Laden, and his words pulsed with quiet urgency. "There is one way for Muslims to defeat our enemies. A single blow so cataclysmic that it changes the world in an instant."

An odd light appeared in Zawahiri's face. *"Inshallah,"* he said. God willing.

Ignoring this, Bin Laden, the poet, remained true to a character that Al Zaroor revered — reflective, almost gentle, with a keen intelligence that required no bluster outside pronouncements crafted for the West. "Still, Ayman's caution is appropriate. After our triumph in 2001, the Americans nearly destroyed us in Afghanistan — only the stupidity of their adventure in Iraq revitalized our cause. Should your plan succeed, the fury of the West would be incalculable."

Al Zaroor looked at their surroundings, his gaze meant to summon meaning from the shadows in which his leader was forced to live. "We are dying," he said bluntly. "*You* are dying. Our operatives' slaughter of Muslims in Iraq stained us in the hearts of many. No longer are you more popular in Saudi Arabia than its king. No longer does your face appear on the T-shirts of the young, or your name grace Muslim newborns. Now the American president means to bind Zionists to Arabs with the palliative of an unfair peace. We are patient men, Renewer, but the years since 2001 have yet to prove our friend.

"What is required now is the ultimate act of asymmetric warfare. We would not be the first — in Hiroshima and Nagasaki, the Americans unleashed the devil's light on men and women and children. How can we do less without becoming cowards?"

Taken aback by their acolyte's directness, Al Zawahiri became as still as a figure in a frieze. Sitting straighter, Bin Laden rearranged his robes, then said calmly, "If time is not our friend, when do you propose to act?"

Al Zaroor repressed his elation. "It will take years, not months, and great adaptability. But I will aim for the one date so symbolic that it will magnify our feat: September 11, 2011, the tenth anniversary of our greatest triumph. To commemorate this at will would fill the world with awe, our enemies with dread."

Hastily, Zawahiri sought to break the spell he imagined that Al Zaroor was casting. "To acquire such a bomb is a task of great complexity, involving the help of many others. How can you guarantee operational security?"

Instead of answering, Al Zaroor met the deputy's eyes. Both men knew what neither would ever say: that, having conspired with others three decades before to assassinate Anwar Sadat, Zawahiri had betrayed them under torture. At last, Al Zaroor said, "You will have it, Ayman. If necessary, I will die to make this so."

Interceding, Bin Laden held up his hand, a gesture that combined blessing with admonition. "To act would be momentous. The power of final approval must be mine alone."

I pray you live to grant it, Al Zaroor thought. He bowed his head, signaling obeisance.

For a long moment, Bin Laden studied him. "God selects few men, Amer, to change the face of history. Perhaps you will be one."

Briefly, Al Zaroor glanced at Zawahiri. With the faintest trace of irony, he replied, *"Inshallah."*

■ ■ ■ ■

PART ONE
THE ATTACK
THE BLUE RIDGE MOUNTAINS —
INDIA — PAKISTAN
AUGUST 2011

■ ■ ■ ■

ONE

Two years after his near-murder in Beirut, Brooke Chandler visited his mentor, Carter Grey, to contemplate his future as a spy.

Headed for Grey's redoubt in the Blue Ridge Mountains, Brooke drove his Ferrari through the rolling Virginia countryside. The air of midafternoon felt hot and close. Timed as an escape from Washington in the steam bath of August, the trip was also a chance to see the couple who, given Brooke's routine deception of everyone he encountered, offered him the respite of intimacy and ease. The Greys had become his shadow family.

North of Charlottesville, Brooke turned off one country road onto another that narrowed to a dirt track winding through wooded foothills, ever higher, until he reached the Greys' retreat at the top of a ridge three thousand feet above sea level. A large wooden structure, it was the work of

Grey's hands, built before the wreckage of his body prohibited hard labor. Now it was home. Jutting from the site, its rear deck commanded a view of forested ridgelines receding in the distance, becoming shadows in a thin low fog that glimmered with reflected sunlight. This was, Grey had explained to Brooke, the fulfillment of a lifelong plan — to drink cocktails in his dotage while admiring a perfect view.

But the home was also the summation of a life. Perfectly maintained, it housed an astonishing collection of pristine guns from wars fought by nine generations of Americans — many forgotten, misconceived, or misunderstood — and carefully chosen rugs, art, and furniture from Grey's assignments overseas. Outside were satellite dishes for the television, computer, and communications equipment through which Grey kept in touch with a world where, usually in secret, he had once maintained the power to change events.

Those times, Grey had remarked to Brooke, were defined by the Cold War and the rise of the American empire, breeding a sense of mission that, while sometimes illusory, had made the work less soul-wearing. Grey was from the Kennedy generation: gentlemen spies whose mandate had been to shape history and who, in the end, were shaped by it. In succession, he had operated in Iran during the Islamic Revolution, served as station chief in Germany at the height of the Cold War, and helped precipitate the collapse of the Soviet empire by equipping a half million Afghans to fight the Red Army — while, he added ruefully, helping train the militia who formed the Taliban. Along the way he became the most decorated agent in the history of the CIA, honored as one of the fifty most important figures when the agency marked its first fifty years. But he had spent the last two decades as an administrator in Washington, barred by age and injury from fieldwork, until the toxic politics of the city had merged with debilitating pain to drive him to retirement. Now he was here.

Brooke got out of his car, savoring the crisp, cool air. At once the front door opened and Grey stepped stiffly onto the front porch. He appraised Brooke, then his expensive ride. "Still driving that toy, I see."

"The agency promised me a life of adventure," Brooke responded. "Now I'm reduced to dodging radar guns."

Grey grunted, a mixture of dismissal and comprehension. Then he hobbled down the front steps, fighting the weakness in his spine to hold himself erect. His head of steel-gray hair was still full, and Grey remained handsome in a way made craggy by age and adversity — if America was replicating the fall of Rome, he had once remarked to Brooke, then he was Roman ruins. What remained young were his clear light-blue eyes and the vigor with which, as always, he embraced Brooke Chandler like a son.

They might have passed for that, Brooke knew. Once, in a moment of remembrance as Grey slept, his wife, Anne, had told Brooke that he evoked her husband before the nightmare of Iran. Brooke had seen the photographs; Carter had combined the can-do alertness of a soldier with the strong, clean features of the all-American boy. Brooke had the same blond hair, a chiseled face that suggested his heritage, and the smile of a generation raised on fluoride and orthodontia. Brooke tried to wear his handsomeness lightly; he knew that he had been born lucky. Until a decade ago, the year before he joined the agency, he had endured no real hardship or disappointment. Despite the years since, he still looked it.

The two men smiled at each other. "I'd say that you seem good," Brooke said, "except that you'd remind me I'm a practiced liar. So how are you really?"

"Good in the morning," Grey said matter-of-factly, "medicated by two. Given that it's four o'clock, and I just got up from my nap, I'm trying to remember who you are."

"Don't worry, Carter. Anne will remind you."

Grey laughed without humor. "Marrying me really was the devil's pact. Twenty good years, and now she's practicing medicine and running a retirement home."

"She'd still make that deal," Brooke answered. "At your worst, you're never dull."

As if on cue, Anne Grey appeared in the doorway. Slight, blond, and quick of movement, Anne at sixty still reminded Brooke of a hummingbird ready to take flight. Grey had met her at the agency; as with other such couples, the secret existence they led distanced them from others, but provided a depth of understanding no outsider could grasp. For years in the field Anne had weathered this life as a partner. Now, moored to Grey by history and devotion, she had taken on living in the mountains as though it were another posting. The balm for Grey's regrets was their harmonious marriage, one Brooke had increasing trouble imagining for himself.

Skittering down the steps, Anne kissed him. "It's so good to see you, Brooke. For both of us."

"You, too. If your face weren't so mobile, I'd guess you were mainlining Botox."

She briefly smiled at Grey, including him in the badinage. "It's the air up here. The life suits us." Taking her husband's arm, she shepherded him back up the steps. "We keep expecting you to bring a woman for us to meet."

Brooke glanced at her, miming disbelief. "So you can watch me lie to her?"

Anne shot him a look of mock impatience. "Marry one of them and none of us would have to lie."

"It's harder than you think," Brooke replied. "I suspect Carter married the only woman who'd have him."

Now her expression mimed the solemnity of thought. "True. I was young and foolish then, easily distracted by sex and talk of foreign travel."

Grey conjured up a scowl of displeasure. "You got here just in time," he informed Brooke. "But it's too early for a drink, and I'm still too full of morphine. Let's attempt a walk and I'll describe the other women in my life."

"I already know about the one with the

navel ring," Anne replied. Kissing her husband, she added lightly, "Don't wear Brooke out."

Brooke heard her silent message: *Don't let him fall.*

"I won't stand for it," he assured her.

Their rear garden, Anne's work, bloomed with flowers and tomatoes. Grey prodded Brooke toward a walking trail beneath the shade along the ridgeline. He moved with determination, but the odd step was halting, marking back injuries and internal damage dating back to the fall of the shah over thirty years before. Risking his life, Grey had shed his cover as a diplomat to give an endangered Iranian agent — a member of the shah's intelligence service — money and false documents to facilitate his escape. On the way back, he encountered two members of the Revolutionary Guard, their loathing of Americans fueled by fanaticism and hatred of the shah's secret police. Mistaking the American "diplomat" for what he was — a spy — the two men decided to stomp him to death. They were well on their way when Grey located the gun in his suit coat. He killed them in an instant.

Spitting up blood, Grey crawled to his car, drove to a safe house, and slept for two days. Then he returned to the embassy, refusing to report his injury for fear of being ordered to abandon his post. When he finally endured the first of a series of operations that kept him alive, the surgeon who viewed his shattered organs and broken ribs and spine had told Anne, "This is worse than the worst car wrecks I've ever seen, and those patients died."

Grey lived on, but as a different man. Years later, he could still describe to Brooke the glittering zeal in his assailants' eyes. "That was when I realized," he concluded, "that America as a nation had no clue about what the hell this was about. Most Americans still don't."

Now they paused, standing on Grey's latest point of pride, a new bridge that crossed a rivulet still swollen with late-spring rains. Leaning on the railing, they watched the ridgelines as they softened in the light of early evening, two men at peace. At length, Grey asked, "So how *is* the Outfit now? For you, I mean."

"You know how it is," Brooke said flatly. "Maybe getting burned in Beirut wasn't a career killer. But being chained to a desk job makes me feel like the living dead. I still perceive everything around me, but can no longer speak or move."

His mentor glanced at him sideways. "They're keeping you safe. Though perhaps in the minds of some, you're serving a stretch in purgatory for the sin of being right."

Brooke shrugged. "Better than getting killed, I'm sure. What a joke of a death *that* would have been, taken out by a couple of amateurs from al Qaeda because my idiot station chief couldn't tell a double agent from his own unfaithful wife."

Grey laughed softly. "You don't get out of life alive. You were hoping to die for a reason?"

"Everyone dies for a reason. I was hoping for a better one."

"At least you helped the Lebanese break up an al Qaeda cell."

"I could have done more," Brooke objected. "When Lorber butted in, there was still work to do."

Grey gazed out at the ridges and valleys. "Dangerous work. Thanks to Lorber's blunder, you're more likely to die in bed at the age of ninety-five. The question becomes how you kill the time between now and then."

"Not this way. Serving as a bureaucrat erodes my sense of purpose. I've taken to reading analysts' reports on al Qaeda just to sate my curiosity."

"Which is a good thing," Grey opined. "You need curiosity, and you need to care about the work. Have you thought about becoming an analyst?"

Brooke shook his head. "I'm a field officer by nature. As long as I'm with the agency I want to serve where it matters. I've been stuck here too long."

"Granted." Grey eyed him more closely. "But I heard another element just now — 'as long as I'm with the agency.' "

Brooke fell quiet for a time. "I've started questioning my life," he acknowledged. "I've always accepted that foreign postings made relationships harder. So does deception. Not that I minded lying to foreigners — that's what we're supposed to do. But now I'm telling Mickey Mouse lies to neighbors, the women I meet, and friends who've spent years believing they still know me. Even my parents think I've got some desk job at the State Department."

"You're allowed to tell your parents, Brooke."

"And horrify my mother? She'd probably leak my identity to the *New York Times*." Brooke paused, then added with resignation, "Feeling distant from my parents is nothing new. But sometimes I visit my friends from graduate school — with sharp wives, and little kids they like — and I want a family of my own."

"Anne told me you were seeing someone. A lawyer, wasn't it?"

"We've broken up. Erin was no fool — she'd started calling me 'elusive.' I had to decide whether we were worth breaking cover for, and concluded we weren't." Brooke smiled a little. "Besides, it takes a special woman to help you live a lie. Which is why, in my expert opinion, Bernie Madoff never told his wife he was a crook."

"Maybe Madoff just liked lying," Grey parried. "I grant you I was lucky in Anne. The life imposes a certain solitude. Further complicated, in field officers, by the rules against romantic entanglements with foreign nationals."

Brooke raised his eyebrows. "I got entangled once or twice in Lebanon — it deepened my cover. But that's all it was."

"You're lucky to have gotten by with it," Grey said dryly. "I remember the case of one of our analysts, a Hindu, who started sleeping with his mother and sister . . ."

"Not at the same time, I hope."

"No. When confronted, our man said his transgressions were a matter of caste — he couldn't find a wife of his station in the entire D.C. area. Nonetheless, we fired him. Not for incest, mind you, but for sleeping with foreign nationals. We have our standards, after all."

Brooke could not help but laugh. "Thank God for that."

"Which reminds me," Carter continued, "wasn't there an Israeli woman left over from your former life? You once were quite attached to her, I thought."

"That was years ago. It's been five years since I told her my last lie."

Something in Brooke's tone of voice caused Grey to appraise him. "What happened to her?"

"No idea. After the war between Israel and Hezbollah, she simply vanished. No email, no phone, no nothing. For all I know she's dead."

Studying Brooke's face, Grey asked nothing more. "About your career," he said at length, "it's time for a think. And a drink." He hesitated, as though reluctant to ask a favor. "Mind helping me get back up the hill?"

Regarding his mentor with fond concern, Brooke resolved to stop complaining. "Anything for a single malt scotch," he said. But he knew Grey had more to say. His mentor had invested too much in Brooke's career,

and in Brooke himself, to remain silent
about his future.

TWO

Restless, Amer Al Zaroor paced a safe house in Peshawar, waiting in the night for a Pakistani general.

The city was a gateway to Afghanistan, a crowded maze where a man could disappear. Outside the building, a tangled web of electrical wires hung over a dusty street. When morning came, motorized rickshaws and brightly painted buses would belch exhaust into air so polluted that it seared the throat. The apartment where Al Zaroor concealed himself was dingy and featureless, with a flea-infested carpet that stank of dog urine, and one small window over which he had drawn a blind. It was not the sense of confinement that chafed his nerves; as a soldier of al Qaeda he had endured far worse, sustained by a vision of the future. But now he was relying on a man he hardly knew, who might have as many loyalties as his failing country had factions, and whose shifting interests might cause him to deliver Al Zaroor to traitors allied with America and the Jews, Pakistanis with even fewer scruples than their masters. His consolation was that this stranger's intermediary was a trusted leader of Lashkar-e-Taiba — the fearsome Pakistani jihadists — who had proved his mettle by planning the devastating attack on Mumbai less than three years before.

Like Al Zaroor, *this* man — Ahmed Khan — had been waging jihad since America had armed Muslim militia against the Soviet occupiers of Afghanistan. The most zealous fighters of that war became a fraternity. Thus, like Al Zaroor, Khan had extensive contacts among al Qaeda, the Taliban, LET, and the Pakistani military intelligence agency — the ISI — which had been among each group's earliest patrons. LET and the Pakistani army recruited heavily in the Punjab region; Khan and the general were cousins. Such was Pakistan.

Al Zaroor's cell phone vibrated in his pocket. When he answered, a man's voice said, "We're about to serve the curry."

A message from Khan.

The line went dead. Heart racing, Al Zaroor switched on CNN.

Nothing yet. The fare remained innocuous, a documentary on micro-financing in India. Watching and waiting, Al Zaroor thought about his first meeting with General Ayub.

They had faced each other one year ago, in this same dreary room.

Dressed in a tailored suit, General Ayub was slender, bespectacled, and wholly unprepossessing. He did not remind Al Zaroor of a warrior.

Ayub sat across from him, fidgeting. For minutes the two men circled each other with words. Finally, Ayub said, "I'm told that you want a device. A special one."

Al Zaroor gave a barely perceptible nod. After a moment, Ayub leaned forward, elbows on knees, hands clasped in the attitude of prayer. Softly, he said, "I control six."

Al Zaroor's alertness quickened. "Where are they?"

"In an underground vault beneath an air force base ringed by troops, sensors, and electrified wire. Like other such sites, it is secret. Few know that it exists, fewer know the precise nature of my responsibilities. Now you are one."

Al Zaroor's mouth felt dry. In a matter-of-fact tone he asked, "Tell me about the properties of this device."

The general took out a British cigarette, lighting it with care before inhaling deeply. To Al Zaroor, who had no such vices, the man had the air of an abstemious smoker, trying to conceal from others that he lived for each carefully rationed cigarette. "It is two hundred pounds," he said at length, "with dimensions suitable for a coffin. It is made to be delivered by plane. The intended target, as you must guess, is within India."

"And its security features?"

"Until it is needed, the triggering package is kept separate from the core. Even when assembled, there is an electronic code that must be activated before the device can detonate. Access to the code is confined to a few scientists and the technician who will accompany the device in flight." A note of entreaty crept into Ayub's voice. "As you can see, the barriers to unauthorized usage are considerable. It might well be easier to buy or steal highly enriched uranium and construct a device of your own."

"I don't want a technological problem," Al Zaroor said curtly. "The Japanese group Aum Shan tried such a project with millions of dollars and a team of scientists. They failed. I prefer to buy off the shelf."

"Then you would need the code," Ayub

parried. "Not even I possess it."

"For now, let's set that aside. How might an interested party acquire such a device?"

The general grimaced. "The most obvious way is to attack a base like mine. But that involves piercing an electrical fence manned by guards, and a second such fence around the vault itself. In between are several hundred soldiers." Ayub drew a breath, as if the thought itself made him weary. "You would need at least six hundred fighters willing to die in pitched battle. That would also create a commotion visible to the American spy satellites. The odds against you are great."

Al Zaroor stared at Ayub. Coolly, he said, "There are other ways, General."

Faced with this tacit reproof, the general spread his arms, trailing ashes and smoke from his burning cigarette. "There could be a mutiny, of course, where a commanding officer takes over a facility. But on what basis does he enlist his troops? Any man who risked this and failed would face execution."

"I would hate to ask such a man to hazard his life," Al Zaroor replied with an edge of irony. "Perhaps it would be best if he gave up the device in secret."

The general's body stiffened. Taking a last

drag, he ground the cigarette on the wooden arm of his chair. "How would this man smuggle it out without the complicity of others? Sooner or later, an inventory would be taken, and his own death would follow." His voice hardened. "I believe in jihad, but not as a martyr. I have no use for seventy virgins in this life or the next."

Al Zaroor smiled faintly. "You take us for primitives, General. Surely there are circumstances where the device is taken from its womb."

Ayub shook his head. "Only during a state of nuclear alert between India and Pakistan. Such accidents of fate are out of my control."

"Nonetheless, what would happen to your devices should Pakistan decide that it might use them?"

Ayub steepled his fingers. "They would be deployed for a possible second strike, from different airfields than the ones we assume the Indian air force would level. In the event of a first strike against India, our bombers would return to the new field. The devices would already await them."

"How do the devices travel there?"

"By secret convoy. Quite probably at night."

"And the location of these airfields?"

"Almost all are in the Punjab, close to India."

Al Zaroor nodded, eyes narrowing in thought. "Before moving the device, do you unite its components?"

"Yes."

"Then that reduces the technical problems, doesn't it. All that remains is to unlock the electronic codes."

Al Zaroor's calm caused a look of irritation to cross the general's face, closely pursued by worry. "You make this sound like a training exercise. The convoy would be heavily guarded."

"Still, General, if one knew where and when the bomb was moving, you wouldn't need six hundred suicidal jihadists to acquire it. A more modest plan might do."

Ayub scowled. "Then you're back to the element you conveniently dismissed — our security code, the so-called permissive action links that prevent accidental detonation."

"PALs," Al Zaroor said. "I've read of them — a clever American invention, designed to keep their own devices in transit from destroying Cincinnati. If the sequences of numbers entered to arm the weapon prove incorrect after several tries, the PAL system disables itself, rendering the device useless.

Rather like an ATM."

"Precisely."

"But isn't it also true," Al Zaroor prodded quietly, "that Pakistan refused to adopt a PAL system provided by America for fear that the Americans would disable its devices? The Pakistani system, in my limited understanding, is simpler. And, as you say, a trained technician from the air force can defeat it."

"That is true, yes. Assuming that you find him."

Al Zaroor kept watching his face. "But *you* could help us locate such a man, couldn't you. Or at least suggest one."

Ayub hesitated. "Perhaps," he conceded in an arid tone. "Then all you'd need is someone to provoke a state of nuclear alert between India and Pakistan."

Al Zaroor smiled again. "Please don't trouble yourself with that. I've asked enough of you, my brother."

THREE

After a dinner of steaks and fresh vegetables accompanied by a good Bordeaux, Brooke and Carter Grey sat on the deck, watching the stars above the purple shadows of the ridgeline. Brooke sipped Calvados; Grey, who now drank sparingly, settled for decaffeinated coffee.

"I don't quarrel with anything you've told me," Grey began. "The life exacts a price. And you got screwed in Beirut, cutting your work against al Qaeda short. Since then, Anne and I have sensed a certain weariness of the soul, the residue of some very hard years." Grey paused, softening his tone. "I also know why you joined, and how personal that is to you. What happened ten years ago could repeat itself all too easily. In a few swift strokes, the trifecta of transnational terrorism, Islamic extremism, and the proliferation of WMD could change the world as we know it — not only our security,

36

but our values. Not many Americans get that. You do."

Brooke took a swallow of brandy. "Does it matter?" he said finally. "As a nation we're addicted to wishful thinking, staggering from crisis to crisis with the foresight of a two-year-old. Think of all the people who nearly bought us a worldwide depression: financial parasites, greedy lenders, cowardly regulators, venal politicians, and millions of gullible folks who lived on charge cards and thought they could buy a house for nothing. Or a massive oil spill, where a soulless company was enabled by a spineless bureaucracy that gave them what they wanted, and a populace too blind to see that oil has become like crack. It's a moral failure on the most profound level, where everyone blames everyone else, and no one looks in the mirror.

"Apply that to our work. Before 9/11 Bin Laden did everything but advertise. Yet he had to blow up the Twin Towers just to get the serious attention of anyone outside the intelligence community." Brooke paused, then finished with weary resignation. "So what did we do? We invaded the wrong country, killed the wrong madman, and too often used the wrong interrogation techniques on the wrong people — all because our leaders lost contact with the truth."

Grey nodded. "A classic illustration of what I call Cheney's Law: Theorists sit in Washington jabbering about the world like the inmates of an asylum, until they create their own reality out of fantasy, never imagining the havoc they'll wreak. As for the Democrats, a lot of them live in the wing reserved for manic-depressives — on any given day, you don't know who they'll be. In either case, we become their whipping boy when things go wrong."

"I'm sick of it," Brooke said bluntly. "The Outfit's job is to prevent the Apocalypse. But what have we learned as a society since Bin Laden took down the World Trade Center? Our political dialogue is even more empty and corrosive. As long as neocons like Cheney invoke terrorism and adopt an air of gravity, the right listens even when they're babbling in tongues. Throw in the Tea Party folks, who think the president is ten times more dangerous than any external enemy. Then there are liberals like my mother and her rich friends, who have no more idea of what we're facing than a gaggle of spoiled children." Brooke's voice quickened with the frustration he could seldom express. "On 9/11 we were badly wounded by men without a country. These people want weapons of mass destruction; sooner or later, they'll have some. And unlike the Soviets or Saddam or the Iranians, you can't find them."

"But that's why you joined up," Grey argued. "In five years, someone like you will be the station chief in a tough place like Beirut. You represent the new breed of talent we've recruited since 9/11." He paused for emphasis. "Even among them, you stand out. You're an artist — imaginative, with a rare combination of operational and analytical skills. You can quote poetry in Arabic. You challenge conventional wisdom. Your guts and instincts kept al Qaeda from taking you out in Lebanon." Wryly, Grey concluded, "With a little extra seasoning, you'll be the equal of any terrorist."

"Or of any desk jockey in Washington."

"That shouldn't have happened," Grey replied. "But now they've brought back Noah Brustein as deputy director. He'll be quick to see you're being wasted."

"And when Brustein goes?" Brooke asked. "Our leadership has become a game of musical chairs where the occupants change at the whim of the political classes. Good or bad, they're gone in two years. And with every change, more good people think about leaving."

"Maybe so. But al Qaeda never quits." Grey placed a hand on Brooke's shoulder. "Give it time. There's nothing more important than what we do, and nowhere else to do it —"

From inside they heard a soft cry. At first, Brooke thought Anne had fallen; fearing both for her and Grey, he rushed inside.

Pale, Anne looked up from her chair. Pointing at the television, she said, "Someone just hit the Taj Mahal."

On CNN, the sacred site was rubble in which the marble domes had vanished, the graceful spires turned to stubs. Shocked, Brooke murmured, "Like Mumbai."

He felt Grey behind him. In a low voice, he said, "Then India will blame Pakistan. Pray they keep a lid on it."

Suddenly the image changed. In a tone he fought to keep professional, Anderson Cooper said swiftly, "Another plane has struck the Indian Parliament at the beginning of its morning session —"

The stately structure, Brooke recalled, also had a dome, this one ringed by ornate pillars. Now the dome was gone, and so must be many lives. Brooke had no more words. The thick black plume of smoke evoked a sickening memory of September 11 — the day had transformed Brooke's life, when he had begun to fear the next attack that could transform the country that had made him who he was.

FOUR

In Peshawar, Al Zaroor watched the television, pulse racing, as the shell of the Taj Mahal crumbled into ruins. When the picture changed, the Indian Parliament was charred concrete surrounded by ambulances whose sirens sounded like squeals of agony. Then the screen caught the anguished features of a female parliamentarian, a Hindu who described the carnage with tears running down her face.

Each image was as Al Zaroor had envisioned. He could almost feel the hatred searing the souls of Indians. His plan had sprung to terrible life.

The summer before, he had met with Ahmed Khan in the tribal areas near the Khyber Pass, a stronghold of the Taliban. Though the jagged hills were cooler, a pleasant change, both men were tired and sore — each had made the last leg of the trip on horseback. But this did not dim their pleasure in meeting again. At first sight they had embraced, smiling, two veterans who had survived the wars of their youth.

Much had happened since. In the time since the Mumbai attacks, Khan's master achievement, Al Zaroor felt an admiration tinged by envy. But he knew that Khan would not be satisfied until Pakistan, not India, held dominance over the Muslims of Kashmir.

The two men sat together on a rock, gazing out at the expanse of valleys and mountains still capped with snow. Studying Khan, Al Zaroor saw a stringy man on whom God had wasted no fat, his look of alertness hardened by time into adamancy. For a while they spoke of old comrades and where their lives had brought them. Khan had more to say: Fortune had given him a family and a home in Karachi, his safety protected by the ISI and friends in the Pakistani military — a difference that both saddened and freed Al Zaroor. As a principle of operational security, he had nothing to lose but his life.

At length, their talk became philosophical. "After all the years and battles," Al Zaroor asked rhetorically, "what have you left to fear?"

"Softness." Khan spat the word. "Our government's, not mine. America's civilian puppets in Islamabad desire a truce with India. The terms will no doubt be shameful: India's retention of Kashmir, which by rights should be a land for Muslims. There will be pressure from the West to shut us down."

Al Zaroor eyed him keenly. "So you're waiting for this to happen?"

"No," Khan rejoined. "And you? Is the Renewer resting on his laurels, watching Iran and the Shia Hezbollah wage their tepid version of jihad?"

The corner of Al Zaroor's mouth flickered at the jibe. "You and I still have much in common, Ahmed. On behalf of Muslim Kashmir, you were at pains to kill Jews and Zionists in Mumbai. We want to banish the Zionist entity from Palestine. Yet matters remain as they were. That should shame us both."

Khan gave him a sideways look. "Bravely spoken."

"We're not done yet," Al Zaroor said flatly. "Nor, I assume, are you. But your patrons grow too circumspect. Perhaps you need an investor to help you strike again." Al Zaroor softened his tone. "You want Pakistan to wrest Kashmir from India. The 'normalization' of relations between the two would utterly defeat your purpose. Despite your masterstroke in Mumbai, you did not succeed in estranging them. That calls for a shot to the heart of India."

Khan appeared nettled. Sardonically, he asked, "What greater act of boldness do you suggest for us?"

"To succeed where al Qaeda failed. On September 11, we dispatched two passenger planes to destroy the World Trade Center. Another damaged the Pentagon, the seat of America's military power. But a fourth plane was meant to level the Capitol and slaughter the senators and congressmen inside. Only a few unruly passengers thwarted us from wreaking utter psychic devastation on America, eclipsing two ruined towers filled with Jewish stockbrokers." He paused, finishing quietly, "Imagine that the face of our attacks was Capitol Hill in ashes. Then ask yourself what the infidels of India hold closest to their hearts."

Considering, Khan flicked his tongue across parched lips. "And you would help finance this?"

"We have the resources, certainly."

"And your reasons?" Khan paused, then added slowly, "I recall introducing you to my cousin, the general."

"Yes. Thank you for your courtesy."

Khan stared at him. "An attack of the kind you suggest would have consequences. The she-males in our civilian government would recoil; even our friends in the ISI might disapprove. The risks are considerable."

"As are the rewards."

"Perhaps. But there is also the question of methods. Do you expect us to hijack passenger planes? The martyrs of September 11 made that much more challenging."

Al Zaroor shrugged. "If this is a matter of airplanes, we can help you acquire your own."

"And fill them with explosives?"

Al Zaroor smiled a little. "You can supply the explosives, along with the martyrs to fly them." His tone became practical. "The Indian air force is very professional. But they have too much territory to cover, and too many sites to defend. In this they are like the Americans."

Eyes narrowing, Khan stared at the mountains. At length, he said, "The Americans are pushing the eunuch who masquerades as our prime minister into further talks with India. The goal is to emasculate our country, forcing it to abandon Kashmir." Khan faced Al Zaroor squarely. "I will use my sources to explore the risks of peace. Then I will meet with you again, if only as a courtesy. Whatever else I do will be in the interests of our brothers in Kashmir."

In the soft glow of the television, Carter Grey lit a cigarette, his first since Brooke had arrived.

Briefly, Anne glanced at him, then resumed watching CNN. Amid the rubble of the Indian Parliament, soldiers and emergency responders searched for survivors or the dead, giant figures on an oversized flatscreen. The images revived the most searing hours of Brooke's life.

"Lashkar-e-Taiba," Grey said without turning. "This is an act of desperation."

Anne glanced at the cigarette burning in his hand. "Why do you say that?"

"It's all about Kashmir. Most Kashmiri are Muslim, but the province belongs to India. The ISI wants to change that: Within the government of Pakistan, the military intelligence service operates as a shadow state of its own. The ISI helped create LET to fight a guerrilla war in Kashmir. A potential détente between India and Pakistan would be a mortal threat to their ambitions. That's why LET attacked Mumbai."

"Why didn't the Pakistanis shut them down?"

Stirring himself from the past, Brooke said to Anne, "The ISI won't permit it. After Mumbai, there were a few 'punitive' measures, all a charade. With the ISI's protection, LET continues to train hundreds of jihadists every year. Pakistan's nuclear arsenal gives LET a shield; if India invades Pakistan in reprisal for the actions of LET, it runs the risk of a nuclear attack." Turning to Grey, Brooke asked, "What odds would you quote me on reprisal now? Or nuclear war?"

Grey watched the picture shift to thousands of Indians in New Delhi, flooding the streets to express their grief and anger. "You know the history," he said wearily. "Before 9/11, LET hijacked an Air India flight to swap hostages for prisoners jailed by India, including an ally of Bin Laden's. A month after 9/11, they launched a failed assault on the Parliament they've now destroyed. That time, only the attackers died. But both countries mobilized for war. President Bush and Colin Powell had to use every ounce of influence to head off a nuclear nightmare."

Anne gently took the cigarette from his hand, grinding it out. "The Mumbai attack was far worse," she said. "Why didn't that cause another crisis?"

"Calculated restraint by India. But LET achieved its immediate goal — disrupting a rapprochement between India and Pakistan." Grey glanced back at the television. "Like this one, that attack involved intricate planning and operational sophistication. The fact that LET didn't claim credit allowed the ISI to protect its operations, using its cover as an Islamic charity. Now this."

In the semidarkness, Brooke forced himself to turn from the screen. "I assume this is LET's reaction to our pressure on Pakistan to focus on the Taliban."

"In part. Some senior officers in the Pakistani military resent that — as does the ISI, which provides the Taliban with clandestine support and allows it to move back and forth across the border to Afghanistan to kill American soldiers. But on a deeper level, this is about who controls Pakistan's nuclear arsenal — the civilian government or the army. Right now, the army does; the prime minister wants some say. My guess is that the army will use this opportunity to remind the civilians who decides when the arsenal gets deployed." As he studied the images of the dead and injured on the screen, both Indians and tourists, Grey's tone became somber. "After Mumbai, the Indians held back. But this time the bombs and missiles may be coming out of their hiding places. God help us if this tragedy goes

49

nuclear."

Turning to the screen, Brooke watched an EMT carry a corpse from the wreckage of the Taj Mahal. Bowing his head, he summoned as much of a prayer as his tattered beliefs could muster.

In Peshawar, Al Zaroor pulled aside the blind, peering into the crowded street. When he saw the car, he closed the blind, pausing only to watch the riot beginning in Mumbai, the faces of Hindus suffused with hatred as they started hunting down Muslims. Then he switched off the television and left.

The operation had begun.

FIVE

As dusk fell, Al Zaroor waited for the warrior so essential to his dream. Back against the thick trunk of a tree, he looked down from rolling hills at a two-lane road that ran through the verdant farmland of the Punjab. The air was hot and humid, very different from the place where he had first encountered Ismail Sharif. But he still recalled the jolt of recognition: in the face of this stranger, Al Zaroor had seen his younger self.

They sat at an outdoor café in the village of Madyan, a Taliban stronghold in the Swat, sampling pastries and drinking thick black coffee. The café was set on a green hillside sloping to a narrow river whose rushing current carried its own echo. Moved by the beauty of their surroundings, so different from the flat horizons of his homeland, Al Zaroor allowed himself a moment of serenity. Then he turned to face Sharif.

Despite his beard, the man looked alarmingly young, with a lineless face and liquid eyes in which pride warred with a curious vulnerability. But by reputation, Sharif was a skilled tactician who had mastered the art of ambush and surprise, slaughtering government troops through swift assaults in carefully chosen terrain. According to Al Zaroor's sources, Sharif was barely more Taliban than al Qaeda, a man impatient with inaction and devoted to God. But Sharif's hatred of the army involved more than principle: Government soldiers had raped his sister and killed a younger brother by driving nails into his skull. The coolness with which he exacted his revenge was a tribute to self-discipline.

For a moment, Al Zaroor looked deeply into the young man's eyes. Then he said, "I bring greetings from Osama Bin Laden, our Renewer, and Ayman Al Zawahiri. As I do, they wish to know if you're unafraid to die."

Sharif's eyes hardened abruptly, casting his face in a new light. "I'm more prepared to kill," he answered coldly. "Were that not so, I would not have killed so many soldiers in this land."

"Are you prepared to kill them in the Punjab?"

Sharif hesitated, then shrugged. "For jihad, it does not matter where. Only who, and why."

Al Zaroor nodded. "The assignment comes from the Renewer himself, and is vital to our cause. It will also require great skill."

"What is it?"

"On short notice, I will ask you to marshal three trucks and fifty or so crack fighters. For safety's sake, you will bring them through Baluchistan, where the army does not go, to a site at the edge of the Punjab. There you will assault an armed convoy of Pakistani soldiers, leaving no survivors, and seize an important piece of property."

Sharif cocked his head. "Gold?"

"It is gold to Osama. That is all I can tell you, my brother."

The young man put a finger to his lips, regarding Al Zaroor with a chill curiosity. Al Zaroor admired his self-possession — Sharif had mastered the human need to fill silence with words. At length, he said, "Describe the site."

"It is a road at the bottom of foothills near Multan, with ditches on both sides. The countryside is agricultural, the road lightly traveled. The convoy will come at night."

"How many soldiers?"

53

"Also around fifty, the best the army has."

Silent, Sharif turned, gazing pensively into the gorge below. Then he faced Al Zaroor again. "I will want photographs of the site, an air map of its surroundings. That will help define the operation. Likely I'll need plastic explosives, claymore mines, and rocket-propelled grenades. That requires money."

"You will have it."

"I'll also need to recruit men. My people prefer to fight in the Swat. Punjab is not their home."

"It is, however, where they can strike a great blow against those who invade their lands. Those who value money over jihad will have more than they've ever imagined."

Sharif studied him. "You're ripe with promises, brother. To what end?"

Al Zaroor gave him a look of deep sincerity. "Only the Renewer and Zawahiri can know. This much I will say to you: Our aim is to wound our enemies on a scale beyond anything you've ever dreamed, or will be able to dream again. Not just the infidels in Pakistan, but the Zionists, the Americans, and the Shia. You will avenge your brother and sister a thousandfold. You might even live."

"I plan to," Sharif said calmly. "We outnumber the army in the Swat. But in the Punjab the soldiers are many, and move with greater confidence. If this prize is as important as you say, an attack will bring them swarming like bees."

Al Zaroor sat back. He dipped his fingers in a bowl of water, removing the sticky residue of pastries. "Bring me a plan," he said. "By the night we carry it out, I will have arranged a great distraction for the army."

When Brooke arose before dawn, Carter Grey was switching from channel to channel. It was reflexive: For decades, Grey had been at the center of crises, making judgments that helped to shape events. Now he took painkillers and watched CNN.

Its focus was India. In communal prayer and protest, Indians filled the streets of major cities. The images saddened Brooke, and the next few sickened him — Hindus with guns and knives slaughtering hundreds of Muslims in Mumbai.

"Bad to worse," Grey said. "The Indians have bombed Pakistani army bases in Punjab. Troops on both sides have mobilized near the border, and there are rumors the Pakistani military has declared a state of nuclear alert."

"What's the White House doing?"

"What you'd expect. At our urging, the UN is meeting in emergency session. The president has asked for restraint. The secretary of state is on the way to New Delhi, then Islamabad, trying to stave off disaster."

Brooke's thoughts moved quickly, the residue of a broken sleep spent arranging puzzle pieces. "Let me try something on you," he said. "Suppose these attacks are about more than Kashmir."

Grey looked up. "In what way?"

"The stakes for LET are high. There'll be international pressure on Pakistan to shut them down; the civilian government will be forced to try. But what if this crisis results in a military coup by commanders sympathetic to Islamic extremists?" Brooke sat down. "To me, it's at least not unimaginable that the attacks in India didn't result from some reckless plan by LET alone, but from an agreement between LET and elements of the ISI, the army, and, conceivably, the Taliban and al Qaeda."

Though his eyes remained serious, Grey gave him a quizzical smile. "An all-star team of co-conspirators? It's possible, I suppose — the ISI is like the center of a wheel with jihadist spokes. It didn't just help create LET. The ISI supported the Taliban when they fought the Soviets in Afghanistan, and introduced its leaders to Bin Laden. Once the Soviets left, the Taliban became al Qaeda's host and protector with the ISI's blessing — when we tried to take out Bin Laden in a missile attack on a Taliban training camp, the ISI warned them in advance. After that the agency realized that the ISI was so riddled with jihadist sympathizers that joint operations were impossible.

"As for LET and al Qaeda, from the beginning al Qaeda helped fund LET. When al Qaeda operatives fled Afghanistan, they hid in LET safe houses. LET operatives helped support al Qaeda's attack on the London underground in 2005. All of which is known to senior leaders within the ISI." Brooke sat across from his friend, regarding him intently. "Consider what happened after 9/11. When we invaded Afghanistan, Bin Laden and al Qaeda took refuge in Pakistan — along with the leader of the Taliban, Mullah Omar, whose presence in Quetta is an open secret. The region where they're hiding out is controlled by the Taliban. We can't find Bin Laden there. The Pakistanis don't even try — there's too much support for al Qaeda and the Taliban within the ISI and the military —"

"No doubt," Grey interjected. "But the

Taliban and al Qaeda aren't synonymous. LET cares most about Kashmir; the Taliban is focused on Afghanistan and Pakistan; al Qaeda dreams of a worldwide Islamic caliphate. Some Taliban despise Bin Laden for bringing America down on their heads."

"True. But LET, the Taliban, and al Qaeda are all Sunni. Their leaders know each other, and many trained together. They're more than capable of making common cause against America or Israel." Brooke's tone became sharp. "When Benazir Bhutto returned to Pakistan with our encouragement, supposedly to stabilize civilian rule, she was assassinated in a crowd of ten thousand people. How do you suppose that happened?"

"My best guess?" Grey said. "A joint operation of al Qaeda and the Taliban, perhaps countenanced by her enemies within the ISI. But no one knows for sure."

Brooke nodded in acknowledgment. "What we do know is that senior leaders in the army and ISI hate America more than ever, as demonstrated once more when the ISI blew the cover of our station chief in Islamabad, forcing him to leave the country. Even moderates resent our pressure for an offensive against the Taliban, believe our buildup in Afghanistan is driving more jihadists into Pakistan, and think civilian deaths from American drone attacks have increased support for the Taliban. No matter that Pakistan is al Qaeda's epicenter, or that our drones have killed key leaders like Bin Laden's lieutenant Al-Masri. Our actions have tightened the operational links between the Taliban and al Qaeda, which may figure into what we're seeing now.

"The WikiLeaks leaks made public what we've known for years: that the ISI is still playing a double game — ostensibly supporting our operations, yet still aiding the Taliban and, at certain levels, al Qaeda. What matters to the ISI is control, which is why they arrested the Pakistani Taliban leader who started negotiating with the Afghans without the ISI's permission. The ISI may not mind weakening the Taliban enough to keep them at bay, while leaving them strong enough to represent the ISI's interests in a future Afghan government once we bail out." Brooke finished his coffee. "In the minds of the ISI and the military, the Pakistani army has a choice — focus on India and Kashmir, or fight a bloody war against the Taliban and al Qaeda. What LET may have done is bring matters to a head."

"Perhaps. But some of your overlords in

the Outfit will suggest you're turning boredom into fantasy."

This was true, Brooke understood. "Still, look at what the parties stand to gain. The military and the ISI can pursue their enmity with India, strengthening LET. The Taliban gets control of huge swaths of Pakistan without having to fight the army. Al Qaeda's haven becomes much safer. But there's far more. A lot of Pakistanis loathe their civilian government, not least for its incompetence in the face of last year's floods. And for Bin Laden, a coup in Pakistan would be a global game changer — a jihadist state. The prize is access to its nuclear arsenal."

For a long time, Grey thought, motionless. "We can be sure about one thing," he said at last. "Nuclear weapons make Pakistan the most dangerous place on earth."

Six

Waiting in the moonlit foothills, Al Zaroor saw a shadow moving toward him, then another, until they became a line of men moving single file, their bodies and weapons outlined against the night sky. Either they were allies or General Ayub had betrayed him. He reached for his Luger, prepared to kill himself or die.

Pausing perhaps thirty feet away, the leader raised one hand. In a quiet but resonant voice, Sharif said in passable Arabic, *"Shalom aleichem."*

Peace be with you.

The younger fighter, Al Zaroor realized, had a certain dark humor. He wiped the sweat off his forehead; even at night, the humid air was searing. "You have the trucks?" he asked Sharif.

"Of course," he answered tersely. "They're waiting near the road."

The men with Sharif formed a semicircle.

61

Turning from side to side, Sharif gave several curt orders. Then his men broke into groups, filtering silently down the grassy slopes toward the road — some carrying rifles, rocket launchers, or pickaxes, others burlap bags filled with claymore mines or plastic explosives. Scanning the hillside, Al Zaroor counted the fifty fighters Sharif had promised.

Now it will happen, he told himself — a kind of prayer.

In the dim light, the road was a dark ribbon on a ridge defined by an irrigation canal and, on the other side, the ditch dug to elevate the road above the farmlands. Men with RPGs and rifles hid in the canal; crossing the road, others vanished in the ditch. Two figures scrambled onto the road with pickaxes, perhaps two hundred feet from each other, and began pounding holes. The blows of metal on asphalt echoed up to Sharif and Al Zaroor.

Toward the bottom of the slope, a tier of men deployed claymore mines at ten-foot intervals. "We tried them on mud walls," Sharif remarked. "Placed in this formation, they should be far more deadly than machine guns."

The men with the pickaxes finished their work. Kneeling, they hastily planted plastique, smoothing the road before stringing wire that ran to the irrigation canal. Al Zaroor's cell phone vibrated in his pocket.

"Is it ready?" he asked.

Ayub answered rapidly, as though not trusting the untraceable cell phone Al Zaroor had provided for this call alone. "The package should reach you just before midnight. The earlier delivery is not for you."

"Will there also be a party?" Al Zaroor asked. Meaning a state of war.

For a moment Ayub was silent. "That is unclear," he finally said, then added in a lower voice, "The sky above you will be quiet; with so much commerce, we have no planes to spare. Receiving the delivery is your sole concern."

The phone went dead. Turning to Sharif, Al Zaroor said, "They're sending a decoy, but no air cover. Darkness will be our friend."

Wincing, Carter Grey approached the shooting station behind his home. He set down the rifle, bending backward to relieve the spinal pain that shortened his useful hours.

"Why not concede now," Brooke said, "and spare yourself the humiliation?"

The jibe — intended as an offer unpoisoned by sympathy — produced a grunt from his mentor. "When I'm dead," Grey said between gritted teeth. "Maybe not then."

Brooke understood. To watch a crisis deepened Grey's loathing of passivity and the injuries that had compelled it; to forfeit their annual shooting match would sharpen his sense of defeat. The hour Grey had chosen, ten in the morning, exposed the diminishing time wherein he continued to function well. "First or last?" Grey inquired.

"Last. That way I'll know how hard to try."

Grey picked up the M-14 that he had acquired during the Vietnam War, scrupulously maintained ever since. Then he turned and aimed at a target stretched over an armor plate sixty yards away. His shot — punctuated by the ping of metal — was three inches from the bull's-eye. Silent, he peered through the scope at the bullet hole, then gave the weapon to Brooke.

Feeling its weight, Brooke wondered how many lives had ended with a twitch of this trigger. The Outfit had taught him many ways to kill, including with weapons like this. But he had saved his own life by crushing an assassin with the door of his car. A pointless end to a mission cut short by a stupid order.

Aiming, Brooke pulled the trigger, placing the shot just inside Grey's.

Eyeing the bullet hole, Grey said, "I passed on our musings to Noah Brustein — attributed to you, of course. I didn't want him to think it resulted from an overdose of morphine."

"Gracious of you, Carter."

"Nonetheless, I've been thinking about this. With respect to nuclear proliferation, the U.S. and Israel worry about Iran. When Iran gets the bomb, the result will be dangerous: a crisscrossing pattern of nuclear armament among unstable Arab governments — some of which collaborate with, or are threatened by, jihadists." Grey took back the rifle. "But Iran itself won't use the bomb. They have a return address, and Israel would annihilate them. The real problem is nonstate actors."

Turning, Grey squeezed off a shot just inside Brooke's. "And that brings you back to Pakistan," Brooke said.

"Inevitably." Grey passed Brooke the rifle. "There's no country with more terrorists per square inch, and its nuclear program has always been a sieve. For twenty years, the founder of its nuclear program, A. Q. Khan, ran a clandestine supersale of technology to the Libyans, North Koreans, and

Iranians — to the worst regimes he could choose. At the same time Khan gave Pakistan an arsenal designed for delivery to India by F-16s and intermediate-range missiles, concealed in secret locations —"

"Secret from us," Brooke interjected, "with some exceptions. As you pointed out, the only people who *do* know where the weapons are hidden, the military and ISI, are riddled with mercenaries and jihadists. Worse, some believe in sharing nuclear technology with their Muslim brothers. One of the reports I read quotes a former head of the ISI as saying, 'The same nuclear capacity that can destroy Madras, India, can destroy Tel Aviv.' " Brooke faced the target. "We know al Qaeda is rebuilding their capacity to carry out operations around the world. That's why I was ferreting out Qaeda sympathizers in Lebanon, at least until Lorber blew my cover. Once they have a target and the means of delivery, all that's left is to acquire a weapon. They only need one."

Brooke aimed the rifle, sighting with greater care. Again his shot was just inside Grey's, the last of four horizontal holes that ended two inches off center.

Grey turned, eyes narrowing as he regarded the target. Then he picked up the rifle, flinching a little before aiming with such stillness he appeared not to breathe. Squinting with the ping of the bullet, Brooke saw the near-perfect bull's-eye. It was a measure of Grey's satisfaction that he made no comment. Instead he asked, "What kind of weapon?"

"A bomb, not a warhead. Stealing or buying a missile powerful enough to deliver a warhead creates too big a problem in technology and logistics. A bomb is easier to smuggle."

Grey looked at him keenly. "So how does al Qaeda lay hands on it? One way, I suppose, is a mutiny — a rogue general takes over an air base with an underground facility, claiming that he's securing it in the face of some crisis. Then the general gives a bomb to al Qaeda."

"Depending on who's in power," Brooke observed, "they'd hang him. No doubt they'd torture him first. He'd have to be truly committed." Holding out his hand, he said, "Care to give me the rifle? Or are you conceding?"

"What's the other scenario?" Grey asked.

"The one we seem to have now — a state of nuclear readiness. The maximum danger of theft is when weapons are convoyed to an air base through a countryside filled with armed jihadists."

"The Pakistani air bases are in the Punjab," Grey noted. "Al Qaeda and the Taliban are concentrated in Baluchistan and the North West Frontier Province. The last thing the army would do is move bombs in either area."

"They won't try. They would only move bombs in Punjab. Which makes the kind of operation we're talking about risky and complex. But not impossible for al Qaeda. And consider what al Qaeda could do if they succeeded." Brooke took the rifle from Grey's hand. "You might suggest to Brustein that we comb whatever scraps of intelligence we're getting for signs of anything suspicious. No way the Pakistanis will tell us a bomb has gone missing."

Again, Brooke faced the target, clearing his mind. No mercy, he decided; anything less would show disrespect for a man he cared for deeply. He aimed and fired with the same deliberation Carter Grey had shown.

Again, the bullet pinged off metal. Taking the rifle, Grey peered through its scope at the target. "Where's the hole?"

"There is none. I put it right through yours." Brooke handed Grey the gun. "Call it a draw, Carter. We've got a nightmare to watch on CNN."

Grey placed a hand on Brooke's shoulder. They walked toward the house in companionable silence.

Suddenly a brief vivid memory flickered through Brooke's mind: the first time he had fired a rifle, years before. The place was a rifle range in Connecticut; his instructor had not been a CIA trainer but the one woman, Brooke realized, whom he had ever truly loved. She had beaten him; smiling, she acknowledged that the Israeli military had taught her well, and that their contest was unfair. But that had been a different time, and Brooke Chandler a different man.

SEVEN

The convoy appeared as dark shapes in the night, their headlights doused — four trucks, led and followed by land cruisers with machine guns mounted on their hoods. Kneeling with Sharif on the grassy hillside above the road, Amer Al Zaroor murmured, "This is not the one."

Through his radio, Sharif said a few words in Pashto.

Below them the vehicles sped past, their drivers oblivious to the men hidden on both sides. Al Zaroor noted with satisfaction that the front and rear of the convoy fit within the stretch of asphalt bounded by the two lines of plastic explosives. Glancing at his watch, he said, "Perhaps twenty minutes. Our target will look much the same."

He knew this from General Ayub. A larger formation, Ayub had explained, would draw too much attention, and their resources were spread too thin. The target convoy would be identical. The land cruisers that led and trailed would be manned by three Pakistani soldiers, a driver, and two machine gunners. The first two trucks were empty, serving as decoys and spares; the last carried twenty rangers from an elite fighting unit founded by the CIA. The third truck concealed the bomb, guarded by ten more rangers. In all, thirty-six skilled soldiers in a convoy moving at maximum speed.

Al Zaroor's mouth felt dry. The attackers' timing must be exact, their discipline flawless. Only on paper were such plans perfect.

Sharif's profile betrayed nothing. Perhaps when young Al Zaroor had been this calm; now he only hoped to appear so. Leadership began with self-discipline.

Sharif cocked his head. "Listen."

Al Zaroor heard the faint snarl of motors, the whisper of rubber on asphalt. At a bend in the road, moonlight caught the shadow of a land cruiser, then a truck behind it. Reflexively Al Zaroor checked his watch: 11:56.

"Yes," he said.

In a clipped tone, Sharif transmitted instructions. His fighters were invisible in the night; Al Zaroor could not tell if they had heard. A prayer formed in his mind.

The entire convoy appeared now, moving

at sixty miles an hour. The vehicles were spaced too far apart, Al Zaroor realized with alarm. Taut, he counted the seconds until the lead land cruiser crossed the first line of plastic explosives. He willed the trailing cruiser to cross this line before the leader reached the last one.

The first cruiser sped on. Thirty yards, then twenty —

"Now," Al Zaroor urged.

As the trailing vehicle neared the first line of plastique, Sharif spoke a single word. Somewhere below, a fighter pressed a detonator.

A loud explosion lifted the lead cruiser upward, toppling it onto its side as soldiers fell to the asphalt. A split second later the next detonation caught the front wheels of the last cruiser, swallowing it whole. With a metallic crunch, the first truck drove headfirst into the smoking crater left by the plastique. The truck behind it squealed to a stop.

Their quarry was trapped.

Cries came from the road. The rear panel of the last truck flew open. Soldiers spilled from the inside, bent low, scurrying with weapons pointed to surround the truck holding the bomb. The trucks on both sides of it shuddered with direct hits from RPGs. Their gas tanks exploded; caught by flames, a burning, writhing figure emitted a wail that pierced the babel of shouted orders. Placing the radio to his lips, Sharif said, "Claymores."

From the hillside thirty mines detonated at once, each expelling three hundred lethal pellets across a five-foot range. The men facing the hillside crumpled like prisoners at an execution. The one soldier not decimated fell to his knees, blindly returning fire before he pitched forward. In the light of the burning wreckage, Al Zaroor saw the heads of Sharif's fighters appear above the ditch on the far side of the truck, their fusillade cutting down the soldiers who faced them. Dying, a wounded ranger staggered into a wall of flames.

The gunfire trailed off. There was a single shot, a fighter putting a bullet through the skull of a man writhing on his back. Then Sharif began loping down the hill, Al Zaroor at his shoulder.

Fighters poured from both ditches, surrounding the only truck that survived. "Take it," Sharif snapped into his radio.

Launched from the shadows, an RPG blew open the rear panel. At once a mass of fighters fired semiautomatic weapons into the truck, the sound of the bullets pinging off metal mingling with the cries of the soldiers inside.

As the firing ceased, Sharif and Al Zaroor climbed onto the road.

Al Zaroor glanced around them. The only word for this carnage, he decided, was "biblical." The rangers decimated by the mines were doughy masses of ruined flesh and khaki, illuminated by the flames of burning vehicles. Al Zaroor stood over a man with no face.

Turning, he followed Sharif to the rear of the truck. With the same eerie calm, Sharif raised a flashlight to inspect its contents. Ten Pakistani soldiers lay around a gray steel container like sacrifices at an altar. The container was shaped like a coffin.

Softly, Sharif asked, "What is this?"

Al Zaroor stifled his awe. "Gold, as I said. With this we wage jihad."

His tone brooked no more questions. Walking away from the truck, he spotted two black vans waiting on the far side of the blast hole. "Carry it there," he called to Sharif. "Quickly."

On Sharif's orders, four fighters scurried into the truck. Within seconds, they had borne the heavy steel box into the irrigation ditch, hurrying along the side of the road. Sharif and Al Zaroor followed, watching them as they labored up the slope toward the vans. "The second one," Al Zaroor instructed.

The men opened its rear panel and shoved the box inside. The first van sped into the darkness, a decoy. As Sharif's fighters began filtering into the night, Al Zaroor looked into the young man's face. "You are a warrior," he said. "But far more."

Sharif's eyes glinted. "Peace be with you," he said. This time without irony.

Al Zaroor jumped into the remaining van beside a nameless stranger half his age. "Go," he directed.

The operation had taken nine minutes.

Two swift miles later, they swerved onto a rutted dirt path. In the shadow of a tree sat a Pakistani van, its surface festooned with the intricate colors favored by freelance truckers.

A squat bearded man got out. He adjusted his turban, then helped Al Zaroor's driver move the box from one van to the other. The first man did not know where the box was going; the second where it had come from. Wheels spinning, the van headed for the highway.

For once, Al Zaroor thought, perfection.

For forty minutes Al Zaroor and his companion drove without speaking, moving at a clip impossible on such a road unless the driver knew it well. The truck slowed to a stop on the banks of the Indus River.

Its broad waters were peaceful. On its far side lay deserts and mountains, the harsh land of Baluchistan; beyond that Afghanistan. The powerboat that would cross the river was moored near its reedy banks.

Two men waded ashore, their pants legs rolled up. Silent, Al Zaroor pointed them to the van. As his driver opened the rear door, they slid the metal coffin from the truck. Al Zaroor thanked the driver, the first words of their journey. Then he drove off, severing another link in the chain.

"We must hurry," Al Zaroor told his new companions.

Helping them lift the container, he felt its weight for the first time. A sharp pain shot from his spine through his leg. Too many battles; too many jolts from horses or pitted roads. Clamping his jaw, he moved with the others.

Knees bent, they descended the bank, then waded into the waist-deep waters, container hoisted like a casket. With a grunt of relief, Al Zaroor helped push it inside the powerboat. One man helped pull him up; the other fired up the motor.

At half-speed, the pilot steered them toward the far bank. But for the thrum of the engine in their wake, the waters were silent and still.

The far bank was flatter. Gliding close to shore, the men slid the bomb from the boat and quickly returned to their craft.

Ahead of Al Zaroor, another dark form appeared in the half-light. The black van stopped in front of him. Jumping out, two al Qaeda fighters greeted him in whispers.

Straining, they lifted the container into the van. As Al Zaroor clambered into the front, he felt the sweat drenching his shirt. All this in an hour, he thought.

They sped into trackless desert, avoiding the Indus Highway and bypassing the low-slung town of Dera Ghazi Khan. Again they used no lights. All Al Zaroor saw were the outlines of mud huts, one no different from another. Only his driver knew where they must stop.

Abruptly, he did. The men leaped out and laid the container on an arid patch of earth. Then the second man drove off, leaving Al Zaroor and the other man on foot.

For grueling minutes punctuated by fleeting seconds of rest, they carried the container to its destination, perhaps two soccer fields away. It was a mud structure like any other — open windows and a door, a wire fence to hem in chickens. Inside the fence was a wooden cart made to be hauled by donkeys.

Getting out, Al Zaroor scanned the skies. He saw nothing but stars; heard only silence. "Move the cart," he ordered.

The young man stepped inside the fence, straining to pull the cart. Its movement exposed a low ridge of fresh dirt and chicken droppings. Stepping over the ridge, Al Zaroor stared into a hole in the earth six feet long and three feet wide, the dimensions of a grave. But this grave was lined with car batteries.

Hoisting the steel box, Al Zaroor and his partner carried it to the hole. The younger man climbed down inside. With the aid of ropes, the two men maneuvered the container into its resting place. Then Al Zaroor pulled his companion out.

Wordlessly, the two men took shovels from the cart and started pitching dirt into the hole. Somewhere in the night, Al Zaroor knew, the van that had left them was speeding toward the Afghan border. The driver believed that the two men and the container were now in a second truck, headed in the same direction, and that his mission was to clear their path. Perhaps the army would catch him, perhaps not. If caught, he would put a bullet through his brain.

As Al Zaroor had told Bin Laden and Zawahiri, it was a matter of operational security.

Zawahiri's words of doubt had echoed in the cave. "Why not exfiltrate at once?" he had demanded.

"They'll expect that," Al Zaroor said evenly. "There will be search parties and checkpoints — if they're not too proud to call the Americans, also spy satellites peering from above. It will be hard to reach Afghanistan; harder to get through the Punjab and out to sea." He faced Bin Laden, his tone quiet but persuasive. "The army will form concentric circles from the site of the ambush, trying to find the bomb. Best to make it disappear."

Bin Laden pondered this. "For how long?"

"Perhaps a month. Enough time for the search to cool off, allowing the hunters to think the bomb has left Pakistan. The last thing they'll believe is that it's a hundred miles from where we stole it."

"And if they find the others, Amer?"

Al Zaroor shrugged. "What could any of them say? None will know the men before or after them in the chain. None knows where the container is headed — a ditch seeded with batteries to prevent detection of radioactive materials —"

"One man will," Zawahiri cut in. "The man who helps bury the bomb."

Al Zaroor faced his antagonist. "With respect," he said slowly, "leave this man to me. I will assure that he's reliable."

Pausing to rest, the young fighter leaned on his shovel, wiping his brow with his shirtsleeve.

Al Zaroor backed two feet behind him. Taking the Luger from his belt, he aimed at the back of the man's skull, hesitating for a last split second. His finger squeezed the trigger. There was the concussive pop of bullet on tissue and bone; the man's arm fell to his side, as though he had finished wiping. Then he toppled into his grave.

Motionless, Al Zaroor gazed down at the body sprawling gracelessly across the steel cylinder. *I'm sorry, my brother. But you are neither the first nor the last.*

Al Zaroor picked up his shovel. With quick rhythmic thrusts, he covered the corpse and the bomb, then concealed the disturbance of earth beneath chicken droppings. The strain of pushing the cart back in place shot fresh pain down his leg. In the distance he heard the whine of helicopter blades.

Hurriedly, he left the fenced area and entered the house.

It was bare save for a mattress, an oil lamp, and enough provisions to last a month. Al Zaroor felt unspeakably tired.

Sitting against the mud wall, he closed his eyes, listening to the whir of Pakistani choppers as they searched for a nuclear bomb.

"He's more tired now," Anne Grey said quietly. "There's no respite from pain, and no time during which Carter has been braver or more stoic. Or, despite my best efforts, more miserable."

Brooke felt a fresh sadness, the confirmation of his instincts and observations. Briefly, he glanced at the muted flatscreen, seeing new pictures of violence in India, then looked toward the door of the bedroom where Grey slept in midafternoon. "Is there a fix for this?" he asked.

"Surgically? Maybe yes, maybe no. But at Carter's age and condition, the risks quadruple." Anne's voice grew softer yet. "Two nights ago he told me, 'I'm staying with you as long as I can. I see no future on the other side.' Carter lacks the consolation of faith. Except in the people he loves, like you."

The words touched Brooke more than he could express. "If there's anything I can do —"

A telephone rasped. Anne stood, then realized that the sound came from a phone used by Grey alone. The third ring was cut short.

Glancing at Brooke, Anne fell quiet. On television, the secretary of state spoke with no sound, her face weary and haggard.

Abruptly, Grey's bedroom door cracked open. Hair mussed with sleep, he hobbled into the great room. "That was Noah Brustein," he said without preface. "We've picked up heightened activity in Punjab — soldiers, planes, and helicopters on the move, a lot of chatter from military communications. We're trying to focus our satellites."

"Where in the Punjab?" Brooke asked.

"Near Baluchistan. In terms of war with India, that makes no sense. And a coup would focus on Islamabad and Rawalpindi." Grey stood straighter. "Brustein wants me to consult," he told Anne bluntly. "Mind driving up to Washington?"

Brooke watched the concern in Anne's eyes commingle with resignation and, perhaps, a trace of gratitude toward Noah Brustein. "I can pack for us in minutes," she answered. "I learned that in Iran."

Facing Brooke, Grey's smile for Anne lingered. "You're coming, too," he said. "I told Brustein that you're intolerable when bored. Trying to fend off Armageddon should keep you amused."

■ ■ ■ ■

PART TWO
THE THREAT
WASHINGTON, D.C. — PAKISTAN —
DUBAI — LEBANON
AUGUST 2011

■ ■ ■ ■

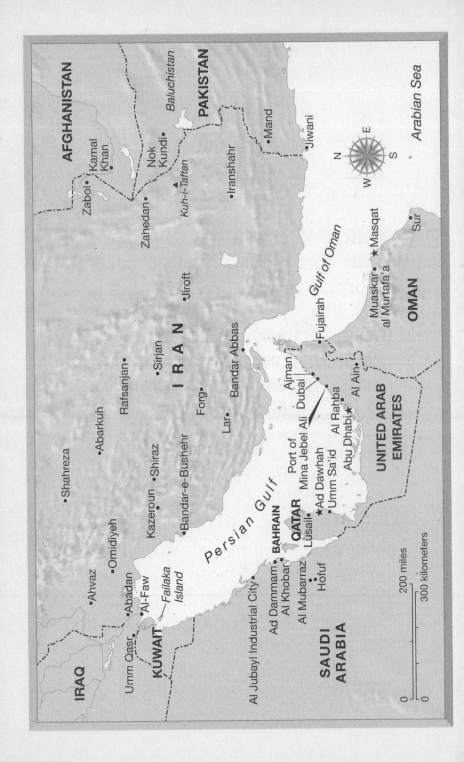

ONE

Just before six the next morning, Brooke Chandler drove from his brick town house in Georgetown to CIA headquarters in Langley, Virginia.

Though cut by the breeze of his convertible, the early morning air felt hot and close, the harbinger of an insufferable day. Switching on NPR, Brooke heard what he already knew — though their troops were massed at the border, the tenuous truce between India and Pakistan was holding. There was no word about the problem that obsessed him.

His mind kept racing, even while registering everything on the highway around him. As he took the off-ramp to Langley, the white SUV in front of him stopped abruptly. At once Brooke slammed on his brakes, glancing over his shoulder for a second car intent on blocking his escape. There was none. As a stray cat skittered from beneath the SUV, Brooke expelled a breath and then laughed softly at himself. His training, and Beirut, were imprinted for life.

In minutes, he passed through the security barriers into the cloistered world of American intelligence, 250 wooded acres banded by electronic fences, sensors, and warning signs. The massive building at its heart, the George Bush Center for Intelligence, was the length of three football fields, a seven-story grid of windows and offices that housed Brooke's unit. He parked, then walked swiftly through the entrance.

His first impression of this vast marble hall remained vivid: the seal emblazoned with an eagle and embedded in the floor; the statue of Wild Bill Donovan, the World War Two spymaster who became the agency's godfather; the ninety stars chiseled on the wall — now increased by jihadist bombings in Afghanistan — commemorating agents killed in service, some of whose identities remained secret. At the rear was a statue of George H. W. Bush, revered within the agency for raising its morale in a time of trouble and adversity. There had been too many directors since, Brooke thought, often faced with much the same mission. As now.

Heading for the elevator, he passed a hall of exhibits limning the history of the CIA. The one that held meaning for Brooke was placed at the entrance — the metal scrap of a safe-deposit box taken from the Twin Towers, melted beyond recognition by heat estimated at 1800 degrees. On the odd day he would pause there, quiet. It was the nearest Brooke Chandler came to prayer.

Today, without stopping, he took an elevator to the seventh floor.

The hallway was long and white and sparsely decorated, its doorways serving as entries to vaults of offices sealed off from the others and locked at night. Brooke's office was also spare, a ten-by-twelve box with a floor-to-ceiling window and an L-shaped desk equipped with a computer, a small-screen TV, and two telephones — one a secure line on which he could call any CIA station in the world. In the corner was a burn bag for disposing of classified documents. The only photograph on the desk was of Ben, his closest friend, and Ben's new bride, smiling at Brooke from the summer of 2001.

Brooke was reaching for his secure line when it rang. "We're meeting in Brustein's office," Grey said brusquely. "You're wanted."

By agency standards, the deputy director's quarters were commodious, with a desk, leather chair, bookshelves, and a seating area containing a couch, more chairs, and a table on which one could place coffee or papers. Crowded around the table were Grey, Noah Brustein, and several administrators with whom Brooke had varying degrees of familiarity: Frank Svitek, head of operations, a stocky, crew-cut man with merry eyes and a doctorate in English literature; Ken Sweder, who ran the counterterrorism center, known for his slender build and perfect dress as the most elegant spy in Washington; Michael Wertheimer, a senior analyst who specialized in Pakistan, and whose keen eyes and gold-rimmed glasses evoked for Brooke an extremely crafty accountant.

The man he knew least, Noah Brustein, was the new deputy director. Though Brustein's name conjured for Brooke an orchestra conductor rather than an operative, the man's appearance fit his reputation. An ex-marine, Brustein was barrel-chested and extremely fit, with close-cropped hair, a trim beard, and ice-blue eyes. Once a storied field agent, Brustein was fiercely loyal to the Outfit, and his return from a lucrative consulting business had cheered an agency buffeted by politics and a bewildering succession of new directors. Shaking his hand,

Brooke remembered another facet of Brustein's reputation — that his grip could maim you for life.

Brustein sat across from him, commencing with the directness he was known for. "We're picking up more indications that the Pakistanis may have lost a nuclear weapon. Carter tells us you've already been mulling this."

"An unlucky guess," Brooke answered. "In a country riddled with jihadists — including in government — it was a matter of time. The best time is when weapons are moving."

"You said more," Wertheimer interjected in skeptical tones. "According to Carter, you posit a possible arrangement among LET, al Qaeda, and the Taliban to bring on a state of war."

Brooke poured some coffee, then faced him. "Tell me I'm wrong, and I'll be happy. Can you?"

Wertheimer pursed his lips. "We don't even know if a bomb is missing. We don't think the prime minister of Pakistan knows, either."

"No surprise there," Ken Sweder put in. "The army thinks nuclear weapons are only for grown-ups. If someone snatched a bomb, their first concern is to protect their

91

own position."

"Are we absolutely certain," Grey asked, "that a faction of the army didn't steal it? Perhaps as a precursor to a coup."

"We're not," Brustein responded. "But what we're seeing is activity in the area of Baluchistan near Dera Ghazi Khan — helicopters, roadblocks, deployments of troops in areas the army usually avoids. It feels more like a manhunt than a mutiny."

Brooke spoke to Wertheimer, the skeptic. "Which plays into a conspiracy thesis, Michael. To steal a nuclear weapon takes meticulous planning — not just the theft itself, but how to get the weapon out of Pakistan. That requires months, if not years, of arranging. You don't just up and steal a bomb because LET blew up the Taj Mahal. Please credit the possibility that LET's attacks on India didn't *precede* the plan, but followed from it."

Wertheimer frowned. "You're suggesting an act of genius."

"A few such geniuses exist." Turning to Brustein, Brooke asked, "What are the Pakistanis saying?"

"Nothing, and we're not pushing yet." Brustein scowled. "As you well know, our speculation about a missing bomb is subsumed by a larger worry — the threat of nuclear war. Right now the president's working the phone with the prime ministers of India and Pakistan, and the secretary of state and the chairman of the Joint Chiefs are ping-ponging between Islamabad and New Delhi. One of the keys is pressing the Pakistanis to roll up LET, which only the army and ISI have the power to do. At least until we have more proof, we can't start accusing them of losing a weapon and covering it up."

For the first time, Svitek spoke. "We're working it," he said with a trace of defensiveness, "and so's the new station chief in Islamabad. We still have our own friends in the ISI and senior command. Problem is, a lot of them are massed at the Indian border, or caught up in planning for war. And we can't start flying surveillance planes over Pakistan in the midst of a nuclear alert."

Carter Grey, Brooke noticed, held himself carefully, the effort to keep his back straight showing in his eyes. "There's another barrier," Grey said. "The senior Pakistani generals are absolutely consumed with India. The last thing they want is to give us an excuse to come in after their weapons. Even if the situation weren't so fraught, we don't know enough to go in uninvited." He looked from face to face, pausing at Brustein. "If our guess is right, whoever took this weapon is smart enough to know all that. They may even hope that we do come in, throwing the country into turmoil and empowering the jihadists. So the immediate focus has to be who took the weapon, and where it may be going."

Wertheimer put down his coffee cup. "As to who has the apocryphal missing bomb," he told Brooke in his driest tone, "Carter says you know that, too."

Brooke inclined his head toward Sweder. "So does Ken — better than anyone. Not the Taliban, LET, or a pack of mutineers."

Nodding, the head of counterterrorism addressed Brustein. "Al Qaeda makes sense, Noah. We're all aware of their self-concept — Islamic warriors fighting to create a caliphate from Spain to Indonesia and, beyond that, to bend the world to their will. In his own peculiar way, Bin Laden is a romantic. But taken on their own terms, Bin Laden and his inner circle are also extremely rational — the exact opposite of the illiterate knuckle draggers who still dominate the Taliban. Bin Laden studied economics, and Zawahiri is a physician. The rate of college graduates among al Qaeda activists is higher than that of Americans. Almost none of them, if you believe our psychologists, has significant mental pathology.

"The result is a bizarre but potent combination — an apocalyptic vision pursued with cold-eyed realism. Their plan is to wear down America and its allies by creating al Qaeda franchises throughout the Islamic and Western worlds, building an infrastructure that can stage attacks so terrifying that we'll beg for mercy. A nuclear detonation would be the ultimate strike."

Brustein listened impassively, then turned to Grey. "What do you think, Carter?"

Grey moved in his chair, as though to relieve his back. "I'm with Ken and Brooke. The Taliban, LET, and the Chechens work within a region — they don't want to blow up their own territory, and don't have the means to strike beyond it. In contrast, we know that Bin Laden is allying with jihadist groups in key countries — that's what Brooke was uncovering in Lebanon. Al Qaeda's history is one of operational daring: not just their greatest successes — the USS *Cole,* 9/11, and the London subway attacks — but the ones we managed to interdict." Grey looked at the others. "The general public doesn't know that al Qaeda smuggled antitank missiles from Yemen to assassinate Vice President Gore in Saudi

Arabia, or put a team in Bangladesh to blow up *Air Force One* and President Clinton with a surface-to-air missile. Bombing shopping malls doesn't interest al Qaeda at all. Their goal is our complete psychic devastation.

"Take 9/11. Khalid Sheikh Mohammad's first proposal to Bin Laden was to fly additional planes into iconic targets like the White House, the FBI, and the building we're in now." Grey's tone became sardonic. "A final plane bearing KSM would touch down in Los Angeles, whereupon he would alert the media and deliver a riveting speech demanding that America transform itself. Practical man that he is, Bin Laden vetoed the press conference and scaled down the hijackings. But what al Qaeda accomplished changed the world as we know it."

For a moment, Brooke stared out the window, frozen by an image far different from the wooded glade surrounding them. "What Osama never dreamed," he heard Svitek interpose, "is that after 9/11 America would go out of its way to save him. Any analyst who wasn't brain dead knew the World Trade Center was Bin Laden's work, and certainly *not* Saddam Hussein's. We had the sonofabitch on the ropes in Afghanistan, and nearly buried him in rubble at Tora Bora." Svitek's voice held a quiet bitterness.

"So what did we do? We redeployed the commandos hunting Bin Laden to find Saddam Hussein; diverted our troops and intelligence assets to Iraq; and gave al Qaeda fresh recruiting opportunities across the Muslim world. In return, Bin Laden created a Sunni–Shia civil war that turned our occupation of Iraq into a bloodbath — all for the pleasure of hanging Saddam. The term 'crack-smoking stupid' leaps to mind.

"Since 9/11, Bin Laden has built the first global terrorist organization in history — cells in over sixty countries, with sophisticated communications and financing. They've struck in London, Casablanca, Madrid, Algiers, Islamabad, New Delhi, Saudi Arabia, Jordan, and Egypt. They took out Benazir Bhutto. Every day they hit targets in Iraq, Yemen, Pakistan. In Afghanistan, a double agent blew up seven of our colleagues. An al Qaeda operative trained in Pakistan tried to blow up a passenger plane over Detroit, another attempted to demolish Times Square with a truckload of explosives, and more seem to be coming at us damn near every week. And we still don't know where Bin Laden is, or even if he's alive."

"Pray he's dead," Sweder said flatly. "Zawahiri is a worker bee, with less operational

97

ability and judgment impaired by hatred. Bin Laden is special."

Grey sat straighter, drawing attention before he spoke. "Alive or dead," he said with quiet authority, "Bin Laden is a rare leader in the history of the world. He lets no personal grudges cloud his thinking — early on, some of us misread him as merely spiritual, even ethereal. But Bin Laden alone had the capacity to envision and create the network we're describing. Viewed with dispassion, Osama Bin Laden is a truly exceptional man. Only a Western capital in ruins would be worthy of his achievements."

The room fell briefly silent, each man weighing his own thoughts. "For twenty years," Sweder reminded them, "Bin Laden has been obsessed with nuclear weapons. He tried to buy highly enriched uranium in South Africa, and he negotiated with Chechen separatists for a bomb they'd stolen from the Soviet arsenal. But Pakistan has always been his focus." Ever meticulous, Sweder paused to straighten his tie. "He has links to A. Q. Khan, the ISI, and scientists within the Pakistani nuclear program. We also know that just before 9/11, Bin Laden and Zawahiri met in Afghanistan with a leading Pakistani scientist and a prominent engineer, both of whom shared his belief that a nuclear holocaust would fulfill al Qaeda's perverted notion of the Koran. They even sat around the campfire drawing up specifications for an al Qaeda bomb. But Carter and Brooke may well be right. Why build your own when you can steal a better one off the shelf?"

Brooke turned to the group again, glancing at Wertheimer. "Michael's principal question," he told the others, "is whether al Qaeda could motivate LET and the Taliban to help. I don't know how much al Qaeda would tell them. But a proposal that empowered jihadists, toppled the civilian government in Islamabad, and got us out of Pakistan and Afghanistan might be too seductive for its brethren to resist. As for using nuclear weapons, people with countries fear retaliation. But men in caves call them 'war winners.' "

Wertheimer, Brooke saw, listened with new intensity. "So what's al Qaeda's plan?" he asked.

"Nuclear disaster," Grey answered crisply. "After 9/11, al Qaeda announced its intention to kill four million Americans to balance the Muslim deaths they attribute to the U.S. and Israel. Then Bin Laden issued a fatwa openly calling for the use of nuclear weapons against the West. A Pakistani bomb would destroy an entire city. That would cause widespread death and devastation, stagger the world economy, unleash a wave of fear that could curtail our civil liberties, and create mass sentiment for withdrawal from the Middle East." Facing Brustein, Grey concluded, "In Bin Laden's mind, such an act would command deep admiration throughout the Muslim world. With America gone, there'd be nothing but a few enfeebled Arab states between al Qaeda and its dream of an Islamic caliphate."

Brustein rested his chin on steepled fingers, then faced Sweder. "Assuming that al Qaeda has its weapon, where do they plan to set it off? Your people ponder that question night and day."

"And weekends," Sweder answered tersely. "Our very long list starts with Washington and New York."

A flash of doubt pierced Brooke's consciousness. But he could not yet work out why.

Two

On entering his office, Brooke took out a map of the Middle East, well thumbed from his service in the region. Perhaps inevitably, his thoughts turned to the woman who had returned there, to Israel, and the year that followed their first encounter, its final day the fault line that divided him from the man he had been before.

They had met on a warm fall night in Greenwich Village. It was September 2000; Brooke was twenty-five then, headed for a master's degree from NYU in Near Eastern Studies. School came easily, and it was early in the semester. So Brooke decided to meet Ben Glazer, his closest friend since Yale, for dinner at Trattoria Spaghetto, consuming pasta and Chianti at an outdoor table while observing the usual array of eccentrics.

"After this," Brooke informed Ben, "there's a student forum on Israel and the peace process. I thought you might be interested."

Ben raised his eyebrows, feigning bemusement as a means of tweaking his friend. On the surface the two were opposites. Blond and athletic, Brooke carried himself with a careless ease — the legacy, Ben insisted, of "six generations of WASPs whose only tragedy was inbreeding." By his own admission, Ben was the antithesis of aristocratic panache — short, round, bearded, and Jewish, a would-be master of the universe at an investment banking firm. But the bluff kindness at Ben's core served a humor and directness that drew men and women alike. It was Ben, not Brooke, who had the smart and beautiful fiancée. And Brooke savored his friend's impatience with euphemism and evasion, his gift for speaking hard truths that sometimes made his listeners squirm. The fact that Brooke was unoffendable did not dishearten Ben at all.

"A disenchanted evening in the Middle East?" Ben asked in disbelief. "Why? They're crazy, all of them — Hezbollah, Hamas, the Orthodox Jewish settlers, the Arab terrorists in caves. By now you must have noticed how much these God-bit visionaries relish killing each other's kids. But sooner or later they'll start killing ours.

102

Fanaticism has no respect for borders."

Brooke repressed a smile, pausing to admire a tall blonde who sauntered by their table. Noting this, Ben admonished, "She looks too much like you. Diversify now, or your children will be idiots."

Brooke gave his friend a look of amiable tolerance. "Entrapping Aviva has made you smug. As for this forum, your world is shrinking. You sit peddling derivatives on the ninety-fifth floor, never noticing the inexorable shriveling of your soul. You need a break from lusting for excessive compensation."

Ben grinned sourly. "My father, the gravestone magnate, always said college professors lived in the ether. You'll be perfect."

Brooke had never doubted that Ben would go with him.

The auditorium featured bright lighting and theater-style seats that, as Ben pointed out, were lacking in soft drink holders. Settling in, he remarked, "We should have rented *Lawrence of Arabia*."

The forum had already started. One of the two speakers, a massive Orthodox Jew from Brooklyn named Jacob Sklar, was vigorously denouncing Arafat, the Palestinians, and the peace process promoted by

President Clinton. Sklar's older brother, it emerged, had emigrated to the no-man's-land at the edge of Israeli settlements on the West Bank, inspired by the biblical God who had reserved it for the Jews. As Sklar finished, Ben tartly encapsulated the man's worldview — Sklar's personal Jehovah had stuck Palestinians on a lower branch of His evolutionary tree. As the landlord of a Greater Israel that included the West Bank, God wished no Arab to be His tenant.

But it was the peace advocate who drew Brooke's attention before she said a word.

Her name was Anit Rahal, the program informed him, an Israeli taking a junior year abroad after four years of service in the army. In an offbeat but arresting way she was extremely pretty — small and wiry, with jet-black hair, dark crescent eyes, olive skin, sharp, well-defined features, and a somewhat sardonic grin. She listened to her opponent with a stillness and concentration that, for Brooke, accented her appeal. Yet he sensed a caged energy about her. It did not surprise Brooke to learn, as he later did, that at school in Tel Aviv she had excelled in track — as a sprinter, he guessed correctly. Everything about her seemed bred for survival.

At last the moderator, a middle-aged

professor, interrupted Sklar's monologue. "How do you respond, Ms. Rahal, to the assertion that Jewish dominion over the West Bank is a biblical imperative?"

"That my God has never mentioned it," she told Sklar briskly. "You see three million Palestinians as squatters. I see them as our Siamese twins. For centuries Jews had no country; now Palestinians don't. There will be no peace until they do."

Her English was flawless. Though Brooke noticed the stray guttural enunciation that marked Hebrew as her first language, someone with a lesser ear would have taken her for a New Yorker — she had the directness of manner to match. Leaning closer, Ben observed, "Gets to the point, doesn't she?"

Clearly, her point was not lost on Sklar. "By a 'country' for Palestinians," he retorted, "you must mean Greater Israel."

Anit waved a hand. "I call it the occupied territories —"

"What you call 'occupied,'" Sklar interrupted, "is the Jewish land of Samaria and Judea. You would mutilate it with borders of your own devising, telling God's children where they can and cannot live. This is sacrilege."

Rahal gave him a thin smile. "Your synonym for sanity, it seems. But this much should be clear to anyone — Israel cannot incorporate the Palestinians on the West Bank and survive as a Jewish state. Unless you mean to deny them the right to vote, like the stateless Palestinians confined to refugee camps in Lebanon —"

" 'Stateless,' " Sklar repeated with palpable outrage. " 'Confined'? For over a decade Arafat and the PLO used Lebanon as a launching pad for terrorist attacks on the diminished patch of earth you define as Israel. Only when we attacked them did we eliminate the threat."

"To what end?" Now Rahal's tone conveyed weariness and disdain. "The slaughter of Palestinians — some women and children — at Sabra and Shatilah by Christian militia empowered by Ariel Sharon? Caging Palestinians in refugee camps that serve as a breeding ground for hatred? Helping to empower another threat to Israel, the Shia terrorists of Hezbollah, through the indiscriminate bombing of Lebanese civilians? There is *no* end, and all our wars provide none."

Rahal's quickness of tongue, Brooke perceived, was enhanced by an intensity of manner that seemed close to aerobic — gestures, nods, swift shakes of her head. But he caught something more: Though roughly

Brooke's peer in age, she seemed older, grounded in a reality harsher than that of the other women he knew. "Don't mistake me," she concluded in a level voice, "Israel has real enemies. I'd sacrifice my life for its survival. But our very existence is threatened by a permanent state of war."

The student audience, Brooke noticed, seemed to pay her rapt attention. Inclining his head toward Ben, he murmured, "The Israelis need a way out of Palestine —"

"War," Sklar was saying, "is the only sane response to terrorists with no regard for human life. The settlers are the Jewish bulwark, our first line of defense. Would you ask my brother to abandon his home?"

"Yes, some must leave," Anit acknowledged. "I know this would be a tragedy for your brother. But if Israel wanted protection, the settlements were a grave mistake. Soldiers leave more easily."

To Brooke, she had captured the nub of the problem — a historic error, maintained through two generations, had placed Jewish families in the way of peace. "Whoever asks us to leave," Sklar said fiercely, "our duty is to resist them — Jew or Arab. Your belief that Palestinians will honor your betrayal is the pipe dream of a child." His words came as swift as gunfire. "They mean to kill us all. Arafat can't make peace — his own people would tear him to pieces. Instead they keep on breeding. The most deadly bombs of all are the wombs of Palestinian women. Their children will come for you unless we expel them first."

"In cattle cars?" Rahal inquired in acid tones. "That's not a pretty image. What destination do you propose?"

Sklar waved a stubby hand. "Australia or Canada. Certainly not the Middle East — even other Arabs can't stomach Palestinians on their land. It's only people like you who haven't noticed."

With genuine fascination, Brooke watched Rahal control her anger, the effort bleeding into the chill of her voice. "One notices many things, Jacob, when not listening for the voice of God. One is that the Palestinians aren't going anywhere. You'd make us and them scorpions in a bottle, bent on consuming each other." She paused, then achieved a calmer air. "There's no safety for Jews in oppressing or expelling others, imposing on Arabs the hardships we've endured for centuries. Our only hope is to create a place where Palestinians have the joys and challenges of a normal life, and the ability to live it. Anything else is doomed."

Ben's expression, Brooke noted, had

become thoughtful and intent. "She's right," he remarked at length. "The Greater Israel people are on a suicide mission. The question is who goes with them."

At the end, the audience gave both speakers sustained applause, especially Anit Rahal. Though she nodded in acknowledgment, her eyes did not change. Brooke swore he could read her thoughts — most of the audience were Jewish progressives, and their approval was foreordained; the rest were equally disdainful of Palestinians and of Jews less militant than they. She had debated for an hour and changed no minds. Brooke supposed this was what fatalism looked like on the face of a twenty-five-year-old woman.

Standing apart, Rahal and Sklar lingered on the stage, speaking with whoever approached. "If you don't mind," Brooke told Ben, "I'd like to talk to her for a minute."

Ben looked at him sideways. "This is novel. You *are* aware she's Jewish, right?"

"Is that a problem?" Brooke inquired blandly.

"Maybe for her. I just thought your taste ran more to deracinated Gentiles from New England. As previously noted, I've resigned myself to being the honorary uncle of kids with sloping foreheads and defective hips."

"I'm more venturesome than that, pal. Ms. Rahal has a certain allure."

Ben grinned. "Beauty isn't everything — yours or hers. *This* woman strikes me as daunting."

"Nonetheless," Brook answered with a shrug, "so goes the lemming to the sea." With that he began a lazy but purposeful stroll in the direction of Anit Rahal.

A claque of admirers still gathered around her. He waited at the outskirts until, at last, they were alone. Rahal looked at him with raised eyebrows; Brooke sensed that she had noticed his presence without seeming to. Extending his hand, he said, "I'm Brooke Chandler."

Her firm grip came with a querying look. "You sound as if I must know you. Should I?"

Brooke was amused, partly at his own discomfiture. In seconds this woman had nailed a sense of entitlement to which, Ben pointed out, Brooke was sometimes oblivious. "I just thought it was good manners," he responded. "I also thought you were impressive. Agreeing with what someone says is one thing; respecting how they say it another."

She nodded briskly. "I should thank you, then. That's good manners, too."

This woman gave no openings. Hastily, Brooke said, "I'm a grad student in Near Eastern Studies. I was hoping we could sit down sometime. I still have a bit to learn."

A skeptical smile appeared at one corner of her mouth. "So you're a scholar, in search of quotidian knowledge."

Caught, Brooke could only laugh. "I thought it was a passable cover story."

Anit Rahal gave him a long look of appraisal before allowing the smile to curl both sides of her lips. "I prefer honesty," she said. "You're certainly nice-looking enough. I can spare an hour to find out if you're smart."

Ben, Brooke thought, would have loved this.

THREE

Three hours after the emergency meeting, Carter Grey came to Brooke's office, his face seamed and pale. Before Carter could speak, Brooke said bluntly, "Get some rest. You can't last this way."

Grey shook his head. "We've confirmed the missing bomb through sources in the ISI. The president has started a task force. I'm taking you."

Standing at once, Brooke went with him to the director's conference room, ready to help if his friend stumbled. Sitting beside Grey, he took in the setting: mahogany walls; photos of former directors; the American flag beside that of the CIA. The room was equipped with secure phones, a bank of computers, televisions monitoring CNN and al Jazeera, and several teleconference screens — a nerve center in crisis. The faint metallic hum in the air, Brooke assumed, was meant to thwart surveillance.

The others were already seated at a long, burnished table. Brooke knew most on sight: Alex Coll, the president's national security advisor; the deputy secretaries of State, Defense, and Homeland Security; the deputy director of the FBI; senior administrators from Immigration and the Drug Enforcement Administration. Among those representing the CIA were Noah Brustein; Ken Sweder of the Counterterrorism Center; Frank Svitek of Operations; senior analyst Michael Wertheimer; and, by teleconference, Carl Holt, the station chief in Islamabad.

Coll ran the meeting. Curtly nodding at the newcomers, he continued speaking to Brustein, "When the president confronted him, the prime minister swore he didn't know. We don't know any more than you've already guessed. Starting from scratch, our job is to stop whoever took the bomb from using it."

Coll did not need to embellish this: An act of nuclear terrorism was what any president feared most. The first — and worst — fear was that the bomb was on its way to this city. Still addressing Brustein, he demanded, "How is the agency responding?"

Watching the two men, Brooke reflected

on their disparity. Slender and dapper, Coll was a smart and polished infighter, with a fierce ambition to become secretary of state; Brustein cared less about himself than agency and country. "We're calling on all our capabilities," Brustein said. "Operations, analysis, signals intelligence, counterterrorism, key people from the Near East Division, analysts with expertise in nuclear weapons systems. Our information systems will redirect all data to a central point, so that no critical information slips through the cracks." Pausing, he inclined his head toward Sweder. "Ken will run this day-to-day, with the assistance of Carter Grey. As to the nature of the search, we're looking for a small group of men with a bomb you can fit in a crate. We won't get much help from satellites. We need to depend on human intelligence: We've alerted our stations around the world to work every relevant source. That's how we'll find this bomb."

Without comment, Coll faced Carl Hobbs of the FBI. "What if it's coming here?"

Hobbs held out a palm, fingers ticking off his list. "We're accelerating investigations of potential cells. We've alerted our counterterrorism unit. We've assigned anyone we can spare to checking domestic sources. We're coordinating with the DOE's detection team to comb wherever the bomb might be —"

Interrupting, Coll turned to Joseph Farella, deputy secretary of defense. "Any plans to go into Pakistan?"

Farella gave a sidelong glance to Francine Andrews, the poised career diplomat who had become the deputy secretary of state. "We'd need to know where it is," Farella answered. "Otherwise we're blind men searching for a grain of sand in a country close to nuclear war. We might well destabilize an already weak government."

"Imagine how destabilized we'll feel," Coll interjected caustically, "when al Qaeda eliminates New York." He caught himself, speaking more evenly. "You're right, of course. But we're less than a month from the tenth anniversary of 9/11. We have to assume this weapon is meant for America."

Hobbs leaned forward. "That's why we'd like CIA personnel reassigned to a joint task force under our direction. That way they can operate domestically."

Brooke saw Brustein bridle. Ignoring Hobbs, he said to Coll, "In this last decade every successful prosecution of a terrorist started with leads from us. We can't bring field officers back from overseas — we don't have enough as it is. We need them to work with foreign agents and intelligence agencies."

"Which ones do you trust?" Coll inquired sharply.

Brustein became expressionless — a method, Brooke divined, of concealing his annoyance. "There's trust, and then there's situational usefulness. We trust the Brits, the Germans, and the Jordanians. They're less likely to leak, and they'll worry the bomb is meant for them —"

"What about the Chinese and the Russians?" asked Francine Andrews. "Both of them have terrorists, and neither wants a nuclear weapon in the hands of al Qaeda or the Chechens. Going to them may be worth the risk."

In a tone of dispassionate inquiry, Brooke asked, "What about the Iranians?"

Coll's eyebrows shot up. "How do you know they're not behind this?"

"I don't. But suppose they're not. What happens if there's a nuclear catastrophe in the Middle East, and the Iranians get blamed for it? Or their clients, Hezbollah and Hamas? The last thing they'd want is an excuse for the Israelis to flatten them. Israel might not need much of one."

Coll appraised him. "We don't know each other, do we?"

"Brooke Chandler." Brooke felt his name and face being filed away. "I work here. I also worked in Iraq and Lebanon. The experience was useful —"

"Brooke's one of our best," Brustein cut in. Sitting back, Brooke saw Grey smile.

"About the Israelis," Coll asked Brustein, "what are we doing with them? Or about them?"

"As Brooke suggests," Brustein answered, "they're worried about Iran and groups like Hezbollah and Hamas, for whom the destruction of Israel is the Holy Grail. Their Middle East network is better than ours, and they'll focus every resource on ensuring their own survival."

"Nevertheless, do I divine a certain distrust between you and Mossad?"

"The Israelis," Brustein answered coolly, "have been known to use false information to manipulate us to their own ends. If that doesn't work, they'll try to steal our secrets. We don't even like having Mossad in this building.

"Fear makes them arrogant and aggressive, inclined to overrate themselves — witness their classic blunder in the blockade of Gaza, where they end up killing eleven civilians on a boat allegedly embarked on a humanitarian mission, infuriating the entire world. In turn, they don't think we're as competent or serious. They also believe that anything we do will get leaked to Congress and the media."

"Imagine that," Grey remarked sardonically.

"In short," Brustein continued, "the Israelis will be an immense pain in the ass. Once they get word of this, they'll want to move their people to Langley, get everything we have, and give us as little as possible. They'll also pressure the White House to make them equal partners in the effort.

"The bright side is that if we find the bomb, the Israelis will do whatever it takes to recover it. The danger is that they'll try to justify any operation they think helps protect them — including against Iran. There's an inherent conflict. Israel will want us looking out for Israel; our first obligation is protecting this country. That means we'll read intelligence differently, and have very different priorities. The fact that we need each other won't make that any easier."

Coll bit his lip. "Let's hope the prospect of a nuclear holocaust concentrates the Israeli mind. In their place, I'd be very afraid of al Qaeda destroying an American city. That would create tremendous pressure for us to get out of the Middle East —

reasonably or not, many voices would blame Israel. I expect the president will make that point to their prime minister. As for the rest of us, cooperation is paramount." He glanced at Hobbs. "That means keeping the CIA overseas, and making sure the FBI works closely with the other domestic agencies. Understood?"

Under the weight of Coll's stare, Hobbs slowly nodded. "Moving on," Coll said to Brustein, "who in your agency briefs who in Congress? We have to get this right."

Brustein leaned forward. "I'll personally brief *selected* members of Congress: the chairmen and ranking members of the intelligence committees of the House and Senate; the majority and minority leaders of the Senate; and the Speaker, majority and minority leaders of the House. I strongly recommend we cut it off there, or else we might as well ask Bin Laden to join us." Brustein looked around the room. "I also suggest that no one else outside this room know that a bomb is missing unless it's absolutely essential. Including at the White House."

Briefly, Coll looked nettled. "Whoever has the bomb," Grey told him emphatically, "won't say so unless and until they've perpetrated a tragedy that dwarfs Hi-

119

roshima. We have the same interest in keeping secret from al Qaeda whatever *we* know or suspect. We're moving toward an election year — once this news gets out, there'll be an orgy of finger pointing, and Bin Laden will have hijacked the campaign to select an American president. Beyond that, any artless or premature disclosure to the public could cause evacuations of our cities, the collapse of the stock market, and a cacophony of political recrimination that mushrooms with each rancid hour of demagoguery on talk radio and cable news." Grey suddenly sounded tired. "It would be a test of national character. I'm not sure we can pass it anymore. I don't relish finding out."

The faces around the table were uniformly grave. Coll puffed his cheeks, expelling a breath. "Any argument with that?"

For a moment, Brooke hesitated. "No argument," he said. "But I'm not sure al Qaeda will keep our secret. If I were Bin Laden, I wouldn't wait for Congress to leak it. *I* would."

Coll's mouth became a thin line. "For what reason?"

"For all the reasons you suggest," Grey responded quietly. "A simple announcement would damage us whether or not al Qaeda succeeds in using the bomb. We couldn't control the Israelis. And if al Qaeda did succeed, it would magnify our sense of fear and powerlessness. Bin Laden, not the president, would become the most powerful man in America."

FOUR

Through the window of the earthen hut, Amer Al Zaroor watched the moon.

For the first time since he began his self-imposed isolation, the new cell phone that had awaited him buzzed. "All is quiet," the woman's voice said. "The baby sleeps."

"I love you," Al Zaroor answered quietly, and hung up — a conversation that, in his own life, he would never have.

It was as he had suspected. The Pakistanis were attempting to conceal that someone had stolen a nuclear weapon. Now he could weave his web of misdirection.

The three men had met again in Bin Laden's illuminated cave. As often happened, Zawahiri had laced his questions with sarcasm. "So while you sit on this bomb, a mother chicken with her egg, how do you divert our enemies?"

At the corner of Al Zaroor's vision, Bin

Laden cocked his head in an attitude of inquiry. "The Americans fear Iran," Al Zaroor responded, "and the Zionists fear them even more. I mean to stoke those fears through a sequence of disinformation planted with the ISI, and cryptic phone messages that the Americans' signals intelligence will no doubt intercept. Together, these snippets will suggest that the weapon is moving through Swat, then Afghanistan, toward Iran."

Bin Laden's eyes were grave with doubt. "The Americans will never believe we'd procure a weapon for Iran."

Al Zaroor nodded respectfully. "They will surely doubt it, Renewer. But they know very well that the Iranians would dearly love to reverse-engineer a Pakistani bomb. For the Zionist entity, Iran is both an obsession and an excuse for their own aggression." He looked at Zawahiri. "All I want is to create a distraction in the first few crucial days. That means inciting our enemies to think that someone other than us may be moving the weapon in a direction different than we intend. Out of Pakistan."

As Zawahiri began to speak, Bin Laden held up a hand. With a finality that foreclosed all discussion he said, "We believe in you, Amer. Completely."

The words that for two decades now Al Zaroor had worked to hear.

When Marwan Said first met the Renewer, transforming his path, he was barely twenty-four.

Bin Laden had summoned him to his sanctuary in Afghanistan. They sat by a campfire at night, the younger man quiet and awed. Among militia leaders in Afghanistan, Bin Laden was said to be an anomaly, combining the global vision of a revolutionary with a rare command of organizational intricacies. In the flesh, the man radiated energy and purpose. Yet he retained the aura of a poet: With his penetrant gaze came an air of calm and stillness that, for Marwan, created its own light. In a deep but gentle voice, the Renewer said, "They say you are a good fighter, Marwan. And, more than that, daring and resourceful. Such a man can choose many paths in life, some more convenient than others. What do you wish for yourself?"

Marwan composed his thoughts. "To wage jihad," he said simply. "Not orating in mosques, but taking actions."

Bin Laden considered him. "You are from Riyadh, I understand. Your father is a wealthy banker connected to the royal fam-

ily. Your own degree is in architecture —
though you dabbled a bit in philosophy." In
the glow of the fire, Marwan saw Bin Laden
smile at the younger man's surprise. "Your
father," he continued, "demands that you
lead a prosperous life as his acolyte, surrounded by wives and children. What makes
you aspire to a life of hardship?"

The leader's directness encouraged Marwan to open his soul. "In the beginning,"
he answered, "it was more feeling than
thought. I was only fourteen —"

"You had an awakening, then?"

"Yes, but not in a mosque. On television a
man was interviewing Palestinian survivors
of the Zionist massacre at Sabra and Shatilah; parents who saw their sons killed, their
daughters raped." Marwan paused, surprised by the impact of memory. "Suddenly
I could see the dead. For the first time it
came to me that I was not just Saudi, but
Arab. I felt myself quiver with anger and
shame — for my people, who did nothing;
for my father, whose only 'act of courage'
was to beat his wife and children. I saw what
he was, and wanted to spit in his face. I
promised myself that I would become a
man, not a tyrant who turns coward outside
the walls of his home."

"And so?"

Marwan bowed his head. "I went to the mosque and prayed for guidance."

Bin Laden straightened his white robe, still gazing at Marwan. "Where you came to the attention of the Muslim Brotherhood. What did you learn from them?"

"Many things. To pray five times a day, to behave modestly with women." He looked into Bin Laden's eyes, seeking acceptance. "More, I learned that the Christians softened men like my father with pleasures while using money from our oil to arm the Zionists. That we bowed our heads like women because the love of Allah, and the willingness to die for jihad, had vanished from our hearts. The West has neutered us."

Now Bin Laden's gaze felt piercing. "That is all?"

Humiliation coursing through him, Marwan understood that his words could have come from anyone. "Not all," he said in a tighter voice. "I saw the rubble of homes destroyed by the Zionist air force in Palestine and Lebanon, the unmarked graves of our Muslim sisters and brothers. And I dreamed that one day I would cause the tallest buildings of the Americans and Jews to become graves for their own people. An act of revenge far more eloquent than speech."

"And more ambitious," Bin Laden ob-

women make you feel?"

Marwan swallowed, then came as close to truth as he dared. "I was frightened of my own weakness. I told myself that whatever I did in America wouldn't matter. But in my heart, I knew it would change me."

"So you returned to Saudi Arabia and repudiated your father's ways."

"Yes." Marwan's voice gained strength. "Always I treat Sunni women with respect. But I know now that I can take no wife. When I envision martyrdom, I don't imagine seventy virgins. I don't think of an afterlife at all. I see the death of a single man — my death — changing the world as we know it. One does not have to live the future to be part of it."

"And this is why you wish to follow me."

"Yes." Marwan closed his eyes, quoting Bin Laden from memory. " 'I am willing to sacrifice self and wealth for knights who never disappoint me, knights who are never deterred by death, even should the mill of war turn against them.' You also said this: 'Oppression and exploitation can be demolished only in a rain of bullets. The free man does not surrender to the infidel.' " Opening his eyes, Marwan said prayerfully, "I wish to be your knight, Renewer. Allow me to be free."

Bin Laden smile_____ steele____
was keen. "Yo_____ ____ and how
Marwan. I'm _____ _n in fro__
planning — th_____ _n as his
training as an a_____ this. I
serve us well." His _____ ppose____
"Islam faces an e_____ use."
crusaders seek to des_____ Lad____
seize our lands, using _____ _ler, s
vanguard. The ultimate _____ _e in
the Koran. But we will a_____ _oo_
Day only by inflicting s_____ to
carnage that those who sur____d mu
the dead."

Marwan felt his skin tingle. _____ ai____
Renewer."

"Then you must be ours al____ __e
Laden's eyes locked on Marwa____
must change your name, becoming ____
new. You can have no home to h____
enemies find and kill you. We will send____
to your family that you've died here.'
Renewer leaned forward, voice softe____
"I'm sorry, Marwan. Perhaps your fat____
no loss to you. But you can never see____
mother or sister again, or anyone fro____
life you've led before. Can you do this___

At first, Marwan could not speak____
thought of losing his beloved mothe____
sister was too painful to acknowle____

served. "Is this why you studied in America?"

Marwan felt himself flush. "I wished to look our enemy in the face."

Though Bin Laden nodded, his gaze seemed more probing than before. "And what did you see there?"

Suddenly Marwan felt the weak man's need to hide behind words. "The place where I studied, Miami, was filled with Jews who cared only for the Zionist entity. The students indulged themselves in drugs and alcohol and promiscuity, as if they were Saudi princes —"

"Saudi princes," Bin Laden interjected tartly, "often disappoint. What about you, Marwan?"

This man could read minds, the young Saudi thought in shame. In a lower voice, he said, "I abstained from drugs and alcohol —"

"But not women."

Marwan briefly looked away. The memory was suffocating: the girl with bleached hair, round and shameless in her nakedness, rolling on her stomach so he could use her as a man, the nausea in his own stomach after this moment of discovery and release, curdled with self-loathing. But Bin Laden's tone was free of judgment. "How did these women make you feel?"

Marwan swallowed, then came as close to truth as he dared. "I was frightened of my own weakness. I told myself that whatever I did in America wouldn't matter. But in my heart, I knew it would change me."

"So you returned to Saudi Arabia and repudiated your father's ways."

"Yes." Marwan's voice gained strength. "Always I treat Sunni women with respect. But I know now that I can take no wife. When I envision martyrdom, I don't imagine seventy virgins. I don't think of an afterlife at all. I see the death of a single man — my death — changing the world as we know it. One does not have to live the future to be part of it."

"And this is why you wish to follow me."

"Yes." Marwan closed his eyes, quoting Bin Laden from memory. " 'I am willing to sacrifice self and wealth for knights who never disappoint me, knights who are never deterred by death, even should the mill of war turn against them.' You also said this: 'Oppression and exploitation can be demolished only in a rain of bullets. The free man does not surrender to the infidel.' " Opening his eyes, Marwan said prayerfully, "I wish to be your knight, Renewer. Allow me to be free."

Bin Laden smiled a little, though his gaze was keen. "You have an excellent memory, Marwan. I'm told you also have a gift for planning — the residue, perhaps, of your training as an architect. This talent could serve us well." His tone became prophetic. "Islam faces an existential threat. The crusaders seek to destroy our religion and seize our lands, using the Zionists as their vanguard. The ultimate battle is foretold in the Koran. But we will achieve Judgment Day only by inflicting such horror and carnage that those who survive it will envy the dead."

Marwan felt his skin tingle. "I am yours, Renewer."

"Then you must be ours alone." Bin Laden's eyes locked on Marwan's. "You must change your name, becoming someone new. You can have no home to help our enemies find and kill you. We will send word to your family that you've died here." The Renewer leaned forward, voice softening. "I'm sorry, Marwan. Perhaps your father is no loss to you. But you can never see your mother or sister again, or anyone from the life you've led before. Can you do this?"

At first, Marwan could not speak. The thought of losing his beloved mother and sister was too painful to acknowledge.

Instead he steeled himself by thinking of his father, and how pitiful he was compared to the man in front of him, offering to embrace Marwan as his own. "Yes," he said at last. "I can do this. I will trust no one, kill anyone who opposes me, and die before betraying our cause."

Bin Laden had placed a hand on his shoulder, sealing their bond —

Alone in Pakistan, Al Zaroor still gazed at the moon, so round and large it seemed he could touch it.

He must prepare himself. Five miles away, a man who did not know him would soon be waiting with a truck. Facing a cracked mirror, Al Zaroor used a straight razor to shave his head and beard, leaving only a mustache. Then he removed his contact lenses and put on gold-rimmed glasses. Save for his clothes, he resembled a lawyer or banker, a semblance of the man his father had wished him to become.

Once again, Al Zaroor thought, he had become a shadow.

As night fell, Brooke and Carter Grey met with Terri Young in Grey's borrowed office.

Blond and pretty, Terri still had the well-scrubbed look of the student body president she once had been. One of her specialties as an analyst was the study of al Qaeda operatives; at times, she could discern who had planned an operation by the intricacy of its details. Now she spread three photographs on Carter's desk.

"If your theory is close to right," Terri said, "the man behind this would need connections to the Taliban and al Qaeda; a web of contacts within Pakistan; a decent understanding of nuclear weapons; and a superior grounding in military tactics. All in the service of a first-rate mind." She looked over at Grey. "Considering the stakes, he'd also have Bin Laden and Zawahiri's absolute trust. Maybe we've never heard of him. But my guess is that he's one of these guys."

"Tell us about them," Grey requested.

She placed a finger beside the face of a heavyset man with a stubbly beard. "Abu Nemir is Jordanian. He has the requisite contacts, and his credits include multiple bombings of embassies and hotels. But sub-Saharan Africa seems to be his specialty, and our most recent information puts Nemir in Somalia."

Grey gazed at the second photograph. "Mahmoud Farhat," he said grimly. "I met him in Afghanistan when all of us were killing Russians. Smart and mean as a snake. He's also Pakistani, which would fit."

131

"And maybe dead," Terri answered. "Our people in Pakistan think we've gotten him with a drone. They're trying to confirm that."

"Don't wait up for it," Brooke said. "Who's the third?"

"This one's worth a closer look." Using her computer, Terri summoned the grainy profile of a man who appeared to be in his early thirties, his body like a blade of tempered steel, his ridged nose in perfect proportion to a sculpted face. "Looks like a film star," Grey remarked. "What's his name?"

"Amer Al Zaroor. At least that's the name he uses."

"What do we know about him?"

Gazing at their quarry, Terri's brow knit. "Regarding his origins, nothing. No past, no family, no country. He seems to have been born as an adult."

Grey grunted. "Adam without Eve. How old is this photograph?"

"Twelve years, at least. Al Zaroor is elusive; according to one of our prisoners, some within al Qaeda call him 'the shadow of God on earth.' The only Amer Al Zaroor we can trace was a friend of Bin Laden's who died in childhood —"

"In other words," Brooke said, "Bin Laden christened him."

"So it seems. His operational fingerprints are rumored to be on some of Osama's greatest hits." She looked up from the screen at Brooke. "We believe he helped plan the attack on the USS *Cole*. We also think that he persuaded Bin Laden to scale down the plan for 9/11, perhaps enabling its success. That speaks to a very cold mind."

Grey studied the two photographs. "What are his connections to Pakistan?"

"Impressive. The last two operations attributed to him were the bombings in 2009 of an army garrison in Rawalpindi, and of a hotel in Peshawar frequented by foreigners — both with massive casualties. There's no doubt he can work on Pakistani soil."

"Those operations were two years ago," Brooke pointed out.

Terri nodded. "No one claims to have seen him since. He could be dead, in hiding, or working on something very deep. With this guy you just don't know."

"What do the Israelis know?" Grey asked.

"According to them, zip. I actually believe that. They've got no resources in Pakistan." She flicked back her bangs. "According to the Indians, who do, they received a vague description of an al Qaeda operative spotted last year in Peshawar — a dark, slender man with a dark beard, perhaps dyed. But no one knows his name.

"Even the descriptions of men sharing Al Zaroor's voice and manner vary markedly in appearance — beard, no beard; glasses, no glasses; dark hair, gray hair. The only thing he's never been is fat." Terri resumed studying the picture. "Somewhere in the world there are multiple images of this same man on security cameras. But no one has any idea they're looking at Amer Al Zaroor."

"What *do* we know?" Brooke asked in frustration.

"We think he's a Saudi, fluent in English. That suggests he may have studied in England or America. But he's completely erased his past." Terri shut off the computer. "My best guess is that the people he fought with in Afghanistan knew him by another name, and that most of them think he's dead. That makes him a needle in the haystack of deceased Saudi jihadists. Assuming that his former family ever knew he *was* one."

It struck Brooke again that he had no family other than his parents, and lied to both of them. "Like a lot of us," he remarked.

Before leaving, Brooke printed out the photograph of Amer Al Zaroor, wondering if he were adversary or illusion.

FIVE

A little after 5:00 A.M. in the Bekaa Valley of Lebanon, Dr. Laura Reynolds knelt in a Maronite Catholic church, seeking peace before resuming her life of secrets.

The church was shadowy and still, candles dimly illuminating its stone walls and worn wooden pews, the tormented Christ set below a stained-glass window. Though new to Laura, this church in Anjar afforded her a fleeting refuge of the soul. On some days, as now, she was accompanied by an intern on the dig, Maureen Strafford, who retained the faith of her Boston Irish childhood. Crossing herself, Laura rose, emerging with Maureen into the first light of morning.

Maureen drew a deep breath of air, too cool at this hour to burn her lungs. "It's so beautiful here," she said.

Though only ten years separated them, the eagerness radiating from Maureen's open face made Laura feel old. The town

135

had lovely aspects, she acknowledged, such as leafy trees and stone houses left by Armenian immigrants. But the quarters they shared with other archaeologists were drab, save for the courtyard where they sometimes ate dinner. Nor could either woman indulge her femininity — in loose cotton pants and long-sleeved shirts, they were as androgynous as clothes could make them, Laura more so because of her slightness compared to Maureen's buxom form. Even their hair — Maureen's bright red, Laura's black and straight — was covered to honor the mores of Islam. Among the Shia, females in pants were suspect.

The two women were part of a dig team financed by a compendium of Polish universities. Altogether they numbered twenty-five, augmented by cooks and housekeepers from Anjar. Maureen had arrived two weeks before, a student from the program at the American University of Beirut that had granted Laura Reynolds her doctorate. Delighted, as Maureen put it, to find herself in the company of an American woman on the right side of menopause, she had appointed herself Laura's friend. For reasons of her own, Laura concealed how little they had in common.

Among the dig team, Maureen was a

welcome pair of hands, learning as she worked. All the rest but Laura specialized in the Umayyad period, a highlight in the archaeological history of the Arab peoples: experts in pottery, geology, botany, and the reading of script; a photographer and a draftsman; and the director, Dr. Jan Krupanski, a man as good-hearted as he was accomplished. As the newest Ph.D., Laura ran the dig house — the nerve center of the project and the source of its supplies — doubling as a member of the survey team. Given Laura's interests, the otherwise mundane assignment was a stroke of luck.

Managing the dig house involved organizing the objects removed from the site while keeping them secure. But among Laura's other duties was ensuring that the dig was well supplied, requiring drives around the Bekaa Valley and sometimes to Beirut. The job, she had assured Jan Krupanski, was perfect for her.

Leaving the church, Laura and Maureen drove toward the site. One hand on the wheel, Laura put on her aviator's sunglasses, a shield against the brightening dawn. "How do you like running the dig house?" Maureen asked.

Implied in the question, Laura knew, was

that she must find it menial. "Pretty well," Laura answered. "For an archaeologist, I'm restless by nature. Instead of being nailed to the site, I'm getting to know the Bekaa."

Turning, Maureen gave her a look of concern so sisterly that Laura fought to repress a smile. "Isn't this a dangerous place for a woman to travel alone?"

"Not really. As a professional and a Ph.D., I'm mostly perceived as a neuter. Even the fundamentalist guys from Hezbollah don't object to me, as long as I don't shake their hand." Laura's tone became rueful. "I've become an honorary man. Given my social life, it's far too easy to maintain the fiction."

Arriving at the site, Laura reflected that one use of fiction involved concealing the fictions that lay beneath.

Two weeks before, Laura had taken Maureen on her first tour of the ruins.

The others were already dispersing through the site, talking in twos and threes. The searing heat defined their schedule. To stay ahead of it they arrived before sunrise. To lessen its impact, they broke for breakfast and lunch in the shade of canvas tents before taking an afternoon siesta, resuming work in early evening until the light of sunset failed. But for Laura, Anjar at dawn had a pensive beauty.

Standing with Maureen, she felt no need to explain this. The site stood in eerie but evocative contrast to the distant mass of the Anti-Lebanon Mountains, the territory of smugglers and Hezbollah fighters. Bordering the ruins, stands of pines and cypress and eucalyptus softened their starkness. The marble arches and fluted columns were gray-white in early light; the Great Palace at their center was made of sandstone, its varied colors richening as they watched. At times Laura could hear the whisper of history. The remnants of once-imposing towers rose from the rubble of walls, reminding her that the Umayyad's fleeting century of dominance, the eighth, had been marked by war and bloodshed. In the foothills beyond was another reminder of the transience of power and the permanence of strife — a graceful mosque of the Shia, whose rise within Lebanon had empowered Hezbollah, helping to fuel the wars with Israel so tragic for so many. The thought made Laura briefly bow her head.

But Laura's thoughts were not Maureen's. In a husky voice, the young woman said, "No photograph could capture this, and no book could describe it. To be here is so uplifting."

139

Laura made herself refocus. "I only hope we can stay. The Poles have a great tradition of archaeology, and absolutely no money. I'm helping them look for grants." Looking around them, she finished, "For however long, we're lucky to be part of this."

Entering the site, Laura led her to where Segolene Ardant, a birdlike Frenchwoman who specialized in pottery, knelt among a team of diggers gathering fragments to inspect. "We wash these by hand," Segolene told Maureen, "and lay them out for a day. Then we try to piece them together, using the profiles of known Umayyad pottery."

"How do you do that?"

"In part by color, and by the nature of the earth in which they're found. The color variations are often subtle; archaeologically they can be profound." She smiled up at them. "As Laura can tell you, the profiles can take years to assimilate. But she's proving a quick study. Her memory and eye for detail are the envy of us all."

Thanking her, Laura and Maureen continued on their tour.

Toward its end, they encountered Dr. Antoine Abboud, a representative of Lebanon's Department of Antiquities. Greeting him warmly, Laura saw that Maureen was hanging back. Including Abboud in her smile, she said, "You can shake Tony's hand, Maureen. As a Christian, he's used to such familiarities."

Abboud chuckled, his eyes merry. "I also bring Laura whisky from Beirut, in the hope it will lead to greater liberties. I trust my failure reflects an unreasonable prejudice against the married."

"It's nothing personal," Laura said with mock solemnity. "When I donned these clothes, I took an oath of chastity. I have no life but archaeology."

Abboud rolled his eyes in resignation. "I've tried to imagine you in makeup and a dress, Laura, but the fantasy is driving me insane. Even in camouflage I can still discern your beauty."

Smiling, Laura said, "You've been too long in the sun," and took Maureen on their way.

"What a character," the young woman said. "Does he come here often?"

Laura gestured for Maureen to sit with her on a wall. "Quite often, but not to see me. It's not that Tony doesn't trust us, but antiquities can be priceless. If you can believe the Lebanese, the Israelis looted sites like this whenever they invaded."

"Do you think that's true?"

Laura shrugged. "Probably. To be sure,

there's a rich history of hatred between Israel and the Lebanese — especially Hezbollah — exacerbated by civilian casualties from Israeli carpet bombing. But the Israelis never joined the UN's feeble effort to fight antiquities smuggling. So the Lebanese suspect the worst."

"That's hard to accept," Maureen objected. "Israel has some of the finest archaeologists in the world, dedicated to preservation."

"Not all Israelis are created equal. As one example, Israel's greatest military hero, Moshe Dayan, was an accomplished antiquities thief." Laura dabbed her brow with a handkerchief. "To be fair, it's also rumored that Hezbollah sells antiquities to help buy the rockets they lob at Israel from the Bekaa. There's enough greed and bloody-mindedness to go around."

Maureen considered this. "Where *is* Hezbollah? I keep expecting to see masked men in jeeps driving around with submachine guns."

Laura shook her head. "Until the next war with Israel, you won't. The core Hezbollah fighters are hidden; others are civilians waiting for the call. But Tony Abboud aside, the Lebanese government is a minimal presence here. When I take you to Baalbek, you'll see that Hezbollah runs the valley."

"I'm not so sure I'll go with you. Call me sheltered, but terrorists scare me."

"No need for that, as long as we don't offend them." Restless, Laura stood to leave. "Fortunately, we're devotees of the eighth century. We have nothing to do with wars between Arabs and Jews."

Later that week, Laura and Maureen traveled to Baalbek with a shopping list from Segolene Ardant.

As they drove, Maureen marveled at the richness of the valley, fertile farmland between two mountain ranges, one marking the border with Syria. Pointing out a swath of green, Maureen asked, "What crop is that?"

Laura grinned. "Do you smoke hashish? If so, your evenings will start looking up."

"They just grow it in the open? I thought that Hezbollah was Shia. The Shia forbid the use of drugs and alcohol."

"In general they do. But as the great Boston politician Tip O'Neill once said, 'All politics is local.' In the valley, good politics means arming yourself against Israel with profits from the drug trade. So sit back and smoke the benefit."

Maureen glanced at her. "You've learned

a lot about this place, haven't you?"

"We're here," Laura answered. "Curiosity helps kill time."

Entering Baalbek, they were greeted by posters of Hassan Nasrallah, the leader of Hezbollah, hanging from telephone poles and streetlamps. As they neared the center of the city, Maureen stared at the wooden replica of a bearded man in combat fatigues, twenty feet high, standing atop the ruined shell of an Israeli tank. "Who's *that?*"

"The late Imad Moughniyeh, assassinated several years ago by an Israeli hit team in Damascus. Back in the 1980s, he planned the bombing of our embassy in Beirut, as well as the barracks filled with our marines." Laura's voice turned cold. "Several hundred died. As an American, and a New Yorker, the lionization of butchers like Moughniyeh challenges my powers of detachment — on 9/11 we saw where that can lead. But Hezbollah is sentimental, so Moughniyeh iconography is huge here. If you like, you can buy a keychain with his picture and send it to your mom."

"No way," Maureen rejoined. "She'd think it was Fidel Castro, and disown me. She has no room for enemies of the Catholic Church."

Laura smiled. "Neither does mine, actually. We still argue about abortion."

They turned down the main street, a crowded thoroughfare in which the posters of Nasrallah were interspersed with the photographs of young men barely older than boys. "Those are 'martyrs,' " Laura informed Maureen, "who died in some action against Israel. Baalbek is where the Iranians set up Hezbollah in the first place. No doubt it remains filled with people from all over who are up to no good. But when I came here as a child, all that I knew was that I loved the food."

Maureen stared at her. "Your parents brought you to Baalbek?"

Laura jammed on the brakes, barely missing a pedestrian. "My mother's family are Maronites, and Beirut is her second home. So I came by my Arabic the easy way. Every summer, Mom brought my brother and me back to visit family." Swerving abruptly, she stopped in front of the Hotel Palmyra, a colonial relic with vines creeping up its walls. "One year, we stayed at this hotel, which I swore was haunted. But across the street were the most astonishing Roman ruins outside of Italy. That's where I first decided to become an archaeologist."

Maureen gazed at the massive arches rising from the site. "How old were you?"

"Eight," Laura said. "My parents thought I was crazy. Now Mom calls me 'a gypsy among the rubble.' The lure of the past eludes her."

Returning to Anjar, Laura dropped Maureen at the site with the dental picks essential to Segolene's more delicate efforts. Before getting out, Maureen sat back, watching the team at their work. Lightly, she said, "I wonder if anyone here is a spy."

Laura gave her a smile of puzzlement. "Why would you think that?"

Maureen's eyes lit with a humorous enthusiasm. "Haven't you read the histories? There's a great tradition of archaeologists as secret agents, like the Englishwoman Gertrude Bell. Maybe Segolene works for French intelligence."

Laughing softly, Laura said, "Why don't you ask her? I can certainly see the advantages — you get to know the language and the people, and have an excuse for being in someone else's country. So why not Segolene?"

Maureen turned to her, interested. "Why not indeed?"

"Seriously? Because she's too good at what she does. You can't fake your way through archaeology, and no real archaeologist would throw away her career." Absent-mindedly, Laura polished her sunglasses, as though considering the matter further. "Gertrude Bell has been dead for decades. These days there's too great a risk of getting caught, so I wouldn't augment your day job by pursuing a life of adventure. Likely you'd be captured or killed. Besides, you're much too competent to work for the CIA."

Maureen had laughed at this. She was, Laura had already divined, a type she knew well from America — the reflexive liberal, an innocent living in a world more complex than she knew. Unless, of course, Maureen was not what she pretended. But Laura knew a considerable amount about lies and liars, and this was not how she read Maureen. One tool of her survival was a gift for separating casual liars from people like herself.

Now, dropping Maureen at the site, Laura drove back to the dig house.

In the next few hours, she would find an excuse to drive off in her jeep alone. She had scheduled another cell phone call, at one o'clock. A new and troubling secret made the call imperative.

SIX

Sequestered in his office before the next crucial meeting, Brooke sorted through his emotions.

For two years in Lebanon, he had acted on his own, operating under nonofficial cover — a "singleton NOC," the definition of a loner. No past or future had tied him to anyone: He became Adam Chase, a young American businessman with a gift for languages and an interest in Arab culture. Chase was free to follow his instincts.

Now Brooke Chandler was a bureaucrat. The central purpose of his existence had not changed: to help ensure that the tragedy still echoing from 9/11 — which had taken so many lives and changed countless others — never happened again. In recent days, fearing an event far worse, he felt his instincts quickening. But instead of acting, he must undertake the slow, patient, often frustrating work of persuading others who, for reasons good and bad, might not listen. He felt like a man in a straitjacket.

But the job, he reproved himself, was not about indulging his likes or dislikes. To be right — if he *was* right — imposed terrible responsibilities. And to fail meant living with a psychic burden too terrible to imagine, turning the last decade of his life to ashes.

Standing, he studied the photograph of Ben Glazer and his wife. "I'll do my best, pal," he promised, then headed for the meeting.

Around the conference table was the core group focused on the missing bomb: Carter Grey, Frank Svitek, Ken Sweder, Michael Wertheimer, and Noah Brustein. It was 7:00 A.M.; each man had a steaming mug of coffee. Projected on the wall were maps of India, Pakistan, the Middle East, and the shipping lanes to North America.

There were pouches beneath Grey's eyes, suggesting a night too racked by pain for sleep. In a rough, tired voice, he asked Brustein, "What's the situation in Pakistan?"

"Still holding. The secretary of state has extracted a promise from the Pakistani prime minister to find and prosecute anyone involved in the terror attacks in India."

Grey snorted. "Does anyone believe that?"

"*I* don't. But it may help to hold off a war, and slow down the wholesale slaughter of Muslims in India. If true, the only nuclear turd is in our pocket." Brustein glanced up at the maps. "The task this morning is to think about where the missing bomb may be going, and how it gets there."

"What are its specifications?" Brooke asked at once.

"According to our sources," Brustein answered, "it contains enough HEU to destroy New York, but can travel in a container about the size of a coffin. The total weight is roughly two hundred pounds, meaning that you don't need a lot of men to move it. Two men, perhaps. You could put it on a van, truck, boat, train, airplane, or conceal it in a cargo container. At that weight, even a small private plane could get it off the ground."

"How detectable is it?"

"Not very. Even the most sensitive equipment probably won't pick up radiation."

"Do we know how it detonates?"

Brustein turned to Sweder. "It has an altimeter," Sweder told Brooke, "set for one thousand feet. When the plane gets above that altitude, you unlock the bomb's security system, then drop it. At a thousand feet, it goes off."

"What's the security system?" Michael Wertheimer inquired.

"The Pakistanis' version of our PAL — permissive action link — a sequence of numbers much like the code to an ATM machine. The purpose is to confine knowledge of the code, preventing unauthorized use." Reflexively, Sweder straightened his tie. "That's some comfort, I suppose. To detonate this bomb, al Qaeda — if that's who has it — would need a technician sophisticated enough to bypass the system, or a Pakistani insider who knows the code."

Grey reflected on this. "That's a critical piece of this. I assume we've asked the Pakistanis for the identities of anyone with the wherewithal to do that."

"Of course," Brustein answered disgustedly. "Repeatedly, and vehemently. But anytime you seriously question a Pakistani about their nuclear program, and his lips start moving, he's lying. And they certainly don't want us tracking people who know the secrets of their arsenal. All they'll say is that the information is 'sensitive' and they're making their own inquiries —"

"Fuck *them,*" Frank Svitek snapped. "I'm sensitive about Chicago."

"Please," Grey said softly, "they're a proud

people." He turned to Sweder. "Is Immigration checking out any Pakistanis entering the country, and the ones already here? Or will that offend their sensitivities as well?"

"They're checking," Sweder said tersely. "If this person exists, we need to find him. Follow him, and maybe we can locate the bomb."

Grey nodded. "Speaking of which, how's our surveillance over Pakistani airspace?"

"So-so. We've redirected our satellites to areas nearest to where the bomb was stolen. Of course, unmanned aerial vehicles would give us better images. But the Pakistanis won't permit overflights of UAVs as long as they're worried about the Indians."

Grey grimaced in disgust. "Whoever planned this is an operational genius, with a sophisticated understanding of how it might play out." He turned to Frank Svitek. "How are we using our assets in the Middle East?"

Brooke watched the wariness steal into Svitek's eyes — this was a classic human intelligence problem, and the agency would succeed or fail based on its network of operatives and sources. Firmly, Svitek responded, "Our station chiefs are pressing foreign intelligence agencies and flogging every source we've got. We're working on suspect jihadist groups, transfers of money,

152

smuggling rings, suspicious convoys, private planes, and vehicles moving at night. We're also questioning informants with ties to al Qaeda, which is how we got Khalid Sheikh Mohammad after 9/11. As for signals intelligence, we're focusing on cell phones in Pakistan, India, and the Middle East."

"That's about a million calls an hour," Brooke observed. "An operative this smart will be talking in code on a series of ghost phones. The only way to sort through all the garbage may be through samples of his voice. Do we have any for Amer Al Zaroor?"

"None." Svitek scanned the group. "We *have* picked up some interesting phone chatter. On the surface, the contents are banal — too banal, perhaps. But from the location of the calls, and the repetition of certain phrases, they could suggest a suspicious package may have moved through Swat into Afghanistan."

"What sense does that make?" Grey inquired. "Except for Bagram Air Force Base, there's nothing in Afghanistan worth blowing up."

"Unless it's headed for Iran," Svitek countered. "For a country developing nuclear weapons, a Pakistani bomb would be a blueprint."

"Then al Qaeda didn't steal it," Brooke

said flatly. "They hate the Shia, Iran most of all."

Brustein looked from Brooke to Svitek. "The chatter could be disinformation," he said, "as Frank well knows. But we can't dismiss it out of hand. I've told Frank that we have to follow up."

Somewhere in the Middle East, Brooke thought, a man without a voice is laughing.

"Nonetheless," Brustein pressed on, "our working premise is that al Qaeda has the bomb, and that it's headed for the United States — possibly through the ports in Long Beach or New York. The principal concerns are Washington, D.C., and New York — although, as Frank suggests, we also worry about major cities like Chicago."

Grey turned to Michael Wertheimer. "What about targets outside the U.S.?"

"There are a number of them. Given the apparent involvement of LET, India is one possibility." He placed a finger on Afghanistan. "If they go after Bagram Air Force Base, as you suggest, Afghanistan actually would make sense."

"Not to me," Grey rejoined. "We've got too many troops there for al Qaeda to risk it. If you want to take a flier, try the Chechens blowing up Moscow. Not that I'd mind."

"There's also every capital in Europe,"

Sweder proposed. "Rome, Madrid, Paris, Berlin, and, most likely, London. If al Qaeda levels any one of those, no European country would help us fight our wars again."

"Are they helping now?" Grey asked innocently. "Please, show me on the map."

Sweder smiled a little. "There's also the Saudi oil fields. Beyond wanting to cripple the world economy, Bin Laden hates the royal family. Finally, of course, there's Israel."

"I'd move it toward the top," Brustein said, "if saving Israel was this agency's job one. But it isn't." He looked around the table. "Taking the targets we've identified, how does the bomb get out of Pakistan?"

"Maybe it doesn't," Grey suggested. "At least not right away. In al Qaeda's place, I might hide it somewhere safe until everyone exhausts themselves looking."

Sweder looked dubious. "Then how would you get it out?" he asked Grey. "Every day of delay gives the Pakistanis more time to turn their attention from India, tightening the net."

"That might be true if al Qaeda was running it through the Punjab to Karachi. The Pakistanis have a functioning government there. But Baluchistan is filled with smugglers and Pashtun tribes who hate the

155

government — the army barely goes there. So the smart move might be to smuggle the bomb through Baluchistan to the Makran coast, then head for open water."

Brustein put a finger to his lips. "And then where?"

"Anywhere. You could fly it in, though that's complicated by distance and the need to keep refueling. Another means is through normal shipping channels. If you're going to America, you might put it in a cargo container and ship it from Dubai." Grey turned to Sweder. "In an average year, how many cargo containers do we inspect once they reach Long Beach or New York?"

Sweder frowned. "About two percent."

"Well," Grey said philosophically, "at least they check my shoes at airports."

Svitek emitted a mirthless laugh. "I think this bomb is coming to America. But a container also works for targets in the Middle East and Europe. If you're headed for the Mediterranean, you could go from Pakistan through the Indian Ocean and the Red Sea. There's too much traffic for any boat to stand out, and you can get to Israel or any port in Europe. The only choke point is the Suez Canal."

Brooke leaned forward. "Why risk getting nailed at the Suez?"

"Depends on what the target is," Svitek answered promptly. "If it's Tel Aviv, you'd go through the Suez to Gaza. Then you'd tunnel it into southern Israel and fly from there."

"Risk upon risk," Brooke shot back. "First the canal, then the Israelis. They'd carpet-bomb every tunnel in Gaza with the bunker busters they've been saving for Iran. After that they'd reoccupy every patch of earth."

"So what's your alternative?" Svitek asked. "For al Qaeda, moving the bomb overland has too many problems. We could intercept the bomb in Afghanistan. The Iranians might take it for themselves. After that there's the Turks, our more or less ally that loathes Bin Laden."

"What about a land-sea-land route?" Brooke got up, pointing toward the maps of Pakistan and the Middle East. "As Carter suggests, you run the bomb through Baluchistan to the Indian Ocean. Then you take a route far shorter than the Suez Canal: through the Persian Gulf straight to the southeast corner of Iraq."

Glancing at the others, Brooke noted the skeptical looks of everyone but Grey. "I know you served there," Brustein told him. "But I wouldn't have picked Iraq."

"Still," Brooke answered, "you know why

157

I did. Our troops are drawing down and confined to certain areas. We're leaving behind one of the most corrupt countries on earth — a fragmented mess riddled with al Qaeda cells and crisscrossed with smuggling networks. You can run anything in or out of Iraq and never get caught. Even a nuclear bomb."

Brustein studied the map. "My bigger problem is with what's next: Jordan or Syria. The Jordanians are our closest allies. Syria, like Iran, has a sophisticated intelligence service and a hatred for al Qaeda. Pick your poison."

"I'd have to guess Syria. Because it's the path to Lebanon."

Brustein gave him a long, considering look. "Iraq. Lebanon. Those are the places you were posted."

Beneath Brustein's even tone, Brooke sensed an accusation: that he was recycling his own past, perhaps out of lingering resentment. Calmly, he said, "The boundary between Syria and Lebanon is a sieve. The Bekaa Valley is a smugglers' refuge, with clans who've been running contraband to and from Syria for hundreds of years. The Lebanese government has no presence there —"

"But Hezbollah does. They'd love to take

the bomb. So would their patrons, the Iranians."

"Hezbollah's all over," Brooke conceded. "But they don't control every inch of the Bekaa. The Anti-Lebanon Mountains are filled with places to hide."

"But what then?" Brustein prodded. "Al Qaeda would have to smuggle the bomb across the border to Israel, which bristles with security."

Brooke sat down again. "Not if they flew it in," he answered.

Brustein shook his head emphatically. "A Lear taking off from Lebanon could never beat the Israeli air defenses. They're the best in the world." He paused, softening his tone. "Your idea has arresting elements. But there are too many gaps, and our primary focus has to be on protecting America. Given that, our challenge is to choose where in the Middle East to concentrate our resources. They're not limitless, and neither are the field officers who know the region."

"Especially in Lebanon," Brooke rejoined. "Before my unplanned departure, I'd started disrupting jihadist cells. Since then, we've been searching for al Qaeda at diplomatic receptions. The work goes slowly."

Brustein stared at him. "Maybe so," he said at last. "But you can't build up an intelligence capacity overnight, or start turning Lebanese off the street into spies. Given what we know, Lebanon isn't a priority. Nothing you've said so far makes it one."

Brooke stifled his frustration. "All I'm asking," he responded in a milder tone, "is that we keep Lebanon on the agenda."

No one answered. Brooke could hardly blame them. He had made mistakes before, notably the one in Beirut that had almost cost his life. Neither he nor his colleagues could know how this might affect his judgment now.

Seven

The rest of Brooke's day — a task force meeting, reviewing emails from the field, ad hoc debates with colleagues — bled well into the evening. Only after a last hour spent running at the CIA gym did he leave Langley. It was close to midnight before he poured a snifter of brandy and sat in his living room, too wired to sleep.

His usual solution was reading. His shelves were full of books; on his night table was the new translation of *War and Peace* and a volume of poetry in Arabic. But he could not stop sifting his thoughts, or asking himself the same questions in a different way. At length, he put on a favorite album from his past, a Brazilian female vocalist with a terrific jazz pianist.

The last time he had seen them live was with Anit. Eleven years later, his thoughts kept doubling back to her, and the country to which she had returned.

■ ■ ■ ■

"The singer is amazing," Brooke had promised her.

They were entering the Zinc Bar, a subterranean nightclub on Houston Street, the air already dense with cigarette smoke and the whiff of marijuana. Brooke and Anit got there early enough to snag a corner table near the stage, giving them time to talk before the music started. As they sat, Brooke caught their reflection in a mirror above the bar: Brooke blond and rangy; Anit dark and exotic in the way Israeli women often shared with their Arab sisters. Sitting across from him, she struck Brooke as compelling.

Quiet, she sipped white wine, studying his face in a way far more direct than he was accustomed to from American women. "So you like jazz?" she began.

"I like all kinds of music — jazz, rock, folk, classical. But opera is my favorite."

She raised her eyebrows in surprise. "Even Wagner?"

Brooke shook his head. "Too much historic resonance. I hear all that atonal thunder and start thinking, 'a little less bombast, and a bit more melody, and the Germans wouldn't have invaded Poland.' I prefer the

Italians — their armies were worse, and the music better."

Anit's expression mixed amusement and interest. "Perhaps I'm prejudiced. But I always thought people acquire a taste for opera when affluence meets middle age."

"Not me. I came by it naturally — my father is on the board of the Metropolitan Opera. Even when I was young, my parents would take me to opening night." Brooke smiled at the memory. "Unlike a lot of his peer group — captains of commerce dragged there by socially ambitious wives — Dad was in heaven. His rapture was contagious."

Anit propped her chin on her hand. "So you're not merely good-looking," she inquired wryly, "but wealthy? How nice for you."

Her directness startled and amused him. "Since you ask, it's my mother who's wealthy — my grandfather Brooke founded an investment-banking business into which Dad married. In Mom's defense, she compensates for good fortune by being relentlessly liberal on every issue there is. What dead Italian composers are to Dad, Democratic politicians are to my mother: an object of charitable giving. Except that Mom can try to tell them what to do."

163

Anit smiled at this. "Somehow I sense less excitement at her enthusiasms."

Brooke sipped his Manhattan. "Less as an adult. I've decided that facts should inform my beliefs rather than beliefs dictate my choice of facts. A healthy bias for a would-be professor of Middle Eastern Studies."

Anit looked curious. "Did your parents hope you'd enter the family business?"

"They don't mind that I'm not. But like most Americans, my parents' beliefs about the Middle East are derivative. This particular enthusiasm is my own."

Briefly, Anit looked around them, her gaze keen and observant. In that moment, Brooke imagined her as an anthropologist, noting differences between this place and a nightclub in Tel Aviv. "I think you're right about Americans," she remarked. "Too often they seem to believe what they wish. Including American Jews."

Brooke nodded. "Some of my acquaintances are more discerning — my closest friend, in particular. But the survival of Israel is too visceral for easy detachment. There's no equivalent for Gentiles I can think of."

"So how *did* you become interested in our benighted area of the world?"

"So many questions," Brooke answered

with a smile. "But I suppose I asked for this. You did threaten to find out if I were smart."

To his surprise, Anit seemed disconcerted, then gave him a sideways grin. "People tell me I'm direct."

" 'People' are right, and I don't mind. As to the Middle East, at first it was more of an intellectual interest. The turning point for me was a junior year at American University in Beirut." Brooke took another sip of his drink. "I decided to travel anywhere there wasn't a war: Egypt, Jordan, Saudi Arabia, Syria, Pakistan. Also the West Bank and Gaza and, of course, Israel. There's nothing like actually seeing places to change the way you view them."

Anit nodded her understanding. "I agree. So how did your travels help?"

"In several ways. There's no 'Middle East,' I discovered, but a number of them. There are sclerotic autocracies like Egypt and Saudi Arabia, with the battle between modernism and fundamentalism roiling beneath. There's Lebanon, a magnet for every troublemaker there is, whose relationship to Israel became so poisoned by war that it spawned Hezbollah. To visit the border between Lebanon and Israel was instructive in itself: Shia badlands on one side, green Israeli farms on the other,

165

separated by an electrified fence —"

"I know," Anit interjected quietly. "I've spent time there. But tell me what you thought of Israel."

Brooke paused to organize his thoughts. "I admired it," he answered. "As a society, it's energetic and contentious, with a great strain of optimism. But I also felt a corrosive fear. You were right the other night: The occupation of the West Bank is a horror — checkpoints seething with hatred between Israeli soldiers and Palestinians who are treated like cattle. I met students who spent three hours making a forty-minute trip from home to school." He softened his tone. "I know why Israel feels stuck there. But you can't stay much longer, or else Palestinians not yet born will die hating Israel. Some will take Israelis with them."

Anit waved wisps of smoke away from her face. "No doubt you're right," she said evenly. "But it is we who have to live the problem. I'm not so sure that history will give us choices."

Despite the mildness of her tone, Brooke felt a touch defensive. "I don't expect to live the problem," he answered. "But that doesn't mean I don't care."

"Believe me, I prefer that you do. And I'm sure you'll be a very good professor." Seeing Brooke's smile, she answered with her own. "Was that too condescending?"

"Depends on how you define 'too,' " he answered amiably. "But in other ways you're right. Life in academia is not a high-stakes enterprise. I'll have plenty of time to write and still lead a very pleasant life."

She flicked back a strand of hair. "Listening to music?" she asked lightly.

"And competing. In high school and college, I played every sport I could. If I were a dog, I'd be the one who goes running after sticks. I can always bait my students, I suppose."

The noise around them was thickening now, the slow build of anticipation in a crowd awaiting music. For his own liking, Brooke had learned far too little about Anit Rahal. "You spent time at the border," he probed. "Was that part of your military service?"

Anit hesitated. "Almost all of it," she said at length. "I wanted to serve in a combat unit, which was not allowed. So I became an officer in military intelligence, stationed along our borders with Lebanon or the West Bank."

"What did that involve?"

"Internal security." She finished her wine, her gaze more distant than before. "Much of our job was keeping terrorists from crossing into Israel. And killing the ones who did."

Brooke stared at her. "You, personally?"

"Not unless you count giving the orders. But I saw enough of the dead — the Arabs killed by our soldiers." She paused again, adding quietly, "As for the Jews who died the time we failed — a suicide bombing at a café — I could only imagine them."

For a moment she studied the table, as if parsing her own memories.

Mustering a dispassionate tone, Brooke said, "It's not easy for me to imagine any of it."

Anit kept her eyes down. "In certain ways one grows hardened. Sometimes, usually at night, our soldiers would kill terrorists as they came in. The first lesson we learned was to pat down the bodies, to ensure they weren't booby-trapped with explosives. Otherwise we might die at the hands of a corpse." Anit looked up at him. "Handling the dead isn't nice, nor were we nice to them. We'd roll the bodies up in a blanket and throw them on a truck to be buried in a wasteland reserved for Arabs. Some nights we stacked them up like firewood."

Brooke tried to envision her doing this. "How old were you?"

"The first time? Nineteen." She shook her head, as if dismissing some painful image. "The harder part was knowing what might happen if we failed. But the work was necessary, and I learned that I was capable of doing it."

A veil, Brooke noticed, seemed to have fallen across her dark, expressive eyes. "That must have been draining," he ventured. "Intellectually and emotionally."

"It's also a condition of our lives, the difference between Israel and America. No one has attacked the American mainland in the last two hundred years. The borders I was guarding were merely cease-fire lines, recognized by no one, with enemies on almost every side." Anit paused, her expression pensive and resigned. "We chose to live in Israel, I know. But it's a little harder to enjoy the shopping mall when a suicide bomber might blow it up."

"And yet you advocate reconciliation."

Anit gave a fatalistic shrug. "What choice is there when the alternative is to remain bound to each other by hatred? Four days ago, Ariel Sharon — the butcher of Sabra and Shatilah — deliberately taunted the Palestinians by setting foot on the Temple Mount, sacred ground to both Jews and Palestinians. The result has been riots and a

169

new wave of suicide bombings." Her tone held quiet outrage. "According to Arafat, they're a spontaneous reaction to Sharon's provocation. This I don't believe. Arafat needed an excuse to pressure Israel through violence; his violence serves Sharon's ambition to become prime minister. Each is the other's doppelganger.

"Many Israelis would disagree. This much I know. In the last few days, nearly a thousand Jews have died. Sharon cannot be surprised."

Brooke detected sadness beneath her anger. "Was anyone you know hurt?"

"No one I knew well. But a cousin of an army friend, a sixteen-year-old girl, was killed walking to school in Jerusalem. And here I am, studying the Arab world in Greenwich Village."

Brooke felt the pulse of sympathy, both for the woman in front of him and the girl he did not know. "I'm sorry," he said bluntly. "But at the risk of stating the obvious, the fact that you're not manning the border has nothing to do with that."

She smiled without much humor. "Oh, I know. Only children believe that their every action affects the world. But Israeli lives are precious to me, and to my family. My great-grandfather was among the early Zionists;

170

my grandmother survived the Holocaust. To us, history is a living thing, and to survive we must continue to shape it." Her smile became more genuine. "No doubt that sounds egocentric. But I expect your ancestors did not flee some pogrom in Poland, but arrived here safely on the *Mayflower*."

"Not quite. Though my great-great-great-grandfather Chandler was a general in the Revolutionary War."

Anit arched her eyebrows. "American or British?"

"American," Brooke answered blithely. "Still, I grant that our history is less immediate."

"And accepting facts more volitional. For Israelis, ours are inescapable."

At the front of the room, a stagehand was adjusting the sound system, suggesting the music was about to begin. Facing this complex woman, Brooke resolved to make himself clear. "There's something I want you to understand, Anit. As a male, as my parents' son, and — above all — as an American at the end of the American Century, I'm fully aware that I enjoy a surfeit of good luck. But it's better to know that than to believe I've earned it. Or to apologize for it."

She looked into his face. "If I've made you

171

feel that, I'm sorry. Perhaps a part of me envies you a little. But I also have my privileges, like studying for a year in America. And sitting in this bar with you."

It was a pretty enough apology, Brooke thought, the more so for its honesty. "So let's enjoy the music," he suggested.

"Let's," she agreed. "In an hour, the world will still be waiting."

For Brooke, that night the performers were particularly delightful, the weave of voice and instruments complex yet infectious. But what made his evening so memorable was the expression on Anit's face, the desire for music to transport her completely. To see her so unguarded was to perceive another woman beneath, carefree and alive to pleasures.

They lingered for a nightcap, Anit asking more about the music, then chatted comfortably on the way to her dormitory north of Houston.

They stood in its shadow, suddenly out of words. "Thank you," Anit said simply, and stuck out her hand.

When he did not let it go, she looked directly into his face, dark eyes questioning.

"I'd like to see you again," he said.

Her look of inquiry lingered, and then she

smiled a little. "All right," she answered. "Next time I'll try to be a little less self-righteous."

On the way home, Brooke decided that she was worth another mention to Ben. He had never met a woman quite like her.

EIGHT

For hours of darkness, Al Zaroor traversed the harsh, rocky earth in the garb of a Baluch tribesman, his path guided by the stars and a GPS.

Shortly before dawn, he reached the road to Quetta. Soon a pickup pulled up beside him. Leaning through the window, its driver inquired in Pashto, "Do you need a ride, brother? Or do you prefer walking?"

Smiling in relief, Al Zaroor spoke the scripted words: "A ride, thank you. I still have far to go."

Getting into the cab, Al Zaroor noted that the man was young, with a beard that partially concealed the chubby face of an infant. One would not guess that he was the trusted nephew of someone who, excluding Mullah Omar, was perhaps the most powerful man in the Taliban stronghold of Quetta. As they drove, Al Zaroor perceived that Abdul Zia had taught his nephew well. The

174

young man knew the virtues of silence.

Bone-weary, Al Zaroor settled down in his seat, allowing himself to be hypnotized by the barren flatness filling the window. His senses came alive only when he saw the barrier ahead, manned by Pakistani police. Glancing at the driver as he braked, Al Zaroor read the indifference in his eyes.

The middle-aged policeman approached the truck with the defeated trudge of a man imprisoned by bureaucracy. Seeing the driver's face, he nodded and waved them through. As with the others at the barrier, he seemed indifferent to Al Zaroor or the contents of the truck. No words were needed for Al Zaroor to know that their salaries were supplemented by Abdul Zia.

As Al Zaroor had told Bin Laden, this was the lifeline of his plan.

A few hours later Al Zaroor and Zia's nephew had reached Quetta, a dusty outpost near the Afghan border run by drug dealers and the Taliban, where the presence of Mullah Omar was an open secret.

Al Zaroor had always found Quetta engaging in a hardscrabble way. It was a frontier town in all respects: The buildings were shabby and dun-colored; the roads potholed and dirty; such trees as existed scruffy; the backdrop of jagged mountains forbidding and severe. Covered women and bearded men in tribal garb, Pashtuns and Baluchs, clustered at open-air markets selling meat and fruit. Much of its quirky appeal, Al Zaroor decided, derived from the bright multicolored buses that rumbled among the camels, motorcycles, and ancient, beat-up cars. Another of its charms was historical: Revolutionaries by temperament, fierce Islamists by tradition, the locals hated the Pakistani army and police. Prudent representatives of government comported themselves so as not to end up dead.

Warlord and smuggler Abdul Zia exercised unquestioned power from a sprawling villa carved into the amphitheater of mountains overlooking the city. As they climbed the khaki-colored hillside, Al Zaroor felt entwined in the weave of ferocity, loyalty, and money that ensured Zia's own survival. Al Zaroor would be safe here; Abdul Zia was a serious man.

He had first come one year before, at night.

The open room where Al Zaroor and Zia had dined on an ornate carpet commanded a sweeping view of Quetta that, despite its squalor, was electrified for miles, its lights casting an upward glow into the clear night sky. Placed before them were generous servings of lamb, chicken, yogurt, okra, bread, and sweets — a roll of deep-fried batter dunked in sticky sugar syrup. If Al Zaroor were to die here, it would be from the desserts.

Their dinner was quiet, the conversation courtly and indirect. In the flesh Zia confounded Al Zaroor's imaginings — he was slender, gray-bearded, and bespectacled, with the subdued, reflective manner of a scholar or an actuary. There was little to suggest the hardened man who could smuggle drugs or arms through Baluchistan at will, or order an enemy murdered because he wished it. Only after several hours did Zia's quiet bitterness emerge — an American drone attack on the Taliban had accidentally killed his oldest son.

Al Zaroor knew this, of course. Hatred had seared into Zia that smuggling drugs held a meaning beyond family tradition — he was poisoning the children of the West. Zia knew, or guessed, Al Zaroor's affiliation: They had come together through a trusted intermediary, a relative of Zia's known to Amer since they had fought together in Afghanistan. Hatred was their bond.

"This shipment," Zia inquired thoughtfully, "it will have great value to you?"

"And to my cause. That's why I seek to entrust it to your protection, and to pay as you deserve." A decorous way, Al Zaroor thought, to describe a million dollars.

Zia nodded his acknowledgment. "You are wise."

"And discreet. No one else can know of its importance."

Zia gave a fractional shrug, a movement of the shoulders beneath his crisp white robe. "To the others, its nature will not matter. Those who move it will be the most disciplined men I have. They will know that any lapse in security will cause their death, and that of their family. No one will sell you to outsiders."

"And beyond Pakistan?"

"This depends on where you wish to go."

Al Zaroor considered his answer. "To start, let us say in and around the Persian Gulf."

Zia touched his lips. "I don't need specifics yet. But in certain Middle Eastern countries my network is ironclad. Allowing for changes in local conditions."

"We have our connections as well. If conditions become more challenging — and I think they will — perhaps our forces can complement each other."

Zia paused to consider the implications of

the statement, and what it might suggest about the shipment. "Are there other considerations we should discuss?"

"Yes. I also wish for you to smuggle *me*."

Zia's mouth moved in the brief semblance of a smile. "I thought as much. Transporting a stranger presents no problem. Such as it is in Baluchistan, the army fears us. So do the police. As generous men, we also pay them."

"Still," Al Zaroor parried, "mischance is random, and strikes us all. How do you arrange safe passage for a specific shipment at a preordained time?"

"That's not how we operate, my friend. We never inform our sources in the government about the time or date of an operation, or what is being moved. We merely tell them that we have activities in their area that should not be disturbed." Zia spread his hands. "You seem to know Pakistan well enough. Low-level functionaries, and their bosses, routinely accept gratuities. When the payment comes from us, they also know that loyalty ensures a longer life." The wispy smile returned. "Those few with moral qualms may guess that this particular shipment of heroin is leaving Pakistan rather than going to the 'shooting galleries' that pervade their cities. What a pathetic ruin

179

this so-called country has become."

A feudal ruin, Al Zaroor thought but did not say, in which you play a part.

Zia snapped his fingers, causing two obsequious menservants to remove their meal. "As to the men who'll guide you," he continued, "they'll be extremely well armed and skilled. Several were trained by the ISI to fight in Afghanistan or Kashmir. Faced with them, officials in Baluchistan know better than to be brave."

Al Zaroor nodded slowly. After a moment, he asked, "If I'm traveling to the Persian Gulf, what route through Baluchistan do you recommend?"

"That depends on where we meet you."

"I don't know yet," Al Zaroor responded with care. "But somewhere nearer to the Punjab."

Zia raised his eyebrows. "Then I suggest you bypass Quetta, taking the back roads edging the Kirthar Range, as you move south to Bela. From there it's east to Awaran, through Turbat, then south to the tiny port of Jiwani."

Al Zaroor felt modest surprise. "What kind of ship would use such a port?"

Zia's smile seemed more genuine. "A dhow — the same ship that has plied these waters for centuries, shipping goods and produce. A modest vessel among countless like it, and therefore inconspicuous. These days, of course, dhows have auxiliary motors." He bent forward, looking intently at Al Zaroor. "You haven't asked my advice about a transfer point. But I suggest a warehouse in the free port of Jebel Ali in Dubai. Dubai is a pirate kingdom, and this port is reserved for ongoing shipments — no customs inspections, and fewer annoying officials. A brief sojourn in a warehouse, and you can ship your package by cargo container anywhere in the world."

"Thank you," Al Zaroor said respectfully. "This is good advice."

Zia's eyes probed his. "But you have other worries, I detect."

"No doubt you've gelded the army and police. But I hear too much about banditry among unemployed young Pashtuns. Men with no future don't worry about preserving one."

Zia shrugged. "Some are reckless. Should they be reckless with us — or you — they will have no future."

"You reassure me." Al Zaroor hesitated. "I'd also like to entrust you with prior shipments — also important, but less valuable. That will allow us to better assess any dangers."

Zia's eyes narrowed in displeasure. "There will be no dangers."

"Nonetheless," Al Zaroor responded firmly, "my masters wish it. They have earned the right to caution, and I have promised them success."

For a time, Zia was silent, his expression indecipherable but for the intensity of his thoughts. Among them, Al Zaroor was certain, was that he would not be running heroin. "As you like," Zia said at length. "As to success, as long as you're under my protection, you will have it."

NINE

At 6:30 A.M., when Brooke reached Langley, Carter Grey was waiting. They sat together in Brooke's office. "You shouldn't be here," Brooke said baldly. "From the looks of you, you'll be dead in a week."

Grey shook his head, resistant. "Maybe I look like a cadaver, but I'm liveliest in the morning. I'm saving my naps for afternoon. Anne will see to it."

"Or I will."

"Not your job," Grey said in a grousing tone. "I liked it better when you were this kid."

Brooke gave a short laugh. "So did I. But here we are. Anything happen overnight?"

"Yes and no. Miracle of miracles, none of our media friends is on to the missing bomb. But the Pakistanis and Indians are standing down. That may create more room to search for the bomb in Pakistan — assuming it's still there." Grey sat back. "I keep thinking about Baluchistan. In the eighties, I ran twenty-five tons of explosives through the region for the Afghans. How much simpler to smuggle a two-hundred-pound bomb to the Makran coast."

"No doubt," Brooke answered. "But we've got almost no assets there now. Since we started using drone attacks on al Qaeda and the Taliban, the locals hate us as much as their own government. That limits us to spy satellites."

"Maybe now the Pakistanis will let us put UAVs over Baluchistan," Grey proposed. "They could send us pictures in real time, day and night. Of course, they'd be looking for a flyspeck — a small group of men, a few trucks, maybe a boat. But it can't hurt to try."

Standing, Grey shuffled out the door.

Brooke turned to the window, briefly allowing his mind to drift.

I liked it better when you were this kid.

So did I.

Before I knew you, Brooke thought now. Before I knew too much.

For their first dinner, Brooke had taken Anit Rahal to Moustache in the Village.

They sat at a copper table beside a plate-glass window that looked out at the street

184

and sidewalk. A waitress bustled among the diners with aromatic dishes of lamb and baba ghanoush. Anit's smile as she looked around suggested that she liked the place; Brooke noted that she had used a touch more makeup to accent her eyes and, another novelty, worn earrings. It seemed almost like a date.

"I assume you like Middle Eastern food," he told her.

"I do. I've been wanting to try some here."

As she looked at the menu, quiet, Brooke caught a hint of distraction. Studying her, he asked, "More news from home?"

She seemed to watch his face, deciding whether he was merely being polite. "The same kind of news," she answered. "Sometimes I feel my country is caught in this endless feedback loop. More riots and now gun battles on the West Bank between us and the Palestinians. They stomp two soldiers to death; we bomb Ramallah. Hezbollah seizes the opportunity to cross the Lebanese border and take three of our soldiers hostage. And so on. None of it is new."

"And nothing seems to change?"

"Except for the worse." Briefly, she looked vulnerable, perhaps in need of understanding. "I don't want to come off as this brooding person. But what's happening now reminds me of when I was on the border. A right-wing Israeli had assassinated Yitzhak Rabin, our greatest hope for peace. So we had an election: Rabin's successor, Peres, who also favored peace, against Netanyahu, a man supported by fanatics like the one I debated. Hamas, which did *not* want peace, launched a wave of suicide bombings to discredit Peres and elect Netanyahu. It worked."

"Barak is prime minister now," Brooke pointed out. "Clinton can work with him. Any president who could get Arafat and Rabin to shake each other's hand in public has a shot at making peace."

Anit frowned, dubious. "I believe in President Clinton," she answered. "But this task needs another Rabin and a Palestinian Mandela. Instead we've got Arafat and Sharon, both stirring up the conflict that began all this. I pray for peace. But if it doesn't come soon, Sharon will rise to power, and the next five years will replicate the last."

"What will you do then?"

"What can I do? I despise Sharon. But my country will need us all."

A liter of red wine arrived, with two glasses. Raising his, Brooke said, *"L'chaim."*

Anit smiled at this, then touched her glass to his. "To peace."

Her smile faded. "Perhaps things are becoming more difficult for America as well. An hour ago, I saw that suicide bombers had struck one of your destroyers anchored in Aden. There were a number of deaths."

Brooke nodded. "Seventeen. A jihadist group called al Qaeda, they think." He put down his wine. "It's tragic, but different. Aden is thousands of miles from here. As you reminded me the other night, we're safe."

Anit played with her gold earring. "Please don't think I was beating on America. But safety makes you different. It's more possible here to live a nice material life, not caring much about anything, and get along just fine."

"True enough," Brooke answered. "When you talked about your time in the military, it struck me that I don't know anyone my age who's served in ours. Let alone anyone who died."

"Again, I envy you. The good part, I suppose, is that so many of us feel empathy for each other." Stopping, she flashed a self-deprecating smile. "Here I go again, the child of one thousand years of Ashkenazi suffering. Why should you suffer with me?"

"Do I look like I'm suffering? This may seem remarkable, but I like that Israel matters to you. I may even like *you* a little."

Anit laughed, semi-embarrassed. "So tell me what's good to eat here."

Afterward, Brooke took her to Chumley's, an old speakeasy that, by tradition, still had no sign — only an unmarked door with one window obscured by grills. Sitting by the fireplace, Brooke ordered coffee for Anit, a glass of port for himself, and then explained Prohibition. "A bizarre outburst of American Puritanism," he concluded. "We have them every couple of decades. This one gave us organized crime, gin so bad that it blinded you, and a whole new generation of alcoholics."

Anit took in the worn wooden floors and dark tables and chairs. "So this is a historic site."

"Very. On the subject of history, I'd like to hear more of yours. We seem to have covered mine."

"You'll be fascinated, I'm sure. But fair enough. Where would you like me to start?"

"As a kid. Before all the suffering began."

Anit looked at the ceiling with an expression of mock concentration, as though striving to separate the momentous from the merely consequential. "I was an only child," she informed him, "and very independent. There's one picture that my mother considers telling. I was two, and very small. My parents had put me in a stiff white dress to be photographed — sitting on the floor, I look like a head and body with no legs. I must have despised the dress: My arms are folded, and I'm staring at the camera with absolute defiance." Anit rolled her eyes. "My parents call it a formal portrait of the demon's seed. They never made me wear the dress again."

"So you were not a malleable child."

"Never. When I was three, and fighting with a cousin, my uncle took me to the parlor and deposited me on top of an upright piano. Then he took the bench away, and left me there, a prisoner —"

"Traumatic, I'm sure."

"Actually, my principal reaction was stubbornness. I sat there on the piano, refusing to call for help even when I wet my pants. My reward was when my mother found me and began screaming at my uncle. In the end, I won."

Brooke found the scene quite easy to imagine. "So you're competitive, too."

"Very. Like you, I love games — soccer, basketball, and especially track. I was fast, and hated losing." She paused, reflecting on her reasons. "Winning was more than fun. It brought me this fierce satisfaction, the best moments I had in school."

"Best? What about boys?"

Anit shrugged. "Not really. Until I was eighteen I didn't give them much time."

"And now?"

Abruptly, her face became more guarded. "There is one, yes." When Brooke said nothing, she continued, "His name is Meir. I met him in the army, and we've been seeing each other ever since. I guess you could say it's serious."

Aware that he had no right, Brooke felt deflated. "So I'm an experiment?"

Anit studied his face. "I don't think of it that way," she answered. "The two of you are so different I don't know what kind of experiment that would be." Her gaze became curious. "Tell me, have you ever been serious about anyone?"

It was something Brooke had asked himself. "I'm not really sure. I've had periods of semi-monogamy, punctuated by moments of random chance —"

"I'll bet."

Brooke laughed a little. "Random or not, it's all felt pretty predictable. Like the rest of my life, I suppose. Perhaps I'm waiting for someone to shake things up a little."

Anit looked at him askance. "Shouldn't that come from you?"

"Mostly. But there's also Chandler's Theory of Romantic Symbiosis."

"Which is?"

"That who you choose to be with helps to define who you are — that each couple is a different entity. So Anit and Meir are different than Anit and anyone else would be. Therefore you become different, too."

"Have you seen any proof of this theory?"

"My closest friend." Brooke sipped his port, warmed by the thought. "Ben Glazer. He's sort of teddy-bearish — warm, funny, blunt, and a great friend. Not to mention smart as a whip. But he's not exactly a movie star, or inclined to blow his own horn. So women didn't always get him."

"But now one does?"

"Aviva — the sharpest and hottest soon-to-be lawyer in Manhattan. I didn't know her before they met. But she sees my friend to the core. Now he's looser, more confident, and way more content — a happier, better Ben. As for Aviva, she claims to be mellower and more grounded. Together, they're great to be around."

His fondness drew a smile from Anit. "You make me wish I knew them."

"Then maybe you will," Brooke answered.

In front of her dormitory, they moved closer to each other. Brooke felt a current of connection he could not remember at other times and with other women. He sensed that this meant something — perhaps about her, perhaps about his own life. But he did not know.

"What is it?" Anit asked.

Without words, he put his hand behind the nape of her neck and drew her mouth to his. He felt the warm, answering pressure of her lips, another tingle of surprise. Then she drew her head back. "And *that* was for?"

"I think you know. Or you wouldn't have kissed back."

She gave him a penetrant look. "You're very certain of your own charm."

"At times. Right now I'm just hoping that I've got at least some charm for you."

After a moment, her lips formed the shadow of a smile. "Enough for another dinner," she answered.

Though it was past ten-thirty, Brooke phoned Ben.

His friend was with Aviva, watching a Kurosawa film on DVD. "What's up at *this* hour?" Ben inquired. "Couldn't be much, seeing that you're obviously alone."

"Sad but true. Nonetheless, there's something going on. I like this woman."

"Ms. Tel Aviv? Have you been drinking, or are you able to discern why?"

"How about that she seems to be wicked smart. Also direct, funny, sensitive, remote, and sometimes a little sad — like an old soul passing through this exotic young woman. Whatever mood she's in, I like occupying the same space."

"Hang on a minute." Waiting, Brooke heard his friend tell Aviva, "Brooke seems to be falling in like."

Aviva's surprise was audible. "With whom?"

"A Jewess, remarkably enough. Not like you — a real one, from Israel."

Aviva said something Brooke couldn't hear. Ben came back on the line. "We think we'd better meet her," he told Brooke.

TEN

Two nights after his second meeting with Abdul Zia, Al Zaroor and Zia's nephew Muhaiddin brought two other men with shovels to exhume the bomb.

This was sooner than Al Zaroor had planned. But tension between India and Pakistan was subsiding, and Zia had his own sources of intelligence. At the end of their last sumptuous dinner, the warlord had remarked, "I understand that the government is looking for something taken from them." Pausing, he surveyed the starry night sky, as though for a specific object. "Also the Americans."

Al Zaroor's tone was mild. "Is this a problem?"

"It's a concern. In the usual case, the government and the army won't tread too heavily in Baluchistan." He turned back to Al Zaroor. "How long will it be, I wonder, until the army stops massing along the border, and gives more attention to this search? Even the most standard operation might receive more scrutiny."

Left unstated was Zia's implication that Al Zaroor's mission might be far from standard. Impassive, Al Zaroor asked, "What do you suggest?"

"That you consider moving your package. The environment may change here, at least for a time. Should you agree, I'm ready to proceed."

However quiet, the last statement was imperative, a warning. Nodding, Al Zaroor said, "Then let's discuss the details."

Zia folded his hands in his lap, his manner businesslike. "Our men will conceal your cargo in the usual Pakistani crate, assembled with scrap wood. Then they'll put it in a van driven by Muhaiddin and start toward the coast.

"This van will meet two others carrying teams of men with automatic weapons. Each van will have stolen Punjab license plates." Zia's tone became pointed. "Given your fear of bandits, three land rovers holding men armed with AK-47s will travel a mile or so behind. That should be safeguard enough."

Al Zaroor hesitated. "There is, perhaps, one more precaution."

"Which is?"

"An identical convoy one hour before. Carrying an identical crate."

A glint of displeasure preceded Zia's measured smile. "You're a careful man, brother."

"And a grateful one. We pay well for extra services."

Zia looked down, fingering his cup of tea without drinking from it. "What package will this new convoy carry?"

"Heroin. To be placed in a dhow and shipped to Dubai, just as the second crate will be."

Once again, Zia seem to examine the sky. "They say you're a survivor," he remarked at last. "It's a skill I respect."

"It's one we share."

Zia turned back to him, his expression grave. "Then for both our sakes, you will have your second convoy."

Now Al Zaroor watched Zia's men dig deeper into the earth. Softly, he warned, "Soon there will be a stench."

The men looked up, silent, and kept digging. Arms folded, Muhaiddin stood beside Al Zaroor. "Was he yours?" he asked.

"Yes."

Muhaiddin's eyes narrowed to slits. He

said nothing more.

Al Zaroor knew at once when they had found the body; one of the diggers put his shovel down and buried his nose in the crook of his arm. "Hurry," Muhaiddin ordered curtly. "There's not much time."

The men kept digging. Moments later the clang of a shovel hitting metal echoed from the ditch.

An hour later, Muhaiddin drove the van into the trackless night, headlights off, Al Zaroor beside him. The crate rode in the wheel well beneath the van. Behind them, Al Zaroor knew, the remaining vans and land rovers were moving into place.

Ahead was a vast ungoverned space — mountainous, rocky, and stark, a moonscape with more stunted bushes than trees. Soon they would reach the back roads traversing the Kirthar Range, dirt scars in the earth hacked from rocks. Few used them. There would be more dust than water; the rivers dried up in summer, leaving only a few springs fed by underground water. Little wonder, Al Zaroor reflected, that Alexander the Great, becoming lost here on his return from India, had left several thousand soldiers rotting in the sun, dead from hunger and dehydration.

There were hours of darkness yet. Any danger would not come from the army or police; at night, the countryside reverted to the Baluch. Most were Pashtun: bearded men in white cloth robes, conservative Sunni who lived by a rigid social structure, a weave of tribes and clans in which Zia's family was intertwined. They would pose no problem. But the chaos in Afghanistan had driven desperate Afghans into a region where too many men already faced poverty. These could be a threat.

Al Zaroor closed his eyes, still thinking of the bomb beneath them.

When a pothole jolted him awake, dawn had broken, and Muhaiddin was talking into a radio. The convoy had fallen into place.

To the side, Al Zaroor saw the jagged mountains of the Kirthar Range, the highest still snowcapped. The road ahead was barely wider than the van and skirted a hillside with a precipitous drop. Al Zaroor wished he had not opened his eyes.

Muhaiddin smiled, still watching the road. "There are reasons we take this route," he said.

"Of course. Who else would?"

They took a hairpin turn without braking. Abruptly, Muhaiddin became taut. Ahead

Al Zaroor saw a barricade manned by uniformed police. Softly, Muhaiddin said, "This is new here."

He glided to a stop. Counting four policemen, Al Zaroor wondered what they made of this caravan appearing from nowhere. Perhaps Zia had paid the men; if not, they would die. The danger was that one might use a radio first.

Muhaiddin rolled down the window. "What is it?"

The policeman wore sunglasses, two black circles obscuring a skeletal face. "We wish to know your business."

Muhaiddin stared at him. "You know us, brother. Our business is the same."

The man hesitated, glancing at the vans behind them. "These are different times."

Without changing his demeanor, Muhaiddin reached for the handgun on the console. "Not for us. And not for you. Unless you wish it."

The man's neck muscles tightened. Al Zaroor tensed, waiting. Then the policeman turned and signaled the others to raise the barrier. "Be watchful," he told Muhaiddin. "More eyes may see you than before."

Including from the sky, Al Zaroor suspected.

■ ■ ■ ■

In late afternoon the path, sloping downward, neared the road just below Basima.

The young man beside Al Zaroor drove so
that Muhaiddin could sleep. They neither
spoke nor stopped; the men in the convoy
pissed and shat at night. Instead they shared
fruit and warm fetid water from a battered
canteen.

The van's radio crackled, then a woman
spoke in Pashto. "There are men approaching."

Surprised, Al Zaroor wondered at the
source of the voice. The convoy contained
no women. "Baluchs?" the driver asked.

"Afghans."

"How many?"

"I count six."

As the van turned another corner, there
was the pop of gunfire. On the stretch of
road ahead, several men on foot were shooting the tires of a Mercedes sedan. The car
settled slowly on its wheel rims. From inside
emerged two couples, men and women,
hands raised in the air.

More of Zia's people, Al Zaroor thought.

He heard the crunch of brakes behind
them, the other vans stopping. Three men

in Afghan robes and turbans approached, AK-47s held at hip level. One signaled for Al Zaroor to roll down his window.

Though young, the man had few teeth, and sun had graven lines like cracks at the corners of his eyes. "You are not Baluch," he said in accusation.

Al Zaroor felt his heartbeat accelerate. "Nor are you."

Spitting, the man said, "Show me what's inside the van."

"Open it yourself."

Glancing at his companions, this man and another sauntered to the back of the van.

Al Zaroor inhaled. The Afghan on the other side held a gun to his driver's head. Watching him, Al Zaroor envisioned the handgun on the console.

He heard the rear door open with a thud. The crack of gunfire sounded. Startled, the man holding the gun to the driver's head fired, a twitch of the finger.

The spray of blood and brains spattered Al Zaroor. With a swift movement of his left hand he grasped the handgun and fired, obliterating the Afghan's face. The rest of him slid down the side of the van.

Staring at the murdered driver, Al Zaroor felt queasy. He took another deep breath, wiping speckles of blood from his face, then slid out the passenger side.

At the rear of the van, two robbers lay in the dirt, bodies stained with red. The Afghans beside the Mercedes had frozen, as though hypnotized by the six armed men who faced them. The only movement was the two couples drifting to the side of the road.

Muhaiddin jumped from inside the van, following the gunmen who had killed the Afghans. Stepping across a dead man, he glanced at Al Zaroor. "You all right?"

Nodding, Al Zaroor gazed at the surviving Afghans. "Kill them."

Muhaiddin spoke a word.

Zia's men fired. The three Afghans twitched with the bullets like sheets fluttering on a clothesline. Then they fell to the ground, still.

Walking to the first van, Muhaiddin rolled the murdered driver onto the ground. Looking at the man's shattered skull, he closed his eyes.

"A friend?" Al Zaroor asked him.

"A cousin."

Al Zaroor felt the heat sapping his energy by the moment. "We must go," he said. "What do we do with the dead?"

"Our men will have to share two vans. We'll stack the bodies in the third, and leave them at night for the vultures." Looking down at his cousin, he murmured, "But not you, Daoud."

"And the Mercedes?"

"Push it into the ravine. Someone will retrieve the passengers."

Laboring in the blazing sun, Zia's men carried the bodies to the third truck. Then they got back into their vans and land rovers and began moving toward the coast.

Just before sunset, they reached the port of Jiwani.

The place was a womanless pesthole, three rusted fishing boats moored beside corrugated shacks electrified by a groaning generator. The sole person in sight was an old wizened man who seemed to have shriveled in place. Al Zaroor wanted to laugh — the grandeur of his plans could end at this miserable flyspeck.

Muhaiddin approached the old man and exchanged brief words. Then he returned to the van and Al Zaroor. "Your dhow will arrive soon."

"And the first?"

"Left two hours ago with its shipment, headed for Dubai."

Walking to the third van, Muhaiddin ordered the men to dump the dead Afghans in the mountains. Al Zaroor watched their taillights vanish in the enveloping dusk.

Darkness fell. Hurriedly, Zia's men removed the crate from the well of the van. Laid beside the truck, it was a haphazard assortment of wood pieces hammered together and stamped as machine parts. The West's future in a Pakistani box.

Someone called out softly, pointing toward the water. Framed in the moonlight, the masts of a dhow were gliding toward the harbor. Muhaiddin and Al Zaroor watched it be moored, a shadow.

"Come," Muhaiddin said.

Al Zaroor followed him toward an old wooden boat that bobbed in the waves nearest the shore. Beside them, three men carried the crate to the sunbaked mud where water met earth.

Knees bent, they placed it carefully in the boat. Muhaiddin turned to Al Zaroor. "This will take you to the dhow."

The two men shook hands. Then Al Zaroor got into the boat, hand resting on the crate, and was steered toward the dhow by a man whose face he could not see.

Palms on the conference table, Grey and Brooke stared at the series of photographs Ellen Clair had placed before them. To

204

Brooke most seemed to capture tiny rectangles observed from a great distance. Several showed what might be the outline of a boat against a black pool.

"What is all this?" Grey asked Ellen.

Through her glasses, the analyst gave him a look of owlish caution. "It's Baluchistan, of course. These last images were taken over the port of Jiwani and the waters offshore." She placed a finger on one photograph, speaking with a librarian's precision. "Collectively, they seem to show an unusually large number of vehicles, six in all, arriving at the port. These specks appear to be men loading something on a boat before it meets a larger craft farther out to sea. A dhow, perhaps."

Brooke looked up at her. "Can we follow it by satellite?"

"Possibly. It's not easy — there are hundreds of dhows in the Arabian Gulf. But the latest images suggest that this one may be headed in the direction of Dubai."

"Jebel Ali Port," Grey murmured, then turned to Brooke. "Care to go back into the field?"

ELEVEN

As dawn broke, Dr. Laura Reynolds drove from the Maronite church alone, stopping to admire an exquisite Roman temple in the hills above Anjar.

Gazing around her, she confirmed that her land rover was the only vehicle in sight. Then she pushed a button, raising the antenna, and leaned closer to the car's clock radio. She could never quite shake the absurdity of talking to a clock.

Nonetheless, she spoke, quietly but distinctly. "Morning, Sam. How was Paris?"

Hearing this, her listener would signal if the photographs she had sent, taken with the cameras concealed in her headlights, were sufficient. "This particular trip," his voice responded, "was a pleasure."

Instantly, Laura felt relief. Though her broadband bypassed the need for satellite transmission, others could intercept a message. This placed a premium on brevity.

"I'm glad," she said, and terminated the call.

Lowering the antenna, she took a last look at the temple, its marble white-yellow in the first streak of morning sun. Then she drove to the dig site.

Her colleagues were already at work. Seeing Laura amid the ruins, her reluctant coconspirator, Dr. Jan Krupanski, gave a wary smile.

From the beginning, Krupanski had been wary of Laura Reynolds.

At the end of her job interview, he had suggested that they stroll through Anjar, stopping by the river flowing through its center. Motionless, he pondered its depths, his pleasant young-old face creased with worry.

"So," he began, "you're the spy UNESCO proposes to plant among us."

"I prefer the term 'retriever of antiques,' " Laura amended. "You must know what's at stake here. Smuggling is a deadly business."

"But is it my business, I wonder?"

Laura waited for two Shia women in head scarves and long robes to pass them on the way to market. Quietly, she answered, "Tony Abboud and I agree that it should be. At last the United Nations is allowing UNESCO to address this crime. So here I am." Hands in her pockets, Laura faced him. "It's not just that they're plundering Lebanon's history. Nor is the cast of characters confined to crooked art dealers selling treasures to rich vulgarians from Texas. This traffic finances terrorists."

Distractedly, Krupanski ran a hand through his graying caramel hair. "Perhaps, Dr. Reynolds. But *my* cast of characters includes the universities who fund me, however badly. For them to know that I was harboring you might interdict this precious flow of parsimony."

"Who'll tell them?" she rejoined. "Not you, and certainly not me. As far as everyone but Dr. Abboud is concerned, I'm exactly who I appear to be — a new Ph.D. looking for an entry-level job. My other interests need not concern them." She paused. "As to money, perhaps we can address that. But I can't leave here in good conscience without making my case."

"Then I'll listen. But only as a courtesy."

Laura gazed at him directly, drawing on an allure of which she pretended to be unaware. Her voice held a throaty undertone of urgency. "We're trying to stem a tragedy," she began. "Terrorists across the region help finance their activities by looting the treasures of countries crippled by war and civil discord. It's happening right now in Afghanistan and Pakistan. When the U.S. ripped apart Iraq, al Qaeda fighters helped pay for killing American and Iraqi soldiers and civilians alike by smuggling antiquities onto the black market. One bunker captured by marines contained guns, missiles, ski masks, night vision goggles, and thirty boxes of statuettes stolen from the Iraqi National Museum —"

"A stupid war," Krupanski interrupted disgustedly. "America responded to September 11 like a wounded beast, thrashing blindly in all directions."

Beneath this protest, Laura sensed resistance warring with the conscience of a man whose most sacred belief was in preserving the past. Curtly she said, "Let's not argue about what can't be changed. But since you mention 9/11, I'll tell you a true story. Before the attack, its ringleader, Mohammed Atta, approached a German professor about selling artifacts stolen in Afghanistan. When the professor asked his purpose, Atta replied that he needed to buy a plane." She softened her voice, still looking into his eyes. "I'm a New Yorker, Jan. I saw the Twin Towers go down, taking with them a friend I'd become quite fond of. Perhaps this traffic paid for his death."

"But who *are* these terrorists? The Taliban is not here, nor have I heard of an al Qaeda presence in this valley."

Laura gave him a level glance. "Al Qaeda still has affiliates in Palestinian refugee camps. But we both know we're talking about Hezbollah."

"Yes," Krupanski answered harshly. "The Islamic 'Army of God.' They're all around us, even when we can't see them. Their green and yellow flag, showing a hand thrusting a semiautomatic weapon skyward, flies over most of the Bekaa. It's rumored they have underground installations very near our site, perhaps rockets concealed for the next war with Israel. Why should I endanger my project and my people by provoking such men?"

Laura stood taller. "They won't slaughter archaeologists," she said crisply. "Hezbollah's public relations sense is way better than that. The only person at risk is me."

"So why endanger yourself by coming here?"

"Because, like you, I care about the rape of history and the mass murder of civilians. One feeds the other. Nine out of ten antiquities plundered from the Middle East are controlled by Hezbollah or other jihadists. Many are stolen here: Lebanon is hemorrhaging its past. That aside, smugglers in the Anti-Lebanon Mountains, some affiliated with Hezbollah, are siphoning stolen Iraqi treasures through this valley. I've come where I'm needed."

Krupanski turned to the river again. "You're one woman, proposing to stick your finger in the dike. How will you perform this protean task?"

"By doing my job well. You've seen my credentials —"

"Yes, and called one of your professors, an old friend. He speaks highly of you. You're more than qualified to run a dig house, if that were all that's involved."

Glancing past them, Laura spotted a bearded man in the green fatigues of Hezbollah militia functioning as a substitute for ordinary police. "It's most of what's involved. Supplying the dig house would allow me to move around the valley, going places and meeting people without drawing undue attention." Her tone became quietly persuasive. "I can also be our ambassador. My mother was Lebanese, so I speak fluent Arabic with a Lebanese accent. When we send out a survey team I can explain our mission to headmen in local towns, assuring them that we're not thieves ourselves. If I also hear about antiquities for sale, or see

211

something that suggests it, I'll quietly pass that on to my superiors and, perhaps, to Interpol. My only weapons will be patience and observation."

Troubled, Krupanski still gazed at the river. Moving closer, Laura stood beside him. After a time, she said, "There's one more thing."

Krupanski seemed to sigh. "And what is that?"

"Money. Without going into detail, I believe I can help supplement the funding for your project. Rather than causing difficulties, I might well extend your time here."

He turned, eyebrows raised in an expression that mingled surprise with fresh suspicion. "You're a very interesting woman, Dr. Reynolds. And very complicated."

Laura smiled faintly. "Thank you. Whatever my complications, they won't make trouble for you."

Still searching her eyes, Krupanski nodded slowly. "Trouble," he said with muted fervor, "is something no scholar needs."

Now Laura stood at the site, returning this man's ambiguous smile. You still have no idea, she thought. At least none you care to entertain.

TWELVE

Thirty-six hours later, Brooke Chandler arrived in Dubai at dawn.

He was glad to be in the field again, however briefly. But this feeling was overcome by deep anxiety: This time the issue was whether a Pakistani dhow contained a nuclear weapon. And Dubai itself increased his restiveness — like everything around him, the site of his hotel, Palm Jumeirah, felt like a mirage. A massive landfill shaped like a palm, it jutted from the coastline of a glistening modern city, the high-rises surrounding its mosques piercing the sky in phallic competition. A special point of pride was a stunningly ostentatious shopping mall built around a ski slope supplied with snow at hideous expense. When Brooke had first come there, seven years before, he had emailed Anit Rahal that Dubai was "Las Vegas without the heart." Then she had vanished from his life.

For another twelve hours, seemingly interminable, Brooke killed time in his room. Repeatedly, he parsed the theory he shared with Carter Grey — that al Qaeda had smuggled the bomb through Baluchistan; that its operatives would try to disappear in the maze of boats that plied the Gulf; that Dubai might be their transfer point of choice, enabling them to move the bomb toward America, Europe, or targets in the Middle East. Were they right, and the dhow they were tracking was al Qaeda's vehicle, the search was over, the prospect of nuclear horror averted.

But to be wrong meant more than a failure of sophisticated guesswork. Inevitably, Brooke's ultimate belief — that al Qaeda had targeted Israel — would hold less credence among his peers. He was restless, others might say, still so angry at the screwup in Lebanon that he imagined al Qaeda's theft of a bomb was related to his aborted work. To lose one's detachment was a sin in an agency where judgment mattered.

When at last the phone call came, Brooke was still questioning himself.

His contact, Nuri Abbas, was a polite and slender man highly placed in the intelligence

214

agency of the United Arab Emirates. The job had its perquisites, Brooke perceived, including the black Lincoln Town Car in which a driver took them to Jebel Ali Port. Noah Brustein had informed Abbas only that Brooke worked for the CIA, and that the agency believed that this particular dhow might contain important contraband. But Abbas was among the elite security officers in Dubai who knew that a bomb was missing, and some things need not be specified. The agency did not send field agents halfway around the world to chase down guns or heroin.

The discovery of a nuclear weapon, both men knew, would change everything. Brooke would call Brustein; calls at the highest level would follow. A hazardous-materials team was already in the area, ready to deal with the bomb. Brooke's best guess was that an aircraft carrier from the Fifth Fleet, with more experts on board, was prepared to relieve the Emirates of its unwelcome nuclear cargo. All this would occur without a whisper.

"A dhow," Abbas murmured with a trace of skepticism. "Very quaint. One might have expected a larger ship out of Karachi, perhaps moving toward the west."

"True," Brooke responded. "But I think

215

we're dealing with a very subtle mind."

Perhaps Amer Al Zaroor, he thought. He had taped the operative's photographs to his office wall. Though captured in a ten-year-old image, the man looked elusive, about to disappear. And so he had.

The waterfront at Jebel Ali Port was filled with freighters and tankers. As Brooke and Abbas got out, a setting sun turned the mist hovering over the Gulf deep orange. From this band of color a two-masted dhow emerged, escorted by three boats filled with armed customs officials.

The dhow docked at the end of a pier, the escorts anchored on each side. Brooke and Abbas watched from a distance as the officials marched the crew off to custody. From a distance, none resembled Brooke's conception of Amer Al Zaroor. There would be time for questions later; the first concern was the cargo.

"Let's take a look," Abbas said.

They walked to the end of the pier as customs officials began offloading crates and boxes. The dhow's hull was commodious; the process long. With mounting edginess, Brooke watched box after box emerge that could not, by their shape, hold a Pakistani bomb. All appeared to contain what their labels claimed — every electronic device known to man. Which was curious, Brooke told Abbas, for an ancient ship from some godforsaken port on the Makran coast.

Abbas smiled tightly, his keen gaze directed at the crates that kept appearing. "The world economy," he responded. "A truly wondrous thing." Brooke could feel the man's tension.

By now the orange dusk was fading into night, and a customs official shone a flashlight on each new crate. None was the right size or shape. As each new crate emerged, the men stacked them in two uneven walls, preserving a pathway to the dhow. "Perhaps there's nothing," Abbas remarked. "I'm not sure what to hope for."

"I am."

Abbas did not respond. "How many more?" he called out.

"Maybe three," an official answered.

Abbas gave Brooke a sideways gaze. Then Brooke saw the crate suggested by Ellen Clair's aerial photographs. Pointing, he said, "It's that one."

Abbas issued an order. The seven-foot-long crate placed before Brooke was a rough-hewn construction that someone had stamped as machine parts. The crewmen had groaned beneath its weight. "Tell them to break it open," Brooke requested.

Abbas turned to him with a questioning look. "It's not a problem," Brooke said. "The people who usually handle these things don't wear spacesuits." Nonetheless, he understood — the thought of a nuclear bomb at his feet filled him with superstitious awe.

Working swiftly, two crewmen pried open the box. What remained was a gray metal rectangle with latches, its size matching the specifications of the bomb. Brooke flipped back its latches, then lifted open the heavy metal lid.

Inside, someone had crammed countless bags of white powder.

Angry, Brooke ripped one open, wet his index finger, and tasted the contents. But he already knew — heroin.

Dryly, Abbas said, "A small victory in the global war on drugs."

Or possibly a decoy, Brooke thought — perhaps even a taunt. If so, someone very clever had undercut him, and the argument for Israel as target with it. Unless, as Brustein had intimated, Brooke could delude himself without help.

He stood and thanked Abbas, preparing for his return to Langley.

■ ■ ■ ■

Al Zaroor sat in the stern of the ship, feeling the ancient vessel forge the dark, trackless sea.

He hated this feeling of helplessness, just as he hated the water. He was out of his element, compelled to trust men he did not know — the taciturn captain, the crew of six Baluchs. His cell phone did not work here. The yawing of the old dhow made him queasy — he had no gift for sailing. Few things terrified him; drowning was one. He did not know how to swim.

The dhow was seaworthy enough, he knew — handsome in its ungainly way, a well-maintained two-masted wooden ship whose design, in the words of its captain, was "older than the faith." What troubled Al Zaroor far more was the as-yet-unseen presence of the American Fifth Fleet, no doubt prepared to board a suspicious craft. The captain did not know that the crate concealed beneath the TV sets and machine parts contained a nuclear weapon.

Little else would have bothered him. The captain was a small man, whippet thin, whose ancestors had plied these waters for generations. Perhaps they had shipped fruit and spices; their descendant smuggled drugs, gold, and women bound for sexual slavery. Now the man thought he was running heroin and a stranger to Dubai.

There was much in Dubai that Al Zaroor wanted to avoid. A transfer to another craft, immobilizing them for precious hours. The security services friendly to America and the Jews. Perhaps a minion sent by the CIA should their spy planes have fallen for his ploy. But it was hours yet before he would act.

He went below to his spartan cabin. After a time he closed his eyes, feeling the boat's fitful rocking until he achieved sleep.

When he arose, Al Zaroor discovered that disequilibrium affected his ability to walk. He inhaled, nauseated again, and then ascended to the deck with the halting steps of an old man.

Mist still enveloped the dhow. Seeing him, the captain pointed to the waters ahead.

In the distance, Al Zaroor saw the massive gray outline of what could only be an aircraft carrier. For an instant, he felt defenseless, imagining the huge ship smashing them into splinters. In a voice not quite his own, he asked the captain, "Is this a common sight?"

The captain gave him a quick, searching glance. "Not common, no. But their business here is pirates and Iranians. Not minnows such as us."

Stomach clenched, Al Zaroor watched the carrier moving toward them, its outline becoming clearer. Perhaps the spy planes had not been fooled; in waters so vast, he did not believe that this encounter was random. "Do they see us?" he asked the captain.

The aircraft carrier loomed larger, still coming toward them. Hand on the wheel, the captain squinted with worry. Then, almost imperceptibly, the prow of the warship seemed to turn away.

In moments it was beside them, perhaps a hundred feet distant. Standing on the deck, a sailor waved to the men on the dhow. Inhaling deeply, Al Zaroor raised his arm in a satiric half salute. Then the carrier receded into the mist.

Spitting, the captain said, "Those devils have no business in our waters."

Al Zaroor checked his watch. "I've decided to change our plans," he said calmly. "We're heading toward Kuwait."

The captain gave him a long, resentful stare. "That's hundreds of miles from here," he protested. "We'll need more provisions and fuel."

"Then get them. But nowhere near Dubai." Al Zaroor's tone became flinty. "You are to accept my orders as Zia's. I'll tell you more nearer to land."

The captain spat again. But he turned the dhow westward and began the odyssey Al Zaroor had plotted from the start.

Hearing his proposed target, Zawahiri had shaken his head. "The Zionist entity?" he asked sharply. "Why not its enablers, the Americans?"

Before Al Zaroor could respond, Bin Laden said, "A fair question, Amer. When I selected New York and Washington, I chose the seats of American power."

Al Zaroor paused to weigh his words. "And yet America survived. It is too vast." He glanced at Zawahiri, a gesture of deference intended as balm for the man's festering insecurities. "A single bomb would surely traumatize the Americans. But then they would seek revenge. And the Zionists would still defile our land."

Bin Laden considered this. "But not if your plan succeeds."

"That's why I propose Tel Aviv." Al Zaroor looked from Bin Laden to Zawahiri and back again. "It will tear out the heart of

Zionism. Last year a poll of the Jews revealed that one-fourth would emigrate if the Iranians develop a bomb. Imagine what they'll do when we annihilate them by the hundreds of thousands, destroying their infrastructure, their economy, and most of all, the romantic myth of their survival in the land they fantasize God promised them. The souls of *these* survivors would shrivel and die." He made his voice quieter yet, causing his two listeners to lean forward. "As for our Muslim brothers, they would turn their faces from the Shia of Iran and gaze at us in wonder. It is worth any risk we take."

Bin Laden fingered his beard. "Including nuclear fallout? The calamity you imagine does not respect borders, and the wind above the Zionists moves east."

Al Zaroor had anticipated this inquiry, consistent with his leader's foresight. "That's true. But the greatest fallout occurs when a bomb does not detonate until it hits the ground, yielding a deadly crop of radioactive debris. A midair detonation will kill many more Jews, yet threaten fewer Arabs.

"Some, of course, will suffer. But probably less than the number of Palestinians and Lebanese killed by the Jews, and surely fewer than the many thousands of Iraqis,

Afghanis, and Pakistanis slaughtered by America. And they will have died so that our dream may live."

"But not in the hearts of the Shia heretics." Zawahiri's voice was etched with disdain. "Not this posturing fool who fronts for the Iranian capitalists and clerics, or the great leader of the Lebanese Hezbollah — Nasrallah, the latter-day Saladin who claims to have fought the Zionists to a standstill. They, too, are our enemies, contesting us for the soul of Islam."

Bin Laden faced him. "What Amer is suggesting, my brother, is that in a single strike we can eclipse them. The specter of the Iranian bomb is symbolic — they do not intend to use it, but merely to deploy it as an emblem of power and a shield to protect their clients, especially the tin soldiers of Hezbollah. By this they mean to spread the Shia apostasy throughout Islam, a more abiding affront to our Sunni heritage than those of Christ or Moses." He inclined his head toward Al Zaroor. "Their forces are many; ours are fewer. Amer proposes to cast a shadow so large that Iran will cower in its darkness."

Zawahiri pondered this. "I dream of even more," Al Zaroor interposed. "A war between the Zionists and Iran, where the death spasms of the Jews consume our Shia enemy. On the brink of extinction, the Zionists will lash out at Iran and Hezbollah in misplaced anger."

Bin Laden's scrutiny became puzzled yet probing. "Even if the Zionist leaders know the deed was ours?"

"Their people will demand revenge," Al Zaroor replied. "But they can't find us, and the Iranians and Hezbollah have long been their obsession. When have the Jews discriminated among their enemies, or used precision in the taking of Arab lives?"

"It is true enough," Bin Laden observed to Zawahiri, "and not only of the Jews. The ultimate elegance of our attack on America is that they retaliated by invading Iraq. As for the Zionists, their history is one of excess — deploying Christian thugs to slaughter defenseless Palestinian refugees at Sabra and Shatilah; carpet-bombing Lebanese civilians for decades; responding to Hezbollah's kidnapping of a few soldiers by invading Lebanon once again. Their psychology of victimhood forever seeks out victims. Why not Hezbollah and Iran?" Closing his eyes, he inclined his head in the attitude of prayer. "For fear of offending Arabs, we could not ourselves murder Shia in vast numbers. But there is a terrible beauty in

225

moving the Zionists to do it. They will seed their Shia killing field with yet more hatred of the Jews."

"Yes," Al Zaroor said simply. "It is in their nature."

Bin Laden's eyes snapped open. "Still, we must consider the Americans. If we destroy Tel Aviv, the Zionist lobby in America will demand our end by any weapon at hand."

"And if they do? I wonder if America will be so eager to listen. Or will its people fear they will be next, and turn away from the Zionists at last? Like any nation, America must look to its own survival." Al Zaroor leaned closer to Bin Laden, speaking in his most seductive tone. "With Tel Aviv in ashes, we can remind America that there are other anniversaries, and other weapons of mass destruction. If our allies take over Pakistan, we could have bombs for the asking. There are loose nuclear materials for sale around the globe — in Russia, North Korea, and Pakistan itself — and soon we'll be able to make nuclear weapons of our own. We can already construct a dirty bomb that could poison the air and water of an American city so completely that, by comparison, the Gulf oil spill will be as fondly remembered as a food stain on an infant's bib."

As though to distance Al Zaroor from Bin Laden, Zawahiri hunched forward to thrust his head between them. "And how would you accomplish these wonders? Or do you imagine it a simple matter to send the Zionists a bomb?"

"I beg your patience," Al Zaroor responded in the manner of a courtier, "as I endeavor to explain."

Watching this exchange, Bin Laden repressed the flicker of a smile. With a curt nod, Zawahiri signaled their petitioner to begin.

For the next half hour, without emphasis or inflection, Al Zaroor outlined his plan.

As he concluded, the three men sat cross-legged on the carpet, a map unfolded between them. While Zawahiri studied the map, Bin Laden observed Al Zaroor.

"I've left nothing to chance, Renewer. In the last six months I've been to all these places, meeting with those we will need. The plan will serve."

Zawahiri looked up. "Too many men, too many countries."

"There are difficulties, Ayman. But my plan will make the operation as simple as possible on each leg of the journey. That means using the customary means of transit to move goods from one place to another, whether or not the goods are contraband. Nothing that will look unusual to the locals on the ground, or to America's spies in the sky."

Bin Laden placed a graceful finger on the map, tracing a line across countries. "Why this route?"

"For its sheer ordinariness, Renewer. Each leg of the journey has existed since the dawn of time; each means of transportation is used by smugglers countless days a year. No one will expect men with a nuclear bomb to move it as our ancestors did for centuries." Al Zaroor leaned forward, addressing Bin Laden with quiet force. "We take established routes. We employ smugglers whose survival depends on the reliability of their agents, contacts, and networks of intelligence. When in the water, we use their ships; when on land, we use their vehicles. In either case, the men moving the shipment will be known to the officials they've paid to be deaf and blind. These men are seasoned and smart. They, not we, know best how to smuggle contraband. Some we used to funnel jihadists and their weapons into Iraq, and to smuggle out the antiquities to pay for them. The Americans did not catch us." He paused for emphasis.

"As to operational security, these men will not know what they're moving. Nor will those who help in one area know the men in the last one, or the next."

Bin Laden stroked his beard. "What do these men believe they're carrying?"

"The same cargo I've had them smuggle before — heroin. That shipment reached our intended destination." He drew himself straighter. "This time I travel with it. At the end, I will dispose of the package myself."

For a moment the men were silent. Then Zawahiri said in a querulous tone, "Your very presence will give us away. The others involved may be familiar to the authorities. But a foreigner will stand out."

Al Zaroor nodded. "Though I'm good at languages, accents will be a problem. Nonetheless, my presence improves our chances. Do you doubt my adaptability or quickness of thought? Or that I would rather die than fail or betray you?"

Zawahiri ignored this challenge. "There's also your chosen path. A route through Gaza is more direct."

"And riddled with Zionist spies. Faced with such a threat, the Jews would reoccupy Gaza in a heartbeat. It would be their opportunity to decimate Hamas —"

"Still," Bin Laden interposed, "why do

you object to shipping this weapon in a cargo container?"

"Because once we put our package on a ship, we lose all control. And we still must find reliable men to offload it when it reaches port. I make no promises, but this route holds the greatest chance of success." Pausing, Al Zaroor looked directly at Bin Laden. "There is, however, one more element that would greatly improve our chances. Something you alone can do."

"And what is that?"

Al Zaroor paused, and then spoke firmly. "You must lie to the Americans. You must tell them the bomb is coming to their shores."

Bin Laden stiffened. "I've said many things to the West, and never once have they listened. But I do not lie, Amer."

"Which is why they will believe you," Al Zaroor said urgently. "With respect, subterfuge is a timeless weapon of war. Such a threat will cripple the Americans with fear. Every resource they possess will be focused on self-protection — their police, their spies, their military, the cowardly politicians who, in their nightmares, will see their ruin in a mushroom cloud. That is how we will succeed." Meeting Bin Laden's eyes, Al Zaroor finished softly, "They may not yet listen,

Renewer. But only *you* have the power to make them tremble."

Bin Laden's gaze seemed to turn inward. Zawahiri leaned forward, his tone hectoring. "You ask too much. Whatever else we do, we can't simply send you off with a bomb, hoping it all works out. How will you communicate with us?"

"As little as possible," Al Zaroor said bluntly. "I'm not a student in a madrassa — constant progress reports would endanger our plan. You must learn to let go."

"Still," Bin Laden interposed in a voice of gentle reproof, "we *are* your elders, and this is a momentous passage in your life. If there is trouble, we must advise you."

After a moment, Al Zaroor nodded his acceptance. "Any messages between us will be through intermediaries in Peshawar, who will post coded messages in an Internet chat room. Throughout the mission I'll use new prepaid cell phones, or ghost phones with SIM cards cloned from the phones of strangers. That should be secure." Al Zaroor paused for emphasis. "If I'm forced to change plans, you will know it. You will know when I have the bomb, and when I'm about to drop it. And you will surely know if I succeed."

Bin Laden folded his hands. With a rare

note of imperiousness, he said, "As I told you before, I must have the final power to approve this act. That I cannot leave to anyone else. Even you, Amer."

Al Zaroor inclined his head in obeisance. "I understand, Renewer."

"Then how will you seek my blessing?"

Al Zaroor pondered this, then found an answer that brought a smile to his lips. "A great perversity of Western culture is that their young seek partners on Internet dating services. Perhaps I can place a message from a lovelorn Jew."

Bin Laden's eyes glinted. "And how should I respond?"

"With poetry." In a tone of fondness and irony, he echoed Bin Laden's praise. "From you, Renewer, one could ask no more."

THIRTEEN

On the flight back to Washington, Brooke treated himself to a first-class ticket. After takeoff he sat back, sipping a double scotch on ice while dissecting the crisis of the bomb with all the dispassion he could muster.

Faced with the same evidence, he would still go to Dubai. But the hard truth was that this failure would discredit him. The harder truth was that the bomb could be headed anywhere. Until there was a break, or the weapon went off, the agency was back to guesswork.

Repeatedly, Brooke's thoughts returned to the unknown operative who had made the bomb disappear. The bags of heroin in Dubai were either the dead end of an erroneous judgment, or a diversion planned by an extremely clever mind. The dhow's crew seemed to know nothing; they were smugglers, paid to pick up contraband in Jiwani. The question was whether the sorcerer Brooke conjured had used them as a cat's-paw. In which case one of his enemy's operational signatures was deploying decoys and feints.

Was he Amer Al Zaroor? In one sense it hardly mattered; unless and until the agency caught him, "Al Zaroor" would serve as shorthand for whoever had spawned this plan. But each uncertainty magnified the danger — a faceless man, a missing bomb, too many targets.

Liquor brought this into a gloomy focus. Brooke saw less the living people around him than the imagined faces of the dead. Of course, he realized, these dead would have no faces. This was a failure of imagination understandable in others, but not in him. He knew too well that death sometimes left no traces, save in the hearts of the survivors.

Yet more faces appeared with his second scotch — Ben, Aviva, and Anit, their laughter captured in a freeze frame. Brooke wished that he could rewind life's tape, stepping back into that picture along with them, innocent of all that drove him now.

In the first moments of their dinner at Café Español, Anit had taken to Ben and Aviva in a way that seemed natural yet surprising, hinting at a cultural affinity. The two "nice Yiddish girls," as Ben referred to them, had a chemistry that raised each other's level of animation — Aviva was tactile, given to touching the arm of someone she liked when speaking; responding to this, Anit seemed more carefree and kinetic, flashing a smile Brooke wished he saw more often. Then it struck him that something more was involved: Anit Rahal wanted his friends to like her.

They clearly did. In short order the three were playing what Anit called "Jewish geography" — relatives and friends who knew each other, or at least lived in the same places. The enterprise that had paid Ben's tuition, Glazer Monuments, had, in his words, "supplied the tombstones of choice for every dead Jew in Philadelphia" — among whom, it transpired, was Anit's late and unlamented uncle. A distant cousin of Aviva, a geneticist in Tel Aviv, accounted for a more vibrant interaction: She had been a bridesmaid in the wedding of one of Anit's friends to a man, Anit sadly reported, with the charisma of a fish.

Relishing his role as spectator, Brooke watched his three companions draw out facets of each other's personas. All shared a lively sense of humor and a blunt way of speaking marbled with a certain fatalism, the sense that no one could expect a disaster-free life. "Except for Brooke," Ben fondly remarked, "who's genetically exempt from the laws of gravity." Waving this jibe away, Brooke mentally compared this dinner to meals with some of his parents' more conventional friends — so many conversational constraints; so many polite euphemisms — and found that it deepened his amusement. It was like remembering polite but mummified couples speaking an obscure language — Americans who needed subtitles. Except, perhaps, for Brooke's far less filtered mother.

Over appetizers, Ben caught Brooke's eye. The two women were ensnared in rapt conversation about police brutality, a particular concern of Aviva's, a new subject of interest for Anit. Ben's gaze flickered from one woman to the other — Aviva, with her sparkling blue eyes, pale skin, and riot of curly red hair; Anit, smaller and darker, with almond eyes that suggested some long-ago Tartar warrior who had jumped the fence — his expression signaling to Brooke that these two spirited females were really something. Brooke smiled his agreement.

When the paella was done, the table talk

turned to Israel.

The intensity remained; the laughter ceased. The Second Intifada — the uprising of Palestinians against Israel — was raging now: No one could miss the daily reports of violence that tarnished the hope of peace, yet made peace that much more urgent. But what Brooke only now discovered was the depth of Ben and Aviva's devotion to Israel, and their discernment about what it faced. Brooke was perplexed that he had not seen this before; he felt as though Anit was his ambassador to two people who, in every other way, he knew extremely well.

"What about Ehud Barak?" Aviva asked her. "I think if there's no peace, he's done. The Israeli hard-liners take over."

"Sharon." Anit spoke the name like a curse.

Ben gave her a somewhat cynical smile. "You should pray for Sharon," he said with his contrarian's frankness. "He's got so much blood on his hands that even the pigheaded trust him. It could be like Nixon to China — only an inveterate Red-baiter could have opened that door."

"Nixon had no principles," Aviva objected. "Sharon does. Bad ones."

Anit nodded vigorously. "I agree."

Ben was unperturbed. "I think you're both

wrong," he said. "With all due deference, Anit, humanitarians like you can't achieve peace by yourselves. You lack the credibility of a mass murderer like Sharon. If you're lucky, he won't want that to be his only legacy."

"With all that excess weight," Anit responded softly, "I've been hoping he'd have a heart attack."

Ben shook his head. "Let him make peace first. Then he can keel over."

A pensive silence ensued, and then Aviva raised her glass. "To Israel," she said.

Anit touched her glass to the others. "To Israel," she said. "Whatever it needs to survive."

Quiet, Ben looked from Brooke to Anit, and back again. Brooke sensed Ben trying to gauge his feelings for this woman and then, for an instant, saw the concern of a friend for the heart of his closest friend.

Dinner broke up with hugs all around, Ben and Aviva exacting promises from Brooke that they would see much more of Anit. "On the other hand," Aviva assured her, "we'll take you without Brooke, too."

"Oh, bring him along," Ben put in. "I enjoy watching diversity in action." Then the couples went their separate ways.

It was mid-October, the night air cool but still pleasant. When they decided to go for a walk, Anit took his hand.

They wound up on a park bench in Washington Square. Facing him, Anit gave him a look that, for once, was less probing than soft. "I like your friends," she said. "Very much."

"Thanks."

Anit shook her head, as though his response was insufficient. "They adore you, I hope you know."

"I do know." Brooke paused, then decided to give voice to his deeper feelings. "I'm an only child, Anit. There's no privilege in life more important to me than having Ben as my best friend. There's nothing I can't tell him, or he me. Now Aviva's part of that. I love them more than I can say."

She took his hand again. "Then they're lucky, too."

The warmth in her eyes drew him closer. Anit rested her forehead against his, as though wishing to hide her face. "You know what's so terrible?" she murmured.

"No."

"That beneath that arresting veneer of charm, good looks, and money, you're actually a very nice person."

"That's 'terrible'?"

"Maybe for me."

Brooke curled his fingers beneath her chin, tipping her head back to see her. To his surprise, the look she gave him was unguarded. "Then why don't we just sit here," he suggested, "and live with it awhile."

They did that, quiet, Brooke's arm around her shoulder, Anit's face resting in the crook of his neck. A breeze, stirring the first autumn leaves, made the air feel cooler. "I guess we should move," he said.

"Yes. I should be getting back."

This did not feel right to Brooke. "It's early yet. Why don't I show you my place?"

Anit hesitated. "Actually, I'd like to see it."

They left the park, holding hands again. Walking back along Carmine Street, Brooke pointed out the foreign movie store, Vinyl Mania Records, the ornate architectural beauty that was Our Lady of Pompeii Church. Just beyond that was Brooke's apartment.

They climbed two flights of stairs to his door. Once inside, Anit looked around, noting the print by Agam, an Israeli artist she admired. But something in her gaze was veiled, perhaps preoccupied. Puzzled, Brooke asked, "Can I get you some wine?"

She shook her head, searching his face now. Suddenly he knew why she had come.

Silent, Brooke went to her. She returned his kiss almost fiercely, body pressing into his. When his mouth found her neck, she shivered. Her body felt tensile and light.

Standing, Brooke undressed her, then himself, their eyes still locked. She was slender yet full, as beautiful as he imagined. As they walked naked to the bedroom, he caught them reflected in the mirror, a glimpse of a man and woman about to become lovers. His throat felt tight.

They fell on the bed together, her eyes suddenly vulnerable, her skin warm to the touch. Brooke placed his lips wherever he wished, her murmurs of approval his guide. Now and then he paused to look into her eyes. As when he entered her.

She pulled him close. When they began moving together, it felt natural, two bodies whose spirits had met. With other women, Brooke had felt divided, half involved in the act of love, half mindful of his obligations as a lover. Now he was a single person who, without thinking, knew how to be with another. At that moment, he understood — without conscious thought — that this was how it should be.

When they were still, he looked into her

face again. "Anit Rahal," he said softly. Like the answer to his own question.

She smiled a little, kissing him. "Let's not try to name this," she said softly.

After that, they saw each other several times a week — sometimes just for coffee, sometimes for a meal, sometimes overnight. She never spoke of Meir.

Brooke became her guide to Greenwich Village, and then Manhattan at large. They stopped to watch the chess players in Washington Square, men hunched against the encroaching chill; bought fresh produce at the farmers market in Union Square. They met Ben and Aviva for dinner in Little Italy at Benito II, and then Umberto's Clam House, where Ben helpfully pointed out the bullet holes that marked the demise of Crazy Joey Gallo. They went to the Bottom Line, where Springsteen once had played, and had Irish coffees at a venerable bar, the White Horse, where Dylan Thomas had labored to drink himself to death. Anit soaked it in with relish, like a woman on sabbatical from care.

Soon they ventured nearer the environs of Brooke's parents, uptown Manhattan. They went to Central Park and the Metropolitan Museum. They scored tickets for the last game of the Subway Series, in which the Yankees beat Brooke's beloved Mets: Anit — who comprehended little of the game — consoled him with a philanthropic kiss. They heard Andrea Marcovicci sing at the Algonquin, and saw *Turandot* at the Met — after which, to Brooke's pleasure, Anit admitted loving his favorite aria, "Nessun Dorma." On the mornings after Anit stayed over, they jogged along the Hudson River. If the weather was good, they would end by drinking coffee in Sheridan Square, where the fierce Union general shared space with larger-than-life sculptures of gay lovers. The one experience Brooke spared her was dinner with his parents.

Instead, over Thanksgiving, Brooke asked for the key to their home on Martha's Vineyard. In her usual commanding way, Isabelle Chandler said, "So you're abandoning us for a weekend tryst. Just when are we allowed to meet this mystery woman?"

Brooke knew his mother well. "At the wedding," he answered lightly, and left her precisely where he wanted — guessing about his life.

The white rambling house in Chilmark sat on the bluff above the Vineyard Sound. Their days there were simple and sweet.

Brooke introduced Anit to lobster and turkey; Anit devoured both. It was a good thing, Brooke supposed, that she seemed to burn off calories just by watching cable news. Not that the news itself was good. Though Bill Clinton was using all his skills to promote peace between Israel and the Palestinians, the goal was proving elusive. That the president's time in office was running out quickly made Anit more anxious.

But these serious moments were leavened with lightness and, it seemed to Brooke, a rising passion. They made love on every soft or warm spot in the house. On the last night, feeling the tentacles of time reaching out for them, Brooke asked, "Would you ever consider living here?"

In the darkened bedroom, he could not see her face. " 'Here'?" she asked softly. "If you mean the world of Brooke and Anit, it's a very seductive place."

"But?"

"But that place must exist in a country. To believe that whatever person you may love is more important than anything is very American. And Americans think that anyone would be delighted to live here."

Brooke touched her arm. "But if there were peace for Israel — a true peace — could you?"

For a time, Anit was quiet. "I love being with you," she answered. "Right now, that's all I know to say."

Her Israeli friend Meir remained a phantom in Brooke's mind.

Over Christmas, they busied themselves in the city — several plays, a concert by the Dixie Chicks, skating in Rockefeller Plaza, dinners with Ben and Aviva. But it was the last such dinner that settled in Brooke's memory.

The two couples had intently followed the peace negotiations at Camp David. As the prospects waned, so did Brooke's hope — shared with Ben and Aviva — that Anit might consider staying. With shameless selfishness, Brooke weighed every new proposal on the scale of his own desires — that Israel yield sovereignty over the Temple Mount; that the Palestinians give up the claim to land in what was now Israel — relating all of them to his prospects with Anit. Unaware of his seesawing calculations of cause and effect, she remained skeptical throughout. "In the end," Anit predicted, "Arafat can't say yes. There's no true greatness in him."

That night, Aviva and Ben had come late to Raoul's, their smiles of greeting perfunctory. Anit caught this at once. "What has happened?" she asked them.

Aviva glanced at Ben. "Camp David blew up," she said flatly. "It's done."

Anit closed her eyes. "Now our future is in the hands of settlers and jihadists."

In that moment, catching Ben's look of compassion, Brooke sensed the beginning of their end.

When Brooke awoke, the plane was gliding into Dulles. Images of Anit Rahal mingled with the residue of a three-scotch hangover.

He had been here before. A few hours' sleep and a shower was all it took.

Getting off the plane, Brooke thought the airport oddly muted. Then he saw a crowd gathered around a video monitor, their faces stricken, their torsos tense and still. His first and terrible thought was that someone had shot the president.

As he edged closer to the monitor, a woman turned from the screen, tears welling in her eyes. Glancing up, Brooke saw the face of Osama Bin Laden.

Though his mouth moved, his voice in Arabic was muted, covered by a stilted translation into English. "Our plan is simple," the voice said, "its implications profound. On September 11, the tenth anniversary of our strike against America, we will destroy one of your cities with a nuclear weapon."

On the screen, Bin Laden looked ill, the intimations of death written on his sallow face. "You have only one way to prevent this," the voice continued. "To withdraw your forces from our lands, and cease your support of the entity known to blasphemers as Israel. Or else hundreds of thousands of your citizens will perish on impact, and that many more from the same poisonous sickness you inflicted on the Japanese. And yet that still will be as nothing to all the Muslims you have killed, and the further revenge we will exact from you in blood."

A woman beside Brooke moaned. Then, beneath the translation, he began to pick up Bin Laden's voice in Arabic, the adamantine tone of a vengeful prophet. "The clash of civilizations is upon you," he intoned, "and it will go on until the Hours."

Die, you sonofabitch. Slowly.

His cell phone rang. Even before answering, he knew it was Carter Grey. "I'm on my way," Brooke snapped.

■ ■ ■ ■

PART THREE
THE PROPOSAL
WASHINGTON, D.C. — KUWAIT —
IRAQ — LEBANON
AUGUST–SEPTEMBER 2011

■ ■ ■ ■

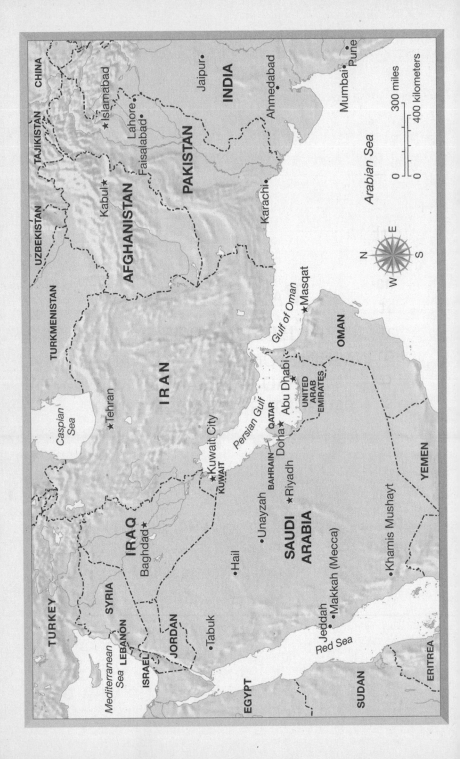

ONE

On the drive to Langley, Brooke learned from NPR that Bin Laden had succeeded brilliantly. In the hours since his announcement, the Dow was down nine hundred points and some New Yorkers interviewed on the way to work said they would leave the city. By the time Brooke parked his car, the stock market was in freefall.

Gathered in the director's conference room were several members of the president's task force, led by the national security advisor, Alex Coll. Representing the agency were Noah Brustein, Carter Grey, and the director himself, Carl Azzolino, a saturnine Washington insider selected for his political skills. When Brooke slipped into the room, Grey glanced up and then continued addressing Coll. "All of us should wonder why Bin Laden has been thoughtful enough to issue a public warning, complete with date —"

"What are you suggesting?" Coll interrupted.

"That we consider what he's accomplished." Grey pointed at muted TV screens showing CNN and al Jazeera. "People in major cities aren't showing up for work. Within days, we'll be conducting searches at every major port, bringing commerce to a standstill." Turning to Coll, he demanded, "Think about it, Alex. Bin Laden has demonstrated his power without limiting his options. The bomb could be anywhere, ready to destroy any major city in the West."

"Maybe so," Coll retorted. "But if one of *our* cities disappears on September 11, Bin Laden will be the most powerful man on earth. Americans will be paralyzed, waiting for the next city to disappear. They won't believe in our government, our system of civil liberties, or even in our future as a democracy. No matter what, we have to keep that from happening." Coll looked around the room. "Tonight, the president will try to reassure Americans that we can keep them safe. We cannot — absolutely cannot — refuse to believe Bin Laden."

On al Jazeera, Bin Laden reappeared, repeating his warning to America. "So what are you proposing?" Brustein asked.

Coll glanced at Deputy Defense Secretary

Joseph Farella. "First, we have to redirect our land, sea, and air defenses — dispersing troops along the border with Mexico and Canada, providing air cover for New York, Washington, and Los Angeles, and deploying nuclear search teams in major ports and cities." He turned to Carl Hobbs of the FBI. "The bureau will exploit every source who can lead us to domestic terrorists; the CAA will restrict the use of private aircraft; ICE will stop all immigration; the coast guard will seize and search any suspicious craft. As for commercial shipping, Homeland Security will search every suspect container traceable to Pakistan or the Middle East, however ruinous that is to commerce. Preventing a nuclear disaster comes first."

Silent, Brooke recognized that the face of the country was already changing. "You mention air security over major cities," Grey prodded. "Is there any?"

Looking at Farella, Coll raised his eyebrows. "Not enough," Farella conceded. "Private aviation is the black hole of national security. A small aircraft could deliver a nuclear weapon to any city in America —"

"Including D.C.?" Grey interjected.

"Especially D.C. In theory, we've got a fifteen-mile no-fly zone around the capital, enforced by surface-to-air missiles and jets

253

at Andrews Air Force Base on a five-minute alert. But thousands of aircraft fly within fifteen miles of the White House — if one crosses the line going three hundred miles an hour, five minutes won't cut it. Truth to tell, multiple planes fly over the capital every year, and we don't spot half of them until it's over." Farella turned to Hobbs. "Right now, al Qaeda could turn the White House into the epicenter of a nuclear blast. The surest way to stop that is to catch the airplane on the ground. Or, better yet, find the bomb."

Plainly discomfited, Hobbs turned on Azzolino. "We don't know that this weapon is even in the country. How are we going to find out?"

Azzolino inclined his head toward Brustein. Crisply, Brustein said, "We're training all our image and signals intelligence on major pathways to the U.S. Now that the threat is public, we can squeeze foreign intelligence agencies and sources for all potential leads. We'll focus on the modes of transfer — foreign aircraft, airports, ships, and ports. Any possible means of moving the bomb —"

"Toward America, I assume," Coll interjected caustically. "We can't be running off to Dubai, chasing down heroin smugglers in the Middle East."

Brooke reined in his anger. "Consult the map," he said evenly. "There are only so many ways to move a bomb to the Gulf, and so many ports with shipping channels to America. Dubai is one. Next time a ship from Dubai shows up in New York, which happens to be tomorrow, you might want to take a look."

Despite the gravity of the moment, Grey permitted himself a smile. Stung, Coll told Brooke, "Karachi would be more likely —"

"Only if you want to get caught," Grey interrupted. "The Pakistani government actually functions in Karachi. I assume you've never been to the Makran coast."

Coll did not respond. Addressing Brustein, Brooke said, "There's one other point I'd like to make."

"Go ahead."

Brooke faced Coll. "I appreciate all the pressure that's building — from Congress, the media, and three hundred million frightened people. But so does Osama Bin Laden. He knew perfectly well the effect his threat would have — he could have scripted the lines for everyone in this room. So he also knows that, in some measurable degree, he's reduced the chance of achieving his stated goal: the destruction of an American city on the tenth anniversary of 9/11.

"That threat carries its own magic: the power to make all of us work to the brink of exhaustion, blaming each other for any prospective failure. The nightmare driving us all will be New York City or Washington in ashes, and maybe dying in the bargain —"

"What's your point?" Coll snapped.

"You ask what the CIA can do. For a host of reasons, some political, we have only thirty-five hundred agents in the field — less than the number of meter maids in New York City. And now they'll all be focused on America." Brooke's voice hardened. "Bin Laden didn't jeopardize his plan because he thought we'd try to save ourselves by abandoning Israel and the Middle East. He warned us because whoever designed this plan isn't targeting America at all. The heroin in Dubai was a decoy, and this announcement is the next one. Two weeks from now, al Qaeda will level a city in Israel or Europe. And we won't have a clue until it happens."

Across the table, Coll leaned forward, closing the space between Brooke and himself. "The 'magic' of 9/11, as you call it, has a certain history —"

"I know it well," Brooke interrupted. "I

saw the Twin Towers go down, and not on television. So you might say I take a personal interest —"

"The towers went down," Coll shot back, "because we ignored Bin Laden's warnings and every scrap of intelligence that should have told us that he meant what he said. Three years before September 11, Bin Laden proclaimed that his mission from God was killing Americans. That same year, your agency called off an operation intended to kill Bin Laden —"

"As I recall," Grey put in, "the plan was more likely to kill a horde of civilians."

"At least they wouldn't have been ours." Coll produced a paper from his briefcase. "In May 2001, Richard Clarke sent an email to the person who then held my job, Condoleezza Rice, predicting that al Qaeda would attack us. Two hours ago, I reread it." He paused, then quoted in a grave tone, " 'When these attacks occur, as they likely will, we will wonder what more we could have done to stop them.' "

"We'll wonder the same thing," Brooke responded evenly, "when they blow up Tel Aviv."

Coll gave him a tight smile. "I can quote another of Clarke's emails from memory. On September 4, he wrote Dr. Rice again, begging her to envision hundreds of Americans slaughtered in the next attack — the very one you witnessed. He concluded by saying that your agency had become 'a hollow shell of words without deeds, waiting for the next big attack.' " He turned to Brustein. "While your subordinates are talking about Lebanon and Dubai, I hope the CIA is focusing on Canada and Mexico, or the possibility they'll fly this bomb from somewhere in Central America."

Brustein's face darkened. "Bin Laden can read emails, too, and the ones you just read are public knowledge. The question is why he's chosen to make everyone in this room relive 9/11."

"A better question," Coll retorted, "is why we're still hoping he dies of kidney failure."

Grey seemed to wince, perhaps from physical pain. "Who says he's still alive?" he asked gruffly. "You don't know for sure when he made that tape, or who may have told him to do it. For all we know it's been in the can for years, waiting for some unknown genius to steal a Pakistani bomb, then air the image of a dead man to make us wet our collective pants."

"He should have died years ago," Coll insisted.

On CNN, Brooke noted, the chairman of

the Senate Intelligence Committee was solemnly addressing the camera. Judging from the closed captions at the bottom of the screen, he was promising to see to it that the responsible arms of government would keep America safe. "The agency will do its utmost," Brustein told Coll. "That includes thinking clearly. The possibility of disinformation exists, and the points Carter and Brooke make are fair ones. Rather than try to shame them into silence, please consider the possibility that they're the next Richard Clarke."

Coll hunched a little, as though feeling the weight of his responsibilities. As he gazed at the table, Brooke imagined this man staring into the abyss — a failure of will or judgment that led to a historic tragedy. "I understand," he finally said. "But the legacy of 9/11 is the most catastrophic failure of intelligence in American history. And that will be as nothing after the destruction of Washington or New York."

"Or Israel," Brooke insisted quietly.

Coll stared at him fixedly. "It's not that I don't care. But we don't bear the responsibility, or the blame, if Tel Aviv ceases to exist. That's what the Mossad is for."

In the silence that followed, Brooke thought not of Bin Laden, but of Amer Al

Zaroor as he imagined him, and how deeply this meeting would amuse his adversary.

Two

In the deep of night, the dhow lowered its auxiliary skiff, and a nameless crew member steered Al Zaroor and his cargo toward a desolate island off the coast of Kuwait.

Nearing the beach, Al Zaroor saw the beam of a single flashlight. The crewman cut his motor, and the prow of the boat kissed the sand. The beam moved toward them. Al Zaroor tensed, his hand on the Luger wedged in his belt. Then the light traced a circle, and Al Zaroor stepped from the boat.

"Allahu akbar," a voice called out. *God is great.*

Now Al Zaroor could see him in the moonlight. Stopping on the beach, he waited until the outlines of three other men appeared at their leader's side. Quietly, the man said, "I am Omar Haj."

Stepping forward, Al Zaroor appraised him. "Haj" was a pseudonym. This man had brought it glory in Iraq; the smile that lit his bearded face did not extinguish the light in his eyes, the look of a fighter prepared to die. "How is it in the world?" Al Zaroor inquired drily. "I've been at sea."

Haj's face became solemn. "The world is much changed. Osama has spoken."

Al Zaroor's face showed nothing. Silent, he watched Haj's men retrieve the cargo from the boat. Then he asked, "Tell me his words."

Haj answered in an undertone that bespoke awe and wonder. "We have a nuclear bomb, my brother. Osama has pledged to destroy an American city."

Relieved, Al Zaroor repressed a smile. "And how was this received?"

"Overnight, the Americans became rabbits. Their stock market is sinking, and panic is spreading. Neighbors inform on neighbors with brown skins." Haj's voice filled with rapture. "The veneer of power slips away. Soon Bin Laden will be their master."

"God is great indeed." Even in his pleasure, Al Zaroor scanned the darkness that enveloped them. "What of this island?"

"Failaka is almost deserted. You have chosen well."

And carefully, Al Zaroor thought. Once

pretty and well inhabited, Failaka Island was a casualty of war, largely abandoned since Saddam had invaded Kuwait more than twenty years before. The Iraqis had moved the inhabitants to the mainland, then used their schools and homes and offices for target practice. Allied bombing of Iraqi positions completed the demolition. What remained was a virtual ghost town — cratered streets and abandoned buildings — lightly populated by Kuwaitis clustered miles from where they stood. "We should take cover," Al Zaroor said simply.

Nodding, Haj gave orders to his men. They lifted the crate, one man grunting with its weight, and began plodding inland through waves of sea grass. The sounds of the motorboat receded, headed for the unseen dhow; Al Zaroor and the bomb were in the hands of al Qaeda fighters who knew their role and nothing more. "No one comes here," Haj assured Al Zaroor. "If they did, we'd kill them."

Ahead, Al Zaroor saw the shell of a building, perhaps an abandoned home. "Is our plan intact?"

"Yes. In two nights' time, we'll smuggle your package by Zodiac boat into Iraq, landing near the harbor at Umm Qasr. A truck will wait there, sent by our Sunni brothers."

"You're still certain they're reliable?"

"Yes. We've used them many times, for men and arms to kill our enemies. Even at the height of the American intrusion, they've had no problem: Our friends pay the police, the army, and the militia — Shia or Sunni." He glanced at Al Zaroor. "As you anticipated, the American withdrawal has aided our cause. They hide in their bases as Iraq descends into chaos. As for the Jews, they have no assets here to speak of. We will leave you nearer your destination, wherever that may be."

Al Zaroor permitted himself a smile. "God willing," he answered softly.

At eight that evening, despite his need for rest, Grey took Brooke Chandler to dinner at the Cosmos Club. "Might as well enjoy my membership," Grey remarked, "while the club is still standing."

The dining room was too empty, a tribute to Bin Laden. But the dimly lit room itself, Brooke judged, had changed little in a hundred years. Waiters of long standing glided among the white-covered tables, serving men who bore themselves with the amiable authority of those whose success had been settled long ago. Raising his tumbler of bourbon to Brooke's martini glass, Grey gave the toast he reserved for members of the agency. "Present company. And absent friends."

Some of those friends had died in service; that Grey included Brooke in their company was a sign of honor. Then Grey said abruptly, "Make me a believer in the destruction of Tel Aviv. Before I start running interference, I need to know why."

Brooke felt his frustration spill over. "Everyone in that room today knows that faking one operation to conceal another is a standard ploy. In World War Two, the Brits concealed their invasion of Sicily by allowing the Germans to 'intercept' communications about their imminent landing in Greece. By comparison, Bin Laden doesn't even flatter us into believing we've stumbled onto a 'secret.' Yet we're tripping over ourselves to do exactly what he wants."

"Perhaps," Grey allowed. "But Bin Laden has always put America first. His goal is to bring down the West and its values. Israel is just an outpost."

"Not so," Brooke said sharply. "For Bin Laden, no crime of the West is more evil than Israel's creation, no wound to Islam more humiliating than giving the holy land of Palestine to Zionists, no threat more imminent than a nuclear arsenal aimed by

Jews at Muslims. Bin Laden may have attacked America. But he also dispatched Richard Reid, the future shoe bomber, to scout Tel Aviv —"

"Concerning holy sites," Grey interrupted, "wouldn't Bin Laden worry about polluting them with nuclear poison?"

"Not if he detonates this bomb from a plane. An airburst will cause less fallout. Tel Aviv disappears; Jerusalem remains." Brooke sipped his martini. "The existence of Israel helped goad Bin Laden into becoming who he is. In his vision of the caliphate, the Temple Mount is sacred ground, the site of the Al-Aqsa Mosque.

"So one of his goals is to liberate Jerusalem. In Bin Laden's mind — and I'm sure in the mind of whoever planned this — Israel's military prowess and nuclear weapons make that close to impossible. But there's an Achilles' heel: a nuclear attack."

Grey parsed this. "I've met with the Israeli minister of defense. He insists, as they all do, that Israel could survive a single nuclear strike."

"Utter bullshit," Brooke snapped. "What did you expect them to say?"

Grey smiled a little. "Precisely that."

"Which, at best, suggests a massive failure of imagination. I dearly hope I'm wrong.

But if I'm right, we'll see what they say after al Qaeda destroys Israel's center of industry and commerce, wipes out its electrical grid, levels its major airport, ruins its sources of coal-based power, and kills ten percent of its population. Except that they won't live to say it." Brooke softened his tone. "But even if you managed to survive, and the center of your bite-sized country was a nuclear desert, what would you do? Take out a building permit?"

Grey regarded him gravely. "The survivors will be angry people with nuclear weapons. Backed by the sympathy of the world."

"The kind of sympathy you feel at a funeral," Brooke rejoined, "which would last about as long. Then what? A country of psychologically damaged people without a future, staring at the ashes of their dream. Would you stay, Carter? Would you ask Anne to stay, or anyone you loved? Would you want your children and grandchildren to even breathe that air? In two years Israel will become a Masada state, populated by a cadre of religious fanatics prepared to watch their families die rather than yield an inch of their atomic wasteland." Pausing, Brooke thought of Anit — already vanished from his life, perhaps about to vanish from this world. "The result would be unspeakably sad — the end of Israel as we know it. It's Bin Laden's only chance to destroy an entire nation, the act of a vengeful Islamic God in a nuclear age."

Grey's eyes were as bleak as Brooke's words. "A Masada state," he finally said, "could respond with a nuclear attack."

"Oh," Brooke retorted glumly, "Bin Laden knows that, too."

Grey sipped his whisky, contemplating the amber liquid that remained. "It's part of Bin Laden's modus operandi, to be sure. Before he pulled off 9/11, Khalid Sheikh Mohammed wanted al Qaeda operatives to recruit pilots from the Royal Saudi Air Force, who would then fly their own aircraft to bomb the Israeli city of Elad. His idea was to incite an Israeli counterattack on the Saudis, pitting two American allies against each other in an all-out war." Grey put down his glass. "Fortunately, we captured him before he could bring this masterstroke to fruition."

"But his concept is timeless." Pausing, Brooke drained his martini. "Two questions, Carter — either of which answers the other. If Israel responds with a nuclear strike, who would they target? And who does Bin Laden despise almost as much as America and Israel?"

Absorbing this, Grey's face betrayed his interest. "Iran, of course. And Hezbollah. They're both Shia, and they've both eclipsed Bin Laden as symbols for Muslims who despise the West." Grey considered this, then said, "So you think Israel would go after the Iranians."

"Quite possibly. They can't bomb al Qaeda — Bin Laden has no known location. But the Iranians do, and the Israeli right is fixated on Ahmadinejad. They might lash out like a wounded beast." Brooke smiled without humor. "We're the prime example of how this works — after all, we pretended that Saddam had his fingerprints on 9/11 so we could invade Iraq. Would Israel be more judicious after suffering an atomic holocaust? Maybe so. But I think whoever planned this imagines the Israelis handing al Qaeda a bonus. The nuclear destruction of Tehran."

Grey hunched in the chair, closing his eyes. For a long time, Brooke thought he was warding off pain. Then he opened his eyes again. "No matter what outsiders think," he began, "the CIA tends to be more rigorous than any other agency of government. There's room to make your case. But you'll have to prevail against some very smart people — some in the Outfit, some not — who believe in their own judgment as much as you do in yours. Not to mention all the others so frightened by the image of a mushroom cloud over Washington that they'll refuse to listen. You'll need a first-rate analyst to back you, and friends in very high places."

"Not Alex Coll."

"Then it had better be Brustein and Azzolino. If need be, they can get past Coll to the president." Grey paused for emphasis. "What you've got is a theoretical case. Now you need to enter the mind of your operative. When you're done, I want you to tell me how he gets this bomb to Tel Aviv."

"Through Lebanon —"

"I'm not asking for directions," Grey interrupted curtly. "You need to figure out exactly how he does this, from beginning to end, until Brustein and Azzolino can believe it — and do that quickly. We don't have much time."

THREE

That night, twenty-four hours after leaving Dubai, Brooke tried to sleep.

This proved difficult. Stirring restlessly, he could not shake his conviction that al Qaeda was deluding his country and its people. His ultimate fear — the nuclear destruction of Tel Aviv and its people — filled his imagination with terrible specificity, its face becoming that of Anit Rahal. He wondered if she were there, and why he could not find her. At length, his thoughts turned to a night, ten years before, when Anit was with him still.

In February, Brooke and Anit had their first dinner with his parents.

As their cab headed toward Central Park West, Anit seemed distant, gazing silently at the foul winter weather. It did not help her mood that Ariel Sharon had been named prime minister of Israel. At last she turned from the sleet-covered window. "I know why they invited us," she said. "But from all you say, we're from completely different worlds. I hope we don't end up sniffing at each other like strange dogs."

"Don't worry," Brooke joked. "My father's like a Saint Bernard. As for my mother, the Doberman, she firmly believes the Holocaust was uncalled for."

To Brooke's relief, Anit mustered a fleeting smile.

Peter and Isabelle Chandler lived in a commodious penthouse above Central Park. The doorman, knowing Brooke, waved the couple to the elevator.

On the way to the top, Brooke imagined Anit's reaction to the man and woman who had raised him. Peter Chandler did, indeed, have the aura of a Saint Bernard turned denizen of Wall Street — a round, pleasant face; gray-flecked brown hair; black, thick glasses; modest jowls to match his paunch. With this came an unruffled air that, at any given moment, could suggest a sound, placid temperament, or complete and utter indifference to what was happening all around him. Brooke, who found his father an enigma, could never quite distinguish his serenity from cluelessness.

Isabelle Chandler was of a different mettle

altogether. Immediately impressive was the blond, imperishable beauty that in Brooke had translated into good looks so strikingly similar that Peter Chandler wryly called himself "biologically irrelevant." What Brooke did not inherit from his mother was the imperiousness of someone who, privileged at birth, could not imagine being anyone else. In the sixties, at Wellesley, Isabelle had discovered a passion for politics, and issues to inflame her sense of rebellion — Vietnam, civil rights, the environment, abortion, and the enactment of the equal rights amendment. Most, if not all, of these causes had Brooke's sympathy. But his mother's politics wearied him; he had never heard her say a surprising thing. And all too often, his mother's statements were stamped with the imprimatur "as I said to Hillary" — or Mario, or whomever. It was not these worthies' fault, Brooke knew, that the toils of fund-raising required them to treat Isabelle Chandler's pronouncements like Einstein's theories, swelling her self-assurance to steroidal proportions. But the fallout was that he had to listen, knowing that dissent was pointless.

"What are you smiling about?" Anit asked as the elevator door opened.

"The human comedy, Chandler-style." He

kissed her forehead. "When all else fails, give yourself up to laughter."

Anit mimed a dubious look, and they proceeded to his parents' door.

Somewhat to Brooke's surprise, it was opened by Peter Chandler himself. He gave Brooke a handshake that managed to be ceremonious yet warm, then did the same to Anit. The look he gave her was appreciative of her beauty without any trace of lasciviousness. Watching Anit relax, Brooke appreciated his father's innate gentility.

The former Isabelle Brooke awaited them on the sofa, her elegant pose worthy of the book-jacket photograph of an author of high-society romances. Then she rose briskly, kissing her son on both cheeks and according Anit a limpid handshake and a swift but thorough once-over cooler than her husband's. It reminded Brooke of her memorable reaction when a girl had made an unsolicited appearance at his sixteenth birthday party. "How lovely to see you, Jennifer," Isabelle had said in her most arid tone. "Had we only known you were coming, we would have invited you."

Now, the greetings performed, Anit and Brooke sat across from his mother while Peter Chandler brought them drinks. Brooke watched Anit absorbing her surroundings

— the sleek Art Deco furnishings, the carefully placed antique vases, the panoramic view of the park, its denuded trees skeletal in winter. Then, politely enough, his mother began to quiz Anit about her life, evoking equally polite but sketchy descriptions of her family, her service in the army, her educational pursuits, her sojourn at NYU, and her worries about the political situation in Israel. At this, Isabelle leaned forward, fixing Anit with a look that combined skepticism and concern. "Do you plan on returning?"

In her perplexity, Anit smiled. "Of course. Israel is my home."

Isabelle glanced at Peter for reinforcement. "What I meant was *should* you go back? Considering the danger."

"But there's never been a time when there wasn't danger, Mrs. Chandler. It's just a matter of degree. What feels more important is that my country is in danger."

" 'Isabelle,' please," Brooke's mother said airily. "Your attitude is very admirable, of course. But I worry about the nature of your enemies, seething with resentment of your manifestly superior culture. Especially given the daunting numbers at which they reproduce."

Anit sipped her Chardonnay. "There are

many concerns," she answered. "But I think most Palestinians would be content to live a normal life. Part of the burden of making peace falls on us. More hope for the average Palestinian means more security for Israel."

Isabelle gave a vehement shake of the head. "It strikes me that your enemies are a different species altogether, with very different values and no respect for life. These suicide bombers exemplify all one needs to know."

Brooke glanced at his father for clues, as he sometimes did during his mother's remarks on the state of the world. Often, as now, he wondered whether Peter's blank expression suggested situational absentmindedness, or the stoic suffering of a martyr nailed to the cross. Despairing of his help, Brooke told Anit drily, "I've spared my mother any disquisitions on the Arab mind. She's far too well informed."

Peter betrayed what might have been a smile. Then, to Brooke's surprise, he placed a hand on his wife's knee. "I thought that's what we pay tuition for, Isabelle — so that our son can know more about the Middle East than we do. Though not quite as much as someone who lives there."

After a moment, Isabelle had the grace to smile. "I don't lack for opinions," she told

Anit. "But I pride myself on keeping up with important issues. One thing that disturbs me is that Israel's location is so dreadful. I wonder if some of the original alternatives, like Uganda, would have been safer."

"Perhaps not," Anit said mildly. "It seems there were people there as well."

"True, though locating Israel in Uganda would have spared us Idi Amin. It's just that starting a new country for the Jewish people is a remarkable undertaking — even under the best of circumstances. And the neighborhood your Zionist forefathers chose is a bad one." Isabelle spread her arms in a gesture of helplessness. "As matters stand, you're surrounded by enemies. Surely you worry they'll get their hands on nuclear weapons."

Anit regarded her steadily. "It's a worry, yes. In the hands of a country like Iran, it might move them to further encourage terrorists like Hezbollah. Nor can you assure that any country with a bomb will be rational." Pausing, she turned to Peter Chandler. "When it comes to nuclear weapons, what scares me more are nonstate actors. It's easier for them to strike, and harder for us to find them."

Peter nodded. "I think of the people who attacked the USS *Cole*. There seem to be a lot of young men in autocracies like Saudi

Arabia who are turning to radical ideas and religious extremism. Sunnis and fundamentalism strike me as a bad combination. I'd hate to see such people with nuclear missiles, or the components of a dirty bomb."

Anit's look of surprise mirrored Brooke's. "I agree," she said. "But most people here don't know that Sunnis are different from Shia."

"I'm one of them," Isabelle said bluntly. "They're all terrible characters, oppressive to women. By our value system, is there any difference that matters?"

A bell rang, the announcement of the dinner prepared by the Chandlers' personal chef, breaking the conversation. In Brooke's mind, this mercy was compounded by the courteous way in which his father shepherded Anit to the dining room.

The first course was sautéed calamari on spinach — organic, at Isabelle's insistence. In the candlelit room, Peter sat across from Anit; Brooke from his mother.

"We were speaking of Middle Eastern culture," Peter said to Anit. "I, for one, know little about it. But I do have the sense that the countries in the region were carved out by colonials, like Winston Churchill, and don't much correspond to how their people see themselves. Am I off-track?"

Smiling, Anit shook her head. "Not at all. Traditionally, Arabs have viewed themselves through the prism of family, then clan, then tribe — and only after that, whatever nation-state they find themselves in." Anit adjusted her gaze to include Isabelle. "As Brooke could tell you, their social bonds are very tight, in contrast to Americans. The role of women is, as you say, subordinate — a terrible waste of human potential. But there are lovely aspects to their culture, including their sense of hospitality. When Arabs invite you to spend time with them, they feel a deep responsibility for your comfort and well-being. And Islam as generally practiced does not inspire violence."

"What about this Sunni–Shia business?" Isabelle inquired. "*Is* there any difference?"

Anit turned to Brooke, inviting him to answer. "Not to the West," he told his mother. "When Churchill started carving up the Middle East with a straight razor, he blithely asked an aide whether the leader he planned to install in Baghdad was a Sunni with Shiite sympathies or vice versa — he could never keep them straight. But to the two branches of Islam it matters profoundly.

"With the death of Mohammed, his followers couldn't agree on his successor.

Those who became the Sunnis chose Abu Bakr, the Prophet's advisor, to be caliph — the leader of a Muslim state. The dissenters selected Mohammed's cousin and son-in-law, Ali, to become what the Shia call the imam." Brooke turned to his father. "The hatred between them dates back to the seventh century, when Ali's son Hussein had the third Sunni caliph murdered. In turn, the Sunnis killed Hussein —"

"That was thirteen hundred years ago," Isabelle interjected with rhetorical astonishment. "Why on earth are they killing each other now?"

"Because the violence and estrangement have only deepened." Brooke glanced toward Peter. "Dad mentioned Sunni fundamentalists. The enemies of Israel include the Iranians and the Lebanese group Hezbollah. Both are Shia — dangerous, to be sure, but also rational. But ninety percent of Muslims are Sunnis. At their most extreme, Sunni fundamentalists imagine destroying 'the unbelievers' — including the West — in order to restore a mystic vision of the caliphate —"

"Magical thinking," Isabelle said with a wave of the hand. "Fit only for children and the insane."

"So one might argue. But the group

responsible for the *Cole* attack, al Qaeda, imagines that very thing. And their leader, Osama Bin Laden, is neither a child nor insane." Pausing, Brooke regarded his mother with deep seriousness. "People with strong belief systems try to create their own reality. Sometimes they succeed."

Isabelle accorded Anit a look of fresh concern. "As I said at the beginning, Anit, all this seems to have profound implications for your country. In their own minds, the Palestinians are displaced."

Anit shrugged. "In the Middle East, Isabelle, displacement is common. Fights over water; the Ottomans' moving people here or there; genocide against the Armenians; the British cramming tribes into artificial countries. All that's different here is that Arabs were displaced by Jews. We're a determined people, but Arabs are a patient one."

"So they have a different sense of time?" Peter asked her.

"Very much so," Anit replied. "To the leaders of Hezbollah and Hamas — and al Qaeda — a few hundred years are nothing. All we can do is endure."

Her words induced a moment of silence. Then Isabelle said, "Thank God we're in America, land of the impatient. Our Supreme Court may have given us Bush, but in four years he'll be an accident in America's rearview mirror."

"Are you that sure?" Brooke asked.

"Absolutely," Isabelle rejoined. "He's Dan Quayle in waiting. In the meantime, with luck, the janissaries of the right will have him too tied up protecting frozen embryos to do any real damage. And he seems to have no taste for foreign adventures."

Looking at Anit, Peter Chandler seemed to register her mood. "For my part," he told her gently, "I hope he'll revive Clinton's efforts at achieving a genuine peace."

Anit smiled at him. "Thank you," she answered. "I pray for that."

Brooke's father raised his wineglass. "Then let's drink to peace," he said.

They did, Isabelle stealing a glance at Brooke as he touched his glass to Anit's.

In the taxi home, Anit rested her head on Brooke's shoulder. "So?" he asked.

Anit hesitated. "It was fine," she answered. "Your mother is much as you described her, but she means no harm. The one who surprised me was your father. Beneath that pleasant surface, he takes in more than he lets on. And you may be more your father's son than you believe."

The observation interested Brooke. "What else did you think?"

He felt Anit inhale. Softly, she said, "That all through dinner I felt homesick."

FOUR

Feeling officebound, Brooke and Terri Young decided to walk through the agency's leafy venues, thinking aloud to each other.

Brooke knew Terri, in a casual but friendly way, as an astute analyst of Israel and its neighbors. Like Brooke, she had learned to view the world through the eyes of Israelis, Lebanese, Syrians, and Palestinians, as well as Hezbollah, Hamas, and al Qaeda. This had led to her suggestion that the architect of the bomb theft might be Amer Al Zaroor. Now, Brooke needed not just her expertise, but her support.

"Lebanon?" she repeated tartly. "You've certainly got that theory to yourself. Nearly getting killed there must have made a lasting impression."

Walking beside her, Brooke shoved his hands in his pockets. "This is about the people who tried to do it," he responded. "Lebanon is very sad, very beautiful, and extremely volatile. It's been a parking lot for outsiders since the dawn of time — Phoenicians, Romans, Muslims, Christian Crusaders, and the French. In the last thirty years you can add Palestinians, Israelis, Syrians, Iranians and their surrogate, Hezbollah. The men who killed my agent were affiliated with al Qaeda, and came from the refugee camp at Ayn Al-Hilweh. A very dangerous place in a dangerous country."

Terri glanced at him, obviously curious. "At some point, I'd like to hear more about what happened to you. But from the longer historical perspective, you can blame the French. They created what we call Lebanon by taking territory controlled by Maronite Christians and adding a stretch of Syria that included both Shia and Sunni —"

"Always a good idea," Brooke interjected drily.

"Then they proceeded to impose a ridiculous constitution that apportioned power among the Maronites, the Sunni, the Shia, the Druze, and fourteen other subsects. What we've got now is an enfeebled state, hopelessly split between factions who distrust if not despise each other. Which is your point, I guess."

"One of them. The Lebanese army is also fragmented, and so is their intelligence service — Sunnis versus Shia versus Christian versus the Druze." Brooke stopped beneath a shade tree. "I spent the first six months there figuring out who I could trust. Frank Lorber never had a clue. But the essence is that Lebanon is paradise for terrorists."

Terri contemplated a patch of grass. "As I understand it, your theory starts with the wars between Israel and the Palestinians. When Israel was founded, a hundred thousand Palestinians fled across the border. The Lebanese government didn't want them, but was too weak to expel them. Many were peaceful. But a hard core within the PLO wanted to use refugee camps as a base for attacks on Israel. Hence the Lebanese civil war."

Brooke nodded. "Exactly. To protect themselves, the Israelis supported the Maronite Christian militias against the PLO. The result was a bloody stalemate. So the Israeli defense minister, Ariel Sharon, decided to invade Lebanon in order to destroy the PLO's power base." His tone became sardonic. "Sharon was never known for his restraint. When someone killed the leader of the Maronites, he directed his army to let the Maronite militia into the refugee camp at Sabra and Shatilah, helpfully lighting their way with flares. The Maronites didn't care who they killed or raped."

Terri gazed at the winding pathway ahead. "I've seen the photographs. Murdered women with their skirts pulled up. Rows of young men shot in the back. Babies tossed in garbage cans. Boys with their throats slashed and genitals cut off. Hands sticking from mounds of dirt bulldozed over the dead. It made me sick."

Terri's quiet indignation reminded Brooke of Anit. "Sharon got by with it," he said. "He succeeded in confining Palestinians to the most squalid refugee camps imaginable, tinderboxes of hatred and despair. Sabra and Shatilah is one; Ayn Al-Hilweh is another. I was working with friends in Lebanese security to clean it up. The work, as you know, was interrupted by Lorber's misjudgment.

"As a consequence, Ayn Al-Hilweh still harbors al Qaeda fighters who might help an operative like Al Zaroor." Pausing, Brooke led her to a bench, seeking further shade against the rising heat of midmorning. "That's one of the unintended results from the Lebanese civil war. Another is that the war expanded the vacuum of governmental authority, especially in the Bekaa Valley on Lebanon's border with Syria. The

Bekaa became the place where every terrorist and foreign agent who wanted to drive the Israelis out of Lebanon set up shop."

"Especially the Iranians," Terri put in. "Once Khomeini came to power, Iranian agents entered the Bekaa, organizing Lebanese Shia into a military force that became Hezbollah, Israel's mortal enemy. Yitzhak Rabin — a man with more foresight than Sharon — said the invasion of Lebanon had let the Shiites out of the bottle, and that replacing the PLO with Hezbollah was the worst thing Israel could have done." She smiled without humor. "Not only did the Bekaa Valley offer Hezbollah financing in the form of drug and antiquities smuggling, but it was full of young men whose model of martyrdom goes back thirteen hundred years to the murder of Hussein in the seventh century. Hezbollah simply brought the concept up-to-date by inventing the suicide bomber." Sitting back, she began ticking off the results on her fingers. "The first bomber hit the Israeli military headquarters at Tyre, killing over a hundred people. The second bomber hit the Marine Corps barracks in Beirut. The third killed hundreds of civilians in our embassy.

"From the start, Hezbollah celebrated these guys as heroes. Their children paid no

288

school fees, and the teachers treated them as living symbols of sacrifice. Particularly touching, Hezbollah gave these kids presents on Father's Day." She stood, restless. "No wonder their martyrs' school for aspiring suicide bombers is such a success. There's even a massive shrine outside Baalbek dedicated to Abbas al-Musawi, Hezbollah's first leader, complete with the burned-out car left when an Israeli rocket incinerated him, his wife, and his four-year-old son. Tasteful."

"And effective," Brooke responded. "Hezbollah's the reason our embassy in Beirut is a barbed-wire fortress, and that Lorber never leaves it. Frank's seen the tape of what Hezbollah did to one of his predecessors, William Buckley, before they were kind enough to kill him —"

"There was a *tape?*"

"Sent by Hezbollah to the agency, to impress us with their seriousness." Brooke paused. "Buckley was a friend of Carter's. It's one reason that Carter — and a lot of others in the Outfit — hate Hezbollah as much as the Israelis do."

Terri looked at him somberly. "Have *you* seen the tape?"

Nodding, Brooke pushed away unwelcome images. "Before I was stationed there. But history marches on. Hezbollah's become a state within a state, a political party with a military wing stronger than the Lebanese army. There'll come a time when we're going to have to deal with them. Distasteful or not."

"That's certainly not our policy."

Brooke shrugged. "Not now. But once again, the Israelis provided us with a salutary lesson: another invasion in 1996, this time to wipe out Hezbollah. The result was a mass exodus of Shia from the south and the indiscriminate killing of civilians by the IDF, whether by accident or design. The worst was when the IDF shelled Qana, where the UN was sheltering Shia refugees." Brooke paused a moment. "As a student in Beirut, I interviewed the UN commander there. What he described was a scene from hell: men, women, and children in pieces, arms and legs, heads without bodies, bodies without heads. Two years later, this very tough man's eyes were filled with tears.

"You know the result. Hezbollah survived. Lebanese of all religions were united in their hatred of Israel. The Shia refugees crowded into a section of south Beirut, making it a Hezbollah stronghold. Their militia cemented its hold on the Bekaa and the south. And four years later, Hezbollah launched the guerrilla war that drove the IDF out of Lebanon altogether, making it the dominant force in Israel's northern neighbor."

For a moment, Terri observed a squirrel looking for nuts. "Israel learned nothing," she argued, "but Hezbollah learned too little. After Israel withdrew, Hezbollah kept on running raids and kidnappings across the Israeli border."

Brooke thought of Anit's service in the army. "It's what the Iranians were paying them for and what they ship arms through Syria to facilitate. Hezbollah's founding raison d'être was enmity toward Israel, and extending Iran's power in the Middle East."

"No doubt," Terri retorted. "But they pushed it too far. Hezbollah should have gone after constitutional reform. Instead they car-bombed Hariri, the Sunni prime minister. When the UN implicated Hezbollah in Hariri's murder, they had it absolutely right."

"Lebanon's a murky place," Brooke cautioned. "Some of my sources think the Syrians killed Hariri, with help from their friends in Lebanese intelligence —"

"*And* Hezbollah," Terri amended. "My point is that they kept on overstepping — kidnapping Israeli soldiers; murdering Hariri; launching rockets into Israel. What happened in 2006 was a massive IDF reprisal. Strikes on roads and bridges; saturation bombings of Nasrallah's headquarters and the home of the Shia grand ayatollah; hundreds of attacks on targets in Beirut and the Bekaa; destruction of part of the country's electrical grids and fifteen thousand homes; thousands of civilians dead. And what did Israel get for that? The intensified loathing of the Lebanese and the condemnation of the world. And the greatest irony of all — increased prestige and power for Hezbollah and Iran, the heroic resisters of Israeli power. Israel helped Hezbollah profit from its own miscalculation."

"Which brings us to my thesis," Brooke replied. "Imagine you're Amer Al Zaroor, or whoever has the bomb. What is it that this man knows about Lebanon?"

Terri rested her elbows on her knees, chin propped on steepled fingers. "Everything we've talked about. The Lebanese government is weak, its intelligence services compromised. The border with Syria is porous. Lebanon is a power base for al Qaeda's Shia enemies. But al Qaeda still has agents among the Palestinians at Ayn Al-Hilweh, whose hatred of Israel goes back to its founding. And Lebanon is the closest state to Israel."

"All true," Brooke said. "But there's more."

Terri looked at her watch. "I'm late for a meeting. But you've got my interest, okay? Come to my place for dinner tonight. If you tell me what happened to you in Lebanon, we can talk about the rest."

"I'll bring the wine," Brooke told her.

FIVE

Terri Young lived in a comfortable apartment on Capitol Hill, suitable to her cover as an environmental lobbyist. Sitting with a glass of sauvignon blanc, Brooke took in his surroundings — a comfortable couch and chairs, two striking prints of ballet dancers, a shelf of books about the Middle East mixed with fiction by writers such as Lorrie Moore, Zoe Heller, and Hillary Mantel, and, amusingly, a football signed by players from the Indianapolis Colts.

Then he turned his attention to Terri herself, sitting cross-legged at the other end of the couch — fresh-faced and pretty, with a keen sense of humor and a sharp, retentive mind. To be alone with any woman inevitably raised for Brooke the question of attraction, with all its mysteries and paradoxes. He had been drawn to Anit before they had said a word; chemistry at a distance, an immediate reaction to how she looked and spoke. What Terri inspired in him was more gentle and benign — a genuine liking largely free of desire. Perhaps it was the incest taboo, the respect and courtesy due a talented woman with whom he worked. If so, in some ways that was too bad. Often men and women in the agency, weary of lying about a job they could not explain, married other agents, bonded by the secret world they shared. Idly, Brooke wondered if it were possible to genetically engineer children for a life of duplicity.

"You were going to tell me about Lebanon," Terri reminded him.

Brooke felt the tug of resistance. "It's the proverbial long story. Maybe I should start with the beginning, and stop with the beginning of the end."

Terri's half smile came with a probing look that searched his face for clues. "It *is* your story, after all. But I'm curious about what happened with Lorber."

Brooke took a sip of wine, and began to explain the life he had led in Lebanon.

He had been Adam Chase then, a junior member in a politically connected consulting firm that counseled American firms doing business abroad. Like Brooke, Chase's expertise was in the Middle East, and he spoke fluent Arabic. This new identity — what the agency called nonofficial cover — allowed Brooke freedom of movement, the chance to apply a sophisticated knowledge of Lebanon at ground level, and access to widening circles of Lebanese. All Brooke had to do was become someone else.

Adam Chase was charming, with an approachability and ease of manner that drew men and women alike. He entertained businessmen and officials, learning about the Byzantine politics of Lebanon on behalf of fictitious clients. Though headquarters did not like this much, he slept with Lebanese women — for information, for cover, and sometimes for companionship. He got to know customs officers, the owners of nightclubs and restaurants, and financiers of all religions — supporters of Hezbollah, or the Hariri family, or the retired general who led the Maronites, or the subtle and clever survivor whose family had overseen the Druze for centuries. He passed out whisky on holidays, for those who drank alcohol, or gifts for wives or children. Sometimes he paid for information; after all, his powerful clients needed it.

Brooke told no one whom he worked for. No doubt Bashir Jameel, the Maronite intelligence officer with whom Adam Chase had cultivated a relationship of cautious trust, understood what — if not who — Adam was. But to the extent possible, Brooke avoided the American embassy.

He had good reason. In 1983, a suicide bomber directed by Imad Moughniyeh of Hezbollah had driven a pickup truck into the lobby of the former embassy. The center of the seven-story building had lifted hundreds of feet into the air, then collapsed in a cloud of dust, rubble, paper, and body parts. Sixty-three people had died, including six from the agency. One was an intelligence officer from the Near East Division who had stopped in for a visit; his hand was later found floating in the Mediterranean, wedding ring still on his finger. The grim coda to this tragedy was the torture and death of William Buckley, taped for the agency as Hezbollah's gift.

But danger was not why Brooke shunned the embassy — it was what the State Department had done to avert danger. The new location was a virtual prison: Sequestered on a hill in the outskirts of Beirut, it was an enormous compound protected by armed guards, razor wire, iron fences, fortified bunkers, machine-gun positions, and rocket screens. The embassy itself had foot-thick steel walls and every security device available. Beyond that was what Brooke thought of as "mini-America" — elaborate recreational facilities, an outdoor basketball court, and housing one might find in a suburban complex. At the entrance was a reminder of why the inhabitants were confined there — a marble memorial engraved with the names of those who had died, with the inscription "They came in peace."

Now they came as prisoners. The prevailing rule was that officials rarely left the compound, and only in reinforced cars with armed guards. The ambassador rated a twelve-car convoy, led by an armored SUV containing a shooter who manned a .50-caliber machine gun. No movements were spontaneous; no one left without permission. If Moughniyeh's purpose had been to confine American officials to a few square miles, he had succeeded brilliantly. The embassy was no place for spies.

Yet that was how most field agents functioned. Under "official cover" as members of the State Department, they worked two jobs, one of which was clandestine. Thus their work oscillated between the boring and routine and the surreptitious and sometimes dangerous. But the straitjacket of official cover in Beirut sharply limited the opportunities for stealth. What remained, in

Brooke's estimate, was the dregs of field-work — trying to recruit foreign nationals at diplomatic receptions. And Brooke saw no good in being spotted at the embassy too much, whether by outsiders or by those who worked there. His mission, and perhaps his life, depended on it.

Then there was the station chief himself, Frank Lorber. That this supposed master of espionage did not know that his wife was sleeping around — including with Adam Chase, if she could have managed it — was the least of it. Lorber affected the sleek manner of a diplomat: well-trimmed silver hair, tailored pinstripe suits, wing tips polished to a sheen. But Brooke sized him up as a bean counter, a man who took small chances for petty gains, mortally afraid that one of his agents might provoke an embarrassing incident by actually doing his job. Carter Grey's assessment was succinct: "At least in Beirut that asshole is off the streets."

Lorber liked Brooke no better. Unavoidably, Lorber knew who Adam Chase was; the station chief was Brooke's nominal boss. But Brooke told Lorber almost nothing about what he was doing, or where he went. In Lorber's mind, Brooke was a cowboy, Grey's reckless clone. He could not wait for Adam Chase to leave Beirut.

Brooke had no intention of doing so voluntarily. By the spring of 2009, after twelve months in the field, he had begun to penetrate the complex layers that existed within the Palestinian refugee camps of Sabra and Shatilah and Ayn Al-Hilweh.

He had started by befriending the UN aid workers who helped sustain the camps. A sympathetic man, Adam Chase had his "consulting firm" ship books and toys for Palestinian children, as well as medical supplies that were difficult to find. This brought him to the attention of the leaders of the two camps, members of the PLO infrastructure. Neither man was a fool; they had enemies both inside and outside the camps and had developed the jaded watchfulness of survivors. Their initial chariness, Brooke knew well, had become the certainty that this American with a mastery of Arabic was more than he seemed.

But they and Brooke had a common interest. Brooke wanted to flush out al Qaeda; both men feared that their camps might harbor al Qaeda cells, bringing Israeli bombs and rockets down on the innocents whose survival was their concern. Nor did the mass of refugees, miserable as their conditions were, embrace the apocalypse promised by Bin Laden. They lived in the hope of securing a homeland or, sadly, of returning to the "home" most had never seen: Israel.

In this, Brooke supposed, they were much like the Zionists who had supplanted them. For this reason, among others, he found their plight affecting. The sharp-eyed leaders of the PLO seemed to perceive this; for whatever reason, both began to give him information about the factions within their camps. The leader at Ayn Al-Hilweh, Khalid Hassan, also seemed to warm to Adam Chase as a person. In time, Brooke learned that Khalid's most fervent wish, other than for a homeland for his people, was that his bright and diligent oldest son attend medical school in America. The unfeeling part of Brooke, the spy who cultivated agents, saw the uses of parental love. Perhaps, Brooke intimated, he could help. And perhaps Khalid could help him.

So their minuet began. Brooke knew well that the more entwined they became, the more danger he was to Khalid. Men had died for less, he told himself, than the love of a son. But Brooke did not just want information to pass on to Bashir Jameel. For reasons coldly pragmatic and deeply humane, he wanted to keep Khalid safe.

The two men now had many contacts; to

keep meeting at the camp would draw notice. Their meetings outside relied on tradecraft — watching for surveillance without seeming to, following no set pattern of movement or behavior. In response to Lorber's inquiries, Brooke said only that he was exploring connections between a handful of radicalized Palestinian refugees and al Qaeda. When Lorber prodded for more, Brooke replied, "Two years ago, four hundred people died at Ayn Al-Hilweh in fighting between the Lebanese army and a group with ties to al Qaeda, Fatah al-Islam. I don't think that was the end."

He did not tell Lorber who his contacts were, or report his nascent suspicion: that within Fatah al-Islam a core of survivors was planning an operation — perhaps an attack on UN peacekeepers on the border with Israel, answering a call by Ayman Al Zawahiri. But on this day, in retrospect fateful, Lorber tried to exercise his authority. One of his agents, ostensibly a political officer, had been approached at a reception by a Palestinian businessman who claimed contacts within Ayn Al-Hilweh. But then Lorber's agent had been transferred to Afghanistan. Now Lorber wanted Brooke to handle this promising new source, a potential entrée into Fatah al-Islam.

At once Brooke's instincts were aroused. "What has he given you?"

Lorber took a list from his desk, handing it to Brooke. Scanning the names, Brooke said, "These mean nothing to me. For all you know, they're PLO, or maybe a kids' soccer team."

Lorber frowned. "This man wants a meeting."

"He can wait, Frank. I've got some checking to do."

But Khalid Hassan had never heard of this businessman, Jibril Rantisi, or any of the names he had provided. "I don't know everyone in the camp," Khalid allowed. "Sadly, there are too many of us. But these names are not among those we believe are Fatah al-Islam."

Nor did Bashir Jameel know much about Rantisi. "He's been in Beirut only a year," Jameel reported over drinks. "Some sort of import-export business." He smiled at this. "Such businesses are always legitimate, of course."

"Of course. Where was Rantisi before?"

"Riyadh."

Brooke raised his eyebrows. "Maybe this particular Palestinian is a Saudi."

Jameel shrugged. "All I know is that my people say he sounds Palestinian."

"When I speak Arabic," Brooke said in that language, "I sound Lebanese."

Jameel's eyes glinted. "I understand your concerns, Adam." The name was spoken with a hint of irony.

Leaving, Brooke resolved not to meet with Jibril Rantisi.

"If he's a double," he told Lorber, "I'm blown. And maybe my agent with me."

Lorber eyed him from behind the desk. "I don't know how valuable your agent is. Or even who he is."

Brooke felt edgy. "Sorry, Frank. I promised him that no one else would know."

Which was not quite true. Carter Grey, for one, knew about Khalid — it was Carter who was shepherding the son's application to medical school. What Brooke had promised was to keep Khalid safe from Frank Lorber.

But whatever Lorber's defects, he excelled at bureaucratic infighting. In a week Brooke had received an order from Langley — the price of keeping Lorber in the dark about Khalid was for Brooke to deal with Jibril Rantisi.

With considerable foreboding, Brooke met Rantisi at a restaurant. The man was plump, pleasant, and seemingly nervous; though he claimed to loathe al Qaeda, his motives struck Brooke as elusive. But over brandy he passed a name Brooke knew — a man whom Khalid had suspected of being Fatah al-Islam. A dead man, regrettably, killed by an unknown gunman the week before.

Brooke took it as an omen. Lorber did not. "You admit that Rantisi was right about this man."

"He was right about a corpse. Maybe we should just read the obituary pages."

Lorber managed a thin smile. "You've spent too much time with Carter Grey."

"Or not enough."

The veiled insult stiffened Lorber in his chair. "You're trying to penetrate Fatah al-Islam, and you know more about them than anyone else. I want you to handle Rantisi. If you're using proper tradecraft, no one will know who your other agent is. And if Rantisi is a double, which I don't believe, you're already compromised."

That was certainly true. "Ever read *Catch-22*?" Brooke inquired.

Lorber did not respond. "Just meet with Rantisi," he snapped.

"As you like." Brooke stood, unable to suppress a jibe that only Lorber could miss. "In the meanwhile, Frank, do give my love to your wife."

■ ■ ■

Adam Chase's evening began not with Rantisi, but with his French-Lebanese lady of the moment, Michelle Adjani.

To anyone who saw them, Adam Chase was an affluent American with a beautiful, sloe-eyed girlfriend, as carefree as any man could be. They had drinks on the terrace of the Albergo in Achrafieh; savored Lebanese food at Al Balad in Gemmayze with a group of Michelle's friends — a three-hour spread of hummus, couscous, lamb, chicken, beef, and the most beautiful tomatoes Brooke had ever seen — finished off at a café featuring noisy Arab music that stirred some of the women to leave off smoking from hookahs to dance with a sensuality that drew wild applause. Only a keen observer — which Michelle and her friends were not — would have noticed how sparingly Adam Chase drank, or that his seemingly random gaze noted the faces of everyone around them. At a little before midnight, pleading the next morning's business, Brooke kissed Michelle and stepped out into the night.

Even at this hour, the cobblestone streets were filled with Lebanese of all kinds, including a few women with burkas and head scarves. His pace leisurely, Brooke chose a quiet street where anyone following him would be visible, or compelled to take a parallel street in the hope Brooke did not change course. But surveillance was not his greatest worry. He did not like the setup for the meeting. He had never carried a concealed gun; in Beirut, he considered it pointless. Tonight he did.

Changing course, he entered the alley where Rantisi was to pick him up. The narrow street was too quiet — no cafés or restaurants, only shops that had already closed. Then Brooke saw the BMW sedan, parked perhaps ninety feet away. As planned, its lights blinked, a signal.

A signal to whom? Brooke wondered. Glancing over his shoulder, he began walking toward the BMW.

Behind him, Brooke heard a motor come to life. He turned quickly. Heading straight for him was a car in which he saw a driver and a passenger. Brooke began running.

Brakes squealed. Brooke's swift backward glance caught the passenger leaping out of the sedan, gun in hand, followed by two men who spilled out the rear doors. Brooke sprinted toward the BMW.

A few feet short, he pulled the gun, aiming at the shadowy head behind the wheel.

"Open the door," he yelled.

An instant later, the passenger door flew open. Brooke jumped in. The lead gunman kept running toward them.

"Back up," Brooke snapped. "Or someone's going to die."

Rantisi stared at him. Then, reflexively, he threw the car into reverse, hitting the accelerator. "Keep going," Brooke ordered tautly.

Framed in the front windshield, the gunman stopped, the two others at his shoulder. Sweat beaded Rantisi's forehead.

They passed the mouth of another street, still careening in reverse. "Stop," Brooke told him. "Take that street."

Rantisi complied. Moments later, they were on the three-lane thoroughfare headed for Achrafieh. His voice shaky, Rantisi said, "Were they going to rob you?"

Brooke kept the gun on his lap. "Drop me near the Albergo," he said quietly. "I don't like our security situation. I think you understand."

Rantisi flashed him a look. Without speaking, he dropped Brooke where he asked.

Swiftly Brooke considered his next movements, and decided that it was time to wake up Lorber.

Hastily dressed, Lorber met Brooke at his

office. "What happened?" he asked.

In clipped tones, Brooke told him. Stubbornly, Lorber said, "It sounds like Rantisi saved you."

"He saved his own life. And his own cover, were I that stupid." He lowered his voice. "They weren't going to kill me, Frank, or they would have. I was going to be the next William Buckley. God knows who's been tailing me since that first meeting, and what I might have missed."

A flicker of doubt appeared in Lorber's eyes. "You can't be sure."

"I am sure," Brooke said in disgust. "I just hope my agent isn't a dead man."

"What happened then?" Terri asked.

Pausing, Brooke drained his wineglass. "If you don't mind," he answered, "I don't feel like discussing Khalid tonight."

At the other end of the couch, Terri nodded her understanding. "What became of his son?"

Brooke gave her a smile that was no smile at all. "He's in medical school, at Columbia. The least I could do."

SIX

Helping Terri prepare dinner, Brooke sipped wine as he turned honey, soy, Chinese mustard, chopped garlic, and basil into a glaze for the salmon. But the drumbeat of cable news from Terri's television peeled the veneer of normality. A half-hour show labeled "Countdown to Terror" reported the state of the country two weeks before September 11, 2011: another dive in the stock market; a run on supplies in major cities; congestion at ports on the East Coast and in Long Beach caused by searches for the bomb; the preemptive arrests of suspected al Qaeda sympathizers in Chicago and Detroit; an increasing flow of migration from Los Angeles, Washington, and New York to less populated areas. A right-wing congresswoman from Minnesota was calling for a suspension of the right to counsel for those "suspected of association with groups opposed to American values." More pressing, a joint committee of Congress had scheduled immediate hearings — some closed to the press and public — in order to grill the secretary of defense and the heads of the National Security Council, FBI, and CIA. There was no mention of Israel or Lebanon.

Terri sliced vegetables. "My parents called today," she said, "asking me to spend the next month with them in Bloomington. The next year, if necessary."

Brooke envisioned Terri's parents, two college professors, anxiously imagining their daughter's incineration. "What did you say?"

"What could I say? That as a committed environmental activist, I'm too concerned about nuclear groundwater contamination to leave my post?"

"So you've never told them what you do?"

"No. They'd think I was wasting my gifts. And I didn't want to make them lie to their friends." Terri began slicing a red onion. "I told them I had confidence in our government. You can imagine how well that went over."

Brooke thought of his mother. "Actually, I can. And if I'm right, our terrorist mastermind — whoever he is — anticipated the panic he's created. I keep wondering if he ever studied here."

"About Al Zaroor, you're not the first one. On the assumption he's a Saudi, we have a list of fifty or so exchange students who are either deceased or impossible to locate. But no one knows if it's a dead end. The man seems to have evanesced." She turned to him. "So finish the case for Lebanon."

Brooke stirred his preparation. "All right. To the average American, Hezbollah and al Qaeda are the same — they despise Israel, they've got a brutal history that includes killing Americans, and they've cultivated 'martyrdom' as a weapon of war. But they're actually very different animals."

"To me," Terri put in, "a fundamental difference is that Hezbollah represents a people — the Shias. As a result they have a territory within a country, Lebanon, where they're seeking more political power. They're also funded by Iran, which has ambitions of its own. Whereas al Qaeda has no territory and is beholden to no one." She trickled olive oil over a Pyrex dish of sliced vegetables. "Even more important, al Qaeda is Sunni; Hezbollah, Shia. In Lebanon, Hezbollah has exploited the universal hatred of Israel by making an electoral alliance with the Maronite Christians, Israel's former ally, against the Sunnis led by the Hariri family."

She glanced over at Brooke. "How soon will the glaze be ready?"

"Five minutes."

"I'm putting these in, then." Kneeling, she slid the dish into her oven. "Both Hezbollah and the Maronites oppose giving the Palestinian refugees citizenship or voting rights because they're predominately Sunni — presumably they'd vote for their Lebanese brothers. Not to mention that Lebanon bars Palestinians from working in the professions, or owning or passing on property, or even attending Lebanese schools. All that intensifies the hatred of Shia among the Palestinians, especially those trapped in that open sewer Ayn Al-Hilweh." She stopped, asking, "Have I followed the subtle workings of your mind?"

"Bin Laden's mind," Brooke corrected. "Hezbollah represents everything al Qaeda hates: the Shia, Iran, tawdry deals with the Christians in Lebanon — all impediments to al Qaeda's mystical caliphate. When I was in Iraq at the height of the war, most of al Qaeda's victims weren't Americans, but Shia. Later, when I was in Beirut, Ayman Al Zawahiri declared that Lebanon should be a front line in al Qaeda's war against Israel —"

"Which is why you were so concerned

about Fatah al-Islam."

"Especially because these people can come and go from Ayn Al-Hilweh." Brooke finished stirring the glaze. "The members of Fatah al-Islam may not be able to vote or hold jobs. But they were capable of trying to kill me in the middle of Beirut, and going anywhere in Lebanon they wanted to. Which our apocryphal Al Zaroor knows very well."

Terri checked the vegetables. "Didn't Fatah al-Islam fire rockets at Israel from Hezbollah territory in southern Lebanon?"

"Yes, while I was there. Hezbollah was furious — the last thing they need is to lose control of their turf and have al Qaeda incite the Israelis into retaliation. They want to kill Israelis on their own schedule, and for their own reasons." Brooke spooned the glaze onto two plump pieces of Atlantic salmon. "One of the ironies of my efforts in Beirut is that Hezbollah was pressing Lebanese security to shut down Fatah al-Islam. When Bashir Jameel and I were working against al Qaeda, we were also working for Hezbollah. Lebanon is a hall of mirrors."

"Lebanon," Terri noted drily, "is where jihadists go to meet, like conventioneers flock to Miami in winter. Our al Qaeda operative could have slipped in and out any time he wanted."

Brooke put both pieces of salmon on the grill, closing the lid. "Four minutes," he told Terri. "There's another aspect to that. The bomb al Qaeda stole has security codes and an altimeter. To use it as intended, they need a pilot willing to undertake a suicide mission. And unless they had someone train one of their own people, they need a Pakistani technician who knows the code, or how to bypass the code. We've been pretzeling ourselves hunting down guys like that in the U.S., or trying to keep them out. But it would be easy for al Qaeda to move them across the Lebanese border. Or into Beirut on a phony passport, like my alter ego Adam Chase."

Bending to remove the vegetables, Terri looked up at him. "So you think al Qaeda would *fly* the bomb from Lebanon to Tel Aviv?"

"Yes."

On cable news, a reporter announced the arrest of two Muslim Americans in Seattle.

"Let's serve dinner," Terri said. "Then tell me how they smuggle the bomb."

They sat at her kitchen table. With a somewhat dubious look, Terri sampled the salmon. "Well?" Brooke inquired.

"It's good, actually. I wasn't sure when you mixed garlic with honey. A residual prejudice from my Midwestern girlhood — Dad didn't cook."

"Neither did my mother — she had a guy to do it for her. I learned from him."

Terri laughed. Then she said, "I'm assuming your path to Lebanon starts in the Gulf."

Brooke nodded. "I think the bomb went through Baluchistan, like the shipment of heroin I found. But instead of going to Dubai, our operative may have headed for southeastern Iraq. The country is a smuggler's haven: fragmented, corrupt, unstable, and riddled with al Qaeda cells."

"We *do* have intelligence sources left there," Terri pointed out.

"Some. But to the average Iraqi, we're another fading imperial power — we came in, screwed up their country, and now we're moving on to the next mess we helped create. If I'm al Qaeda, I figure on getting to Syria undiscovered."

Terri took a second bite of salmon. "Syria's a police state," she objected. "They'll seize the bomb, or they'll want to keep this kind of trouble off their doorstep. Either way, al Qaeda would be smart to avoid them."

"I understand. But Hezbollah smuggles Iranian arms and rockets to Lebanon through Syria, and antiquities from Iraq —"

"Only because Syrian intelligence is complicit. This is different."

"Suppose al Qaeda recruits an insider who knows how all that works, or has an agent who does. That's what they must have done in Pakistan."

Terri considered this. "Pakistan is easier," she replied. "But let's put Syria aside. Your 'Al Zaroor' is clearly headed for the Bekaa Valley, which is controlled by Hezbollah. You're piling risk on risk."

Brooke felt a rising urgency — if he could not persuade Terri, he might fail altogether. "Long before Hezbollah existed, the Jefaar smuggling clan ran contraband through the Anti-Lebanon Mountains into and out of the Bekaa — hashish, guns, antiquities. Even now, Hezbollah doesn't control every inch of territory —"

"But assuming you can smuggle in the bomb, how do you get it to Israel?"

"By private jet from the Bekaa."

"From an airstrip? Improbable."

"From anywhere," Brooke responded. "According to Carter, back in the seventies the Outfit helped foreign arms dealers supply the Maronite militia. They'd fly into the

Bekaa at night, land in an open field, trade the guns for hash, and take off in fifteen minutes. Our operative would know that."

"What about the Mossad? They've got an intelligence network in the Bekaa looking for Hezbollah rocket sites and underground military installations."

"Less so now. When I was there, Lebanese intelligence — with information from Hezbollah — rolled up a network of informants working for the Mossad. Do you really think those Lebanese didn't give up their Israeli handlers? Mossad's been wounded, including in the valley. Our operative knows that, too." Brooke put down his fork. "His problem in the Bekaa is Hezbollah. But their presence is also a temptation. Al Qaeda has already launched rockets at Israel from Hezbollah-controlled territory. What would happen if a plane from the Bekaa Valley demolishes Tel Aviv? Especially if Israel — as they undoubtedly would — knows where the plane took off?"

Terri stared at him. "You think they'd attack Iran with nuclear weapons."

"And Hezbollah, destroying Shia power while setting the stage for Bin Laden's caliphate."

Terri rested her chin on her palm. "Have you tried this on anyone else?"

"Carter. He didn't challenge my thesis; he simply directed me to get the bomb through Lebanon to Israel. I just did."

Silent, Terri poured more wine for both of them. At length, she said, "I'll comb our shop for whatever our signals intelligence people might have, or anything strange in Syria or Iraq. But you want something more."

Brooke hesitated. "Your support."

"I'd assumed that. But for what?"

"I want to go back to Lebanon."

Terri sat back, puffing her cheeks before she expelled a breath. "Some people will say this is personal to you. In a word, that you're obsessed."

Though he was not surprised, Brooke felt stung. "Do you think I am?"

"Honestly? Perhaps. You haven't told me the end of your story — the death of your agent, or the incident that got you pulled out of Beirut." She paused a moment. "But that doesn't mean you're wrong. If you want my help with Brustein, you've got it."

SEVEN

On the night he was to enter Iraq, Al Zaroor paced the beach on Failaka.

Haj was late. One hour passed, then another, Al Zaroor fearing that his design had been shattered. He felt helpless, despising himself for that. At last, near 2:00 A.M., he heard the low thrum of a motor, and wondered if this were enemy or friend. He backed from the sand into the low grass, preparing to hide.

The prow of the motorboat slid to shore, its motor silent. A flashlight traced a circle in the darkness.

Al Zaroor moved forward, his steps feeling heavy in the sand. The form of a man stepped from the boat and, seeing Al Zaroor, came toward him.

"Allahu akbar."

Haj's voice. Closing the distance, the two men embraced. As he pulled back, the fighter's face was grave. "There's trouble," he said. "I couldn't risk calling you."

"What trouble?"

Haj grimaced. "The dummy shipment was intercepted at a checkpoint, by the American fools who search for drugs. Perhaps they were groping in the dark. But your caution may have surfaced an informant."

Al Zaroor felt the coldness coming over him. "Then you must kill him."

"I would, if I knew who he was. But I can't say whether he belongs to the truckers or to us. Or even if he exists." Haj's voice became apologetic. "This may be an accident, nothing more. But I can no longer assure you of safety."

Al Zaroor imagined Americans scouring Failaka with their Kuwaiti stooges. Steeling himself, he said, "Have you come here only to report your doubts?"

Haj stood taller. "We know our business, brother. We're working on an alternative."

"How long?" Al Zaroor snapped.

Briefly, Haj bowed his head. "I ask your patience for two more days."

Two precious days, Al Zaroor thought. "So I wait with my package for whatever comes."

In the half-light, Haj's face had a determined cast. "You will wait for *us*," he answered. "If anyone dies before then, it will be the person who betrayed us."

Al Zaroor closed his eyes, schooling him-self to patience. His plan had provided for treachery and mischance; that was why he had embedded decoys. "It doesn't matter who else dies," he said. "I did not come this far to fail."

Haj looked him in the face. "Nor will we fail you."

Driving home from dinner with Terri, Brooke watched the rearview mirror. He supposed he always would. But another level of his consciousness slipped further into the past — a winter afternoon in New York City; a warm night in Mexico. Way sta-tions to the life he was leading now.

On a blustery Sunday in March, he had gone with Anit to the Film Forum. The of-fering was *Point of Order,* the venerable documentary about Joe McCarthy's witch hunt for "traitors" in the army. Anit emerged fascinated by the vulpine persona of Sena-tor McCarthy, bullying and blustering his way through the ruin of his victims' lives until, too late, he was ensnared in his own excess. Emerging from the theater into a bitter, chafing wind, Anit said, "How could such a man wield so much power?"

"Paranoia. The Soviets had stolen the secrets to our atomic bomb. So every Communist sympathizer — real or imagined — became part of this 'conspiracy.' " Brooke put his arm around her. "Frightened people aren't always discerning about who their enemies are. McCarthy was clever enough to exploit that, and amoral enough not to care about who got hurt."

As they walked, Anit burrowed into him, sheltering her face from the weather. They decided to stop at an espresso bar. Safely inside, she conceded, "I'm not built for winter, I guess."

"Just as well. It's hard to imagine you as a Swede." Brooke studied the snowflakes spattering the window. "Truth to tell, I suffer from seasonal affective disorder."

Anit nodded in recognition. "SAD, I've discovered they call it — and no wonder. It's like becoming trapped in an endless Bergman film."

"True enough. Though some people claim that winter helps them savor spring."

Anit shrugged. "Do they also need pneumonia to enjoy its absence?"

Smiling, Brooke considered her. "There *is* a solution for us," he proposed. "A place in Mexico, Cabo San Lucas. It only rains there eleven days a year. So far I've missed them all."

She gave him an amused, affectionate

323

look. "The charmed life of Brooke Kenyon Chandler. Do you ever run out of 'places,' I wonder?"

"Not with you, I hope. Why don't we go there?"

"You can just do that," she said flatly.

He felt slightly embarrassed. "As you say, I'm lucky."

"I no longer mind," she assured him. "But it bothers me not to pay my way."

He took her hand. "Let me do this, Anit. You're what luck is for."

She smiled at this. "What would we do, I wonder, with all that sun?"

"Use our imaginations. Maybe take some time to talk."

She seemed to follow his unspoken thoughts. Softly, she asked, "About what?"

"Our lives," Brooke answered simply.

She loved it. Swiftly, Brooke discovered that Anit Rahal was a nature sensualist — just as endless winter deflated her, sun and warmth and endless ocean exhilarated her. She seemed to shed her cares with the first layer of clothes. Grinning as she ran into the surf, she proclaimed, "I'm a child of the Mediterranean."

Brooke grabbed her hand. "I think you're a child of the shtetl," he joked, "haunted by ancestral memories of Russian winters."

She gave him a sideways look. "Don't forget pogroms," she said, and dove into the water.

She swam with savage energy, as though she were fleeing her enemies, or bent on winning a race. At that moment Brooke knew that he wanted her for the rest of his life. Right now they had a week.

Brooke had found a casita overlooking the Pacific. In its walled garden was a pool where they could swim without clothes. They ate breakfast and dinner on the porch above, shaded by a palapa made from palm leaves as they watched the first and last sunlight tint the water shades of yellow and aqua. They jogged along the shoreline in midmorning; walked the hills in later afternoon. In between they read and made love and slept naked in the warmth. Anit seemed to devour the days.

In two months, Brooke well knew, she was due to return to Israel.

The knowledge shadowed his pleasure. Away from New York, their conflicting attachments to different lives, he felt the life they could have together. His need to say this nagged at him. Cabo San Lucas, he felt certain, was more for them than a state of mind.

On the fourth morning in Mexico, they walked in the surf. Abruptly, Brooke asked, "What do you tell Meir?"

She gave him a guarded look. "About what?"

"Us."

She turned her gaze to the surf ahead. "That I've met someone I like. That we spend time together."

"That's all?"

"Not all." She stopped, facing him. "What would you have me say?"

He was not quite ready, Brooke realized; perhaps he was afraid. "Let me sleep on that," he said. "Then maybe we should talk."

"All right," she responded matter-of-factly, and continued marching through the surf. But in the next days, there were moments when she seemed subdued. Silence made Brooke a keen observer of her moods.

Two evenings before the end of their time in Mexico, they took a picnic to the beach at sunset. Shoulders touching, they shared cold lobster and ceviche and a chilled bottle of Mexican Chardonnay. As darkness enveloped them, they slipped out of their clothes. "I want you," she whispered. "Now."

They made love with a new, almost desperate intensity that seemed to come from Anit. Afterward, she lay on his shoulder.

The night sky was crystalline with stars; the air smelled faintly of salt. Perhaps Brooke only imagined the silent tears he felt where her face touched his bare skin.

The next morning, they climbed on a rock and sat watching the water glisten with first sunlight. After a time, Brooke said, "You asked what I'd like you to tell Meir. As hard as it may be, I have an answer."

Though trained on the water, her eyes seemed troubled. "What is it?"

Brooke paused, then spoke with far more confidence than he felt. "That you've decided to finish school at NYU."

She faced him now, her gaze hooded yet unsurprised. "Why would I do that?"

"So we can live together."

She smiled a little, though this seemed tinged with sadness. "And then?"

He took her hands in his. "And then the next year, and the next. The beginning of our life."

Her hands were limp, as though all her energy were absorbed by their words. "Where do you imagine us living?"

Brooke tried to feel encouraged. "We'll pick a place together," he said lightly. "Somewhere warmer than New York."

"But not Israel."

"That's not what I was thinking, no."

Anit stiffened. "So this life of ours requires that I abandon my homeland."

Pausing, Brooke framed his answer. "Without being sentimental, America is everyone's place. For a host of reasons, Israel is a Jewish place; that's its reason for being. It's not meant to be my place."

"And our children," Anit asked bluntly. "Will they be Americans, too?"

Brooke shook his head. "If we're both academics, we could spend the summer in Israel. Our kids would be dual citizens." He summoned a smile. "If both of us don't start cross-breeding, our descendants will have sloping foreheads and crossed eyes. We owe this to the species."

She shook her head with a mixture of fondness and dismay. "You would say that, Brooke Chandler."

"Actually, Ben said it first."

"Then maybe I'll take it more seriously." The trace of humor vanished from her eyes. "I promise to think about all you've said. But I can't talk about it now. Just give us this time, okay?"

Hopeful and deflated, Brooke pledged that he would.

A decade later, in a city fearful of extinction, Brooke Chandler drove to Langley in sparse commuter traffic. The exodus was swelling.

He worked alone for several hours, refining al Qaeda's route from Iraq to the Bekaa Valley. In midafternoon, Terri Young opened his door.

"Good news," she told him, "if you can call it that. I've found something — two things actually. They may help you look a little less like Captain Ahab."

EIGHT

For an hour, Brooke and Terri reviewed their theory with Carter Grey. At the end Grey, satisfied, called Noah Brustein to request a meeting.

The deputy director's schedule was jammed: after huddling with the president's task force, he was scheduled to brief leaders of the House and Senate. All Brooke could do, Grey told him, was to prepare himself for whatever time Brustein could spare.

Brooke worked into early evening, outlining his thoughts on paper in anticipation of challenges and questions. At last, confident that he had done his best, he let his mind go where it would.

Often, this was useful. He had long since learned that the subconscious, left to itself, surfaced insights that the conscious mind passed over. But on this night, as often lately, his thoughts returned to Anit Rahal.

Whatever had become of her, it was not

what Brooke had wanted.

Three weeks after their return from Cabo San Lucas, the first breath of spring, breezy and temperate, had inspired Brooke to call her — a round-trip on the Staten Island Ferry was one of the city's undiscovered pleasures, and free at that. Though she sounded subdued, Anit had agreed.

The ancient boat they took was a triple-decker with its bottom deck devoted to cars, and a top deck where passengers on long wooden benches could take in Manhattan from the water. Rounding the tip of the island, Brooke and Anit gazed at the stunning, solitary heights of the Twin Towers, impressive even at a distance. "Have you ever been there?" Anit asked.

"Twice. Once to visit Ben; once with my parents to the top-floor restaurant. Both times, the height seemed unnatural — I couldn't shake the feeling that the damned thing was destined to topple over. To be that high flattens everything out." Brooke sipped his beer. "I told Ben that his view was a metaphor for the financial community: too much distance, too little perspective."

"What did *he* have to say?"

"He patted me on the shoulder, promising never to forget the little people."

Anit smiled a bit. "That's so like Ben."

Something in her tone sounded valedictory, as though recalling a friend from her past. Warding off this intuition, Brooke pointed out landmarks — Ellis Island, where both Ben's and Aviva's ancestors had arrived from Poland; the strange, deserted landscape of Governor's Island; the Statue of Liberty, which Anit confessed that she found mysteriously forbidding; the tugboats shuttling barges filled with trash, or oil from refineries in New Jersey. But beneath the surface of the day, Brooke feared the drift of Anit's thoughts, wondering if she had decided their future. Lately he seemed to think about little else. As troubling as Anit's silence was Ben's reticence when Brooke spoke of her; beneath his banter, Ben was a tender and perceptive man. Brooke had been too cowardly to probe this.

Beside him, Anit had fallen into a trance, so still that the only movement was the breeze rippling her black curls. He looked around them, assuring himself that no other passenger could hear. "Are you okay?"

In profile, she shook her head. A single tear trickled down her cheek.

"What is it, Anit?"

"So many things. There was a suicide bombing, in Haifa. A classmate from high school, Jordana, was celebrating her parents' anniversary." Anit closed her eyes. "Jordana was an only child. Her parents lived. It's unnatural for a family to end in such a way. And yet it keeps happening to us."

Brooke felt a torrent of emotions: horror and pity for this man and woman he did not know; revulsion for the "martyr" who had done this, and the ideology that compelled him; a selfish relief — shameful even in the moment — that Anit's response did not damn his hopes. But when he put his arm around her, she did not respond.

"I'm sorry," he said helplessly.

"Whenever I hear such stories, I shrink inside. But this is someone I knew." Her voice caught, then steadied again. "If I were still on the border, I find myself wondering, would we have caught him? Then I tell myself not to be stupid — that you can't measure each day by what you've done to prevent someone else's tragedy. I can even hear your voice in my ear." She turned to him, finishing quietly, "But then I hear my own. It's one thing to seek your own happiness, another to make that your only reason for being."

"What are you saying, Anit?"

In that moment he saw naked sadness in her eyes. "I can't be with you, my love.

However deeply a part of me may want to."

Brooke steadied himself, determined not to give this woman up. "Then either way, Anit, you lose."

Her eyes dampened again. "Do you think that I don't know that? Do you imagine that some other woman laughed with you, made love with you, told you when she was happy or sad? That was *me,* Anit Rahal." She softened her voice. "This is not about Meir. I wish it were — that would haunt me less, and perhaps you would accept it more easily. It's that you're so American, while I'm completely and inescapably what I am. The terrible thing is that I love you for who you are, and yet can't live in your world. I'd lose too much of myself."

Desperate, Brooke took her hands. "I love who *you* are — all of it. There must be some compromise —"

The tears on her face stopped him. "I'm begging you, don't ask me this again. It will only hurt us both." She swallowed, then went on. "I already know I'm hurting you as you've never been hurt before. But I was selfish, imagining my time with you as this special gift. I hate myself for that, and for letting both of us feel as we do. My weakness has taken this too far."

Hearing the finality in her voice, Brooke

334

felt a surge of bitterness. "As you say, I've lived a lucky life. No point spoiling it with excessive feeling."

She looked into his face with a compassion close to pity. "You don't mean that, Brooke. With or without me, you'll live a happy life. You're like America — it's in your nature."

Brooke could not imagine a future beyond this moment. "You overestimate me, Anit. I'm less impervious than you think."

Her chest shuddered. "Someday, I hope to know I'm right. Please give us time alone — weeks, maybe months. Then I'll call you from Israel. If you feel you can talk to me, I want that." Tentative, she leaned her forehead against his. "I'll always love you, Brooke Chandler. Whatever else happens."

Brooke gave her the only response he could. "And you. That's why I can't talk about friendship. At least not now."

She nodded in silent understanding. It was the last day he ever saw Anit Rahal.

An hour later, they parted on the dock. Anit went to her dorm, Brooke to his apartment.

Usually he was good at being alone. Now he could not stand it. But the only people he could imagine seeing were Ben and Aviva.

Aviva was at Ben's place. Hearing Brooke's voice, and then his news, Ben canceled their social plans for the evening. "This calls for an emergency meeting," he said firmly. "Dinner's on us, so you can drink all you want."

They took him to Da Nico for the suckling pig, one of Brooke's favorites. He barely touched it. But that was not true of the wine. "I know all this suffering is juvenile," Brooke said. "But I don't think I'll ever meet anyone like her again."

"You may not," Ben responded evenly. "We agree she's terrific. But there are other great women out there, with qualities of their own. You're just going to need some time."

Brooke gazed at his friend. "You thought this would happen, didn't you?"

"I hoped not. But yes, I did." Ben paused, trying to describe his instincts. "She's more than very Jewish. She's very Israeli. For Anit, dying for her country is a concrete possibility — if she had to make the sacrifice, she wouldn't flinch. Life for her is existential in a way we can't imagine. However she feels about you, she's not the kind of woman who could live for someone else."

Brooke felt the wine dulling his senses.

"That's pretty much what she said."

Aviva touched his hand. "I like her, too, very much. But when you told Ben she was an old soul, that seemed right."

"And I'm not."

"None of us is," Aviva answered. "We're quintessential Americans."

"And you're you," Ben added gently. "One of your greatest strengths is confidence — the world you see is a malleable place, which you can mold to suit you. Most days you're right. But sometimes an intact self-concept isn't enough. A person of lesser gifts would have taken one look at Anit and known that."

As Ben had, Brooke realized. His assessment now — which included them both — was so accurate that Brooke had little more to say. Managing a smile, he asked, "Then how do you explain Aviva?"

Glancing at his fiancée, Ben laughed. "I imagined being you, and went for it."

Aviva grinned at him. "Maybe I should marry Brooke. But we've hired the caterer, so I guess it's too late now."

"In fact," Ben told Brooke, "that's the only reason we're putting up with you tonight. We've got a favor to ask."

"Which is?"

"Best man in our wedding, in case you

hadn't guessed." Ben's voice softened. "Seriously, pal, neither of us can imagine doing this without you. Seeing how we love you in our own platonic way."

As often, Brooke was moved by Ben's ineffable kindness, expressed less in words than in actions. As painful as it was to lose Anit, he could not imagine life without his closest friend. But that he could always count on.

"Are you kidding?" Brooke answered. "I've already planned your fiftieth anniversary party at some awful place in Florida. Wheelchair races included."

Ben smiled. "You can skip the wheelchairs. But fifty years sounds like a good beginning."

In August, Brooke served as best man, the high point of a celebratory weekend in the Hamptons. For the most part, buoyed by his friends' happiness, Brooke succeeded in quelling his own envy. Anit had been three months in Israel, and never called. Perhaps friendship was too much, or Brooke hoped, too little.

NINE

At ten o'clock that evening, Brooke and Terri Young met with Carter Grey, Deputy Director Noah Brustein, and Frank Svitek, head of operations. That Grey looked tired was expected: His face was chalky and he sat in odd positions, trying to ward off the spinal pain that shot through his back to his legs. But there were also smudges of fatigue beneath Svitek's eyes. Even Brustein — the toughest and fittest of men — showed his strain in the terseness of his remarks, as though speech drained him of reserves. Brooke could understand this: The demands of briefing the White House and anxious leaders of Congress were eating into the time he spent trying to save an unknown American city. That he was willing to give Brooke a precious hour was a sign of regard and, Brooke suspected, his respect for Carter Grey.

For the first twenty minutes, Brooke

argued his thesis as tightly as he could: that Israel, not America, was al Qaeda's target; that a nuclear strike would eradicate the Jewish homeland; that the psychological effect of Tel Aviv's destruction would transform America's policy and terrify its populace; that Lebanon was the optimal launching pad; that al Qaeda had allies at Ayn Al-Hilweh; and that the safest route to the Bekaa was through the Gulf, Iraq, and Syria. Brustein and Svitek focused on two telling questions: How would al Qaeda get through Syria, and how could it defeat Israel's air defenses? Even to Brooke, his answers were not wholly persuasive: He argued that any attempt to detonate a bomb — whether in America, Europe, or Israel — would have weak points, and that these two risks were surmountable. At the end, Brustein said in a neutral tone, "All theory, no fact."

Brooke glanced at Terri. "Two facts," she told Brustein. "Yesterday afternoon signals intelligence picked up a cell phone call to someone in or near Ayn Al-Hilweh. The message was suspiciously brief: 'The party is delayed —' "

"Did they get the cell phone numbers?" Svitek asked.

"Yes. As far as we know, they've never

been used before."

"Ghost phones," Grey suggested.

Terri nodded. "So we think. But the call came from somewhere near southeast Iraq."

Svitek looked at the others. "What about the voices?"

"The caller spoke Arabic — we think with a Saudi accent. His listener said nothing at all." Terri glanced at Brustein. "We don't have a verified voice sample for Amer Al Zaroor. But for what it's worth, we believe he's a Saudi."

For a moment, no one spoke. "The second piece," Terri continued, "results from the DEA's famous war on drugs. They have an informant in a trucking company who may smuggle arms and men into Iraq for al Qaeda. This source tipped DEA that a 'secret shipment' was coming through Iraq — prearranged by a stranger who'd slipped into Iraq months before, who he heard talked like a Saudi —"

"So he never met or saw this guy?" Svitek interjected.

"No. And the shipment turned out to be a hundred cartons of cigarettes."

Svitek snorted. "Which tells us what, exactly? That the DEA is full of shit?"

"The DEA thinks this guy is reliable," Brooke replied, "and that he's fascinated by

his association with the world's super-
power."

Svitek laughed softly. "He'll learn. Probably about a minute before al Qaeda saws
his head off."

"Maybe so," Brooke countered. "But suppose this isn't a lousy tip, but a ploy."

Brustein gave him a skeptical smile. "Like
Dubai?"

"Like Dubai," Brooke insisted. "There
may be a pattern here, a glimpse into the
mind of a clever and cautious operative. You
can argue that, twice now, our mastermind
has sent dummy shipments to throw us off
the track, or to probe for potential danger."
He faced Svitek. "The shipment of cigarettes was discovered a day before the call
to Ayn Al-Hilweh. Both occurred in or near
the Iraqi port of Umm Qasr. That's one
place, among others, where a boat piloted
by al Qaeda through the Gulf could offload
a nuclear weapon."

Wincing, Grey turned in his chair. "It's
plausible, Noah."

Though Brustein rubbed his eyes, obviously weary, Brooke could feel the intensity
of his thought. "We'll alert the Iraqis," he
responded, "as well as our people there.
Also the Syrians, the Lebanese —"

"For whatever good that does," Grey said.

"They're worthless in the Bekaa —"

"There's also the Mossad," Brustein continued. "We'll go to them, of course."

Brooke shook his head. "When Hezbollah and Lebanese intelligence rolled up Mossad's network two years ago, they found a bonanza of retired generals, government officials, and businessmen — all recruited to ferret out Hezbollah's underground installations. The Mossad can't rebuild those assets overnight. Especially given that its last recruits are either dead or in prison." His tone became caustic. "I suspect the Israelis are almost as feeble in Lebanon as we are. Though not quite."

Brustein's eyes narrowed. "And your point is?"

"That Lebanon is full of people who were, are, or would be happy to become informants. Its politics makes Chicago look like a hamlet in Vermont — they don't just jail political rivals, they blow them up with car bombs. You can't believe anyone completely, or be certain of their motives." Brooke paused. "Even if you had a bunch of people to send there — which you don't — they wouldn't know Lebanon from Disney World. It's not a place for neophytes."

Svitek bristled. "We already have operatives there."

"In the embassy. No matter how smart they are, they'll never find the bomb through social networking. Most Sunni and Shia don't do cocktail parties."

"We also have people under nonofficial cover," Svitek said defensively. "Lorber insists he has a strong relationship with Lebanese and foreign intelligence, and that he's getting good information."

"How would Frank know?" Grey inquired. "He can't speak Arabic."

Brustein smiled without humor. "What are the alternatives, Carter? We've got thirteen days until Bin Laden's deadline, and our orders are to focus on America. There's not enough time for Frank to acquire a second language."

"And no need for it," Brooke said. "I speak Arabic quite well."

Brustein appraised him. "I thought this was where we were going."

Glancing at the others, Brooke replied, "Because it's logical. I have sources of information that aren't transferable —"

"Why not?" Svitek shot back. "Agents should be loyal to the Outfit."

"I wasn't paying them. They trusted me, at least to a point, and I could usually figure out where the line was." Brooke faced Brustein. "I know people in the Ministry of

Defense, civilian and military intelligence, the PLO, politicians, journalists, businessmen. I know Lebanese who can get me to other Lebanese. Who else ever developed enough information about Fatah al-Islam to get some of them arrested?"

"You did good work," Brustein said. "You also nearly got yourself killed —"

"Lorber nearly got me killed."

Brustein's face lost all expression. "Whatever the case, Adam Chase had his cover blown. What do you propose to do about that?"

"Nothing."

As Brooke expected, the one-word response caused a skeptical silence. "If I'm lucky," he continued, "the only bad guys who know for sure that I'm a spook are Fatah al-Islam. I won't be knocking on their door to ask about a missing bomb." He looked around the table. "We don't have time to invent another legend and all the pocket litter that goes with it. As Adam Chase, I already have a passport, credit card, Internet identity, and all the rest. I could slide into my own old existence, with freedom of movement and renewable contacts. All we need is to update my life since 2009."

Brustein gave him a level look. "It won't

surprise you that I anticipated this. Lorber doesn't want you there. He's also enlisted the support of the ambassador, who has the ear of Alex Coll. As you learned, Frank has his ways."

"Does he also have reasons?"

"Several. That he doesn't need you. That your cover is blown. That you're likely to get snatched, or murdered in some horrific way —"

"Frank should know," Brooke snapped. "That's why I'm not going anywhere near him — no meetings, no reports, no phone calls."

Brustein held up his hand. "Then let me speak for myself," he said tiredly. "You're smart and resourceful, a valuable asset that we're going to redeploy. I like you. But even if I didn't, I don't want you tortured like William Buckley, or beheaded like Danny Pearl. I've seen that film before."

"So have we all," Brooke amended with equal softness. "To quote *The Godfather,* 'This is the life we've chosen.' "

"A life of calibrated risk," Brustein objected, "not recklessness. Frank says that knowledge of who you are is broader than Fatah al-Islam."

"Really? Who else did he tell?"

Grey emitted a bark of laughter. "Cut the

346

crap," Brustein said. "You were virtually declared to Lebanese intelligence —"

"To Bashir Jameel, a man I came to trust."

"I thought you said that no one in Lebanon is to be trusted."

Engaged in debating his superiors, Brooke had forgotten Terri Young. Now he saw her look of quiet concern. Exhaling, he answered, "But what if I'm right, Noah? Both you and Frank Svitek risked your lives in the field. Carter nearly died there. Everyone in this room would have sacrificed his life to prevent 9/11. Now al Qaeda's got a bomb that could annihilate hundreds of thousands more." He paused, looking from Brustein to Svitek. "If I get killed, the Outfit's lost a single man. I'd prefer that not to happen. I'd also prefer that al Qaeda not evaporate Tel Aviv."

Brustein gave him a dubious look. "Suppose, as you suggest, that al Qaeda gets this bomb to the Bekaa. How do you attempt to find it without alerting Hezbollah? Do you want Hezbollah to seize a nuclear weapon? Or worse, give it to the Iranians? I can assure you that Israel doesn't."

Brooke shrugged. "Would you rather al Qaeda has it? They've got nothing to lose; Hezbollah and the Iranians do. That's why the Soviets didn't destroy New York."

"You forget the history," Svitek remonstrated. "Hezbollah has killed more Americans than any group except al Qaeda."

"I know that. But with all respect to the dead, Hezbollah bombed our embassy thirty years ago. Rumor has it that the Outfit exacted a measure of private revenge." At the end of the table, Brooke saw Grey smile grimly. "We all know Hezbollah is on the terrorist watch list," Brooke continued, "and that it's illegal for anyone in our government to talk to them. We also know there are times that we need to. That's part of what we're for — to preserve the virginity of the moral men and women who employ us."

"You can't just go to Hezbollah willy-nilly," Svitek objected.

Brooke still looked at Brustein. "I don't expect to. Anything I might do with Hezbollah goes through Langley first."

"Good," Brustein said sardonically. "That way we can all be prosecuted for violating federal law. Those 'moral men and women' are prone to second-guessing. If Hezbollah winds up with a bomb, I'm not sure I could blame them."

Brooke could not quarrel with this. "You've heard my reasons, Noah."

Brustein gazed past him. "We can't just

do this," he said at length. "Your proposal would need approval at the highest levels."

"That starts with our director," Grey urged. "Azzolino took this job because the president trusted him. This is what his juice is for."

For a long moment, Brustein considered his old friend. Then, slowly, he nodded. "I'll talk to Carl," he told Brooke. "You'll just have to wait."

TEN

His thoughts consumed by the meeting, Brooke could not go home. Instead he returned to his office and began to study a detailed map of Iraq.

Where was this man? he wondered — by now, even the slowest ship would have made it from Baluchistan to Iraq. If Brooke was right, and the shipment of cigarettes was another feint, his enemy had chosen to hide and wait. But where?

Unless there was no such man — at least no bomb headed toward Lebanon — and Brooke had constructed an elaborate fiction based on his own past. Which, in other contexts, approximated the definition of insanity.

Sitting back, Brooke considered the only known photograph of the man believed to be Amer Al Zaroor. Have I imagined you, too? he wondered. I don't even know if you're dead or alive.

But someone in southeastern Iraq, a Saudi, had placed a cryptic cell phone call to Ayn Al-Hilweh.

Brooke closed his eyes. *If I get killed, the Outfit's lost a single man. I'd prefer that not to happen. I'd also prefer that al Qaeda not evaporate Tel Aviv.*

Once again, he wondered what had become of Anit. Then, inevitably, he found himself studying the photograph of Ben and Aviva.

This is the life we've chosen, he had told the others. But only Grey knew the reasons for Brooke's choice.

At 7:00 A.M. on a Tuesday in September, the beginning of his final year in graduate school, Brooke went running along the Hudson. As sometimes happened, he felt the shadow of Anit running with him.

But the day itself was uplifting, a sunny, crisp morning, its angled light foretelling autumn. Brooke ran easily, lighter of spirit than on most days, nodding to runners and pedestrians headed the other way. As usual, he ended the run at Sheridan Square, his breathing still deep and even.

He checked the time on his cell phone. Noting that he had two hours until his first class, Brooke bought a bagel and black coffee at the Gourmet Garage, then sat on the bench where the young Dylan had posed for a famous photograph. Pouring from the subway stop for NYU, students headed for earlier classes. Content not to be among them, Brooke gazed south toward the Twin Towers, their windows glinting like chips of mica. Feeling the first jolt of caffeine, he wondered if Ben was already fueling America's financial engine from his aerie in Tower 2.

From above him a deep roar pierced his consciousness. A young woman on the sidewalk set down her briefcase, gaping at the sky. Looking up, Brooke saw a silver passenger plane framed against the blue, so unnaturally low that he could identify the airline. With a deep, thunderous roar it passed over the town houses and low-rises of the Village, heading inexorably toward the towers.

Brooke stood, his sense of something gone horribly wrong warring with disbelief. As though hypnotized, pedestrians froze in fascination as the plane moved toward Tower 1. In its last moments of flight Brooke grasped what was about to occur.

A woman shrieked.

The silver projectile struck near the top of the tower, wedging in its side like a spear in some wounded beast. Flames burst from broken windows. Then black smoke commingled with pieces of white, papers fluttering in the wind like tiny kites. All around Brooke, people began moaning or crying out. As if awakened, Brooke pushed the memory button on his cell phone, praying that his friend was late to work.

It took fifteen minutes and repeated calls for Ben to answer. His voice was jittery yet stunned. "I'm in my office," he began. "A plane hit Tower One —"

"Get out," Brooke urged him. "Now."

Brooke heard the same roar, but more distant, then saw a second airplane turning in a glide pattern toward Tower 2. "There's another plane," he shouted.

A few seconds passed, the plane coming closer. Then he heard Ben's strangled voice. "Oh, my God —"

As the plane hit, Brooke closed his eyes. He heard a woman reciting the Hail Mary, then forced himself to look. By his horrified reckoning, the plane had struck below Ben's office. Brooke's phone had cut off.

Instinctively, he began running toward the towers.

Traffic had stopped. Weaving through traumatized witnesses, Brooke pushed on for over an hour, cell phone clasped to his ear. Perhaps Aviva was already at school; perhaps she was in the subway. In some insane precinct of his mind Brooke imagined rescuing Ben for them both.

His phone buzzed. "Brooke? Are you still there?"

Thank God. "Yeah," Brooke managed to say.

"We're trapped here. I can't reach Aviva."

"Try later," Brooke pled. "Look for a way out."

"I can't." Ben's voice hovered between stunned and resigned, as though Brooke's anguish had imposed the obligation of calm. "I have to try her again."

The line clicked off. Brooke kept heading for the towers as though in an endless nightmare, one block becoming another until he reached the plaza. From thickening smoke, flames pierced the sky. Men and women ran from the building without looking back. A man in a suit jumped from above the ruined floors, twirling in the air like a rag doll before his body hit concrete.

Stunned, Brooke felt the phone buzz in his hand. "I still can't find her." Ben's voice was preternaturally calm. "Guess the honeymoon's over."

"Hang on," Brooke encouraged him. "Those towers are built to hold."

"They will or they won't," Ben answered in a monotone. "Whatever happens, I want you with Aviva. Take care of her, all right?"

Another man jumped, then a woman, her skirt billowing as she plummeted to earth. More survivors sprinted from the towers as the gawkers around Brooke groaned or spoke frantically into their phones. "I will," Brooke promised in a parched voice. "But they'll find a way to save you —"

"Easy for you to say." For a final moment, Ben hesitated. "I love you, too, Brooke."

The phone went dead in Brooke's hand.

As if drawn forward, he edged closer. Then he gazed up at the crumbling floors that imprisoned his friend. He made himself call Aviva.

Her phone rang six times, then went into the message center. "Hi," the recording said. "This is Aviva Schecter —"

Brooke dialed again. "Ben?" someone cried into the phone.

It was Aviva, yet not Aviva. Mindful of his promise to Ben, Brooke tried to speak calmly. "It's Brooke, Aviva. Where are you?"

His tone seemed to affect her. Dully, she said, "At the law school. I saw —"

More bodies hit the sidewalk. Sirens filled the air; firemen entered both towers, passing those who fled. Aviva began sobbing.

"Wait for me," Brooke urged. "I'll be there soon —"

Above him, Brooke heard a sharp crack, followed by a sound like a massive waterfall, thousands of glass panes shattering. The side of the tower facing him began to buckle. Then the roar of rolling thunder split the air as the tower cascaded downward.

Around Brooke men and women screamed or wept or ran away. It came over him that one hundred floors were becoming a pile of steel and rubble and ruined flesh that encased his closest friend. Then he realized that the shrieks he kept hearing came from Aviva.

Belatedly, he spoke into the phone. "Aviva —"

"Who is this?" a man's taut voice demanded.

"Brooke — Brooke Chandler. A friend of Aviva's and Ben's."

The man's voice lowered. "She can't talk now. As soon as we can, we're getting Aviva to her parents."

The phone clicked off.

People kept running from Tower 1. But Brooke's last indelible memory was of the uniformed firemen marching like warriors single file into the tower just before

356

it collapsed.

For several hours, Brooke sat alone in his apartment.

Aviva's parents had come for her. She was at their home, sedated; there was nothing he could do for her. Or, when he called them, for Ben's disconsolate parents.

Aviva was a widow, Brooke realized. The word was strange to him.

In midafternoon, his father phoned, inquiring after Ben. Peter Chandler was gentle and consoling. No, Brooke said, he could not come to their penthouse. He could not seem to move.

More hours crept by. Though he tried, Brooke was unable to watch the news. He knew what had happened — terrorists had murdered his friend, and thousands of others. Tomorrow would be soon enough for details.

When Brooke's telephone rang, he forced himself to answer. In the days ahead, someone would surely need him.

"Brooke?" she said.

Even now, Anit's voice jolted him. Foolishly, he asked, "Are you all right?"

"Yes. But are you? I'm worried about Ben."

Brooke's stomach clenched. "Ben was in

his office," he told her. "He can't have lived."

"Oh, Brooke," she exclaimed. "And Aviva?"

"She's with her parents. That's all I know."

For the next moments, Anit was quiet. "Do you want me to fly there?"

Yes, he wanted to say. *Please, God, yes.* Then he realized that seeing Anit come and go would cause more heartache than a broken heart could stand. He breathed deeply, then said, "I'll be okay."

She was silent, as though wondering how to respond. Then she said, "I understand. Please know that I care for you."

"And I you," Brooke heard himself answer.

Anit's voice remained gentle. "Perhaps you can give me Aviva's number. I'll find the right time, I promise."

Brooke repeated the number. Softly, Anit wished him whatever solace he could find.

With all the warmth and grace his friend deserved — or at least so Brooke hoped — he spoke at Ben's memorial service. In the days thereafter, he sat shiva with Ben's parents and Aviva.

Gaunt and pale, Aviva struggled to be sweet. But he sensed that it pained her to look at him. He was too much a part of the friend he had outlived.

Brooke said nothing of his own grief. There would be time for that, in his own private way. He had never believed that a single moment could redefine one's nature. Now al Qaeda had made the life he had planned seem shallow. Perhaps, at last, he understood Anit Rahal.

After graduation, Brooke Chandler entered the CIA.

As instructed, he told his parents and Aviva that he had joined the State Department. He said that to Anit in one of their emails. It did not surprise him to learn that she had reenlisted in the IDF.

Brooke chose to become a case officer, one of only sixty trained that year. In the months that followed, he learned to jump from airplanes; strip and fire a range of weapons; destroy a vehicle with a homemade bomb; kill a man with a gun or knife or his own hands; drive a car so as to smash through barriers and escape entrapment or pursuit; become another person with a different life. The last part, he sometimes thought, had begun on September 11.

All of this merged his natural gifts — curiosity, analytical skills, a competitive nature — with a life of purpose. He would try to prevent such horrors as he had witnessed or, failing that, to ensure that the architects paid a price. In this he had no illusions. His work might never come to much; the capacity of determined men to combine inventiveness with a lust for the apocalypse might outstrip the efforts of those who believed as Brooke did. But he would live this life as though it mattered.

He served two tours in Iraq, moving into and out of the Green Zone. Brooke excelled there. But the war was a bloody mess, a misbegotten mélange of savagery that destabilized a country and gave new life to al Qaeda. What he learned was the infinite capacity of decision makers to delude themselves, and the need to question their wisdom.

Now and then he emailed Anit in his guise as foreign service officer. The mills of life ground on. Anit became engaged to Meir, now a helicopter pilot in the army. Brooke was still in Baghdad when Aviva emailed that she was marrying a widower whose wife had died as Ben had.

In his last year in Iraq, 2006, Israel began its own misadventure, the Lebanese quagmire with Hezbollah. He contacted Anit at once, hoping for her safety and that of her fiancé.

He got no reply. After two months, he tried again. But his emails bounced back, and she was no longer listed in Tel Aviv. He did not know where she had gone.

Six months later, the agency sent Brooke Chandler to Beirut as business consultant Adam Chase. His transformation was complete. Anit Rahal had vanished from his life.

ELEVEN

When Terri Young knocked on his door, Brooke was staring out the darkened window. Momentarily startled, he stood swiftly. Seeing Terri, he inquired, "Doesn't anyone around here sleep these days?"

"I'm not in the mood." She sat down. "Frankly, I'm wondering if I just facilitated a suicide attempt."

"You facilitated a dignified escape. When Washington goes up in flames, I'll be drinking martinis in Beirut."

Terri did not smile. "I want to know what happened there. The rest of it."

Her crispness did not hide her concern. He owed her that, Brooke supposed — at least some of it. This seemed to be a day for exhuming his past.

Reluctantly, Brooke began to speak.

Even at this remove, his memories were vivid.

On a beautiful Saturday in June, Brooke and Michelle Adjani had driven his convertible along the Corniche. The palm-shaded promenade was filled with lovers and tourists admiring the sparkling azure of the Mediterranean, the bright flowers dividing the avenue. A breeze rippled Michelle's hair. Stretching like a cat, she lay back against the headrest, smiling with her eyes shut as the sun warmed her sculpted face. She was lovely in a way that only Lebanese women can be: almond eyes; long, jet-black hair; a lissome figure. A clothing designer and the daughter of a wealthy man, she lived for beauty and pleasure. Innocent of Brooke's life of secrets, Michelle seemed to have no secrets of her own, no sorrow to impinge on her zest for life. She was twenty-five, Brooke reflected, the last year of his own age of innocence.

"Tell me, Adam," she murmured, "can you imagine a world better than this?"

"I no longer try," he answered. Which was true enough.

They had lunch at the Sporting Club, consuming enough wine, lamb, and fresh vegetables to call for a nap on the beach. But Michelle, like Anit, craved the sea. When her feet touched the sand she inhaled deeply, then ran toward the water, young and carefree and alive. Watching, Brooke had a quick, piercing memory of Anit. After eight years, he thought, her image should not be so strong.

Michelle reached the water, her bikini concealing no more than it should. There was something lovely, Brooke thought, about a woman whose innocent pleasure in life's gifts embraced her own body.

It's a shame that I don't love you, he thought. But even if I could, the rules for Adam Chase forbid it. So Michelle was part of his cover — to the extent Lorber had not blown it — unaware that the beach enabled Brooke to gauge who might be watching him.

Later, he would meet with Khalid Hassan. That he feared for Khalid, and for himself, was no longer a matter of routine caution.

Michelle was scampering toward him. She kissed him swiftly, her damp hair and skin smelling of salt. "Stay with me tonight, my sweet."

Brooke cupped her face in his hands. "For a while," he said gently. "I'm meeting a colleague for breakfast."

Michelle gave him a look. "On a Sunday? Is your colleague a woman?"

Smiling, Brooke shook his head. "An

American. In America, commerce never sleeps."

Michelle lived along the water in a high-rise apartment, a gift from her father.

Brooke left near midnight, the scent of their lovemaking still on his skin. Instead of retrieving his car, he took the elevator to an underground garage, then slipped out a service entrance and into the cab whose driver performed such services on call.

They took a circuitous route to Achrafieh, Brooke watching the sideview mirrors. Beyond the loyalty he owed Khalid, Brooke felt empathy and even a measure of affection. The PLO leader was his asset not simply because he despised al Qaeda, but because he did not want his oldest son ensnared in the squalor of Ayn Al-Hilweh. It seemed the wrong reason for this man to die.

When the cab dropped him, Brooke entered a restaurant, exited the back, and walked two blocks to a sedan parked near the Albergo. Sliding in, he checked the thin briefcase lodged between the driver and passenger seats.

Brooke drove for ten minutes, for no purpose except to shed or expose a pursuer. Satisfied, he placed a call on a ghost phone and let the other phone ring twice before hanging up. Then he braked abruptly in front of a nondescript hotel. Inside one of its rooms was a suit and a latex mask that turned Khalid into an American businessman. There were times, Brooke reflected, when his life seemed lifted from a book for boys, except that the violence was real. "Bizarre as this sounds," he had told Khalid on a secure line, "it works. I knew a gorgeous six-foot blonde, stationed in Hong Kong, whose mask and silk robe transformed her into an aristocratic Chinese male. Many women desired him."

Khalid had not sounded amused. "Did 'he' also speak Mandarin?"

"Of course, in the voice of a middle-aged man. What do you take us for?"

"Don't toy with me," Khalid said abruptly. "You're worried."

More than you know, Brooke thought. "I'm concerned," he had temporized. "Part of my job is to keep you safe. When you come out of the hotel, a silver Mercedes will be parked in front. If it's facing south, I'll meet you there. If not, I'll pick you up in front of the Abdel Wahab restaurant. We'll talk in the car — even if someone suspects me, they won't recognize the man I met. When I drop you off, you'll be yourself again."

Khalid had assimilated a degree of trade-craft. Nervously, he asked, "Wouldn't a dead drop be safer? I can leave the photographs somewhere secure."

"That won't do," Brooke said coolly. "I have your son's visa."

For a long moment, Khalid was silent. "As you wish," he said at last.

At twelve-thirty, Brooke stopped in front of the Abdel Wahab. An American in a linen suit tailored to Khalid's short, stout frame stepped into the dimly lit street and slid into Brooke's car. Seeing the briefcase, Khalid asked, "Is that for me?"

Despite his tension, Brooke could not help but smile. "No," he said. "It *is* you."

The pseudo-American regarded him in puzzled silence. Then he reached into his jacket pocket and handed Brooke a roll of film. "These are the men, the best photographs I could get. It wasn't easy."

Brooke quickly turned down another street. "Who are they?"

His latex face caught in the headlights of a passing car, Khalid instinctively flinched. "Outsiders," he answered quickly, "from Tripoli. They met with the man we believe heads Fatah al-Islam. We're certain they're al Qaeda."

Glancing in the rearview mirror, Brooke reached into the pocket of the Italian suit he kept at Michelle's apartment. "This is Imad's visa, Khalid."

As Khalid took it, Brooke turned down another street leading out of Achrafieh. "And the other provisions?" Khalid asked.

"Are complete. When Imad books his flight to New York, his ticket will be paid for. Friends will meet him there. His tuition and housing are arranged, as well as a bank account to be replenished every month. He'll be fine."

Brooke's agent placed a hand over his heart. "Thank you, my friend."

Briefly, Brooke pictured the man beneath the mask — a mustached Palestinian, years of disappointment betrayed by the sag of his chin, the dark rings around serious brown eyes. Quietly, he said, "So now we're done, Khalid."

Khalid stared at him. Quite reasonably, he had believed that Brooke would use Imad for leverage, extracting more information as long as the boy remained in America. Until Lorber's intervention, this had been Brooke's plan. But Brooke himself had changed it. *My agent is resigning,* he had told Lorber. *If you don't like it, complain to*

Langley. Maybe you can get me fired.

"I'll look after Imad," Brooke assured Khalid.

Brooke imagined Khalid's emotions, a complex mix of worry and relief. Passing a double-parked car, he swerved down a cramped street. "In less than a minute," Brooke said, "I'm taking another street and braking at the mouth of an alley. For about fifteen seconds, no one behind us will see you. Peel off the mask, strip off your coat, and jump out of the car. A cab will be there. Take it."

Turning again, Brooke accelerated down a cobblestone lane. Doors and streetlights shot by, Brooke glancing in the mirror. Then he braked suddenly. Shedding his mask and struggling free of his coat, Khalid left the car without words, a man hoping never to see Adam Chase again. The light of a taxi glowed in the alley.

Before Khalid had disappeared, Brooke placed the briefcase on the passenger seat and pushed a button. The head and torso of a man popped up, Khalid in his American disguise.

Brooke stomped on the accelerator, peeling around one corner, then another, taking a narrow one-way street of shuttered stores toward Gemmayze. In seconds he spotted the car behind him, emerging too quickly from a side street. He knew what would happen before the second car appeared, heading toward him in the wrong direction.

Reflexively, he hit the accelerator, willing his mind to turn cold. The car in front swerved sideways, half-blocking the street. Gauging the width of the sidewalk, Brooke kept speeding toward the car. Thirty feet, then twenty. Two men with guns leaped out behind the doors.

Ten feet now. A bullet shattered Brooke's window as his car struck the open passenger door, crushing the shooter and snapping his neck back against the roof, his open eyes caught in Brooke's headlights. Then Brooke clipped the rear bumper, spinning the car into the second man. He cried out, crumpling to the cobblestones.

Skidding along the sidewalk, Brooke sped up still more, glancing in the mirror. The car he had struck was sideways now, blocking the car behind him. He careened through the side streets, then veered into the artery that fed the highway from the city. Sweat dampening his forehead, Brooke threaded through traffic as quickly as he could. Horns blared at his recklessness; anyone who kept up was doing so to catch him. He would deal with that then.

Damn Lorber, he thought. That he might be killed was the least of it. Worse was what might befall Khalid, or what al Qaeda would do to Brooke while he still lived. Perhaps they would share this on the Internet.

Instead he made it to a safe house. In three days, Langley ordered him home.

Brooke gave his photographs and information to Bashir Jameel. One of the shooters was dead, Bashir told him; the other had vanished. "I'll miss you, Adam," Jameel said. "Not every business consultant kills a man on the way out of town."

The dead man was Fatah al-Islam; the men in the photographs were confirmed to be al Qaeda. Forced to act swiftly, the Lebanese army arrested seven men at Ayn Al-Hilweh. None revealed their confederates. Frank Lorber's source, Jibril Rantisi, disclaimed any knowledge of who they might be.

"And you don't believe that?" Terri Young asked now.

"With good reason," Brooke answered softly. "A month later Khalid Hassan was found dead, garroted in an alley in Ayn Al-Hilweh. We flew Imad back for the funeral."

TWELVE

Waiting for an answer, Brooke felt the hours slipping away. To bolster his argument, he and Terri Young reviewed new scraps of intelligence from Iraq, Syria, and Lebanon. But there was nothing of interest. If their unknown operative was in the region, his activities were well hidden.

"Suppose," Brooke said, "that the cigarettes *were* a decoy, designed to sniff out our surveillance before he moves the bomb. Where would it be safe for him to hide?"

Terri looked at his map. "A populous area. Perhaps a safe house in Basra."

Studying the topography of southeastern Iraq, he again noted the two Kuwaiti islands off its lip, Bubiyan and Failaka. Pointing them out, he asked, "What's there?"

"Not much. They were pretty much abandoned after the first Gulf War." Terri looked up at him. "That would involve an extra step. But, sure, someone could hide there, waiting out events."

Sitting at her computer, Terri emailed Brustein and Carter Grey. "Ask the Kuwaitis to search these islands," she recommended. "Sooner rather than later."

The Bekaa Valley, Dr. Laura Reynolds reflected, felt even more stifling and hot.

The dig team was wilting in the sun. Just before they broke for lunch, Laura found Maureen Strafford silently weeping at the edge of the ruins. "Still worried for your parents?" Laura asked.

Maureen nodded. "They won't leave Boston. 'This is our home,' they keep saying."

Laura sat beside her. "Parents are like that," she said gently. "If it's any consolation, I doubt Bin Laden is likely to target Boston. Only Bostonians think it's that important."

As Laura intended, Maureen managed a half-smile. "What about *your* parents? Aren't they in New York?"

"They are. I implored them to visit our family here. No luck."

Falling quiet, Laura allowed herself to imagine the horror of her parents' destruction, the end of a world she had loved since childhood. Tears surfaced in her eyes.

Maureen took her hands. "I'm sorry."

"Don't be," Laura said. "We'll all feel better when September 11 passes."

Later that afternoon, Laura drove to Baalbek for supplies. When Maureen offered to keep her company, she demurred, pleading the need to reflect.

She bought paper and inkjets for their fax machine and printers, art supplies for Segolene Ardant's assistants. Turning a corner, she nearly bumped into a spindly Shia man.

Smiling, Laura pantomimed surprise and delight. "Habib," she exclaimed in Arabic. "How long has it been?"

Though they did not touch, Habib conveyed his pleasure with a ceremonious half-bow. "Dr. Laura — God is good indeed." His face clouded. "But not to your country, it seems. Do you fear this threat?"

At once, Laura's face changed. "For my parents, and for everyone in America."

His tone filled with compassion. "You must find it hard to work."

"Very hard," Laura affirmed softly. "But all I can do for them is pray."

"Then I will, too. I hope a Christian can accept the prayers of a Muslim."

"With gratitude, and thanks."

Pedestrians walked around them. Moving

out of the way, Laura said audibly, "Please, though, tell me how your children are."

Habib smiled. "Demons," he replied with zest, as though every parent would want several. "Growing too fast." Lowering his voice, he added, "There is a shipment coming through Syria, as before. But this one seems different."

As a member of the Jefaar clan, Laura knew, Habib must be taken seriously. Miming interest in some pleasantry, she murmured, "Antiquities?"

"No one knows. But there are differences that suggest a great impatience." He smiled again, the dissonance between demeanor and speech apparent to Laura alone. "It was arranged by a stranger, I am told. A man no one had ever seen."

"What nationality?"

"I don't know, except that he wasn't Lebanese. But it is rumored that a lot of money came to members of my clan. It seems that he possesses some great treasure."

Laura tried to control her expression. With a casual air, she asked, "Do you know where he's going?"

Mindful of those passing, Habib shrugged in a pretense of fatalism, a man dismissing trifles. "I do not."

"Please keep listening," Laura directed in a low voice. "This could be important to those of us who value the past."

Smiling, Habib said, "May God bless you, Dr. Laura."

"And may you and your family prosper." Meaning, they both knew, his secret account at a bank in the Christian section of Beirut.

In the first hours of night, Al Zaroor, Haj, and a helmsman left Failaka by powerboat. His cargo rested between them. Beneath the thud of the motor, Haj cautioned, "You're leaving too soon."

"Perhaps," Al Zaroor said. "But we stayed on Failaka too long. An island is no place to hide."

Both men fell silent. An hour passed, the boat feeling to Al Zaroor like flotsam in the vast darkness of the Gulf. A low mist settled over the water, shrouding them from the moon, now a faint half-disk. When they passed it, the island of Bubiyan was barely visible, a shadowy object squatting on the surface. Turning, Al Zaroor saw the first faint lights of Umm Qasr, the Iraqi seaport near the border with Kuwait.

A smugglers' haven, Haj had told him. *But much nicer now. USAID spent thirty million U.S. dollars deepening the harbor so their*

376

Iraqi stooges could have a real port. Which, of course, made the beneficiaries even more corrupt.

"What will happen?" Al Zaroor asked him.

Haj's face became grim. "For another day and night, we'll hide you. It can't be helped."

Edgy, Al Zaroor watched the harbor as they neared Umm Qasr, slipping between the massive hulls of tankers and freighters at anchor. He must rely on Haj's judgment, Al Zaroor reminded himself; he had chosen him with care.

The helmsman cut the motor, lowering its sound. Slipping past the last freighter, they docked at the end of a deserted pier.

Three of Haj's men awaited them. Using ropes and pulleys, they hoisted the wooden box onto the pier. They bore it down the catwalk like pallbearers at a funeral. Haj and Al Zaroor followed, quiet as mourners.

At the end was an abandoned warehouse with a steel panel in front. By some unknown agency the panel lifted, exposing a bus painted with religious slogans and gaudy colors. "Your chariot," Haj said drily. "Two days from now, you will commence a tour of holy shrines with pious Shia women. There are several such stops before we return our pilgrims to their husbands in the north. A guided tour of heresy."

Al Zaroor stifled his disgust. "Who's the driver?"

"One of ours. The truckers who were to help us know nothing of this change."

"And my cargo?" Al Zaroor asked tartly. "Do we tie it to the roof of this abomination?"

Smiling, Haj shook his head. "Beneath it, in a compartment welded to the center of the tire rack. Be grateful your cargo goes there instead of you. Some of our fighters have found the trip unpleasant."

THIRTEEN

In early afternoon, Brustein summoned Brooke to his office.

Grey was with him. Both men looked grave. "Beware of what you wish for," Brustein said without preface. "You're a singleton NOC again — Adam Chase. For whatever that cover is worth."

Sitting, Brooke glanced at Grey. "How did this happen?"

"We persuaded the White House to cover its tail," Brustein answered bluntly. "As Alex Coll put it, 'In circumstances like this, no one can ignore a dark horse. No matter how dark the horse —' "

"Put another way," Grey added succinctly, "they don't want anyone saying they protected D.C. by sacrificing Tel Aviv."

Brooke felt an odd mixture of relief and apprehension. "When do I leave?"

"Midnight, out of New York. You'll be in Beirut tomorrow afternoon." Seeing

Brooke's surprise, he added, "We've updated your legend. Your identification and credit cards are waiting in Adam Chase's old apartment in Manhattan. Not, as I say, that it matters."

"It may," Brooke said tersely. "What about Lorber?"

Brustein's expression was opaque. "You'll report to Carter and me." He paused, saying in a lower voice, "Neither of us is thrilled about this. If we didn't think your theory was possible, we'd never risk sending you back there."

"I understand," Brooke said. "If the stakes weren't so high, I wouldn't go."

Grey walked him to the car. Leaving the building, they circled the CIA insignia, observing the ritual Grey had taught him — that it was bad luck to step on the eagle.

Standing by Brooke's Ferrari, Grey winced. "You all right?" Brooke asked. "Or do you still hate my car?"

His mentor stared at the pavement. Then he withdrew a small wooden elephant from his pocket and pressed it into Brooke's hand. Grey was not a demonstrative man, Brooke knew, but he had deep reserves of feeling. The elephant was his good luck charm, which had seen him through great peril in Moscow, Afghanistan, and Iran. Gruffly, Grey said, "I don't need this anymore. But that doesn't mean I don't want him back."

Giving Brooke a swift hug, he walked stiffly away, squaring his shoulders to stand taller.

Brooke flew to New York, picking up the emblems of his new life. On the way to JFK, he stopped at his parents' apartment.

His father mixed him a double scotch. Sitting across from them, he perceived his mother's tension. "I don't suppose," Brooke told them both, "that I can persuade you to go to Martha's Vineyard. After all, I'm bailing. Why wait around for September 11 with your thumb in the dike?"

His father's face assumed a hard cast that Brooke had seldom seen. "I'm an investment banker," he replied, "the member of a suspect class. But we used to have integrity. What would happen to the ship of commerce if we all swam away like rats?"

Brooke turned to his mother. "If not a rat," she admitted, "I'm a mouse. Your father has urged me to go. But from all I read about this Pakistani weapon, it won't be a lingering death."

Brooke smiled a little. "It's just that I'd

miss you, oddly enough."

His mother gave a flutter of the hand, dismissing any threat of sentiment. "So you're off again. What for this time?"

"They're short-staffed at the embassy. The political officer has swine flu."

"And you're pinch-hitting?" Isabelle said in bemused exasperation. "I must say I never understood all those comings and goings, or what you're doing lately." Glancing at Peter, she added, "You could still join your father. Forgive me, but at least your career wouldn't seem like such a cul-de-sac."

"I do what I can," Brooke responded drily. "Perhaps you should mention my dilemma to the secretary of state. She'd be horrified, I'm sure."

Isabelle looked nettled. Her husband touched her knee, forestalling any retort. "Isabelle," he said, "we've been married for forty years. For all your quirks, I love you dearly. But sometimes your obliviousness impresses even me."

She turned to him, piqued. "What on earth do you mean?"

"Has it never occurred to you that Brooke is a spy?"

More than surprised, Brooke studied his father, then met his mother's startled eyes.

"Is this true?" she asked.

Brooke nodded. "Score one for Dad."

She shook her head, as though clearing cobwebs. "Why didn't you tell us?" she protested.

Brooke caught his father's smile. "My job carries certain strictures," he informed his mother. "I do recall you labeling my colleagues 'sadists and buffoons.' But I'm barred from revealing which category I'm in."

A rare look of chagrin crept into his mother's eyes. Matter-of-factly, his father inquired, "I take it this trip is about the bomb."

Brooke shrugged. "It could be about nothing at all." He glanced at his watch. "I really do have to go."

His mother's eyes misted. "I'm very sorry, Brooke. And very frightened."

Brooke kissed her on the forehead. "I'll be fine," he assured her. "I've been doing this for almost a decade now."

Peter walked Brooke to the door. In the privacy of the alcove, he said, "I've always been proud of you, son. You should know that."

Touched, Brooke regarded his father with affection and curiosity. "When did you scope this out?"

"Pretty much from the beginning. That was a bad year for you — first the young woman, then your friend. I could see the changes."

Brooke shook his head in wonder. "You should have been in my business."

"Actually, I considered it. But I'm happy with the life I made. I'm left to hope that you are."

Brooke pondered his answer. "I guess the word is 'satisfied.' At least when the work is good."

Peter nodded. "Keep safe, son. Call us when you get back."

Brooke promised that he would. At midnight, he began his journey to Beirut.

■ ■ ■ ■

PART FOUR
THE RETURN
LEBANON — IRAQ — SYRIA
SEPTEMBER 3–6, 2011

■ ■ ■ ■

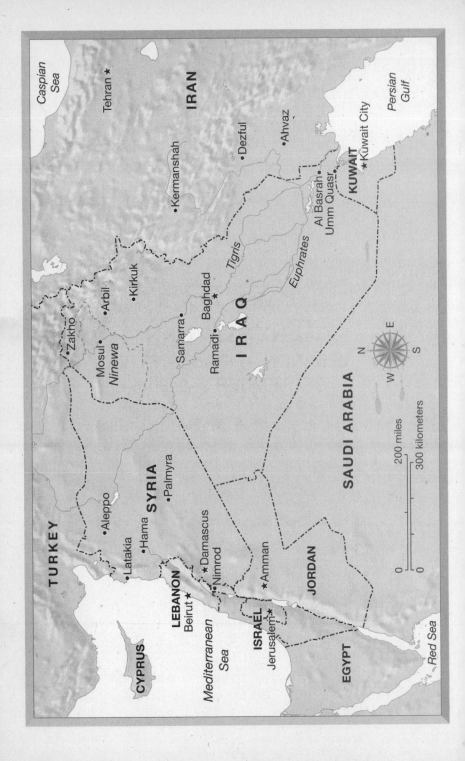

ONE

Within moments of landing in Beirut, Brooke found himself edgy, yet absorbed in his return to Lebanon and to the field.

As before, Brooke was struck by the city's startling juxtapositions: south Beirut, the dominion of Shia and Hezbollah, was wholly Middle Eastern, with signage in Arabic, covered women, and a profusion of Hezbollah iconography — posters of Nasrallah, Moughniyeh, and various martyrs. The Sunni section was similar, but the symbols of Hezbollah were replaced by representations of Rafik Hariri, in whose assassination Hezbollah was suspect. Minutes away, the Christian area of Beirut was quite European, featuring highly sexualized advertisements — often in English or French — and the shops, restaurants, and high-rises of a thriving cosmopolitan city. These worlds coexisted — to the extent that they did — on a knife edge. All this Brooke had to navigate in the guise of Adam Chase.

In late afternoon he checked into his favorite hotel, the Albergo. A historic landmark in a flavorful section of Christian Beirut, Achrafieh, it was a tall, alabaster structure guarded by palm trees. His room was a sybarite's dream: sumptuous bed coverings; fine colonial-era artwork; a multicolored crystal chandelier; pink walls with green trim; an elegant sitting room with a marble table, intricate Persian rug, and commanding view of the Beirut skyline. Bolting the door, Brooke checked his communications equipment — an encrypted cell phone that continuously switched channels, a "tempest-proof" computer that scrambled messages and gave no signal. Then he resolved to test his reflexes in the cobblestone streets of Achrafieh.

On the surface, it was an enclave of stately buildings, smart shops and restaurants, and exclusive hotels — built, in an unintended nod to Lebanon's complex history, on the Roman city of the dead. But now and then Brooke saw walls scarred with bullets fired in the Lebanese civil war, or rubble left by an Israeli bomb. This was Lebanon as Brooke knew it — tragedy amid beauty, death warring with vitality, the place where he had almost perished.

In his seemingly aimless amble through Achrafieh, Brooke took narrow streets, stopped frequently, and turned as if on impulse into other narrow streets — tactics that exposed an enemy, or compelled him to conform his own pattern of movement to Brooke's. He spotted no one. Satisfied, he returned to the Albergo and took the venerable screened elevator to the roof garden.

Each table was screened from the others by artfully arranged plants and trees, yet all had views of the city and, on one side, the Mediterranean. As a pastel twilight fell, the Muslim call to prayer wafted over the garden, reminding Brooke of a trip with Michelle Adjani to the ancient city of Byblos. They had wandered among the Roman ruins, visited a small gem of a Christian church, then had lunch overlooking the Mediterranean. As they did, Brooke heard the call to midday prayer through a loudspeaker system. He had enjoyed his sense of two religions side by side until the call was replaced by a sermon, delivered in the hissing tones of hatred, calling for the death of Americans and Jews. Michelle, a dedicated heathen, promised to intervene on his behalf.

What was she doing now? Brooke wondered. He would not call her; there was no time, no explanation for his sudden departure. Gazing out to sea, he recalled that beautiful, fateful day in June.

"Adam," a smooth voice said. "So thoughtful. Am I interrupting some deep reverie?"

Brooke smiled up at Bashir Jameel. "A near-death experience," he answered.

They embraced with a warmth tempered by irony. Jameel was a trim, handsome man in his forties, elegantly tailored, with the first touch of gray in his black hair and a smile that came and went in an instant, never quite touching his dark, watchful eyes. But Jameel was one of the few men in Beirut that Brooke trusted. A Maronite Christian, he despised American policy in the Middle East, loathed Israel for its works in Lebanon, and wished devoutly that the fractious people of his wondrous, forlorn country would stop killing each other, or being killed by whatever outsider chose to lay waste to some patch of earth and whoever occupied it. Lebanon, Jameel once told Brooke, was Satan's playground. He was sick to death of it.

The two men sat across from each other, drinking gin and tonics brought by a white-jacketed waiter. "How are Janine and the kids?" Brooke asked.

Jameel's thin lips framed the same swift smile. "Janine is great," Jameel said. "As for the twins, they reverse the old expectations of gender — our daughter is intense and ambitious, our son beautiful and languid. Only his soccer skills redeem him."

"Boys ripen slowly," Brooke assured him. "If I'm an example, there's hope."

"If it's all the same to you," Jameel said evenly, "I'll seek hope in other places."

"You're a wise father, Bashir." Brooke paused, then asked in a lower voice, "Who knows I'm here?"

"No one *I've* told. You know the problems in my shop. My former boss reported to the Syrians, our new director to God knows who. Some of our Shia answer to Hezbollah; our Sunni to the Hariris; our Christians to the Maronites." Jameel reached for his drink, exposing an elegant silver cufflink. "Fortunately, the few men aware of your concerns share them. They don't want our country to be a launching pad for tragedy, even against a country we loathe. Humanity aside, we've experienced your Israeli friends' penchant for collective punishment."

"Which al Qaeda hopes to see repeated," Brooke answered. "What's the situation at Ayn Al-Hilweh?"

Jameel put his drink down emphatically, a

gesture of disgust. "Fatah al-Islam retains pockets. The problem festers. Two years ago, when that cretin Lorber aborted our work, we also lost our best sources of intelligence."

As a young couple passed, obviously Americans, Brooke briefly switched to Arabic. "There was only one source — the PLO. Khalid's murder was meant to warn them."

Jameel lit a cigarette. "Consider them warned. The new leader at Ayn Al-Hilweh gives us the sweat off his balls. Which is more than we offer Palestinians."

Brooke felt his old anger resurfacing. "Perhaps he thinks life is for the living. Still, I may have a way to him."

"And if you do? Al Qaeda won't launch a nuclear attack from Ayn Al-Hilweh." Jameel waved his hand, trailing cigarette smoke. "Our problem is as before. Each group within government has its own intelligence — the civilians and the army. So do the Maronites, the Druze, the Sunni, and, most formidable, Hezbollah. Depending on what you want, and where you're looking, you'll need help from any or all of them."

"And they'll be more than happy to give it, I'm sure. Hezbollah most of all."

Jameel flashed a quick, mirthless smile.

"A few Sunnis may like you. As for the rest, when they see America they see Israel. Images of the dead follow swiftly."

Brooke shrugged. "We haven't time for politics, Bashir. Whether or not you believe Bin Laden's deadline, time is short. I need the quickest route to the best information, from anyone who has it."

Jameel signaled a waiter for a second round of drinks. When they arrived, he considered his in silence, as if deciding whether he wished to taste it. "The place to start," he said at length, "is with the leader of the Druze. Hassan Adallah."

"A classic survivor," Brooke remarked.

"A good trait in a man whose father and great-grandfather were killed by assassins. Adallah's life depends on the quality of his information." Jameel stubbed his cigarette. "For the moment, Adallah has a relationship of convenience with General Caron, his counterpart among Maronites — who, in turn, is allied with Hezbollah. To complete the skein of complicity, both have ties to the supreme leader of the Shia, the grand ayatollah, al-Mahdi. Al-Mahdi is a deeply spiritual man. But he maintains contact with the world as we know it. Some consider him a gateway to Hezbollah."

Brooke sipped his drink. "Some might

also say he holds a grudge. Al-Mahdi thinks that William Casey, as head of the CIA, tried to have him murdered."

"Is he delusional?" Jameel inquired tersely. "The Americans claimed to believe that al-Mahdi gave religious sanction to Hezbollah before it bombed your embassy. That piece of history aside, the Israelis bombed his home five years ago, hoping to succeed where Casey failed."

"So what makes you think he'd help me, whoever the intermediary might be?"

This time Jameel's smile was a twitch. "As I say, al-Mahdi is a spiritual man. Bombing foreigners on Lebanese soil is one thing; incinerating them in their homeland is another, even if the locus is Tel Aviv. It was at al-Mahdi's insistence, I understand, that Hezbollah condemned al Qaeda's attack on 9/11."

To Brooke's ear and eye, Jameel was not wholly unsympathetic to this distinction. "In any case," he went on, "Hezbollah won't want al Qaeda using their backyard to launch a nuclear holocaust which, quite swiftly, might consume them and the Iranians. You know all that, of course. Now you're looking for a way to use it."

"By law," Brooke said blandly, "we're barred from dealing with Hezbollah."

Jameel emitted a bark of laughter. "Surely not Adam Chase, business consultant. Be serious with me. Dealing with the devil is what men like us are for." He softened his voice. "In southern Lebanon and the Bekaa Valley, Hezbollah is a state within the state — the government, the police, the dispenser of welfare. In those areas our government hardly has a pulse; any intelligence network worth the name belongs to Hezbollah. You've always been a realist, and so are they. They may strap explosive belts to teenage boys. But mass suicide strikes them as undesirable."

As dusk was becoming night, a waiter lit the candle on their table. "You know the conventional wisdom," Brooke said. "If the bomb is here, Hezbollah will lie to us, then steal it for Iran."

"Fuck the conventional wisdom," Jameel answered matter-of-factly. "If you're right, what other choices do you have?"

Brooke perused the wine list. "Dinner, Bashir? It's on the company."

The last phrase induced in Jameel another arid smile. "With thanks, we should split the bill. But I think we've more to talk about."

"We do. If I'm right, al Qaeda needs more than a bomb and some gunmen from Fatah al-Islam. They'd need a pilot and a plane — preferably flown in from somewhere else rather than bought here where it might attract attention. Even more fundamental, they'd need a technician who can bypass the security codes on a Pakistani bomb, or work the codes himself. No technician, no detonation." Reaching into his breast pocket, Brooke produced a CD and placed it on the table. "For weeks now we've badgered the Pakistanis for information on who al Qaeda may have recruited. For weeks, they've stonewalled. This is a belated gift from the Pakistani ISI — the résumé, passport, personal history, and photograph of an air force nuclear technician who seems to have gone missing. They hate our guts, of course, but they've begun to wonder if losing New York might cause us to take measures beyond reducing foreign aid. If this guy materializes on security cameras, or going through passport control, your hair should stand up."

Jameel put it in his pocket. "Would they be so blatant, I wonder?"

"They might. This man isn't a jihadist, accustomed to traveling in the false bottom of a truck. Were I al Qaeda, I'd bring him in on a phony passport."

Their waiter brought the menus, unfolding them for inspection. As he perused the offerings, Jameel's shoulders sagged. "I hope you're wrong. Not just about the details, but that the bomb is coming here."

"But if I'm right," Brooke answered, "our operative is in a hurry. He knows very well that his world is a treacherous place. So he'll make mistakes."

"We can hope." Jameel met his eyes. "On the subject of mistakes, there's one I should mention. I have little doubt that Jibril Rantisi was a double agent. He's disappeared from Lebanon. Not so the men who tried to kill you.

"We know they're from Ayn Al-Hilweh. Whoever and wherever they are, they know who you are. No doubt that's why Khalid Hassan died in such an unpleasant way." Jameel's tone was flinty. "That makes you Typhoid Mary — dangerous to know, dangerous to be. We can't always protect you. So have a care, Adam. Under any name, it would be a pity if you wound up like Hassan."

Brooke fell quiet. After a moment, he raised his glass to Jameel. "Present company," he said softly. "And absent friends."

TWO

Apprehension melding with a sense of irony, Amer Al Zaroor fidgeted on a bus outside the great Shia shrine of Karbala, erected by these apostates to honor the Prophet's grandson, Hussein, on whose "martyrdom" rested thirteen centuries of idolatry.

Even in early morning, the searing heat caused the air-conditioning on what Haj labeled the "heretic express" to groan with strain. But Karbala was flooded with pilgrims, the men soberly dressed, the women in black burkas reminding Al Zaroor of shuffling Shia beetles. Among them were his fellow passengers, moronic women from the north, their jabbering reduced to awe by this shrine to a false prophet.

As architecture, he conceded, the shrine raised vulgarity to art, with its gilded dome, gold spire, graceful minarets, and filigreed walls, ten gates boasting archways and arabesques. For the Shia, ostentation was

sacred, and this spot reeked of the divine —
the site where Hussein and his half brother,
Abbas, were killed in battle by Al Zaroor's
Sunni forebears. A good day's work, marred
now by wretched excess.

Inside this shrine was the tomb of Abbas,
before which his traveling companions
would prostrate themselves in dumb adora-
tion. For a moment, Al Zaroor entertained
a black comedic vision, reflecting an Iraq
sundered by Sunni–Shia hatred since the
Americans had "freed" them — a massive
explosion turning the shrine to ash and
rubble as lethal as the Twin Towers. A man
could dream, Al Zaroor supposed.

But he had a greater dream — one that
would eclipse 9/11, changing the course of
history by destroying an entire nation. So
he chafed here, silent, while the beetles
banged their foreheads before a heretic's
marble tomb.

Below him, concealed by the tires that surrounded it, was his weapon. He sat just
behind the driver — a young fighter,
vouched for by Haj, whose devotion to al
Qaeda allowed him to affect the beard and
manner of a Shia. Tariq knew only that Al
Zaroor was beloved of the Renewer, charged
with cargo precious to his cause. He could
imagine no higher honor, he had assured

his passenger, than transporting him safely through Iraq. These were the first and last words they had spoken.

At last the women filed out, their heads still bowed — thirty-five of them, steeped in Shia piety. Perfect cover, Haj had assured him; even most Sunni would treat these women with reserve. No one would imagine they were transporting contraband along with feckless prayers.

Mute as donkeys, they filed onto the bus. As was proper, Al Zaroor did not look at them, and they sat well behind him and the driver. Earlier this morning, Tariq had explained Al Zaroor to the tour guide, also fully covered, as a cousin who was traveling to a wedding. Al Zaroor said nothing — none of the women had heard his voice, or looked into his face. He could hardly wait to be rid of them.

But not too soon. For the mission's sake, Al Zaroor must suffer the next thirty-six hours, a period two times as long as that which he had budgeted for Iraq. They would drive through southern Iraq, stopping overnight in the dangerous city of Baghdad, so that these foolish women could shop and rest. Then, tomorrow morning, a drive north to Mosul, at last discharging every passenger but one. That final leg would be taken in darkness to the bank of the Tigris River. The border between Iraq and Syria.

Haj's reasons for this masquerade were sound. If someone in the network had betrayed them, they must bypass the network. But that did not address Al Zaroor's greatest worry — checkpoints. Not all Americans were fools, and prone to missing clues. If some minion among the U.S. drug enforcers had been tipped off to a "special" shipment, and discovered only cigarettes, he might pass that fact along to their intelligence agencies. And some other American who was focused on the missing bomb might perceive the hand of his quarry. Once Iraq had looked simple; now it felt dangerous and filled with risk.

Tariq started the bus, heading toward Baghdad, the heart of this newly menacing country. Sourly, Al Zaroor reflected that Karbala was, after all, a place for him to pray. Closing his eyes, he did that.

At 9:00 A.M., by arrangement of Bashir Jameel, Brooke drove to the ancestral home of Hassan Adallah, leader of the Druze.

As did most of his people, Adallah lived in the vastness of the Chouf Mountains, a natural fortification against intruders. Their religion was an offshoot of Shia Islam, its

401

power derived from the secrecy surrounding it — conversion to or from the faith was prohibited, and its doctrine was contained in seven holy books, existing only in handwritten copies available to a select few. But the political power of the Druze owed much to the Lebanese constitution, which accorded them a proportional share in governance, and the worldly skills of Hassan Adallah, a maneuverer as unsentimental and sophisticated as Niccolò Machiavelli. The proof was that he had lived to age sixty.

Jagged, sheer, and green, the Chouf was his retreat. As Brooke climbed the twisting roads in his Mercedes, the mountains, though steeper, boasted massive sandstone homes, many built in the style of French châteaux favored by wealthy Druze. The panoramic views went on for miles. It would be easy enough for an enemy, situated above him, to follow Brooke's ascent. Easy enough to run him off the road, or shoot him as he slowed for a hairpin turn.

The final curve was marked by an elaborate garden. A hail of bullets had killed Adallah's father as he rounded it, moments from home, his shredded body falling from the car onto the patch of earth where flowers now grew, the work of his son.

Brooke passed it without incident. Minutes later he stopped at an iron gate guarded by three men with submachine guns. A sturdy guide relieved Brooke of his car keys, patted him down, and shepherded him inside the gate.

Hassan Adallah waited at the head of the drive, dressed in a sport shirt and jeans. Brooke had seen his photographs many times, but they did not quite capture the interest of Adallah's countenance. His crown was bald, with long hair in the back and sides that accentuated the downward pull of his face, drawn and dour. The corner of his drooping eyes had a melancholy cast. But the eyes themselves, grave yet droll, seemed to look right through this stranger who approached him.

The complex mien, Brooke reflected, of a man bred for complexity. For the last four centuries, an Adallah had led the Druze — a warlord-prince among his people, a man of influence in his country, a target for assassins when his reach thwarted some other man of influence. Adallah, who had loved his father deeply, later dined with the men who had engineered his death, the agents of Syria. Such was the price of survival.

Adallah greeted Brooke with a brisk handshake. "You'll forgive the security," he said in flawless English. "But it would be

403

foolish to allow those who guard me to make exceptions. In this, as in many things, I'm the ultimate conservative."

"For some," Brooke answered, "trust is a luxury. One might as well choose suicide."

Adallah gave him a meaningful glance, as if to acknowledge a certain kinship. "Come," he said, "let me show you my home."

The comment seemed superfluous — the home showed itself. A three-story sandstone structure with sprawling wings and several porches built on pillars, it was perhaps sixty thousand square feet, occupying a territory somewhere between castle and château. Shaded by pines, it had been built in the mid-seventeenth century, the work of the first great Adallah. Climbing the steps outside to a massive cedar entrance, they passed the windows of an enormous library, its twenty-foot-high shelves filled with books. Once inside, Adallah led Brooke through a series of equally remarkable spaces: one evocative of a chapel, its walls hung with portraits of Adallah's mother, father, and the bodyguards who had died trying to protect him; another filled with paintings of striking character, most notably a heroic portrayal of Soviet soldiers on horseback stomping on a Nazi flag, observed by ghostly representations of Stalin and Lenin — an amusing reminder that Adallah, in his youth, had found it convenient to assume the guise of a Communist; the next holding a museum-quality display of Phoenician, Roman, and Christian relics, including a medieval baptismal font; then a repository of swords, rifles, and ancient maps of the Middle East and Palestine; then the vaulted reception area, thirty feet in height, where Adallah heard the petitions of Druze seeking help. "A pleasant pastime," Adallah remarked, "and a respite from the dangers and betrayals of Beirut. To grant some small favor feels oddly purifying."

Brooke nodded. "Your home is astounding."

"And redolent of the past." Adallah glanced at him sideways. "I believe in the lessons of history. With respect, Mr. Chase, your country is antihistorical. You run through the world breaking china, believing yourselves unique. But the Romans, Spanish, and British came before you, and the Chinese will take your place. Time punishes the vain."

"True enough. But the deadline of mortality tends to make a man shortsighted. Or you wouldn't spend time in Beirut, or trouble yourself with bodyguards."

A glint of humor surfaced in Adallah's

eyes. "Time also punishes the pompous," he replied. "But sooner. Come, let us enjoy the garden."

He led Brooke into a shaded patio, which was enclosed, Brooke saw at once, by wings of the house as well as a sheer rock hill, affording no sight line for an enemy with a high-powered rifle. Through the center of the patio babbled a man-made stream, fed by a waterfall that spilled from the hillside behind them, disappearing in a culvert beneath Adallah's home. The waterfall and stream combined to create a splashing sound that echoed through the culvert. "An invention of my great-great-grandfather," Adallah advised Brooke. "It made conversation harder for the servants to overhear. He took no one's loyalty for granted."

"How long did he live?"

"Until he died of lung cancer. I gather he also fancied this garden as a place to smoke." He gestured for Brooke to sit. "In any event, it's pleasant to receive an American. These days I seem to be less popular."

Smiling, Brooke answered, "It must be your alliance with people on the U.S. terrorism watch list. You forgot to ask permission."

Adallah shrugged. "As so often, your government looks at another country and sees only itself. And too often, as now, the faction supported by the U.S. — the Sunni — is hopelessly corrupt. But in America they have become George Washington, democracy's friend. So I must be mistaken."

The remark was accurate enough that Brooke laughed aloud. "Still," he retorted, "reasonable minds may wonder why Hezbollah, which defies the government and arms its own militia, is any better. Of course, one needn't steal if one is funded by Iran."

Adallah's arid smile confirmed his preference for pragmatism. "Our population is now forty percent Shia, tied to Hezbollah. By allying with Hezbollah, and seeking to reform our electoral process, we offer them a choice — are you Lebanese patriots or are you clients of Iran and Syria, using our soil as a base? We shall see.

"On the same subject, your allies in Israel provide Hezbollah with excuses for not disarming — their periodic slaughter of our civilians, and their relentless oppression of the Palestinians. Given a choice between stupidity and brutality, they opt for both."

"Fortunately for the Palestinians," Brooke said sardonically, "the Druze, Hezbollah, and the Maronites care deeply. Though not enough, it seems, to let them vote or hold jobs. It's far easier for Hezbollah to lob rockets at Israel in the name of an 'oppressed' people they insist on keeping in hellholes. Forgive me if I miss the subtle difference."

Adallah gave another shrug of his thin shoulders. "This is not their country. Were it to become so, the Palestinians would empower the Sunnis, making them a permanent majority. So they must go."

"But where?" Brooke inquired. "Israel offers them nothing. So camps like Ayn Al-Hilweh make Lebanon a breeding ground for Fatah al-Islam. To men like these, caught between you and the Israelis, only al Qaeda offers a vision. This game of realpolitik you play carries risks. The catastrophe I fear now could consume you."

"Let me ask you this," Adallah responded mildly. "Al Qaeda attacked Washington and New York. But what has Hezbollah done besides killing the Americans you sent here? Have they blown up your buildings? Have they kidnapped or killed Americans in other lands? Or have they simply done to you, albeit with a certain cruelty, more or less what your forefathers did to the British?

"Any day now, you and Israel may need Hezbollah, and all your delicacy about 'terrorists' will mean nothing. In turn, I hope the United States will stop presuming to tell us what is good for Lebanon." He gave Brooke a probing look. "Despite my remark about Americans, I acknowledge that you are one — a man in a hurry. In this case, I cannot blame you. So let us not mince words. While the rest of your countrymen are building bomb shelters, you believe the threat lies here. I have no love for Israel. But as a conservative and a survivor, the idea of Lebanon playing host to another breaker of china appalls me. Especially one obsessed with breaking china on such a massive scale."

Brooke accorded him a deferential nod. "Then our interests coincide."

"For the moment. So let me remark on the profound stupidity of America's policy toward Lebanon. On the one hand, the U.S. wants the Lebanese army to absorb the Hezbollah militia. Yet because the U.S. gives the army its most antiquated weapons, they cannot match Hezbollah's weaponry. As a result, only Hezbollah can fight Israel. And now you — Adam Chase — may need Hezbollah to retrieve this missing property."

"It's not that simple."

Adallah's melancholy eyes were sober. "No indeed. Hezbollah will want things, and so will the Iranians. Should the worst occur, Hezbollah will want security from Israeli reprisal; the Iranians may want America's sufferance for their oh-so-peaceful nuclear program."

"I can't arrange that," Brooke said bluntly.

Adallah raised his eyebrows. "Not in exchange for Tel Aviv? Then the outcome may be a terrible cosmic justice." For the first time, Adallah's tone became sharper. "Iran will develop a bomb, whether anyone likes it or not. Not even the Israelis believe their own nonsense about destroying Iran's nuclear facilities — they're too widely dispersed, and too far underground. The real purpose of Israel's bleating about Iran is to distract your government from Israel's crimes against the Palestinians, not to mention its adamant refusal to give them a country of their own."

The cool eye of a realist, Brooke thought, ever looking beneath what is said for what is sought. "There's also the question of who gets the bomb."

"If the bomb reaches Lebanon," Adallah said simply, "all you may have is a choice of enemies. Do you want it in the hands of Hezbollah and Iran or al Qaeda?"

"It's a problem," Brooke answered laconically. "What do you suggest?"

"I can do nothing with al Qaeda. But if

you choose to approach Hezbollah, I will seek out my Lebanese friends of the moment: the Maronite general Caron and the Shia grand ayatollah al-Mahdi. They can help you with Hezbollah — time is too short for you to start from scratch." Adallah smiled a little. "Oh, I know — al-Mahdi is also on the U.S. list of terrorists. If listing enemies were the path to survival, your empire would last an eternity."

This required no comment. "There is one other favor," Brooke ventured.

"Yes?"

"Before the bomb reaches Lebanon, it must pass through Syria. These days you have 'friends' there as well. Perhaps they'll listen to you, or tell you things they may not say to us. That could spare us all a tragedy."

Adallah's eyes became hooded. "Syrian intelligence is formidable," he said in a dispassionate tone. "After all, they planned the murder of my father and Rafik Hariri. So, yes, I will mention this to them."

Brooke thanked him and headed for the refugee camp of Sabra and Shatilah.

THREE

Al Zaroor stared through the windshield at the roadway bisecting the flat, featureless terrain of southern Iraq.

Behind him, the females babbled incessantly about nothing. Sweat soaked his clothes; the sclerotic air-conditioning, though noisy, did not relieve the 120-degree heat that conjured vapor from the asphalt. His fears were simple — that somewhere on this road, an Iraqi stooge of the Americans would not be gulled by a garish bus filled with Shia women. His greatest hope was that the spell cast on America by Osama Bin Laden had kept their intelligence agencies from guessing his true path.

Stop obsessing, Al Zaroor told himself — *you do nothing by exhausting yourself with images of failure.* He closed his eyes and allowed blackness to envelop him.

The squeal of brakes wakened him with a start. A traffic checkpoint manned by Iraqi soldiers had blocked the vehicles in front of them — a small truck, then a van. A soldier with a gun slung over his shoulder spoke to the truck driver through his window. Al Zaroor's driver, Tariq, watched stoically.

"Is this usual?" Al Zaroor whispered.

Tariq did not turn. "We'll see."

They watched a minidrama unfold like a silent film: Prodded by a young mustached soldier, the driver left the truck, shuffled sullenly to the rear, and opened the corrugated panels. This soldier and another began inspecting the contents of the truck. "No," Tariq said quietly. "This is not usual."

The cost of subterfuge, Al Zaroor thought, was helplessness. His planning did not matter. All that counted now was the thoroughness of this search.

Five minutes passed, then five more. Traffic sped in the other direction without stopping. Whatever its purpose, this inspection was directed only at vehicles headed north.

At length the soldiers completed the search and raised the long wooden barrier, permitting the truck to pass beneath. The barrier lowered, and the ritual began again, the next driver ordered from his van and compelled to open the rear door. But this time Al Zaroor saw the sandy-haired American in sunglasses and lightweight shirt and pants talking with an Iraqi lieutenant. Taking out penknives, the soldiers sliced open one box, then another. "Not usual," Tariq repeated in a tighter voice.

As if to confirm this, the American and the lieutenant sauntered to the back of the van as the soldiers kept opening boxes. After a few more, the American spoke to the lieutenant, who spoke to the soldier, who stopped his search. What came over Al Zaroor was not relief, but a deepening worry: Perhaps the American had cut short the inspection because none of the boxes could hold a bomb. Behind him, the women continued babbling about husbands, unmarried daughters, and the excitement of visiting Baghdad. Fingernails on a blackboard.

The driver of the van closed the rear panels. The American spoke to the young soldier with a mustache. Scowling, the soldier lay down on the steaming asphalt and slithered beneath the van. Al Zaroor's mouth went dry.

If this procedure was repeated, al Qaeda's dream could end in failure. Vainly, Al Zaroor imagined means of escape. But he already knew there was none.

Face shiny with sweat, the soldier slid from beneath the van and sat on the asphalt, shaking his head. "A bad assignment," Tariq murmured.

His calm surprised Al Zaroor. But perhaps the young man was a fatalist; fighters did not expect a long life.

Again the barrier rose. The van drove on, leaving their bus next in line.

The mustached soldier approached the window. When Tariq rolled it down, he shot Al Zaroor a brief look, then told the driver curtly, "Get out."

Tariq did. The two men exchanged more words. Tariq opened the cargo hold in the side of the bus, exposing the suitcases of the women.

To the side of the road, the American and the Iraqi lieutenant stood in the blistering heat, watching two soldiers stack suitcases on the asphalt. In this silent, burgeoning nightmare, the lieutenant spoke to the same young soldier. With a look of resignation, the man sat down on the road and began sliding on his back beneath the bus. Standing apart, Tariq stared at his feet. Al Zaroor forced his mind to go blank, then filled it with prayers for his afterlife. But another image pierced them — the soldier staring up at the metal casket hidden between spare tires.

At length, his head appeared from beneath the bus, then the rest of him. He was still for a moment before he stood again, facing his lieutenant. Trapped, Al Zaroor awaited the end.

Slowly, the soldier shook his head.

The lieutenant turned to the American. More words passed. Then the Iraqi waved Tariq back into the bus.

He got on, still not looking at Al Zaroor. In seeming slow motion, the barrier was raised, and the bus drove through. A fever of relief seeped through Al Zaroor. "What happened?" he murmured to Tariq. "The Iraqi must have seen our cargo."

"We pay him not to," Tariq answered. "His lieutenant also."

Al Zaroor sat back. He took a deep breath, and tried to sleep again.

At two in the afternoon, Brooke Chandler took a taxi to the Sunni section of Beirut.

Within minutes, he entered a different culture — the women covered, the streets jammed with stalled traffic and carts peddling fruit and goods, horns honking in a cacophony that produced nothing but more horns blaring. Brooke got out well short of the entrance to Sabra and Shatilah and began browsing. If anyone had followed him, he concluded moments later, he was skilled.

At length, he entered the camp, a prison without walls — the home to sixty thousand Palestinians allowed no other home.

A guide waited to take him to the camp's leader. They passed through a rabbit warren of cramped dirt alleys, concrete or cinder-block buildings with corrugated doors and roofs, tangles of electrical wires doubling as clotheslines. The gray squalor was relieved only by the bright signs of shops, posters portraying Palestinian martyrs, and the flags of rival factions — the secular Fatah, party of Arafat; the Islamic militant Hamas. Now and then Brooke saw buildings pocked with bullet holes from factional fighting or, even more grim, the thirty-year-old massacre of four thousand people by the Maronite militia, the Falange, unleashed by Ariel Sharon. Next to Ayn Al-Hilweh, this was the worst Palestinian refugee camp in existence, a crowded slum with no potable water, no hospital, a single clinic, and too few schools serving children with no future. By law, the Lebanese barred the Palestinians from citizenship, voting, or holding jobs outside the camp. The results were plain enough — the young man in one corner carrying a submachine gun, the children's pictures depicting dead bodies killed by planes or missiles Brooke had seen in one of the schools. Though Brooke's job required dispassion, this place always made him angry.

But when Brooke stepped into his office, Sami Assad looked less angry than two years wearier. The burden of the camp had etched new lines around his sad eyes and full mouth and streaked his black, wiry hair with gray. Selected by the PLO as leader of Sabra and Shatilah, he was charged with ameliorating misery while animating the sixty-year-old dream of life in a better place — which, in too many minds and hearts, meant a return to the country all maps but theirs called Israel. Whatever Assad's doubts about Adam Chase — and they were no doubt grave — Adam and his consulting firm had been benefactors of the camp. "So," Assad said with a trace of reserve, "you're back."

Nodding, Brooke felt like a bird of ill omen — the death of Khalid Hassan hovered over the room. "As of yesterday," he answered. "I came to see how you are."

Courteously, Assad waved him to a chair, then sat behind his cluttered desk. "We are what we were," he said with resignation. "The world's orphans. Most dream of returning to homes lost by their parents or grandparents, which they know only through the romance of other people's memories. Some are willing to settle for a new land of their own, the West Bank. But that alternate 'homeland' is run by Israeli soldiers and infested with settlers determined to expel the Palestinians already there. Hope shrivels."

For a moment, Brooke allowed himself to step outside his role. "I'm sorry."

Assad nodded slowly. "It is remarkable to me, Adam, that so few in these camps channel their despair into violence. God knows the Zionists have a gift for breeding enemies, one generation on the other. Yet they believe they can stonewall until we settle like mangy dogs for whatever scrap of land they choose to throw us — if any. Someday the hatred they spawn will consume them."

Once again, Brooke imagined Tel Aviv in ashes, a terrible turn of history's wheel. Evenly, he said, "As before, my company wants to make contributions to the school and clinic — books, medicines, whatever you might need."

Assad's mouth twisted. "Can you give us a homeland, or the chance to work and live in dignity? Then we can care for ourselves."

Suddenly and clearly, Brooke remembered Anit at the student forum. *Our only hope is to create a place where Palestinians have the joys and challenges of a normal life, and the ability to live it. Anything else is doomed.* "If I could buy you a homeland, instead of books, I would."

Assad smiled slightly. "Forgive the flights of rhetoric. We have great need in the here and now."

Brooke nodded. "I hear conditions are still worse at Ayn Al-Hilweh."

Assad studied him. "More violent, certainly. You know of Fatah al-Islam. Two years ago they killed many PLO at Ayn Al-Hilweh. Now, it is said, our Sunni brothers in Lebanon provide them money, perhaps to keep trouble from their own door. Once again we are betrayed. We are not people, but playthings."

And now there's me, Brooke thought. "Perhaps I can help with that, as well. But first I'll need information."

Assad regarded him fixedly. "Of what kind?"

"Intelligence on Fatah al-Islam. Names, faces, who may be coming and going, who may have disappeared."

Assad picked up some paper clips off the desk and put them in a bowl. Then he looked up at Brooke again. "There's a new head at Ayn Al-Hilweh, Ibrahim Farad. You may recall that the former head was killed."

"Yes. I recall." Brooke kept his manner calm. "Would a meeting with Farad be possible?"

"Should it be?" Assad pointedly inquired. "Your haste in coming here is worrisome. Were you that haunted by the thought of tattered schoolbooks?"

Brooke met his eyes. "Many things haunt me, Sami."

"Perhaps they should. Now America itself is threatened. But there is a belief among many that America is not a grateful friend, but a lethal one. So often your embrace becomes deadly to others."

The murder of Khalid was very close to the surface now. "That isn't my intention," Brooke answered.

"Indifference," Assad said coolly, "is deadly, too."

"And so is inaction," Brooke rejoined. "There's trouble coming that could consume many innocent people. As usual, your people are not exempt."

Assad studied him awhile. "As always," he said softly, "we appreciate your concern. Right now I can say no more."

At three o'clock, Al Zaroor saw the smudged skyline of Baghdad.

When the bus entered, he felt the soot and

chaos envelop them. As at the height of war, Baghdad was plagued by sectarian violence, the ethnicity of its victims classified by the manner of death — the Sunnis favored beheading; the Shia preferred power drills. In a city segmented by ethnic cleansing, he was condemned to stay among the Shia.

They let off the women at a hotel noted for its piety. But the quarters for Al Zaroor and Tariq were two rooms above a hardware store. Al Zaroor's room was dingy and ill furnished, with a worn chair, a mattress on the floor, and a lightbulb dangling from the ceiling. This was fitting, he supposed — he had chosen an ascetic's life as a prelude to a martyr's death. It made the transition easier.

A cell phone waited under the mattress. Removing it, he placed a call.

"Yes," the careful voice said.

Relieved but wary, Al Zaroor asked, "Is the trip still on?"

A moment's silence. Then the Syrian answered, "I'm honored to be your guide."

From his room at the Albergo, Brooke phoned Brustein and Grey.

To start, he summarized his meetings with Bashir Jameel, Hassan Adallah, and Sami Assad. "So they don't like our foreign policy," Grey responded sourly. "What a surprise. Sometimes I don't, either."

Brooke glanced out at the lights of a city prone to late-night pleasures. "They're saying something else, Carter. That all roads go through Hezbollah."

"Not yet," Brustein admonished. "You're tugging at disparate threads — sources at Ayn Al-Hilweh, the whereabouts of this Pakistani nuclear technician, indirect lines into Syria's intelligence. I want more before considering whether we need Hezbollah." His voice betrayed anxiety. "However, we've got something for you. According to the ISI, our missing Pakistani technician flew to Dubai, checked into a hotel, then vanished. If he's in Beirut, it surely elevates the pressure. He's the man who facilitates detonation."

Brooke felt his sense of urgency quickening. "That's another reason for taking this to Jameel. If I'm right, this Pakistani is almost as important as the guy who's running this operation. I'd like to find him — fast."

"And if you do?" Brustein asked.

"We interrogate him," Brooke answered tersely. "Or, if I have to, kill him. Once he touches that bomb, it's operational."

FOUR

The next morning, through the intervention of Sami Assad, Brooke headed for the coastal city of Sidon to meet the PLO leader at Ayn Al-Hilweh.

The security measures were elaborate. Brooke ducked out a service entrance of the Albergo, took a cab to the airport, walked through a terminal, then caught another cab that drove him to the outskirts of Sidon. There he met a stranger in a blue shirt and sunglasses. The man drove him through crowded streets, dropping him in an alley where another Palestinian hurried him through a maze of streets before they entered a nondescript building with no signs or address. At any point, Brooke was prepared for danger: The last encounter between Brooke and Ibrahim Farad's predecessor, Khalid Hassan, had led to the attempted murder of one, the assassination of the other. Of the four men who had tried

to ambush Brooke, he had killed only one
— the others could identify him on sight.
To go near Ayn Al-Hilweh increased the risk
of his death or capture, just as it created
dangers for Farad.

This was among the several reasons
Brooke did not enter the camp itself. By
Jameel's reckoning, it was the most dangerous place in Lebanon, ringed by army units
prepared to subdue violence. To enter,
Brooke would have required the permission
of the American ambassador and the Ministry of Defense, drawing more attention than
he wanted. But a single visit in 2009 had
been sufficient. Within the walls of wire and
concrete were jammed seventy thousand
Palestinians, including members of Fatah
al-Islam, living in a maze of alleys so narrow that Brooke could touch the houses on
either side. The alleys often doubled as open
sewers; the electricity was so spasmodic
that, at any hour, the camp could be
plunged into darkness. Hassan had died in
such an alley, no doubt betrayed by the men
who guarded him. But he was one of many
killed here, before and since — whether in
gun battles between factions, or between
the army and Fatah al-Islam, which could
assault its enemies before vanishing in the
maze. So Brooke preferred following a

stranger up a back stairwell perfect for ambushes.

On the third floor an unmarked metal door with a peephole was guarded by another man, with a handgun in his belt. He patted Brooke down, then rapped sharply on the door. It was opened by a stout man with liquid eyes, a mustache, and the bearing of a man in charge. Nodding curtly to Brooke, he said in Arabic, "Come in."

Brooke did so. Inside, the room was bare save for two chairs, a couch, a desk, a window with opaque glass, and a wall hanging of Yasser Arafat — a man as dead as his dreams. The door shut behind him, and the two men were alone.

With a peremptory gesture, Farad motioned Brooke to a chair, then sat across from him, his eyes unwelcoming and hard. "I'm told it's important that we talk."

Brooke nodded. "I appreciate your precautions."

"I do it for my people," Farad responded mordantly. "Personally, I no longer fear death — I took up arms in 1967, was jailed three separate times, shot at more often than I can remember. But look at what we've accomplished for those who live at Ayn Al-Hilweh. What would they do without me?"

There was nothing Brooke could say. "Of course," Farad continued, "a camp is less than a country. But in a mere forty-five years I've progressed from revolutionary to a salaried employee of the European Union, which helps fund the place that has served as a 'homeland' for the two generations after mine. True, it's not the Galilee, my father's home, or even the West Bank — the Zionists who took our land do not allow us to live in either place. But it's only twenty years since the Jews promised us a country of our own. So the people I represent have every reason to be grateful — with luck, they'll simply get rid of us rather than strangle us in our beds." Farad's lips curled in a bitter smile. "Of course, you care deeply about all this. Isn't that why you've come?"

Suddenly the room felt hot and close. "No," Brooke said bluntly. "I'm here because men from Ayn Al-Hilweh may be involved in a very dangerous activity. They've already killed some of your own people —"

"Including my predecessor," Farad interrupted with sudden softness. "Whom, I believe, you may have known."

"I met him," Brook responded blandly. "At the camp."

Farad's eyes bored into Brooke's. "At least

427

his son does well. That's very rare, you know. In the camp we have but two elementary schools, run in shifts. Only a handful go to college, knowing no jobs in Lebanon await them. But Khalid's son is in America, studying to be a doctor." He paused, then added coolly, "Perhaps God, seeing the murder of a father, intervened on the son's behalf. How else to explain such luck? But I have no sons, Mr. Chase."

The lethal remark put Brooke on edge. "You have seventy thousand 'children,' " he replied. "The danger involves them all."

Sitting back, Farad eyed him with disdain. "As to the camp, Fatah al-Islam is a relative handful. Maybe they're capable of killing me, should they find a reason. But they can't endanger seventy thousand people."

"If they're a 'relative handful,' " Brooke retorted, "and capable of killing you as they did Hassan, you've made it your business to know who they are."

"And now you wish to know." Farad's tone became clipped. "How many times, I wonder, will I play the fool for men like you. Two years ago a man from Lebanese intelligence, perhaps a friend of yours, asked for my help in rounding up Fatah al-Islam. In turn, he promised money for development within the camp — a clinic, a school. So I

428

gave him names and the army came for them. I'm still waiting for my funding."

"I'm not this man," Brooke said simply. "Nor do I represent his government."

"Oh, I know. You're American, and worried about al Qaeda. So you may prefer a story about the CIA. Perhaps, from time to time, you've dealt with them."

Brooke said nothing. "As you suggest," Farad continued, "we have our own sources of intelligence. Around the time of the Camp David negotiations we learned that al Qaeda was planning to bomb American University." He nodded toward the portrait of Arafat. "Tell the Americans, our leader said. President Clinton is trying to help us, so we will help his country.

"This was not an act of charity, but of hope. So we enabled the CIA to prevent a tragedy that would have harmed Americans and Lebanese alike. Then Clinton's term ended, and America supported Israel in whatever it did to us." Farad's tone sharpened. "And now you're here. On whose behalf, I have to wonder."

Brooke met his eyes. "I'm an American, as you see."

"Don't play with me, Mr. Whoever-you-are. Nothing that happens at Ayn Al-Hilweh poses any threat to America — certainly not

429

the danger promised by Bin Laden. You're here because the 'dangerous activity' you mentioned involves our immediate neighborhood. Only my analytical genius allows me to guess the target." Farad smiled grimly. "So let's consider the supposed threat to my people. Should I give you names, the army will enter our camp in force, spraying bullets right and left. They'll gun down fifteen innocents for every fighter from Fatah al-Islam."

"I don't want soldiers to invade the camp," Brooke rejoined. "I'm looking for men linked to al Qaeda who have left in the last two weeks. As for the rest, I want the army to keep them here."

It was less than true, Brooke knew: a third possibility, arrest and interrogation, might involve some risk to others, and Fatah al-Islam might kill anyone linked to Adam Chase. From Farad's silent stare, all this was obvious. "If these men are so dangerous," he said dismissively, "I should be happy to see them go. Then I really would be safe." His tone assumed the same chill quiet. "A sixth sense has allowed me to survive. It tells me that the greatest danger is sitting three feet away."

And yet I'm still here, Brooke thought. "If that were true," he answered, "we'd all be better off. But it's not."

"No? You're asking me to collaborate with Israel. Protecting Jews is not my job, nor any way to secure my safety."

"Then let me pose a hypothetical," Brooke said calmly. "Suppose that men from Ayn Al-Hilweh help al Qaeda turn the Galilee into a nuclear wasteland."

After a telling silence, Farad summoned a derisive smile. "Perhaps the Jews will give it back to us. But more likely they will carpet-bomb our camp, killing noncombatants on a scale dwarfing Sabra and Shatilah. If I provide corroboration for your theory, real or imagined, it will serve as a pretext for a mass murder from the air."

"What if al Qaeda succeeds," Brooke prodded, "and some of the plotters are from Ayn Al-Hilweh? In Israel's place, you'd carpet-bomb this camp into oblivion. That leaves one question for you to answer. Do you believe that men in Ayn Al-Hilweh could be part of a plot to detonate a nuclear weapon over Israel?"

Farad's face and body became still, as though the intensity of thought were consuming all his energy. "I've survived by knowing who to watch," he said at length, "whether agents of Fatah al-Islam or a stranger from America who once knew Kha-

431

lid Hassan. For the moment, that's all I choose to say."

Brooke gave him the business card for Adam Chase. "Call me," he advised. "You don't have much time."

At midday, Brooke returned to the Albergo. When he turned the key in the lock, his room's door was chained from the inside.

Half-expecting a bullet through the crack, Brooke slid sideways. Quiet laughter followed him. "I thought this prudent," a familiar voice said. "You might have killed me before noticing who I was."

Opening the door with a gesture of mock hospitality, Jameel ushered Brooke into the room. "How did you get in?" Brooke asked.

"I took the precaution of obtaining a passkey. Let's hope your enemies aren't as resourceful." Jameel's lean, handsome face was filled with concern. "I apologize for giving you a start. But I have something I didn't want to say on the phone, or anywhere we might be overheard."

Which meant that Jameel feared his phone and office might be bugged, his movements followed. Brooke did not bother wondering by whom — it could be the Syrians, Hezbollah, the Sunnis, or the Saudis. "About the Pakistani?" he asked.

Jameel took an envelope from his suit coat. "You're looking for someone with certain technical abilities. This photograph is from a security film taken at Beirut airport six days ago."

Surprised, Brooke removed the picture of a man appearing to hurry past the camera. Though his image was imperfect, he resembled the technician whose photograph Brooke had already seen. "Do you know where he is now?" he asked.

"No. As you know, the Pakistani who surfaced in Dubai has disappeared. A day later this man entered Beirut on a passport from the UAE with a different name altogether. He also seems to have vanished." Reading the worry in Brooke's eyes, Jameel added, "He could just be touring. But we can't find him, and the UAE claims to have no record of such a passport being issued. Except for a modest beard, he resembles your missing technician."

Brooke's sense of alarm quickened. "What are you doing to find him?"

"As much as possible — alerted the police and army, sent inquiries by email to hundreds of hotels." Jameel paused. "You know the problem. There are areas of Lebanon we don't control, including in the south and the Bekaa Valley — that's Hezbollah, of course. But if he's still within our reach, and part of a conspiracy, he's only as free of a trail as whoever he meets up with."

Brooke thought of his meeting with Farad. "That may depend," he answered, "on who has left Ayn Al-Hilweh."

FIVE

After Jameel had left, Brooke began weighing his choices.

He started with two suppositions — that the Pakistani technician had entered Lebanon, and that the al Qaeda operative would try to move the bomb through Iraq, then Syria. The question was where they would meet.

It made no sense for al Qaeda to bring the bomb anywhere near Beirut — every mile it traveled increased the risk of detection. The same risks, Brooke believed, would discourage an effort to smuggle it into Israel across Lebanon's southern border, patrolled by UN peacekeepers. So the optimal base of operations remained the mountainous edge of the Bekaa Valley, where Hezbollah was the only source of intelligence. In Brooke's surmise, that was where the operative planned to meet the technician, along with anyone else involved in the plot.

If he were right, only Israel's bitter enemy, Hezbollah, could help prevent al Qaeda from trying to destroy the Jewish state. But approaching Hezbollah would blow whatever cover he had left, make him their hostage, and — quite possibly — facilitate their acquisition of a nuclear weapon. The sparse facts Brooke knew would not persuade Brustein and Grey to run such risks. Which left him to decide how far he could go without seeking their approval.

He pondered this for an hour. Then, with grave misgivings, he called the leader of the Druze, Hassan Adallah.

In the late afternoon, after hours of hot and uneventful travel, Al Zaroor's bus deposited its Shia pilgrims in Mosul.

Watching them shuffle off the bus, Al Zaroor felt relief mingle with apprehension. In his soul he was happy to be rid of them. But their witless innocence offered perfect cover. Only the shrewdest mind would imagine them sitting atop a bomb.

Now Tariq and Al Zaroor were alone. The fighter drove on, wordless, his worry showing in the tense hunch of his shoulders, the tightness around his eyes as he pushed the bus harder. The terrain flew past, flat and dry and featureless save for the biblical cities they passed — Nimrod, the walled city of Nineveh. Al Zaroor welcomed the embrace of dusk, shrouding the distant mountains of Kurdistan.

Near the border town of Zakho, he issued his first instruction.

Turning off the headlights, Tariq left the road. For endless minutes, they drove across sun-baked earth toward a slice of the Tigris between Iraq and Syria. Al Zaroor felt his apprehension growing, a knot in his gut he despised but could not control. Syria would be the most dangerous part of a journey based on calculated risk, an eighteen-hour trip through a country run by a ruthless regime that saw al Qaeda as a threat to its survival. He could succeed only by adopting its coloration.

At last they reached the river, in silver moonlight as black as a ribbon of spilled ink. Al Zaroor stood on the bank. A light appeared on the water, its movement toward them accompanied by the chopping of an outboard motor.

Al Zaroor remained still. As its motor cut off, the boat hit the edge of land. The outline of a man ascended the sloping riverbank. When he became visible, he wore the uniform of a Syrian intelligence officer, his gun aimed at Al Zaroor's head. His face was young and hard and wary.

"I've come to arrest you," he said.

Heart still racing, Al Zaroor nodded.

In twilight, Brooke took a taxi to southern Beirut, the domain of Hezbollah, to meet Grand Ayatollah al-Mahdi.

The Shia section was even poorer than that dominated by the Sunni, its Middle Eastern character so absolute that Brooke could not square it with the upscale Western luxuries of Achrafieh and Gemmayze. Since Israel's bombing campaigns against the rural south of Lebanon, a Hezbollah redoubt, Shia farmers had crowded into what they called "the belt of misery," raising its population to almost a million people. There were no road maps or street signs; makeshift buildings defied all laws of architecture or safety; a tangle of cables ran from structure to structure, providing makeshift power. In the endless web of alleyways, the smoke of smoldering garbage mingled with the aroma of roasted chicken and skewers of lamb kebobs, and carts of fruits and vegetables clogged arteries already crowded by motorcycles, cars, covered women, men in shabby clothing, and Hezbollah militia struggling to avert gridlock. The Lebanese government held no sway here, nor did the Sunnis. But what most distinguished this from Sunni Beirut was not the posters of Hezbollah martyrs, but the blocks of bombed-out buildings destroyed by the Israelis in 2006, rubble amid reconstruction projects financed by Iran. More than a thousand people had died here. Among the survivors were Grand Ayatollah al-Mahdi and Hassan Nasrallah, the leader of Hezbollah, whose homes were leveled by targeted air strikes. But with respect to possible assassins from Ayn Al-Hilweh, Brooke was probably safer here than in Achrafieh.

On a crowded corner that looked no different from any other, a man in a sport coat signaled Brooke's cab to stop. Up close, the man was fortyish, with a graying beard and a firm handshake. Casually, he said, "So you're visiting from America," and led Brooke through the knot of pedestrians to a Volkswagen minibus.

Once the door closed behind Brooke and his escort, Salim, the driver negotiated a series of twists and turns designed to confuse Brooke as to where they were. He gave up on following this — he had entered al-Mahdi's world. Even while chatting with Salim, the most amiable of men, Brooke reviewed what he knew about the spiritual leader of the Shia.

Even for Lebanon, the portrait was complex and contradictory. Beyond doubt al-Mahdi was — with Sistani of Iraq and Khameini of Iran — one of the three most revered clerics in the Shia world, and the greatest figure among them: a theologian who had written extensively on Islam's dialogue with other religions, an authority on Islamic law, a poet of considerable skill, and the founder and patron of charities funded in part by a pristine restaurant where Brooke had once taken Michelle Adjani. He was also believed by the CIA to have given religious sanction, thirty years before, to the suicide bombings of the Marine Corps barracks, the American embassy, and the Israeli military headquarters at Tyre. For this, many believed, while head of the CIA, William Casey had tried to have al-Mahdi killed. Despite this, al-Mahdi had severely condemned the al Qaeda attacks on 9/11. But to the State Department, al-Mahdi remained what he had been for three decades — a murderous cleric with whom American officials were barred from meeting.

None of this troubled Brooke at all. His concerns were practical — whether, by meeting al-Mahdi, he was exposing himself

440

to Hezbollah, exceeding his orders and jeopardizing his life. But time had forced his hand. Seven days remained until September 11, and the risks of failure dwarfed any risk to Brooke.

At length, the bus reached an iron gate at the end of the alleyway, behind which trees partially concealed a one-story building that, transplanted to a modest American suburb, might have housed the local accountant, insurance agent, or divorce lawyer. "Not precisely the Vatican," Brooke remarked to Salim.

"It's true, alas. But no one bombs the pope."

Inside the building, Brooke passed through a metal detector, giving up his watch and, with greater reluctance, his cell phone. Then he was led to a large interior room with parquet floors, sumptuous carpets, and two severe black chairs. Facing them was Grand Ayatollah al-Mahdi.

A man in his midseventies, al-Mahdi was dressed in a white tunic, a yellow-gold robe, and the black turban reserved for descendants of the Prophet Mohammed. He had a long, steel-gray beard, and his eyes were grave and penetrating. But what struck Brooke was his utter stillness and serenity, an aura of peace so profound that he seemed to repose in his own illumination. Brooke looked for a trick of lighting, and found none.

Salim introduced Brooke in Arabic as a visitor from the United States, familiar with the commercial and political circles of its capital, who had come under the auspices of Hassan Adallah to seek the grand ayatollah's observations on issues of mutual concern. Throughout this nonsense, al-Mahdi regarded him with a look so calm yet piercing that, from someone less beatific, Brooke might have perceived a threat. As with Hassan Adallah, Brooke had no doubt that this man knew exactly what he was — a member of the agency that, al-Mahdi believed, had tried to kill him. When Salim had finished, al-Mahdi continued appraising him for a silent moment, then waved him to a chair with a slight but graceful gesture of his hand. As Brooke sat, a smile played on al-Mahdi's lips.

"Aside from Jimmy Carter," the grand ayatollah remarked in a deep but mild voice, "you're that rarest of visitors, an American. It seems that I'm on a list of 'terrorists' with whom officials of your government are forbidden to speak. How fortunate for me that you do not work for them."

Repressing his own smile, Brooke nodded

gravely. "And for me, Your Holiness. I would regret missing the chance to hear your thoughts."

"And to what purpose, I wonder." Although still quiet, al-Mahdi's tone gained intensity and force. "I have said that Saddam Hussein was evil. I do not support the tactics of the Taliban. I condemn al Qaeda and its works as contrary to Islam. I seek no clash of civilizations. Yet again and again your military — in Iraq, Afghanistan, and now Pakistan — creates misery and chaos, just as the Zionists did here. Your leaders embrace 'democracy,' then send aid to kings and dictators across the Islamic world. And after all that, your government deems us unfit for one moment of conversation."

"I didn't compose the terrorist list," Brooke answered simply. "But it's based on more than differences in viewpoint."

On the surface, al-Mahdi ignored Brooke's tacit reference to the murder of Americans. But his eyes bored into Brooke's, underscoring the passion of his words. "There is also the matter of Israel. As a man of faith, I cannot believe that God gave Palestine to Jews alone. But your country enables the Zionists to treat Palestinians as your ancestors treated the Indians, expelling them from their native land and dividing them on the West Bank as though creating reservations. Nor did God grant Jews the right to invade this land and kill or maim its people — it is America, not the Almighty, that supports them." Al-Mahdi's voice softened. "So what principles does your country live by? And who, I might ask, are the terrorists?"

However elegantly, they were edging closer to raw truths. "I can only speak for myself," Brooke answered. "But one definition of a terrorist is someone who straps a bomb to himself and kills innocent people. The first such actions took place here."

Briefly, al-Mahdi's stare turned cold. "I trust you are not condemning Islam as a religion of violence. We did not kill the Jews in World War Two, or bomb the Japanese in Hiroshima and Nagasaki." He paused, modulating his voice. "But you are speaking of Hezbollah, of course, and perhaps of me. There are many ways in which its leaders and I disagree, though I do not wish to tell you what they are — or were. But what Lebanese do in defense of Lebanon adds a layer of moral complexity, at least with respect to Israel and those who aid it. You must agree, Mr. Chase, that if the Soviets had tried to occupy America, your people would have claimed the right to kill them in their offices and encampments. That, regrettably, is the most effective way of persuading an occupier to leave."

This was, Brooke sensed, as close to a defense of Hezbollah's beginnings as the grand ayatollah would advance. For himself, he thought it prudent to pass over the car-bombing of Rafik Hariri, or the deaths of Israeli civilians caused by Hezbollah rockets. "You and I may not always agree," Brooke said. "But be assured that I'll convey what you've said to my friends in Washington."

Silent, the ayatollah regarded him with an expectant look. "In turn, is there anything else you wish me to know?"

"There is, Your Holiness. A great evil may be coming here, with terrible consequences to America and Israel, but also to Lebanon and, especially, the Shia." Brooke leaned forward, speaking to al-Mahdi in a clear, emphatic voice. "I believe outsiders mean to provoke a deadly war between Israel and Hezbollah and Iran. I know that you and Hezbollah are separate. But, as Shia, they look to you."

"What guidance would you have me give?"

"To watch for strangers, and to listen. If these men succeed, hundreds of thousands will die. And that could be the least of it."

Al-Mahdi's expression became impenetrable. "That sounds much like Bin Laden's threat against America."

"So it does."

Nodding, al-Mahdi seemed to withdraw his attention, a signal that the audience was done. As he left, Brooke glanced back over his shoulder. The grand ayatollah was again utterly still, his eyes closed, as if returning to a place of peace or, perhaps, absorbing the troubles of the world.

Six

In a cab provided by the grand ayatollah, Brooke returned to the Christian section by an equally circuitous route. Out of caution, he had the driver drop him in Gemmayze.

The night was warm and pleasant, the cobblestone streets crowded with young people and couples hardy enough to be careless of their hours on a weeknight. Passing by a nightclub that pulsed with festive Lebanese music, Brooke briefly regretted the loss of a carefree life. But his mind kept working on different levels — wondering if he had told al-Mahdi too much or too little, searching for some way to secure information on Fatah al-Islam. The phone buzzed in his coat pocket.

Several thoughts struck him at once: that few people had his number; that the call might be critical; that he had parted with the phone during his time with al-Mahdi; that the caller might wish to divert his attention or stop his movements, setting him up to be shot or snatched off the streets. Maintaining the same pace, he put the phone to his ear.

"How was the grand ayatollah?" Jameel asked.

Of course, Brooke thought — Jameel had ties to Hassan Adallah. "Looking out for me, Bashir? Then I hope you're on your cell phone."

At the reference to his obvious fear that his phone was bugged, Jameel answered drily, "A new one." He paused, then said, "There was an arrest at the entrance to Ayn Al-Hilweh. The driver had a bomb in his car."

Involuntarily, Brooke stopped moving. "Fatah al-Islam?"

"We think so, yes. The man was from the refugee camp in Tripoli."

Brooke began walking again. "Who was he after?"

"He's not talking. But Fatah al-Islam has one overt enemy within the camp."

The PLO, Brooke thought at once. He wondered how this would affect Ibrahim Farad's assessment of his own safety. "You've got security cameras at the entrances to Ayn Al-Hilweh," he said. "I assume you're reviewing all the tapes from

448

the past two weeks. Not just to see who entered, but who left."

"Of course."

With that, Brooke got off, moving at the same pace toward the Albergo.

Close to midnight, Al Zaroor, Tariq, and the Syrian carried the bomb in its casket to the powerboat. After giving Tariq his hurried thanks, Al Zaroor and the stranger, Yusif Azid, crossed the Tigris into Syria.

A van waited there. Sweating, Al Zaroor and Azid loaded the bomb into the van, then covered it by turning the powerboat hull upward. Before dawn, they had transferred their cargo to a diesel-belching truck driven by a Syrian smuggler, and Al Zaroor had dressed in a uniform identical to that which Azid already wore. But Azid was who he appeared to be, an officer in military intelligence. He was also a Sunni fundamentalist, secretly worshipful of Osama Bin Laden, and had done al Qaeda crucial favors in the past. But he could manage this very large favor only by taking a few days' vacation time, then behaving as though he were still on duty. Or so he said — Al Zaroor could not quite trust him.

Not that he had a choice. In the abstract, the plan was the best he could design for

Syria. The chubby and phlegmatic trucker, Hussein, thought he was smuggling antiquities to Lebanon for the usual shadowy purposes, most likely to finance Hezbollah. By early morning, they had entered the normal stream of commerce — the main highway through the north of Syria. The bomb was concealed among crates of machine parts covered by falsified Syrian documentation. The three oddly assorted companions occupied the cab, exchanging awkward conversation beneath the spasmodic wheeze of feeble air-conditioning. As in Iraq, the drive was long and flat and hot; as in Iraq, they faced the risk of checkpoints. But the Syrians, unlike the Iraqis, were purposeful and suspicious. This made Azid necessary.

For miles, they moved in a line of vehicles — trucks, vans, beat-up cars, a few luxury vehicles. Shortly before eleven, traffic slowed abruptly. Though Al Zaroor did not yet see a checkpoint, there could be no other reason.

He glanced sideways at Azid. If the Syrian planned to betray the mission, a mass of soldiers might be waiting at the checkpoint. Azid would be promoted; Syria would have the bomb; Al Zaroor would be tortured and executed or left to rot in a stinking Syrian prison. Unless he used the gun in his holster to put a bullet through his temple.

He had a long time to weigh his choices. The massive truck in front of them inched forward as the unseen checkpoint cleared one vehicle at a time, even as the traffic in the other direction passed unimpeded. It felt too much like the checkpoint in Iraq. Al Zaroor breathed deeply, willing his tension to subside.

At last the truck, creeping ahead, exposed the ends of a mobile barrier that otherwise remained invisible. Al Zaroor watched a uniformed official speak to the driver, then casually scan his papers. That no one searched its cargo made Al Zaroor more, not less, apprehensive — it suggested that the Syrians were looking for a particular truck. Azid's face showed nothing. Al Zaroor would not betray his nervousness by asking if this procedure was routine.

When the truck cleared the checkpoint, Al Zaroor saw that it was manned by only two policemen. The official walked up to their van, motioning for Hussein to roll down his window. Then he saw Azid and froze.

With a thin smile, Azid held up his identification. In this ambiguous moment, Al Zaroor touched his gun.

"Move on," the official said, and the truck

451

rolled through the checkpoint.

Brooke got up early and ordered breakfast in his room. He felt trapped and useless, craving some activity that would get him out. But pointless movement carried only risk. So he stayed there, sending a report to Langley that omitted any mention of al-Mahdi. Then he saw the email from Terri Young.

She had little new — the checkpoints in Iraq had yielded nothing, nor was there any report from Syria. Her most concrete news was that Washington was emptying out, with Republicans blaming Democrats for a catastrophe that had yet to occur. When Brooke's cell phone buzzed, it came as a relief.

The man spoke with the accent of a Palestinian. "At three o'clock this afternoon, Mr. Chase, you will visit the Crusader Sea Castle in Sidon. Perhaps you can learn from the past."

The caller clicked off, leaving Brooke to wonder whether this message came from Farad or Fatah al-Islam. But he would not scare off Farad by calling back.

It was a little past eleven. Time enough to wander the streets of Sidon, then meet whomever waited.

■ ■ ■ ■

The day grew hotter, the cab so suffocating that Al Zaroor, sitting between Azid and the trucker, could smell the noxious mix of sweat with aftershave that no doubt served as Hussein's substitute for bathing. To kill time, the trucker produced photographs of his wife and two sons. Perusing them out of politeness, Al Zaroor saw a doe-eyed woman, pretty from what little her cover revealed, and two handsome boys in soccer uniforms. Life held many mysteries, Al Zaroor reflected — the latest being how such a dull-looking beast could spawn such sons. Murmuring compliments, he passed the snapshots to an equally bored Azid.

"My boys are keen athletes," Hussein informed his companions. "Also readers — especially the Koran. Sharia has raised them well."

Still apprehensive, Al Zaroor watched the traffic ahead, moving steadily across the scrub and khaki terrain. "Have you a family of your own?" Hussein inquired.

Al Zaroor thought of Salwa, the one woman he might have loved. But that was very long ago; like his parents and sister, no doubt she thought him dead. Perhaps his parents were dead, too, and Salwa thickened by bearing some other man's children. "No," Al Zaroor responded. "That was not God's wish."

Clearly not, Azid's silent look said. Al Zaroor felt his fleeting sadness become resentment of both men. Perhaps it was only that they assisted jihad on vacation from the comfort of their lives. He willed his mind to leave his body, envisioning the path ahead.

As planned, they turned sharply south, passing Aleppo and the ruins of ancient cities, rendered more haunting because no one knew why the cities had died. They continued without pause, sharing soggy pita pockets provided by Hussein. At length, they reached the outskirts of Hama, a pretty place along the Orontes River, its banks lined with trees and gardens — another place Al Zaroor had no time for. To his irritation, Hussein stopped at a stand outside the city.

"What's this about?" Al Zaroor demanded.

Oblivious, Hussein smiled. "Halawat," he said. "Want some?"

"No," Azid interjected curtly. "Thank you." The intelligence officer, Al Zaroor realized, also felt jumpy. He hoped their reasons were the same.

Debating which man to watch, Al Zaroor got out with the driver, pretending to stretch his legs. Standing in line, Hussein talked to no one. From where he stood, Al Zaroor could not observe Azid. Silent, he fidgeted while Hussein consumed the pastry, a combination of cheese-based dough and ice cream soaked in honey and topped with pistachios. The remnants glistened on his fingers.

Here I stand, Al Zaroor thought, watching a fat man clog his arteries while a nuclear weapon sits in the back of his truck, uncertain of whether the second man is a traitor to his uniform, or to me. "Let's move," he prodded Hussein.

When they went back to the van, Azid put away his cell phone.

Ten minutes later, they hit a second checkpoint.

This one was different, Al Zaroor knew at once. The traffic ahead was not backed up, suggesting that the checkpoint had just appeared. In front of it stood six soldiers and an officer.

For the few seconds he had, Al Zaroor watched Azid's eyes, wondering whom he had called. A muscle twitched in the Syrian's face. "Open the door," Azid told the driver.

As Hussein slid out, then Azid, Al Zaroor touched the gun in its holster. On the steaming tarmac, Azid walked up to the slender young officer. Their voices were faint, fragmentary; Al Zaroor tried but failed to read lips. Then Azid took out his identification.

The officer studied it, then demanded Hussein's papers. Scanning them, he faced Azid again, his voice now audible. "Let's look inside."

As Hussein shrugged, Azid sighed with a theatrical impatience that did not conceal his apprehension. Al Zaroor wondered which man — if either — had betrayed him.

Swiftly, he got out. At the rear of the truck, the officer and Azid watched Hussein open the steel door. Nodding to the officer, Al Zaroor stood to the side. The false identification in his pocket was his only shield.

Inside the truck were crates of auto parts. Summoning his soldiers, the officer ordered them to remove each crate, eyeing their contents through the cracks. Al Zaroor watched as if in a waking dream, knowing that the process would uncover his anomalous cargo.

At last the rectangular crate was exposed. "What's that?" the officer sharply asked

Hussein.

The driver shifted his weight. "Machine parts, like the rest."

"It looks more like a coffin. Or a box for concealing men."

To Al Zaroor's surprise, Hussein laughed. "I hope not. If he's dead, he's rotten. If he's alive, by now we can smell his shit." He turned to a soldier. "Try to lift that, for the love of Allah."

With one of his men, the officer climbed in, seizing each end of the crate. They started to pick it up, feeling its weight. Then the officer peered through the crate at the steel casing. He got out again, this time facing Azid. "What is this?"

Paling beneath his olive skin, Azid summoned the stare he had first given Al Zaroor. "As I said, it's a matter of state security. We have friends who await this."

Hezbollah, he might as well have said. The officer regarded him, as though gauging the consequences of offending a man who outranked him, a member of the military's most fearsome branch. Facing his soldiers, he ordered, "Load up the truck again."

Arms folded, Azid watched them do this. Al Zaroor looked from Azid to Hussein, surprised and appreciative. The two men had proven themselves as actors.

When the soldiers were done, Hussein closed the truck, then climbed back into the cab with Azid and Al Zaroor. The officer waved them through. Shaken, they headed toward the Anti-Lebanon Mountains.

SEVEN

At a little before two, Brooke arrived by taxi in the coastal town of Sidon, the site of Ayn Al-Hilweh.

Brooke wore a polo shirt and blue jeans. Before leaving, he had put Carter Grey's elephant in his back pocket; now he wandered through the streets close to the waterfront, choosing a route designed to expose anyone who followed him. But this assured him of little; teams of trackers with cell phones were harder to spot than a single man. Nor, in this case, did his methods matter much. The danger lay less in what he did before three o'clock than that he was meeting an unknown person at a specific place and time, a setup for being kidnapped or killed.

At two-thirty, half an hour early, Brooke abruptly flagged a cab and asked to be dropped near the Sea Castle.

Brooke had been there before: If someone

meant him harm, he had chosen well. Built by Crusaders in the thirteenth century, the sandstone ruins faced the sea, connected to land only by a narrow stone causeway roughly fifty yards in length. To Brooke's advantage, no one could follow without being seen. But the only means of escape was to dive into the Mediterranean. Even if his enemies were not equipped with boats, he could not swim fast enough for that to matter.

Approaching the castle, Brooke glanced around him. The roadway along the waterfront was lightly trafficked in both directions, enabling an assassin to shoot him from a car; the cafés had outside tables where a lookout could watch for him; three men were idling near the entrance to the castle. Without breaking stride, Brooke gave himself permission to turn around. But this was not what he had returned for.

He reached the entrance. Without seeming to, he noted the faces of the three men, the seasoned, watchful look of bodyguards or killers. What confirmed his instincts was that none looked at him as he passed.

Walking at a measured pace, he started down the causeway. Halfway to the castle he stopped, hands on hips, turning sideways to gaze at the water. In the periphery of his vision, he saw that the men remained at their posts. Then he headed toward the castle again.

Though in the seven centuries since its abandonment, parts had toppled into the sea, much remained — turrets, a parapet, walls with small windows through which defenders could peer, a wing with three intact stories of shadowy rooms that offered relief from the harshness of sun, a stone pier in front of the structures from which sentries could watch for enemy ships. At the end of the causeway, Brooke climbed sandstone steps to the top of a wall, a vantage point from which he could scan much of the ruins. A few Westerners meandered into and out of the castle; he saw no one who seemed threatening. But in this place he would never spot a professional in time. Then he saw a man sitting at the end of the stone pier, gazing out to sea.

Brooke took the steps down to the pier and started toward the lone man. Briefly turning, he saw two other men emerge from inside the castle. Though Brooke's footsteps were audible, the man he was approaching did not interrupt his contemplation of the ocean. Only when Brooke sat beside him did Ibrahim Farad say, "You're very brave, or very stupid. Not that they're mutually exclusive."

"True. But I'm neither. The odds were that the call came from one of your people, not Fatah al-Islam. They may not know I'm in Lebanon."

Still Farad did not turn. "No? A matter of time, then. It seems you were right."

Brooke studied his impassive profile. "The car bomb was meant for you?"

"We believe so, yes." Farad gave a heavy shrug of his shoulders. "Perhaps they resented your visit."

Brooke felt defensive; Farad's remark raised the specter of Khalid Hassan. Evenly, he said, "I wasn't followed."

"As you like."

"And yet we're meeting."

Farad turned, eyes boring into Brooke's. "Like you, I believe they have a mission outside Ayn Al-Hilweh. They don't want you, me, or anyone to sniff that out. That's why they tried to slip a car bomb past the army." His voice softened. "Ironic, isn't it. I don't wish to die like Khalid Hassan. And yet, like Khalid, I find myself dealing with you."

"Are we dealing?"

Farad did not answer. "Fatah al-Islam," he said slowly, "cares nothing about a homeland for my people. Their ambitions

462

transcend our petty concerns. Oppression hasn't broken them; it's made them insane."

Best to let Farad talk, Brooke concluded. "What do they offer al Qaeda?"

Farad looked at him keenly. "Foot soldiers, unafraid of death, with access to sophisticated Internet and cell phone equipment. They may not be allowed to hold jobs outside the camp, but they can leave at will. That means they could be anywhere in Lebanon."

"I need names. Or faces."

Farad smiled faintly. "Ahmad Duri, Ismail Qurai, Yusuf Harani. Perhaps they've all gone fishing. But no one has seen them in a week."

"Can you describe them?"

Reaching into the pocket of his pants, Farad produced a BlackBerry. In rapid succession, he displayed three photographs of men clearly caught without their knowledge — one with soft eyes, barely more than a boy; another with a fleshy, sullen face; a thirtyish man with scruffy beard and slits for eyes. "Duri, Qurai, Harani," Farad repeated. "For all I know, these were the men who tried to kill you." Seeing Brooke's expression, he added, "You thought I didn't know this? A few days after you left Lebanon, sensing that death awaited him, Khalid Hassan spoke to me — not of everything, but some things. Once you came to see me, I knew you must be Khalid's grim reaper."

Brooke was silent. At length, he said simply, "I liked Khalid. I mourned his death."

Farad gave him a cold smile. "Do men like you mourn anyone?"

"You'd be surprised. I have these odd moments of sentiment."

Farad studied his face and chose to say nothing.

Evenly, Brooke said, "I'd like to borrow your BlackBerry."

From the same pocket, Farad produced a FlipDrive. "Consider these pictures a remembrance of Khalid. Perhaps one of them strangled him with that piano wire."

Brooke took the drive, putting it in his pocket with Grey's elephant. "I appreciate your help."

"Your 'gratitude' is nothing to me," Farad answered. "You're an operative, without influence. But perhaps you will mention our help should it aid you in protecting a few hundred thousand Jews from a nuclear holocaust."

The hopelessness and disdain beneath Farad's words was palpable. Abruptly, he stood. "Which one of us should leave first, I wonder."

Silent, Brooke shrugged.

Farad's smile was grim. "I thought as much. After all, it was only Khalid who died."

Without more, he turned and headed for the steps up to the causeway, his two body-guards at his side. Standing, Brooke watched him go. Both men knew that if someone had followed one of them, or the other, the first man to leave might draw their attention. If someone had to die, Brooke preferred that it not be he.

Gazing out to sea, he let ten minutes pass. Then he began climbing the same steps.

Near the top, a terrible sound made him flinch, then duck. He knew it was a car bomb before the shiver of fear finished running through him.

Steadying himself, Brooke stood. Perhaps a hundred feet from the entrance of the causeway the shell of an unidentifiable car spat flames through shattered windows. Wedged into its side was a van, partially obscured by thick black smoke. No one inside either vehicle, Brooke felt certain, could have lived.

He began moving down the causeway, ignoring the traffic jam on the road ahead, the cries of pedestrians running from the blast. By the time he reached the road, two policemen on motorcycles had arrived at the wreckage. Brooke moved swiftly in the other direction, pulse pounding in his throat, half-expecting to be shot. Instead he spotted a cab parked in front of the hotel across the street. Weaving swiftly among the cars stalled in the lanes headed toward the blast, he waited for a break in the opposite lanes, then slid inside the cab.

"What happened?" the cabbie asked in English.

"No idea," Brooke answered in an uninterested tone. "Can you take me to Beirut?"

As they headed north, away from the wreckage, Brooke heard the sound of sirens. His stomach felt hollow.

Get a grip, he told himself.

After a couple of minutes, he took out his BlackBerry. There was a message from Carter Grey — the Counterterrorism Center had picked up a telephone transmission in Syria. An intelligence officer, supposedly on leave, might have helped a truck through a checkpoint. Now the Syrians were looking for him.

Of course, Brooke thought. That was how al Qaeda would get the bomb through Syria. Sitting back, he hoped against hope that the dead he had left behind did not include

Ibrahim Farad. He reached the Albergo without knowing.

Taking the elevator to his room, he locked the door and put the FlipDrive in his computer. As Farad had promised, the three Palestinians appeared. Brooke sent the photographs to Langley, then Jameel. In Jameel's message, he requested that Lebanese security check these images against the tapes from Ayn Al-Hilweh. Two more faces consumed his thoughts — Khalid Hassan's, then Ibrahim Farad's.

Close to six, Jameel called him. "We got the photographs," he said, then briefly paused. "There was a car bombing today in Sidon. A leader of the PLO was killed."

Brooke touched his eyes. "Ibrahim Farad," he said softly. "I was there."

There was silence, Jameel absorbing this. "We need to talk, Adam."

"Where?"

"Someone will contact you." Jameel paused again. "My wife and I had planned an evening out. Maybe she'll bring her sister — you will like her." His tone softened. "We go only to the best places, and only with minders. This is not a celebratory occasion, I know. But we have matters to discuss in person."

Hanging up, Brooke heard another voice,

Ibrahim Farad's.
After all, it was only Khalid who died.

EIGHT

At dusk, Al Zaroor and the bomb reached a road near the foothills of the Anti-Lebanon Mountains.

Tersely, he ordered Hussein to cut off the headlights and leave the road. For perhaps a mile they drove slowly along the edge of the hills in failing light, until the only illumination came from an almost full moon. Spotting two large boulders, Al Zaroor told the trucker to stop. Edgy, Azid said, "I must get back soon."

"We're almost done," Al Zaroor assured him.

Hurriedly, they got out, clambered into the rear of the truck, and moved aside the crates of machine parts. Al Zaroor felt his apprehension deepen — in a few hours, should the Syrians not hunt him down, he would be clear of this accursed country. Straining, he and his companions laid the coffin-shaped container beside the truck.

He took out his new cell phone and pressed a number. When someone answered, relief coursed through him. He ended the call without speaking.

"One more task," he told the others.

Together, the three men began bearing the crate away from the truck, Azid in front, Hussein holding up the middle, and Al Zaroor in the rear. The air was still hot; sweat dampened Al Zaroor's skin. He could hear Hussein panting with effort. Under his breath, the man murmured, "After this, I can't wait to see my family."

"A little farther," Al Zaroor urged.

In minutes, should the plan hold, his new allies would materialize from the darkness. As their clan had done for centuries, they would guide him into the mountains, harsh and bleak and rocky, on paths hacked by men as hard as the terrain, as disdainful of Hezbollah as they were of governments or borders. As Hussein and Azid labored in front of him, he visualized the next few moments.

Al Zaroor readied himself. "This is far enough."

In the shadows of the foothills, the three men lowered the crate to earth, Hussein grunting with effort. Azid faced Al Zaroor.

"You've done a great service," Al Zaroor

told him.

The Syrian nodded. Stiffly, they embraced, and then, with more reluctance, Al Zaroor let the sweaty trucker clasp his shoulders. Wordless, the two men started toward the truck — Hussein to return to his family, Azid to take a separate car, arranged by Al Zaroor, after Hussein dropped him in a nearby town. For the sake of security, they had all agreed, it was essential that they separate.

Treading softly behind them, Al Zaroor took out his gun.

Azid first, he had decided. He squeezed the trigger. The security man stiffened; the shot jerked him upright, and then he toppled to his knees. As though puzzled, Hussein stared down, then saw his new enemy facing him across the fallen officer.

"Why?" the unarmed man bleated in protest.

Silent, Al Zaroor shot him through the heart.

Hussein fell at once. Groaning, Azid writhed in the dirt. Al Zaroor knelt and put a bullet through his temple. A spray of blood dampened his hand.

He permitted himself a brief moment to feel the weight of his choice. Though a hireling, Hussein's playacting might have saved him; without Azid's allegiance, his willingness to risk all, the bomb could not have crossed this police state. But that was the problem — if arrested and tortured, either or both could have described Al Zaroor and his cargo. The Syrians would surmise its nature, and act to protect themselves and Hezbollah, exposing Bin Laden's warning to America as a ruse. Had the two men at his feet known they were transporting a bomb, they never would have helped. Now they were corpses.

In the distance, from the hills above him, headlights flashed and vanished. He waited by the bodies.

Moments later, the van found him.

Four men emerged, of varied shapes and sizes. When they were close enough to be seen, three were young, the fourth a gaunt man with seams of experience marking hooded eyes as he stared down at the bodies. In the phlegmy voice of a smoker, Rasul Jefaar said, "What do we do with these?"

"Make them disappear."

The man nodded. His three underlings loaded the crate into the van, then threw the bodies in beside it. "The keys are in the truck," Al Zaroor said and pointed. "You'll find it in that direction."

One of the underlings began walking. His

job, easy enough for such men, was to conceal the truck. Al Zaroor got into the van with the others and began his clandestine journey into the mountains.

Still weary after a long day following a sleepless night, Dr. Laura Reynolds studied the faces on her computer screen. Hastily, she printed the photographs. Then she slid them into her purse, slipped out of her room, and drove to the Sunni enclave of Shawtarwah.

Parking on a street of modest storefronts, she entered a place that said "Internet Café" in English and Arabic. Inside were metal tables at which a few men sat staring at computers, some with cups of coffee.

It was a long shot, she knew. But in the Bekaa Valley, predominately Shia, there were few places where Sunni men gathered or where strangers felt at ease. Though a man or two looked up at her, perhaps surprised to see a woman, the owner gave her a friendly nod from behind the coffee bar. She had come here before; knowing such places was important to her work.

She bought a cup of black coffee, exchanging greetings in Arabic with the grizzled proprietor. Selecting a corner station, she began sipping coffee and tapping out emails to friends from graduate school.

A few other men, arriving, noted and dismissed her. Now and then, she stretched in her chair, casting an idle glance around the room. Though she committed them to memory, no faces matched the photographs. But the exercise was crucial. In place after place, she had learned to type strangers on sight, distinguish Shia from Sunni or Lebanese from outsiders, spot Republican Guards from Iran who had filtered in to meet with Hezbollah — just as, when younger, she had learned to separate Mississippians from Californians before they spoke. Tonight, it seemed, no men of interest would oblige her by walking in.

She sent another few emails, waiting for the customers to thin. Then she went to the bar and ordered another coffee. "Business is good?" she asked the proprietor.

He held out his hand, wiggling his fingers. "So-so."

She took a sip of coffee. "I was hoping to meet friends here," she said. "Visitors from Beirut. Perhaps they misunderstood."

He gave her an upward glance. "Perhaps. Tonight I've seen no strangers."

She took the photographs from her purse, placing them on the counter. "These are my friends. Have you seen any of them in the last few days?"

The owner scrutinized them closely, placing a finger on one. "This man, I think, maybe yesterday. I knew he was not from here." He looked up at Laura, asking quietly, "If I see him again, shall I say you were looking?"

"That's all right. I'm sure we'll find each other."

Settling her bill, she slid money across the counter for more than she owed him for the coffee.

NINE

A little after nine, Brooke met Bashir Jameel and his wife, Janine, at Mayrig, a lively Armenian restaurant in downtown Beirut. With them was her sister Raina, a dark-eyed beauty in a sleek black dress that, on some other night, might have provoked in Brooke an imaginative leap or two. Over drinks, he discovered that the exotic Raina was studying to be a surgeon. Glancing at her in a way intended, and accepted, as an expression of humor, Brooke said with a smile, "Only in Beirut."

Raina laughed. "What is your business?" she inquired wryly. "Bashir has told me so little about you."

"Nothing that interesting. I give commercial and political advice to anxious Americans looking to invest abroad. In that way, like Bashir, I'm a collector of information. But the stakes are only money, and not even mine at that."

She gave him an amused but skeptical look. No doubt she, like Brooke, was conscious of the guards parked outside, the security men stationed at a nearby table. But dinner went on like that, pleasant chatter with an attractive woman and a bright and amiable couple, enjoyable but for Brooke's sense of foreboding, the image of a man in the last moments of his life. Washing down meze and lamb with earthy Lebanese wine, Brooke fought to repress the imprint of Farad's smoldering car.

"You look pensive," Raina said.

Brooke forced another smile. "I travel a lot, and often I see great privation — the Palestinians here, for one example. The next moment I'm enjoying nights like this. Sometimes my life seems unreal."

Raina nodded her understanding. "On nights like this, I try to accept that. As a doctor, one can see a week's worth of misery in an hour. But that is my calling."

Brooke touched his glass to hers. "Good luck."

She held out her hand, steady after several glasses. "Luck has nothing to do with it," she said with a touch of pride. "I have the nerves of a surgeon."

Smiling fondly at Raina, Janine gave the presumptive Adam Chase a speculative look. Americans had fallen in love with Lebanon before.

"The night is in its infancy," Jameel announced cheerfully. "I have a table at the Music Hall."

A cavernous nightclub, the Music Hall featured an eclectic parade of acts that went deep into the night. Plush couches surrounded lacquered tables offering Perrier, Veuve Clicquot, Jack Daniel's, arrack, nuts, cigarettes, and cigars. The crowd was sophisticated and almost wholly Christian, the women in low-cut blouses and blue jeans or short skirts or dresses. Between acts, recorded rock music pulsed through the smoke-filled air.

Brooke and Raina drank champagne; Bashir and Janine, arrack. In swift succession they saw a Lebanese vocalist backed by electric ouds; a sexy young Frenchwoman performing cabaret-style; a folksinger covering Dylan's "Knocking on Heaven's Door"; an Arab tenor who billed himself as Saddam Hussein's son; and a bearded group in tribal garb called the "Rockin' Taliban." Twenty minutes away, Brooke reflected, Grand Ayatollah al-Mahdi lived in ethereal quiet, surrounded by pious men, women in cover, and Hezbollah militia. He expressed this to Raina.

"We're a country of contradictions," she said, "often poised on the edge of catastrophe, either through our own divisions or as the 'gift' of outsiders. This is a place where Christians come to enjoy their privilege, to believe for a moment that they can define their own world." Frowning, she added quietly, "Most of all, to forget that our power is slipping, that our compatriots are emigrating out of insecurity or fear, that the next tragedy may only be days away. Even Bashir does this."

As though on cue, Jameel leaned across the table. "Forgive us for a moment," he asked of Raina. "I've some business to discuss with Adam."

Prompted by Janine, the sisters went off to dance to the piped-in beat. Nodding toward his sister-in-law, Jameel murmured, "She's a prize, that one," and then his social veneer vanished utterly. "I have more information," he said bluntly. "The suicide bomber who killed Farad was from Fatah al-Islam. You could be next."

Though chilled, Brooke managed to shrug. "No surprise there."

"No. But the photographs tell us more. We've gone over the security tapes from Ayn Al-Hilweh. Those three men left six days ago, we don't know for where." Jameel looked at him intently. "We surmise that one or more were among those who tried to kill you in 2009, and perhaps killed Khalid Hassan."

Brooke found himself staring at his flute of champagne. "You might look for them in the Bekaa Valley."

"If we could, we would." Jameel glanced around them, then added quickly, "We also have a tip from Hassan Adallah, courtesy of his 'friends' in Syria. The missing security man still has not been found. There is some concern about his loyalty."

"They need to find him."

"Of course. But it seems he was with a second man, also dressed as a security officer. No one knows who this other man is, or what their business was — not running guns to Hezbollah, it seems clear."

Assuming a pose of casual conversation, Brooke scanned the crowd. "If they're headed for the Bekaa, they'll need help."

Jameel smiled for whoever might be watching. "Hezbollah may control the valley, but it's not hermetically sealed. There are Sunni pockets here and there which have no love for Shia. Also, in the mountains, the Jefaars. They know paths no one else does, well enough to move at night."

"If al Qaeda were moving this weapon, would they trust a clan of smugglers?"

"One might wonder. But whom else to trust? The Jefaars run their business with a thief's perverse sense of honor. If you assume the Bekaa is a desirable destination, and the mountains an optimal place to hide, you'd need them."

"Do you have sources within the clan?"

"Sources, yes. Good ones?" Jameel answered himself with a shrug. "All this is probably nothing. Perhaps Washington will say as much. But you might tell your Zionist friends to watch their border. As for me, I'll worry for my country."

Brooke nodded. After a moment he said, "Thanks, Bashir. For everything."

Jameel gave him an ironic look. "Such as it is. Or appears to be."

The women returned. "Done?" Janine inquired. "You seem so serious."

"Only me," Brooke answered. "I have a text message. It seems I have to go."

Janine made a pouty face. Gallantly, Brooke kissed her on both cheeks. "I'll see you out," Raina told him.

They walked together toward the exit. Brooke paused at the door; he did not want her seen with him on the sidewalk. "I enjoyed tonight," he told her. "Very much."

She looked into his eyes. "So did I. I hope I see you again."

"If I'm lucky."

But Brooke knew that he would not be — Raina did not fit with the life he led. He hoped he lived to regret this.

Alone, he stepped out into the night. He walked several blocks, then turned into an alley. The cab he had arranged was waiting.

Lying on his bed, Brooke called Langley at once. But it was ten minutes until Brustein patched in Carter Grey, another ten before Brooke explained what he had learned in the hours since Farad's murder.

"Worrisome," Brustein said bluntly. "As is what's happening here. The FBI has come to the president with information it believes is credible — domestic sources, provocative phone chatter. They believe that bomb is in D.C."

Brooke gazed up at the chandelier, the reflection in its crystal shards distorting pieces of the room. "Are they sure this isn't an al Qaeda plant?"

"No. But that's the problem, isn't it? Who wants to assume it is?" Brustein spoke soberly. "You've developed enough to give your theory credence. But you can imagine what Alex Coll will say with our capital on the line. That your bits and pieces are circumstantial. That Palestinians leave refugee camps all the time, and kill each other copiously. That acts of smuggling in Lebanon occur many times a day. That governmental officials are bribed, including in Syria, several times an hour. That all this is probably nothing, or at least different than you think it is. And that Israel's security is, first and foremost, Israel's responsibility."

Brooke felt his frustration spilling over. "Guess I'm lucky to be in Lebanon, out of harm's way. You might intimate to Coll that if al Qaeda destroys Israel, protecting his reputation won't be too high on my list."

"Calm down," Grey admonished. "We're all under strain, doing the best we can within well-defined priorities. The problem is that Tel Aviv is someone else's capital."

"I'm aware of that," Brooke retorted. "Sure would hate to lose it, though."

"So would I," Grey said softly. "I'm sorry about Farad, Brooke."

Brooke felt his anger dissipate. "I'll be sorrier if his death was pointless."

"We have two items for you," Brustein said at length. "The first is vague information from within the Jefaar clan suggesting that an unspecified 'important shipment' was coming into the Bekaa. The second is more recent. Two nights ago, one of the men in Farad's photographs may have been spotted in Shawtarwah."

"According to whom?"

"I don't know, specifically. I just told you what I could."

"Then I need to go to the Bekaa." Sensing skepticism, Brooke added, "I have a Shia friend who has lived there all his life. There's no one he doesn't know."

"That's all you've got to go on?"

"Until and unless I can approach Hezbollah." Brooke's voice became firm. "Maybe this threat about September 11 is subterfuge. But four days from now we'll know."

There was silence. "Look out for yourself," Grey told him. "We can't help you from here."

■ ■ ■ ■

PART FIVE
THE SEARCH
LEBANON
SEPTEMBER 7–11, 2011

■ ■ ■ ■

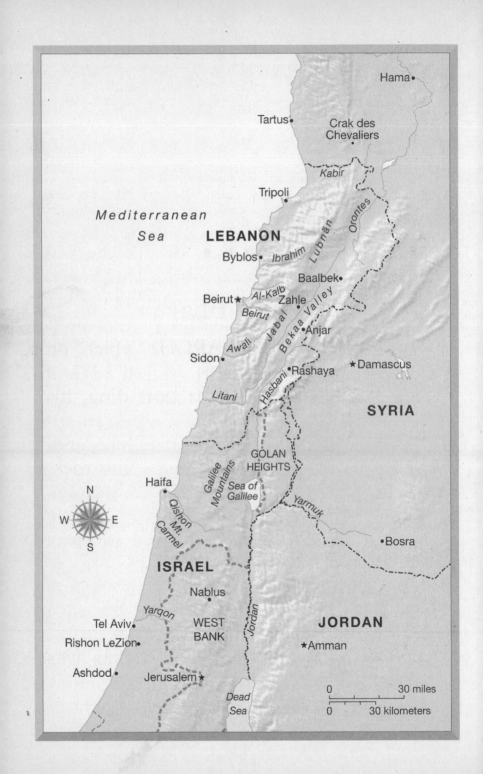

ONE

On a warm, clear morning, Brooke checked out of the Albergo, picked up a land rover, and began the drive toward Baalbek.

Outside the city, he took the road ascending the Mount Lebanon Range, which, on its other side, formed the western edge of the Bekaa Valley. Steep and winding, his course was bordered by shade trees, sumptuous homes, broad vistas of bare hills, and, briefly, an old monastery carved into rock. Now and then he slowed to pass through villages beside the road. At last, reaching the crest, he saw the green-brown sweep of the Bekaa.

Less valley than plateau, the rich expanse stretched in all directions, its eastern edge demarked by the Anti-Lebanon Mountains. As with Lebanon itself, the Bekaa was defined by its contradictions: the yellow flags of Hezbollah with a green hand grasping a semiautomatic rifle; the omnipresent posters of Hassan Nasrallah and Imad Moughniyeh, its living and dead icons, who, in Israel and the West, were labeled terrorists and murderers; vast fields of hashish, in theory an affront to Islamic piety; the sprawling villas of drug lords and farmers; junkyards full of rusting cars; majestic ruins from the Roman and Arab past. But its recent history was defined by the mountain range Brooke saw in the distance.

Dotted with caves and half-concealed pathways, in the early 1980s these stark, red-brown mountains had become the gateway for Iranians who filtered in to train the militias of Hezbollah. Other terrorist groups formed encampments there; after his confrontation with jihadist Islam in Iran, Carter Grey had sought permission to go to the Bekaa. Citing the dangers, his superiors had refused. Shortly thereafter, the torture and murder of William Buckley — a special project of Moughniyeh — had effectively put the area off-limits. When Brooke first visited there in 2007, adopting the guise of a tourist, he became a rarity within the CIA — an agent who had seen the valley at firsthand.

His purpose, as on subsequent trips, was to travel the area and make acquaintances where he could. Brooke had found the

Hezbollah iconography jarring; he had seen the tape of Buckley's torture. But by 2008 the images of Moughniyeh inspired a certain black humor: that spring a team of assassins, no doubt from the Mossad, had blown him to pieces in Damascus. In Baalbek, Brooke had purchased a keychain that featured an image of the newly minted martyr and sent it in a diplomatic pouch to a colleague who, for years, had conducted a fruitless effort to determine Moughniyeh's whereabouts. With it, Brooke had enclosed a note: "Funny — I found this guy in five minutes." Then, it had seemed amusing; now, four days from September 11, Brooke thought his joke puerile. For him the Bekaa had become a place of terrible danger.

Reaching the outskirts of Baalbek, he saw the majestic colonnades and arches of the most impressive Roman ruins outside Italy, then the rectangular Temple of Bacchus, its massive pillars still intact. As Brooke expected, Baalbek offered more evidence of the martial spirit of Rome than of Hezbollah. While its yellow flags were everywhere, the only soldiers in sight were images of the dead that hung from buildings or lampposts. Some fighters were in the mountains; others in underground installations beneath the valley or near the southern border; still others conducted civilian lives, awaiting the next war with Israel. Their rockets and armaments were hidden from view. But their intelligence agents, while also invisible, were ubiquitous, as was the job and social service network that, in Baalbek alone, employed forty thousand people. It was Hezbollah, Brooke knew, that had uncovered the Mossad's agents in Lebanon — some now dead, others in prison. It would mark Brooke's presence here before an hour had passed.

Bypassing the city, he drove into the rolling hills above it. For whatever reason, his Shia friend Fareed Karan had not answered emails or calls to his cell phone. This provoked anxiety, but not alarm; a freelance journalist who often worked for Reuters or Agence France-Presse, Fareed often disappeared for days. But that compelled a visit to Fareed's sprawling house near the village of Jamouni, five thousand feet above the floor of the Bekaa.

Brooke found only his wife, a reticent woman who wore a black head scarf. Unlike Fareed, who knew everyone in the valley — Iranians, smugglers, Christians, Shia, Sunni, and the key figures of Hezbollah — Azia was homebound. She knew only that Fareed was elsewhere, and professed to have little sense of when he might return. At his chosen time, Fareed would just appear.

Frustrated, Brooke left Adam Chase's card and drove to the Palmyra Hotel.

It was past six o'clock. With no choice but to await Fareed, Brooke decided to take a room there. He parked the land rover in front and walked into the lobby.

The Palmyra was a sandstone monument to faded grandeur, perhaps the most flavorful of the colonial relics dotting the Middle East. Its door was a graceful archway and its sitting room had marble floors and plush but worn furnishings. The lobby leading to the restaurant featured a painting of Kaiser Wilhelm II commemorating an imperial visit in 1898, and its peeling plaster walls were lined with photographs of other long-ago guests: Lawrence of Arabia, Charles de Gaulle, Kemal Atatürk, Leopold of Belgium, Jean Cocteau, Ella Fitzgerald, and the general staffs of two armies — the Germans in the First World War, the British in the Second. Upon checking in, Brooke went to a drafty room with a view of the ruins, scanned his email, and called Fareed's cell phone without results. Restlessly deciding to seek out the proprietor of a Shia restaurant, a particular friend of Fareed's, he returned to the lobby. He could feel time running through his fingers.

Near the entrance, a woman in khaki shirt and pants gazed into the street.

Brooke paused for a moment, wondering who or what she might be. From the back, she gave an impression of tensile alertness that evoked a sliver of steel. Her head was covered by a black scarf, and her jet-black hair was caught in an efficient ponytail. Her posture suggested vigilance; hearing his footsteps, she turned abruptly.

She was dark, slight, near Brooke in age, and — despite an absence of adornment — strikingly pretty. Completely still, she stared at him, not bothering to conceal this, just as Brooke could not conceal his own scrutiny. Their seconds of silence seemed longer. Then her expression became puzzled and, it appeared, embarrassed. "Can I help you?" Brooke asked.

She shook her head with brisk impatience, as if to clear it. "Sorry," she said in the accent of the American eastern seaboard. "For a moment, I thought I knew you from somewhere. You're not an archaeologist, someone working here?"

Brooke smiled at this. "Hardly. All I know about these ruins is that they're very old. Are you an archaeologist?"

"Yes. And you're a fellow American, obviously." As though remembering her manners, she extended her hand. "I'm Laura Reynolds."

Brooke took it, cool to the touch. "I'm Adam Chase," he told her. "I was in Beirut on business, and decided to become a tourist."

The corner of her mouth flickered upward. "That makes you a novelty. You weren't frightened?"

"Only of getting lost. But here I am, in Baalbek, with Rome across the street." He angled his head toward the bar. "I don't want to impose on your obvious good nature, but I don't know a soul here. If I buy you a drink, could you tell me where to go and what to do?"

She raised her eyebrows. "Me? You really are lost." Swiftly glancing at her watch, she said, "Fifteen minutes, then. My fee is a glass of arrack."

"What do I get for two?" Brooke inquired.

High in the Anti-Lebanon Mountains, Al Zaroor watched the sunset from beneath the edge of a cave.

He had been here since the first light of dawn. The night before, Rasul Jefaar had driven upward in the darkness, headlights off, taking a dirt path so precarious that at

493

times Al Zaroor could see nothing but the black void of the next sheer drop. He stopped looking — after all these years he had mastered, but not banished, the fear of heights he had discovered in Afghanistan. Only at Jefaar's suggestion did they stop.

Getting out, he pointed to an indentation in the mountainside. "We'll leave them here," Jefaar said, "where the vultures will draw less attention."

With help from the nameless younger man, they carried the bodies of Azid and Hussein into the darkened aperture. Hauling Hussein by his arms, Al Zaroor discovered that the trucker, once so doughy, was already stiff.

Emerging, he saw the distant outline of a mosque against the foothills, a reminder that he was now approaching the land of the Shia and Hezbollah. But by tradition and necessity, the Jefaar clan, an extended family of ten thousand people, recognized no authority but its own. He could only trust that this would hold.

They got back into the van. Reaching the crest of the mountain range, they began descending toward the Bekaa, bent on reaching their destination before daylight. Al Zaroor began feeling a quiet elation. He had been here months before, and found a place that met his needs. Now he was on the cusp of history.

At dawn they had reached the site, traversing the last half mile of scrubby hillside above it without the benefit of a road. Standing here six months before, Al Zaroor had memorized the landscape. A hundred yards below, a dirt road wound toward the valley; a quarter mile farther this artery passed an aqueduct that was dry in summer. Behind Al Zaroor was the mouth of a cave.

This morning, Rasul Jefaar had backed inside. After thirty yards the cave was but two feet wider than the van; Al Zaroor got out, guiding him deeper. Suddenly the cave opened. Illuminated by a generator were two black vans of identical make. Near them were caches of food and weapons guarded by three Palestinians, who sat cross-legged, and three al Qaeda fighters from Iraq who had crossed the border weeks before.

The last man, a former member of the Pakistani air force, had met the Palestinians in a Sunni town known for its lack of watchful Shia eyes. Seeing Al Zaroor, he composed his features in a mask of resolve. Alone among the smugglers and the men waiting in the cave, he knew what Al Zaroor had brought with him.

Al Zaroor embraced each man in turn. None were strangers to him; all but the Pakistani had sworn their loyalty to al Qaeda. Each had met Al Zaroor on a single occasion — the Palestinians in Beirut; the Iraqis at a safe house in Basra; and the Pakistani in Peshawar, through the good offices of General Ayub. This man had been chosen for his secret sympathy for jihad, his lack of a family, and his willingness to assume the new identity and life of ease Al Zaroor had promised him. "You are as essential as the prize I seek," Al Zaroor had assured Hazrat Jawindi. "All I ask is that you prepare it to be used."

The bomb technician had shifted from side to side. "How long will our mission take?" he asked.

"A week at most," Al Zaroor had promised. "Then you can begin a better life."

In paradise.

Two

The room was dark and snug, with a few tables, a long wooden bar, and shelves stocked with Western whisky. Brooke and Laura Reynolds sat at the bar, sipping from glasses of arrack served by a slight, balding man with a thin mustache who then busied himself polishing glasses. Laura gave the man a sharp glance before laying a worn map on the bar. "What are you interested in?" she asked Brooke.

"Everything. I'm a connoisseur of experience."

Silent, Laura looked him in the face, then placed a finger on the map to trace a route. "For a man of such broad interests, there's a lot to see. If you like architecture, you can easily drive to Zahle, a Greek Catholic enclave with wonderful Ottoman era stone houses. Then there's the Ksara winery nearby, a scenic place that produces lovely whites. Closer to Baalbek, there's a small but exquisite Roman temple, perfectly preserved, near the remnants of an ancient mosque." She glanced at the bartender, then continued moving her finger on the map. "If you're not sick of ruins, I'd recommend a trip to Anjar."

"What's in Anjar?"

"An absolutely stunning site from the Umayyad period. In the morning light, it feels almost haunted by those who lived there." In profile, a reflective smile played on her lips. "Sometimes, when I'm alone, I imagine the city as it was. It's quite magical, really."

Brooke kept watching her face, at most times guarded, at odd moments lovely and expressive. "How did you come to work there?"

She took a sip of arrack before answering. "It's not as long a road as you might think. My mother is Lebanese, a Maronite. She met my father in Beirut — he's a New Yorker who worked for the State Department. They lived in Saudi Arabia until my mother told him she could deal with New York, but not Riyadh. The solution was a new job for Dad in Manhattan, where I was born, and trips to Lebanon every summer. So I grew up bilingual, with a foot in two cultures."

"Where did you go to school?"

"For prep school, Hotchkiss, then college at NYU —"

"NYU? When were you there?"

Laura regarded him curiously. "I graduated in 2000. Why do you ask?"

"Because I got my master's there, at about the same time. Did you ever take any courses in Middle Eastern studies?"

"No. But I did go to some seminars at the Kevorkian Center, just out of curiosity."

Brooke nodded. "I spoke at a program there, and attended several others. That could be why I look familiar."

Gazing at her arrack, she smiled faintly. "That seems so long ago. Doesn't it to you?"

"Yes. So does everything before 9/11."

Laura did not look at him. At length, she said, "I lost a friend there."

"In various ways, I lost three." Brooke paused, then added quietly, "But I interrupted your story. You never told me how you got here."

She seemed to ponder the question. "I wanted to leave the U.S. for a while. Maybe what happened was part of it." She turned to him. "In any event, Lebanon is my second home. I went to American University, got a doctorate in archaeology, and started looking for work. So what about you, Adam Chase?"

The barman, Brooke noted, was still polishing glasses, his back turned to them. "If I can buy you dinner," he answered, "I'll tell you my story."

She gave him an appraising smile. "Do you often bribe women to listen to you?"

"Nope. I'm just old-fashioned."

"So it seems. Our 'relationship' is a half-hour old, and you're trying to pay for everything." Briskly, she drained her arrack. "I may be a scholar of sorts, but I'm not impoverished. If you agree to split the bill, I'll consider it."

The restaurant, too, bespoke its history, with venerable rugs and brass plates on the walls, sturdy beams bracing the ceiling, and white tablecloths fatigued by years of use. Save for an elderly English couple, the restaurant was empty. They sat down at a table looking out at the garden, ordering their appetizers and entrées from a squat, attentive waiter. To go with their fresh trout, a specialty of the Bekaa Valley, Laura recommended a bottle of Ksara Chardonnay.

Over their first glass, Brooke outlined Adam Chase's life and career — much of it, like Laura's, spent in the Middle East. She listened attentively, as though parsing every nuance and detail. "So you prefer Lebanon?" she asked.

"Definitely. Everywhere in the Islamic world is fascinating — up to and including Afghanistan. But too often the weather's terrible; you can't touch the women; and the residents want to kill you." He spread his hands to indicate their surroundings. "How many places have a great story, ethnic diversity, nice weather, terrific food, beautiful women, and a rich cultural heritage? Lebanon has them all."

"Yes," Laura said tartly, "and also a tragic history. Which everyone — especially us, the Israelis, the Syrians, and the Iranians — seems intent on adding to."

The waiter, hovering nearby, refilled their glasses. "If I sounded glib and stupid," Brooke said, "I'm sorry. Like you, I don't want to see this country destroyed. I take it that all the young men on the posters I saw in town are Hezbollah martyrs."

"Yes."

He frowned. "I don't understand the cult of martyrdom. Killing yourself to take the lives of others is very strange to me."

Abruptly pensive, Laura gazed at the table. "And to me. I excuse nothing — not the suicide bombings, the rocket attacks on Israel, or the kidnapping and murder of

Israeli soldiers and civilians. But the Shia have a story of their own, filled with poverty and neglect. Hezbollah filled the void."

He watched her face. "It must be tiring," he said at length, "listening to other people's ignorance."

She looked up at him with a perfunctory smile. "That's not what I was feeling tonight." She hesitated, then added softly, "The truth is that my life here is way too solitary."

"How so?"

"Cultural differences, for one thing. Many Lebanese Christians don't leave home until they're married. So you see forty-five-year-old men marrying women two decades younger, having lived all their lives with Mom. Not a rich dating pool for an independent woman in her thirties."

"What about your colleagues?"

She neatly cut a piece of trout. "They're nice, not to mention interesting. But there aren't many single people of either sex, at least anyone my age. We have a new intern, twenty-five, who reminds me that a decade of life makes all the difference in the world. I mean, think of us when we were twenty-five." Looking into his face, she concluded softly, "So no, Adam, this has been far from tiresome."

"Or for me." Brooke hesitated. "I don't know how long I'll be in Lebanon. But I'm very much enjoying your company. Do you think we could stretch this out with a drink?"

She tilted her head. "At the bar?"

Brooke glanced at the waiter. "My room, I thought."

She studied her plate, then gave him a long, cool look. "All right."

They settled the bill, preoccupied with their own thoughts. Brooke felt the waiter watching them. Leaving, they walked into the lobby, Brooke lightly touching her arm. "I'm on the second floor," he said.

They climbed the stairs. Though they were close together, she said nothing, nor did she look at him. To Brooke, she seemed to occupy a separate space.

The second floor had a sitting area with lush rugs and antique furniture. Near his door, someone had left a large wicker basket on wheels, designed to transport used sheets and towels. Moving it aside, Brooke gauged its weight, too light to contain a man. Laura observed him in silence.

Looking about them, Brooke opened his door. He turned to Laura, standing aside for her to enter. Their eyes met, and then she stepped inside the room.

Brooke switched on a light. She looked around her, seeming to register her surroundings — a Cocteau print, a rug, a double bed, an old table, the open door to a tiny bathroom, a window that overlooked the Roman ruins, lit at night. Brooke went to it, drawing the curtains. Then he walked to the door, turning its lock, then inserting the chain on its latch. "Now we have privacy," he said.

Laura faced him. He moved close to her, gazing into her face. Then he placed his hand behind her neck and kissed her gently on the lips. As though by instinct, she returned the kiss with equal softness, extending it for a last moment. Then he raised his head back, looking into her dark, stunned eyes.

"So this is what happened to you," Brooke said quietly. "If I didn't know you, I might not have guessed."

Anit Rahal gazed back at him. "Nor I about you." She hesitated. "And so?"

He looked around the room, to suggest a fear of listeners, then gestured at the bed. They sat beside each other, silent for a moment. Touching his hand, she murmured, "This isn't how I imagined it."

His throat felt tight. "Did you imagine it?"

"Many times." She shook her head in

504

wonder, then spoke in the same near whisper. "Then I saw you tonight, and it was all I could do to maintain cover. When did you start this work?"

"After Ben died. But at least I didn't vanish."

Her shoulders twitched. "I had my reasons." She paused, then took his hand. "I think that's all we should say now."

"There isn't much time."

"I know. But there are people we must speak with, things I'm not free to discuss. Let's agree that I'll give you a tour of these ruins tomorrow, in early evening." She smiled a little. "My doctoral studies included the Roman period."

"Impressive." Leaning over, Brooke undid her scarf and ponytail, freeing her hair. "Sorry, but I needed to mess you up a little."

"At least you left my buttons alone." Anit stood abruptly, then looked down at him. "I'm not going to sleep very well."

"Nor I. Though given what I'm here for, I wasn't before."

Standing, Brooke walked her to the door. She opened it, scanned the hallway, then turned to him again. For a moment, all he wanted was to look at her. Then he rested curled fingers against her face, saying,

"Good night, *habibi*" — Arabic for "my sweet."

For a last moment she looked into his eyes. "Good night, Adam," she said, and left.

THREE

For the next twenty hours — precious by his reckoning — Brooke was frozen in place. He kept trying to track down Fareed, until his friend's scratchy phone call from Amman informed him that he would return tomorrow. The rest of his time was spent worrying that the bomb was now in Lebanon, rechecking his room for surveillance devices, scanning emails, and wondering how Anit's life had brought her to this place. He felt anew the force of seeing her again; he could only imagine the reverberations of their chance encounter within their agencies. Reporting it to Grey and Brustein, Brooke explained, "We had a relationship at NYU."

"Define 'relationship,' " Brustein prodded.

"More than meeting for coffee. Though sometimes we had coffee in the morning —"

Sharply, Grey interjected, "This is the woman you told me about."

"Yes. The question now is if and how we work together."

"What do you suggest?"

Brooke gazed out his window at the ruins. "Last night, we played at becoming involved for show. Maybe we should play that out."

"What about the 'human factor'?" Grey inquired. "Where does that come in?"

"It can't. We both know why we're here—"

"Her masters may object," Brustein cut in. "Your cover is threadbare; hers may not be. You could end up getting both of you killed. Or worse."

Brooke knew this all too well. Quietly, he replied, "What are their priorities, Noah? If they think I'm right, and that time is short, I know what mine would be."

There was silence on the other end. "We'll let you know," Brustein said.

An hour before he was to meet Anit, Brooke received his answer. "We've reached an understanding," Grey advised him. "At least for today. But they're not going to like where I know you're headed."

"I think they're out of choices," Brooke rejoined.

■ ■ ■ ■

She stood at the entrance to the ruins, appearing as composed as the woman she pretended to be. Only the brief look she gave him, fond yet apprehensive, suggested the complexity of her feelings. They entered the site together, cognizant of the tourists in pairs or guided groups. After a moment, Brooke took her hand.

"So you've heard," she murmured.

He looked around them. "Yes. We're lovers again, in public, by order of our governments."

"Why not? We only get fired if it's real." Her voice softened. "So much has happened. To both of us, it seems."

They stopped, gazing at the remains of a city built two thousand years before — massive temples to Jupiter, Venus, Mercury, and Bacchus, a huge courtyard with an altar for sacrificing animals. Above the ruins, the haunting sound of the Muslim call to prayer echoed from the jagged ridges of the Anti-Lebanon Mountains.

"This is amazing," Anit said. "The greatest temple complex ever conceived."

"Why here in Baalbek?"

"Political savvy and imperial arrogance. A

line of emperors decided to build a monument to Rome's power, while incorporating tributes to certain local gods." She glanced at him. "Building all this took two and a half centuries, a hundred thousand slaves, and countless tons of sandstone and marble hauled from throughout the Middle East. As you'll see, the Romans used a pure stone masonry technique, excluding mortar. Instead they strengthened the joints with iron clamps, coated with lead to avoid oxidation. They truly meant this place to last forever."

Brooke raised his eyebrows. "You actually know archaeology, don't you?"

"Of course. I may not be real, but my doctorate is." Her voice lowered. "I also learned that nothing lasts forever. But I hope this isn't Israel's time to vanish."

Taking his hand, she led him from structure to structure, commenting on each for the benefit of whoever might overhear them. In the failing light, the pillars, colonnades, and archways cast shadows at their feet. At length, she guided him up the steps of the Temple of Bacchus, the best preserved of the structures. Sitting there they could watch the site, Brooke saw at once, noting anyone who approached them. It reminded him of whom Anit Rahal had become.

"What happened to you, Anit?"

She continued keeping watch. "Laura," she corrected. "A lonely American archaeologist, having a fling with you. The least you can do is remember my name."

Brooke ignored this. "The last I heard you were getting married. Then nothing."

Still not facing him, she spoke in a monotone. "And then the war in Lebanon," she answered. "Our political losses were great, but our casualties relatively light. A little over one hundred." She paused, then finished. "One was Meir, a helicopter pilot in the reserves. I remember telling you that I would die for Israel. Instead my fiancé was killed by a Hezbollah rocket."

Brooke grasped her hand tighter. "I'm sorry," he said. "I'd imagined you living a happy life."

"So did we. When Meir was called up, he was thirty, a promising architect. I was quitting the army to start a family." She faced him. "And when I imagined you, as I often did, you were working for the State Department."

Brooke shrugged. "September 11 changed things. For the past nine years I've been lying to everyone outside the agency. But you know how that goes."

Anit studied him. "Have you ever wished

for an ordinary life?"

"At times. But it's so hard to go back to who I was. There are days I envy other people, yet feel detached from them. It's like I lost my innocence so they can cling to theirs." He heard a tinge of bitterness in his tone, and stopped himself. "So when Meir was killed, you were ready for the Mossad."

Her eyes became distant, as though recalling another life. "They'd kept extensive data on me — IQ tests, psychological profile, language skills, intelligence background, travel abroad. And, of course, my commitment to Israel —"

"I remember it well. I used to think it had cost me a wife. Perhaps a life."

She gave him a level look. "After all these years, are you still angry?"

"Angry? No. Right now I'm feeling a little sad for us both."

Turning, Anit gazed at the ruins. "Our lives may be an accident, not what we intended. But I try never to look back. What I knew after Meir died was that I had no spouse, no children, and could pass for an American." She paused. "In defense of my colleagues, they didn't want someone with a death wish, or who was acting out of revenge. I was able to convince them I wanted to serve Israel."

"So you chose the hardest work there is." Brooke's tone became crisp. "I know a fair amount about the Mossad. No other agent knows your identity. You're allowed to kill, and are trained to do it well. And, if need be, to carry out assassinations."

Turning away, Anit was silent. At length, she said coolly, "We took our oath of allegiance at Masada, where a cadre of Jews killed themselves rather than surrender to Rome. We're sworn never to disclose the details of our work.

"That means not just to you, but family or friends. If I'm involved with an Israeli man, no matter how well I deceive him, after three months I must report it. Better to have no relationships at all, unless it's inside the Mossad." Her voice gained intensity, as though, against her will, she was feeling a surge of repressed emotion. "The ideal agent is a loner who's willing to give up her life and disappear at will. In fact, the best of us are arguably insane — fanatic patriots with a pathological gift for deceiving others. Not to mention becoming someone else."

"How long have you been Laura Reynolds?"

"Four years now." In profile, her lips formed a smile without humor. "I can tell you more about Laura's childhood than my own — school friends, the clothes I wore, what Mom put in my lunchbox, favorite movies and TV programs, my date to the junior prom. I have a transcript at NYU, created by a gifted hacker; a credit history in New York; and a hard-earned doctorate from American University. As you well know, I need it all. It's easy enough for an Israeli spy to get killed in the Bekaa Valley, and too many people willing to compete for the honor. Especially Hezbollah."

"Do they suspect you, I wonder?"

"Before you showed up?" Anit answered pointedly. "I gather people keep trying to kill you."

"Only twice, and only Sunnis. But don't think I'm not concerned for you."

"Nor I you," she said more softly. "But caring isn't our job, is it? As for whether my cover is working, one seldom knows until it's too late. But it's elaborate enough. I'm a genuine archaeologist who, my boss believes, is moonlighting for UNESCO."

Brooke laughed out loud. "You're joking."

"Hardly. UNESCO thinks that, too. Which allows me to delve into smuggling out of purer motives than the locals would attribute to the Mossad." She faced him, her voice becoming somber. "As you'd expect, it gets complicated, even unnerving. And now I'm sleeping with Adam Chase, an American business consultant."

Once again, Brooke felt a stab of fear for her. "I take it you're here to watch Hezbollah."

"Of course. Knowing smugglers helps me divine when Hezbollah is bringing in arms and rockets from Syria. My travels for the dig have allowed me to guess at where they're hiding their command centers — if only from the places they don't allow me to go. So when the next war comes, we'll carpet-bomb those sites, and Israeli commandos will kill their leaders." Her tone became harder. "As I told my recruiters, I'm not doing this to avenge Meir. Nothing can bring him back. So instead of counting our children, perhaps I can count the dead commanders of Hezbollah, and imagine the families I've helped save from their rockets."

Brooke repressed a chill. "Do you know who their leaders are?"

"They're very secretive. But yes, we know some of them."

Once again, Brooke looked around them. In the dusk, the tourists had dwindled. Quietly, he said, "But now you're searching for a nuclear weapon."

Anit nodded. "Al Qaeda has turned my work on its head. Suddenly I'm looking for

515

smugglers who aren't connected to Hezbollah; places al Qaeda might hide from its network of spies; or strangers who aren't from the Bekaa Valley —"

"So the tip about an 'important shipment' came from you. As well as the possible sighting of a man from Ayn Al-Hilweh."

Anit regarded him gravely. "And it was you, I now understand, who originated the theory about an attack on Tel Aviv."

"Yes. I think Bin Laden is pulling off a massive hoax, and that by now al Qaeda has moved the bomb into Lebanon. Perhaps within miles of here."

Briefly, Anit touched her eyes. "But that's the problem, isn't it? We can't send commandos into the Bekaa looking for a bomb that could be anywhere. Hezbollah would slaughter them before they found it. And if they did find the bomb, Hezbollah would take it." She shook her head. "Ten years ago, when we were lovers, I never imagined us wondering how to save my country from al Qaeda."

You already know, Brooke thought. You're just not ready to face it. But all he said was, "I have a source. Tomorrow I'm going to see him."

"If it's not too late," she answered. "How

many days or hours, I wonder, do we have left?"

FOUR

Deep within the cave, Al Zaroor studied the photograph on his laptop. Around him, the three Palestinians talked among themselves.

"Who is this man?" Al Zaroor asked.

One of the Palestinians, Mohammad Hamzi, spat at the stone floor. "An American who calls himself Adam Chase. He pretends to be a businessman. But he's an agent of the CIA."

Al Zaroor looked up. "How do you know this?"

"We tried to kidnap him two years ago, in Beirut. He killed my partner and got away. Then he disappeared." Hamzi's voice turned hard. "Before that he recruited the first PLO lackey we eliminated, Khalid Hassan. Chase's target was Fatah al-Islam."

Al Zaroor felt a jolt of fear. "So this is the same man who met with Farad?"

"We think so, yes."

Al Zaroor studied the American's face

518

more closely as he absorbed the meaning of his presence here. That people within the CIA did not believe Bin Laden's threat was predictable. But this man had come to the Bekaa Valley. Al Zaroor wondered what he knew, and what the Zionists might learn as a result. At once his thoughts moved to the two dead Syrians. The risk of killing them was that their disappearance had raised questions; the benefit was that neither man could answer them.

"You say this photograph was taken in Baalbek," Al Zaroor said.

"Yes, just before he checked into the Palmyra Hotel. As you asked, we put several of our comrades in strategic places, watching for strangers. The man who sent this knows the American on sight." Hamzi paused, then said in a lower voice, "We should eliminate him at once."

Al Zaroor sat against the wall of the cave. If they knew "Adam Chase" was here, he reasoned, so did Hezbollah. By himself, the American was not a serious threat — there was only so much he could glean in the next seventy-two hours. But Hezbollah could pose grave dangers. In the CIA's place, he would set aside its historic loathing, and go to Hezbollah. And if he were Hezbollah, he would snatch this agent off the street.

All this he thought without speaking. Except for the Pakistani, no one in the cave knew the contents of the coffin — Al Zaroor had let the others believe it was gold. But the Iraqis and Palestinians eyed the technician with suspicion. They, too, were capable of thinking the Renewer had lied, and they knew far more than this American. So for Hamzi to be snared by Hezbollah would pose the greater threat. The question was whether he could kill the American without getting caught.

At length, Al Zaroor said, "If you murder this agent, you must leave the valley at once. I don't want you followed back here, or caught in the act. Unless you can take him out swiftly and silently, let him live."

Hamzi folded his arms. "Our man is watching him now. He can call me when the American is alone."

Al Zaroor considered this. Then he dug into a duffel bag and took out a new cell phone. "If you succeed, or leave Baalbek without trying, call the number I'll give you. Let it ring three times, then hang up. If I hear the telephone, I'll rest easier." He paused, then added coldly, "If not, I'll hope this agent killed you. You cannot fail and live."

Hamzi's jaw worked. "I won't fail," he

answered. "The American will die as Khalid Hassan did, unable to make a sound."

Darkness shrouded the Temple of Bacchus, relieved only by a three-quarter moon. Above the wall surrounding the ruins, Brooke and Anit could see the lights of Baalbek, more lights scattered in the hills above. The tourists were gone, and they were alone. By the grace of Dr. Antoine Abboud, Laura Reynolds had a special pass.

"This Shiite friend of yours," she asked, "how can he help us?"

"He can't, directly. But he knows everyone in the valley — who they are and what they do."

Though the light was dim, he saw her face set. "Hezbollah, you mean. And then what? You'll just knock on their door?" Anit emitted a short, bitter laugh. "Perhaps I can accompany you, with an introduction from the Iranians —"

"You bargain with Hezbollah for the dead," Brooke cut in softly.

"Yes," she said with lethal quiet. "They exchanged the charred remains of my fiancé for six imprisoned fighters. So how can I object?" Her tone remained cool. "There are, however, certain practical barriers to my involvement. My agency has invested a

521

considerable amount of time and money in preparing me to be here — in part, to replace the network snuffed out at Hezbollah's direction. If Hezbollah finds out who I am, they could treat me with the same consideration they accorded William Buckley, with variations appropriate to my sex. And if they try to swap me for a busload of would-be suicide bombers, my agency has warned me, the price is too exorbitant." Her voice softened. "If I die, I'd like some good to come of it. If I live, I don't want to go slowly insane in a Lebanese prison, reduced to the pathetic hope that my country will retrieve me by releasing terrorists who, sooner or later, will murder other Jews."

Watching her, Brooke ached at how completely they had changed since they were lovers. "If I go to Hezbollah, Anit, I won't involve you."

"A little late, don't you think? Who do you suppose that waiter and bartender work for? The best I can hope for is that they're debating whether I'm an American spy or simply an American slut."

"Let's leave it that way. Just tell me this — who else but Hezbollah could find this bomb?"

Anit gazed at the moonlit ruins. "Many in my agency don't believe a strike would come from here. Some think al Qaeda will cross the border into Galilee. Others believe the bomb will come by sea —"

"And then what does al Qaeda do? Smuggle a nuclear technician into Israel, then drive the bomb to Tel Aviv? As to the border, forget the twenty-foot fence bristling with Israeli soldiers and surveillance equipment, or the UN troops who patrol it. For the last fifty miles southern Lebanon is controlled by Hezbollah, and filled with land mines planted by your army. Only a fool would run a bomb through that." Facing her, Brooke finished emphatically, "Al Qaeda won't. Once they're close enough, they'll fly it into Israel. The Bekaa is close enough."

Anit shook her head. "Our air defenses are too good."

"Even the best can be beaten — including by amateurs who penetrate no-fly zones by accident. Our operative is no amateur, and he's stolen a two-hundred-pound bomb designed to detonate at one thousand feet. He'll try to use it exactly as intended, working a nuclear variation on what LET did to the Taj Mahal and New Delhi —"

"That was India," Anit retorted. "Our air force has standing orders to shoot down a suspicious plane, and signals intelligence that can follow air traffic from any airport in Lebanon."

"How many planes can you watch? Chances are al Qaeda will use a private jet, take off from an airstrip no one uses, and fly literally beneath the radar. If I'm right, within three days' time."

Reflexively, Anit glanced around them. "So you think this will happen on September 11."

"Unless it's sooner. Al Qaeda is drawn to symbolic dates. September 11 became symbolic only after they couldn't bring off the attacks that summer, when Ariel Sharon came to Washington." Brooke's voice softened. "If they had, Ben would still be alive. The week Sharon visited, Ben took time off to help Aviva with the wedding."

The reference to Ben, instinctive and unplanned, seemed to cause a change in Anit. Quiet, she looked down. "I'm sorry for what I said to you all those years ago — about not being a serious person. Only a very serious person would risk his life to come here."

"For better or worse," Brooke answered, "we've become the same person."

"No. We're fictitious people, pretending to be lovers when we can't be. My overseers have cautioned me never to forget that."

She faced him again. "When I entered the Mossad, I had to disclose every sexual relationship I'd had. So you were already in my file."

Brooke smiled a little. "How thick is it?"

She did not smile back. "You took up a fair chunk. But that was when I could remember how I felt, and how hard it was to leave you. That man and woman are dead now."

The last words pierced him. "Not dead," he insisted. "Just dormant. And the part of me that still loves Anit Rahal won't put Laura Reynolds at risk."

Anit turned away. In a monotone she said, "I'll report what you said about Hezbollah. Then they'll tell me what to do."

Their conversation was done. After tonight, Brooke realized, he might never see her again.

Silent, they walked through the ruins toward the exit. A guard opened the metal door. Together, they headed down the dirt road, deserted at night, which wound to the outskirts of town.

Anit's jeep was parked by the road. "Can I give you a ride?" she asked.

"No. If anyone is watching me, best we split up here."

Anit nodded. But instead of getting into

the car, she stared down, hands shoved in her pockets. Gently, Brooke cupped her chin, raising her head so that she looked into his eyes. "One last time," he said.

She did not answer, or turn away. When Brooke kissed her, she pressed her body into his. Then she pulled back abruptly, sudden tears glistening in her eyes.

"Who just kissed me?" Brooke asked softly.

"Anit Rahal." Swiftly, she turned away and got into her car.

FIVE

Walking down the darkened road, Brooke was acutely aware of his solitude. The terrain surrounding him was open; the distance to the outskirts of Baalbek — perhaps one hundred yards — too great to cover swiftly. A sniper with a rifle and night vision goggles could shoot him; enemies in cars could snatch him off the road. The only factor in his favor was that Baalbek, by its nature, would not be crawling with operatives from al Qaeda. But for his fears for her, he should have accepted Anit's offer of a ride.

Brooke kept moving — looking to each side, listening for sounds behind him. Seventy-five yards left, he calculated.

The piping notes of Arabic music issued faintly from the town. Aware that his hearing was compromised, he stopped near a grove of trees, trying to listen more intently. Then he heard the footsteps on the gravel, and knew too late that this was a mistake.

Before he could react, he felt the wire around his throat, the pressure of a strong body against his back as the wire twisted tighter. He tried crying out and could not. So this is how I'll die, he thought — unable to breathe, starbursts in his eyes, wire slicing his skin. A weak gurgle issued from his larynx.

He felt the attacker flinch, then heard him gasp. Gagging, Brooke wrenched himself free and turned to face his assassin.

The Palestinian's eyes were wide. From behind him, a hand had jammed a pen into the man's windpipe; a slender arm wrenched his torso backward as the palm bracing the pen shoved it deeper still. Over the Palestinian's shoulder, Brooke saw Anit, her eyes slits of effort and concentration as the pen punctured her victim's spine.

The man sank to his knees, unable to take a breath, all muscle control lost. Strangling in his own blood, he stared up into Brooke's face like a supplicant seeking absolution. As Brooke's vision cleared, an image flashed before him — a man jumping from a car to block an alley in Beirut. The same man pitched forward at his feet.

In a taut voice, Anit said, "Have you never seen a corpse before?"

Inhaling, he stared at her across the body.

"Not one you've killed."

"Neither have I."

She was breathing hard now, a shiver running through her. "We need to get rid of him," she snapped. "Drag him behind those trees."

Brooke grabbed the dead man's feet. As she ran to the car, Anit's footsteps faded in the night.

Brooke lay the man in the grove, then hid behind a tree. Moments later, he saw Anit's jeep, headlights off. She stopped, leaping out to open the trunk. Hoisting the corpse's deadweight, Brooke stumbled to the car and threw the body inside. The man's skull thudded against the trunk.

Slamming it shut, Anit said, "Get in."

He was barely in the passenger seat before she gunned the engine. Leaving the dirt road, they drove along the outskirts of the city, Brooke watching for anyone who followed. "I know this man," he said. "He's Fatah al-Islam, from Ayn Al-Hilweh."

"Then he died like a fool," Anit said curtly. "Now we're sure they're here, and want you dead. He's enhanced your credibility."

And strengthened Hezbollah's hand, she must know. Brooke could feel the welt across his throat. Softly, he told her, "You

529

saved my life."

"I'm aware of that." Anit paused, then said in a lower voice, "I was worried, so I decided to follow you. Are you always that careless?"

"No."

"Then you should keep your mind on work."

From her arid tone, he could not tell if she were serious or using black humor to stave off horror. They drove in silence into the darkness of the valley, passing apple orchards and broad swaths of hemp plants that provided hashish. Anit glanced into the rearview mirror, then abruptly stopped beside a field.

They got out, scrambled to the trunk, and hoisted the corpse by its limbs. Brooke remembered Anit's description of her service on the border, disposing of the dead.

Twenty yards into the hemp, she said, "We can leave him for the vultures."

They dropped the body, concealed by the waist-high plants, and scurried to the jeep. In seconds they were headed back toward Baalbek. "If all we have is three days' time," Anit said, "this should be all right. No one in Lebanon cares about Palestinians when they're alive; few in the Bekaa will care about a dead one. Though Hezbollah may wonder how he got here."

Still in darkness, they could see the reflected glare of Baalbek softening the night sky. Her tone remained cool but level. "Even if Hezbollah hasn't pegged me yet, al Qaeda surely has. I don't want them following me to the dig house."

Once more, Brooke felt how gravely he, and al Qaeda, had endangered her. "So our 'affair' is on again?"

"Just for tonight. Laura's been too lonely for too long."

Reaching town, they parked near the Palmyra and got out, each looking from side to side. As they entered, Brooke took her hand.

There was no one in the lobby, one couple in the bar. Brooke saw the barman note them passing through.

They took the stairway to the second floor. The sitting area, too, was quiet, and lit only by moonglow through its windows. Approaching his room, Brooke turned to Anit, signaling her to follow. Then he unlocked the door, stepping inside.

Quickly, he looked into the bathroom. Anit slipped in behind him, opening the closet door. No one was there. When he switched on the lights, he heard her lock the door, then set the latch. "We should be all right," he said. "Even if they have bodies to spare, al Qaeda won't try to kill us surrounded by Shia lookouts."

Anit sat on the bed, slumped, staring at nothing. Though the room was warm, she hugged herself.

He sat beside her. Though she remained quiet, he felt Anit's shoulder against his. Turning, he touched her cheek with the curled fingers of his hand. "Are you all right?"

"Of course," she answered in a toneless voice. "Yesterday, after ten years, I encountered a man I once loved deeply, discovered we're both spies, and learned that he might blow my cover. Tonight a Palestinian tried to garrote him. So I killed the Palestinian — a first for me. Now my former lover wants to cut a deal with Hezbollah, which killed my fiancé, and which I'm spying on at terrible risk. And in a day or so, al Qaeda may obliterate Tel Aviv, erasing my family and friends and everyone who lives there, and ultimately destroying my country. Why shouldn't I be fine?" Suddenly her voice trembled. "Don't say a word, Brooke. Just hold me. I remember liking that."

Silent, they lay on the bed, Brooke's arms encircling her slender body, her face against his shoulder. For a long time, they remained quite still. Brooke could feel her breathing.

After a time, she burrowed against his neck. Her lips grazed his skin.

He turned to her, questioning, as she looked into his eyes. Then he understood what he saw in hers — there wasn't much time left, for anything.

When he kissed her throat, his lips could feel her pulse.

Slowly, he undressed her. Once again, he discovered Anit Rahal's body, lovely still, yet belonging to someone he no longer knew. But she remembered how to touch him. Just as he remembered what to do.

His mouth and hands went where they would. As he slipped inside her, he looked into her face. Her lips formed the shadow of a certain smile he last had seen long ago.

They used the moments given them, unrushed. In the darkness, she stifled her last cry. Then she moved with him, his partner again, until he shuddered against her.

Afterward, they lay beside each other, faces close. After a time she murmured, "Two hours ago, I killed a man. But it's only now that I've committed a firing offense."

"Then maybe we should send them pictures."

Anit did not smile. Softly, Brooke asked, "What will you do on the other side of this?"

"If I still have a country?" she asked. *And*

if I survive, she did not need to add. "Stay here, if I can. Finish the work I came for."

"And then what?" His tone was urgent. "I've known deep-cover agents who never came in from the cold. In the end, they give up everything."

Anit looked away. "Do you think that's news to me?"

"No," he said bluntly. "I think it's like a widow throwing herself on her husband's funeral pyre. Once you wanted children —"

"Maybe that's not given to me." She paused, then finished in a weary tone. "I used to hope for peace. Now all I hope for is our survival. I mean, look at what we're doing here."

"But why do we do it, Anit? Not just for an idea, or a country, but because people are entitled to the joys and sorrows of a life that's fully realized. The nihilism al Qaeda wants would wipe all that out. Why should we do it to ourselves?"

"Because that's what we're for." Her voice became gentler. "For many reasons, I needed you tonight. But however we might feel, you and I can't be together for a day, or even an hour, after this is done." To stave off his protest, she kissed him. "No arguments, please. To be with you, an American agent, I would have to give up my citizenship and my country. As long as Israel exists, that's impossible for me. Let's be grateful for the hour we were given."

A part of Brooke felt leaden. "Now isn't the time to argue, I suppose."

She gave him a wispy smile. "An understatement," she said. "Right now we should sleep."

After a time, she managed this. Once she stirred and cried out. Still awake, Brooke wondered about her dreams.

Her breathing deepened. Walking softly, he went to the bathroom, closed the door, and called Noah Brustein. "There's something you need to decide," Brooke told him. "I know now that I'm right, and this won't keep."

SIX

The morning of September 9 dawned warm and clear and bright.

In first light, Anit drove to the Temple of Venus, Brooke following in his land rover. He knew without asking that she was calling Tel Aviv. When he arrived, Anit was leaning against the jeep as she scanned the area. The site of the ruins, Brooke saw at once, provided a sweeping view of the terrain. It was as good a place as any to have this conversation. Their lovemaking seemed very long ago.

"And so?" she asked.

Brooke sat on the hood beside her. "On one level," he said flatly, "this is simple. The essence of spying is outsourcing the problem. The problem here, we both believe, is that al Qaeda has concealed a nuclear bomb in some secluded area of the Bekaa. We'll never find it. Hezbollah can.

"You know that better than I. Before the

536

last war, they began sealing off areas near the border. After the war was over, your soldiers discovered vast military complexes beneath the earth, some covering two square miles, equipped with air-conditioning, sleeping quarters, medical centers, communications systems, and caches of rockets and weapons. And no one saw them do it, because they worked at night —"

"What's your point?"

"The leaders of al Qaeda have no plan except to bring on the apocalypse. But Hezbollah is the most dedicated, disciplined, and farsighted terrorist group in the world. For them, violence is a means to achieving long-term goals —"

"Which makes them the most deadly enemies we have."

"Not today, or tomorrow. No doubt Hezbollah, like their patrons in Iran, wants Israel to vanish from the earth. But the Shia have lived here for a thousand years. Lebanon is their home. A retaliatory nuclear strike from Israel would depopulate this land as surely as al Qaeda's bomb would destroy Tel Aviv."

Anit turned from him. "These people killed Meir, then kept his body to trade for living terrorists. I came here to stop them from killing our civilians. And now you say

I should go to Hezbollah for help."

"What does Tel Aviv say?" He waited for her to face him. "Thirty years ago, Anit, an Israeli missile incinerated the first leader of Hezbollah, along with his wife and four-year-old boy. Fifteen years later, Israeli forces killed the teenage son of Hassan Nasrallah. Do you think Nasrallah would refuse to deal with Israel to save his people from destruction? I don't."

Anit's jaw tightened. "Do *you* think Hezbollah would just give us a nuclear weapon? They'll keep it, or hand it over to Iran. In either case, it's an existential threat to Israel. They won't drop this bomb on New York."

"They won't drop it at all," Brooke retorted. "That's the definition of suicide."

Anit put on her sunglasses. "Perhaps not. More likely, Iran would use this bomb to deter us from attacking their nuclear facilities while they develop bombs of their own. Then they'll have impunity to fund Hezbollah in Lebanon, and Hamas in the West Bank and Gaza, surrounding us with terrorists."

Brooke shrugged. "They'll do that anyhow. But I suppose this is Israel's call. Maybe your air defenses really are that good."

Anit stared at him. "There's an alternative," she said more evenly. "Without involving us, our governments can leak their suspicions to Iran. Hezbollah will search for the bomb; our satellites will watch them from the sky. Then we can step in."

"With what? You can't start bombing a nuclear weapon. Nor can you send enough commandos to snatch it. Hezbollah would slaughter them. And there's also the time all this would take." Sliding off the hood, Brooke stood in front of her. "Right now you've got two risks — that al Qaeda drops the bomb in days or hours, or that Hezbollah steals it. The alternative is going to Hezbollah ourselves."

Anit folded her arms. "Is this where I tell them, 'Keep me if you like, but please don't keep the bomb'?"

"This shouldn't involve you," Brooke answered. "Instead our governments will warn Hezbollah that taking the bomb carries too high a price."

"Such as?"

"Why spell it out? Hezbollah knows we're using drones to kill the leaders of al Qaeda. And the Iranians know, as my agency does, that Israel has three nuclear submarines parked off their coast." Brooke paused, then asked with quiet force, "Why didn't Hezbollah seek revenge when the Mossad blew Imad Moughniyeh into pieces in Damascus? It isn't like Nasrallah doesn't know who did it."

Anit smiled faintly. "Maybe it was the Syrians — one hears they didn't like him. After all, they car-bombed Rafik Hariri."

"With help from Hezbollah," Brooke cut in. "Be serious, Anit."

She shoved her hands in her pockets. "What do you want from me?"

"For the moment, two things. First, that you survive this. Second, the names of Hezbollah's political and military leaders in the valley."

Anit regarded him. "So this Shia friend of yours — the man who knows everyone — could help you approach them."

"With the approval of our governments. I've asked mine not to think too long."

"Then we both have people to talk with, don't we." Her voice flattened. "I should go back to the dig. I've got an identity to reassume, for whatever that's still worth."

Anit opened the door of her jeep. Pausing, she looked back over her shoulder. "Please try to stay alive, Brooke. I worry about leaving you alone."

Brooke took Grey's elephant from his pocket and held it out in his palm. "I'm never alone," he answered. "I have this lucky charm from a friend."

Anit eyed it quizzically. "Did it keep your friend alive?"

"Barely."

For a last moment, she looked at him. Then she got into the jeep and drove away.

Al Zaroor sat at the mouth of the cave, gazing out at the valley.

The Palestinian Hamzi had not called. Perhaps he was still waiting for his chance. More likely, he was dead, or a prisoner of Hezbollah. In the first case, this agent from the CIA would now be certain of his instincts; in the second, Hezbollah might find this cave. Even men as remorseless as the Palestinian sometimes faltered in the face of torture — they knew too well what to expect. Sometimes they even told the truth.

Behind him, Al Zaroor heard the others, talking quietly among themselves.

Where was his mistake? he wondered. His thoughts kept fixing on the two dead Syrians; crossing Syria had always been the weak link in his plan. But he had little choice, he told himself, and less time to wonder.

Glancing around, Al Zaroor used a ghost phone to call a man in Belgium. The man answered on a phone reserved for such a call. In a light, nervous voice, he said, "What is it, Uncle?"

"Your aunt is very sick. Can you visit before Sunday?"

"That is sooner than I was planning. Already it is Friday."

"Yes. But she may not last until then."

The man was silent. He understood that there was a problem, but could not ask what it was. He knew only that the hour of his death was coming sooner. "Perhaps Saturday evening," he said at last.

"God will reward you for it," Al Zaroor answered softly.

In midmorning, Brooke drove into the hills alone. As he did, he saw vultures circling over a field, and knew they had found the Palestinian. A reminder that his own fate was enveloping him.

Fareed waited in his shaded garden. "What happened to your neck?" he asked.

"A shaving accident," Brooke answered in his blandest tone. "Embarrassing."

Waving Brooke to a chair, Fareed regarded him amiably. In Brooke's previous time as Adam Chase, Fareed had been an entertaining friend and, on occasion, an informal access agent — it was less that he always knew some secret than that he often knew who did. He had lived in the valley all his life, and his extended family of a thousand people was spread over four generations. From an early age, Fareed had learned to navigate sectarian tensions with skill; as a journalist, unlike some men of his culture, he knew when to get to the point. After a moment, he said, "I don't see you for two years, and now you're desperate for my company. Should I be flattered?"

"Complimented. I have urgent business, and only you can help me."

"Business with whom?"

"The men who run this valley."

Fareed's face darkened. "These are not the kind of men who have offices, or announce their role to others — even to me. Do you have names?"

"I'm working on that."

Fareed raised his eyebrows. "Strange work for a business consultant. What interest do these men hold for you?"

"We have mutual interests. Should my home office authorize a visit, they will find themselves grateful."

Fareed appraised him. Neither man had mentioned Hezbollah, nor had Brooke stepped outside his cover. But Fareed no longer doubted, if he ever had, who Brooke worked for. "Whomever you may want to see," he said at length, "I know them well."

This was as Brooke suspected. "And you would recommend me?"

Fareed took a long sip of coffee. "My old friend Adam Chase?" he answered sardonically. "What harm in introducing him to a few old schoolmates." He waved a hand. "But go, please. There will be other times to catch up. It seems you're in a rush."

Moments later, Brooke was driving back toward Baalbek when his cell phone buzzed. "I've been to the powers that be," Brustein told him.

The White House, this could only mean, as well as the Israelis. "What did they decide?" Brooke asked.

"It's delicate," Brustein answered. "We've sent someone to see you."

SEVEN

Three hours later, Brooke arrived at a medieval monastery in the hills north of Beirut. Given the speed at which he had driven and his disregard for safety, he was certain no one had followed him.

Stepping into the crisp mountain air, Brooke gazed out at the Mediterranean, struck once more by the contrasts of this compelling but dangerous country. Through the windows of a shadowy chapel, he heard male voices chanting in a haunting Latinate cadence. Below were groves of cedars and quadrants of rich farmland. There was no sense of Islam here; this was a place for Christians. The Bekaa seemed distant, every hour precious. Brooke wondered what message from Langley must be delivered only in person, and by whom.

He went inside. In a small room lit by candles lay the tomb of a local saint, Charbel Makhlouf, revered by Maronites as a source of miracles. A half century after his death, the devout had opened his tomb and found his body uncorrupted, cementing his reputation. As Brooke approached the tomb, a familiar voice remarked, "They say this man performs wonders from the grave. Do you think he could find the bomb?"

Turning, Brooke saw Carter Grey sitting on a stone bench, back held stiffly. "Not in the Bekaa," Brooke answered.

"Then there's no point in keeping him company. Let's go outside."

Grey stood, then walked with halting steps into an open courtyard. He rested his elbows on a low stone wall, easing the pressure on his spine, and pretended to admire the blue of the Mediterranean through the cedars. Brooke joined him, saying, "What the hell are you doing here?"

"I'm all that Langley could spare. Everyone else is preparing for Sunday's annihilation of Washington."

The answer was, Brooke understood, accurate but incomplete. "So they're still on that," he said.

Grey gave his familiar grunt. "How could they not be? The president has decided not to evacuate — it would spread mass panic and elevate al Qaeda to new heights. So everyone is moving heaven and earth to track the bomb."

"Have you told them it's in the Bekaa Valley?"

"We've told them what you think. The White House can't afford to believe it. That leaves Brustein and me."

Brooke felt himself tense. "What about enlisting Hezbollah?"

"The Mossad doesn't like it — they're obsessed with Hezbollah, and think you'll compromise their agent. It also bothers them that you used to sleep with her —"

"Too bad. I only wish I'd had more foresight."

Softly, Grey asked, "How are you doing with that?"

"Can I stop caring for her? No. But that's not what matters now. Are the Israelis that confident al Qaeda can't detonate this bomb over Tel Aviv?"

"I'm not sure. Let's say they're considering their military options."

"They have none. Their only option, if it is one, is to track Hezbollah and me while we're looking. If we find the bomb, then they can try to send in a strike force."

In profile, Grey's seamed face was haggard. "In which case, you'll be as expendable as Hezbollah. Bombs, rockets, and bullets don't discriminate."

"Not to mention that I'd have to wear a tracking device, or use a cell phone to communicate where I am." Brooke kept gazing at the water. "Hezbollah may decide to kill me before the Israelis get their chance, just to keep me from functioning as a human GPS."

Grey turned to him. "Speaking for the agency, the thought you'll wind up dead troubles us a bit. Alex Coll is less sentimental. His concerns are legal and political —"

"Let me guess," Brooke cut in. "A congressional hearing to investigate why I handed the Iranians a bomb. Laws are invoked; headlines blossom; Rush Limbaugh hyperventilates. Heads roll, including Coll's. Far more important to me, the Outfit gets the shaft. Does that about cover it?"

Grey took out a cigarette but did not light it. "For you to approach a designated terrorist organization violates all sorts of laws. That it's Hezbollah makes it worse. It isn't just that they murdered Buckley, blew up our embassy, and slaughtered our marines. People like Coll believe that Hezbollah is a bigger long-term threat to Israel and American interests than al Qaeda ever will be —"

"If al Qaeda destroys Tel Aviv," Brooke snapped, "they'll be pondering the future of a nuclear desert."

"They know that. But they're stymied trying to figure out the angles. If all we have is forty-eight hours, they can't change the law, or insulate themselves by approaching Hezbollah through intermediaries like the Germans."

Brooke felt anger overtaking him. "Who's making the call on this, for Godsakes?"

Grey regarded him with a bleak half smile. "The president of the United States and the prime minister of Israel. Or no one."

Brooke stared at Grey. "That's what you've come to tell me, isn't it? No one has decided that I can't talk to Hezbollah. And no one will tell me that I can."

Grey lit the cigarette, taking a deep drag. At length, he said, "If you go off the books and deal with Hezbollah, you assume the risk. If anything goes wrong — anything at all — it's not just your career. You could be prosecuted for violating American law. Assuming, as you say, that Hezbollah or al Qaeda doesn't kill you."

Though Brooke had expected this, to hear it stated baldly jarred him. "What would you do, Carter?"

Grey's eyes narrowed. Brooke could not tell whether this reflected his question or the pain that, at odd moments, shot through Grey's body like a current. "What it comes down to, in the end, is whom you answer to — other people or your own sense of what's right. I learned that early on. There were times when my personal compass led me off the books. I knew the risks, and chose to live with them." Facing Brooke, he softly added, "That's why Noah sent me. He knew that you'd ask me, and he knew what I'd say. Part of me wishes that we both aren't who we are."

At once, Brooke understood — it had been easier for Carter to take chances for himself than sanction the chances Brooke might take. "But we are," Brooke said simply.

Slowly, Grey nodded. "Still got that elephant?" he asked.

"Of course. It saved my life in Baalbek."

"With the help of an Israeli woman who wields a wicked pen. She must be quite remarkable."

"She always was. But now she's very different."

"She's a deep-cover agent, Brooke. You know what that does. At some point the person they once were slips beyond anyone's reach — including their own." He paused again. "I guess that hasn't happened yet. Instead of following you that night, she could have driven away. The Israelis know that, too."

Feeling the divide in his soul, Brooke could say nothing. "Keep the elephant," Grey advised. "With luck, Ms. Mossad won't give you the names you need. Then you might survive this."

Brooke placed a hand on Grey's shoulder. "Thanks for coming," he told his friend. "It matters that the message came from you."

Restless, Anit prowled the site at Anjar while the others sought shelter from midafternoon sun. She felt time slipping away in the arc of its decline. Before this, these ruins had made her feel the expanse of history, the slow passage of years and decades. Now she imagined Tel Aviv in ashes.

She ached to call her parents, or her friends. But they were Anit Rahal's friends, and she was Laura Reynolds. The only person she could talk to was someone who might die. Laura could not care for him too much.

Where was he? she wondered. Perhaps they would call him back to Washington. Viewed with detachment, that would be best for them both.

Still, she admitted, their stolen hour had been precious. An hour, too little and far too late. Now there was only the bomb.

Her cell phone rang. She snatched it from her pocket — perhaps it was Brooke, or her contact in Tel Aviv.

"Dr. Reynolds?"

Habib's voice, though familiar, surprised her. "I'm glad to hear from you."

Though he was surely alone, Habib spoke in a lowered voice. "If the whispers are true, the shipment I mentioned has arrived."

"When?"

"Perhaps three days ago. It came at night, one hears, with a stranger. But only the men who guided him know for sure."

"Do you know what it is, or where?"

"No. All this is very secret; I don't even know who among us helped this man. But such security is unique."

"What does that suggest to you?"

Habib began speaking quickly. "That this shipment is very special, and the man who brought it very powerful, or very rich. That is all I know."

"Thank you," Anit said. "May your family prosper."

The phone clicked off. But Anit knew that Habib, her only source within the Jefaar clan, would alter the calculus in Tel Aviv.

Looking around her, she called her contact.

■ ■ ■ ■

In early evening, Brooke met Anit outside the ruins. The crew was working again; a young red-haired woman, no doubt the intern Anit had mentioned, watched as they embraced. Anit held him for a moment longer than playacting required.

He smiled into her face. "Miss me?"

Her eyes remained grave. "I was hoping never to see you again."

Brooke watched her. "What's happened?"

"I've heard from someone within the Jefaar clan. Two days ago a mysterious shipment arrived. My agent has no names, contents, or location. But he says that kind of secrecy has no precedent." She moved closer to him, pretending to straighten his collar. "If this is the bomb, they're on schedule for September 11."

"So what will Israel do?"

" 'Israel,' " she amended, "is a lot of anxious people in a closed room, trying to guess for the prime minister whether it's more likely that al Qaeda will succeed or that Iran will get this bomb." She shook her head. "If we knew exactly where it was coming from, or how, al Qaeda would have no chance at all. But we don't."

"Is anyone quoting odds?"

"No. But they know very well the consequences of Tel Aviv's destruction." She paused, then asked, "What does Langley say?"

Weighing his answer, Brooke was silent.

She looked at him sharply. "They've cut you loose, haven't they?"

"I'd like those names, Anit. Israel's out of time."

She turned from him, as though in sudden anguish. Brooke rested his hands on her shoulders. "I'll keep you out of this, I promise."

"That's not the point." Her voice was thin. "I have no permission to do this."

"I know. That's not how they work."

She stood straighter. "When can you see your friend?"

"Tonight."

For a long time, Anit said nothing. Then she spoke two names.

EIGHT

To Al Zaroor, the atmosphere in the cave was claustrophobic. The two remaining Palestinians, Walid and Asif, were silent, as if muted by the likelihood that Hamzi had been killed or captured. In contrast, the three al Qaeda from Iraq — Said, Chihab, and Abur — were voluble, using words to kill the time that passed too slowly. The Pakistani, Jawindi, sat near the coffin like a mother hen, his watchfulness unsettling to the others. No matter how carefully Al Zaroor had planned, his design rested on how each man would perform and whether, in the alchemy of varied natures, they would inspire or diminish their fellow operatives. But the man on whom all depended was not yet with them.

Restless, Al Zaroor walked to the mouth of the cave. In the dying sun, he traced their plan in his mind, gaze focused on a field barren of crops. Ten minutes at most, he told himself. If only they could move to-night: Every instinct told him that, despite the bucolic scene below, unseen enemies were closing in. Perhaps this American — or Hezbollah, or the Jews. Someone.

Al Zaroor hated this passivity, a paralysis not of will, but of means. He felt like a foolish woman waiting for a lover to rescue her before an angry father discovered their affair. He willed his man to call.

The American stalking him had killed one man, and perhaps another. No matter that his country cowered, Adam Chase had not been fooled. From the photograph, Al Zaroor had conjured the inner landscape of his enemy — an intuitive and determined man unafraid to die, filled with loathing for al Qaeda. How much did he know, Al Zaroor wondered, and how would he try to thwart al Qaeda's dream? The capstone of this vision, the iconic date, must be sacrificed to its achievement.

The phone vibrated in his pocket. Anxious, Al Zaroor answered. "Nephew?"

"Tomorrow evening, Uncle."

Tightly, Al Zaroor said, "No sooner?"

"Impossible. But assure my aunt that I will shower her with kisses."

He sounded calm, Al Zaroor thought, for a man who was choosing the hour of his death. No doubt it was his commitment to jihad.

"Allah will reward you," Al Zaroor replied.

They had met only once, at a safe house in Brussels. Outside, a bleak, sleeting rain seemed to permeate the streets, deepening the gloom of winter. But Salem Rajah's dark eyes held a molten glow.

Rajah was in his early thirties, with dark curly hair and the nerves and sinews of an athlete. He had been a fighter pilot in the Royal Saudi Air Force; sitting across from Al Zaroor in a worn chair, he projected the alertness of a man trained to fly at sickening speeds. Now he wished to fly only for al Qaeda. When Al Zaroor explained his plan to destroy the Zionist state, Rajah remained impassive.

"Where do I acquire the plane?" he asked.

No emotion, Al Zaroor thought approvingly; rather, a practical inquiry on an essential point. His tone was quiet and authoritative, suiting his sense of Salem Rajah. "In Belgium," he answered. "When the time comes, we'll provide you with the money and a Lebanese passport. On the night of the mission, we will meet you at the field we have chosen, timing our movements to coincide with your arrival. In less than ten minutes you'll land, acquire the weapon, and take off for Tel Aviv."

Rajah's thin smile carried the hint of amusement. "Just like that, attracting no attention."

"If all goes well. You will file a normal flight plan showing a route from Beirut to Baalbek." Leaning forward, Al Zaroor looked intently at the pilot, reading his expression as he spoke. "You'll take off from a private airstrip, flying at a low altitude. In the last few minutes you'll turn off the radio and land in a darkened field. Can you do that without lights?"

"Yes, by means of GPS. I would need lights only at the very last instant." Rajah frowned in thought. "How much does this bomb weigh?"

"About two hundred pounds."

Rajah raised his eyebrows. "Light," he remarked. "That expands our choice of aircraft. Considering the Zionist air defenses, that's important."

Al Zaroor had expected this. "They're the best in the world, I'm told."

"In most ways, yes. The Jews are prepared for an attacker coming at the highest speeds, from less than a hundred miles. The commander of the air force and his deputies have authority to order an intruder shot down." Rajah paused a moment, reviewing his knowledge. "The heart of their air defenses is a sophisticated radar system that picks up virtually anything in the sky, even gliders. In order to respond more quickly, the Jews divide their airspace into zones. Within each zone they have at least two pilots who can take off in sixty seconds, as well as antiaircraft missiles they can fire off even quicker. Once they see you, you're dead."

Rather than daunted, the pilot sounded as though he were coolly assessing a challenge. "So how do you beat them?" Al Zaroor asked.

Rajah smiled at this. "By not doing what they expect. At the height of the Cold War, when Soviet air defenses were second to none, a demented Finnish teenager flew a private plane from Helsinki to Moscow and landed in Red Square. The Russians weren't prepared for an aircraft flying at low altitude. If he'd had a bomb, that kid could have reduced the Kremlin to rubble."

"That was thirty years ago," Al Zaroor rejoined. "The Zionist air defenses are much better."

"Better, yes. But good enough?" Again Rajah's lips curled. "Like the Russians', the Zionists' defenses aren't designed to pick up small, slow-moving objects whose flight pattern is obscured by ground cover, glare, or weather. Five years ago Hezbollah put up an Iranian drone, flew it for ten minutes over the Galilee, then returned it to southern Lebanon intact. Even the Jews admitted it was like trying to catch a mosquito with a net."

Gazing up at him, Al Zaroor asked mildly, "So what aircraft would you use to destroy the Zionist homeland?"

"A Cessna 185," the pilot answered promptly. "A single-engine propeller plane."

"What about payload?"

"The payload on this Cessna is roughly eleven hundred pounds. I'd need a hundred pounds of fuel. Add two men — four hundred pounds at most — and a two-hundred-pound bomb. That leaves four hundred pounds to spare. We'll get to Tel Aviv."

"In how long?"

"That depends on the flight plan. I'd fly thirty feet above the ground, so that it's hard for the radar to pick me up, and I'd choose a path where I can use hills or trees for cover." Rajah stopped, making a mental calculation. "From the Bekaa, that could take me half an hour."

"What about Zionist spotters on the ground?"

Rajah shrugged. "At night, they won't know what we are. We could be Jews in a private plane, or the drones the Zionists use to spy on Hezbollah." He paused. "The greatest danger is from an AWAC — a plane stuffed with radar that can pick up objects below it. But they'd have to know that we were coming."

Satisfied, Al Zaroor said, "I'll make sure the Jews know nothing."

Rajah sat down again. For the first time, his tone of voice suggested a trace of awe. "Tell me about the properties of this bomb," he requested. "That will affect our final moments."

Slowly, Al Zaroor nodded. "The bomb will have a nuclear core, surrounded by explosives that are triggered by a very precise electrical system. When the trigger goes off, it ignites the explosives, causing the nuclear event. Once the bomb starts falling, the trigger detonates it at one thousand feet."

Rajah frowned. "A weapon that detonates on impact would allow me to stay lower. Less chance of detection; less chance of getting shot down before I can drop the bomb."

"I understand. But much of the energy of a groundburst is spent digging a useless hole. An airburst maximizes the damage to the target area." Al Zaroor paused for emphasis. "That is why I chose this weapon. Tel Aviv, and everything around it, will cease to exist."

Rajah bent forward, considering the problem. "All right," he said. "Let's assume we fly in undetected. When we reach Tel Aviv, we suddenly go straight up. In about forty-five seconds we'll reach one thousand feet. Even when they see us, it will be too late. The bomb will detonate before they can react."

Al Zaroor stared at him fixedly. "In a single flash of light, Rajah, you will have destroyed the Zionist state. Perhaps its death throes will take a year, perhaps two. Then maps will be rewritten, the word 'Israel' removed. Only your sacrifice will live."

Rajah fell quiet. The reality of his death had entered the room. Softly he said, *"Inshallah."*

As night fell, Al Zaroor called an operative in France. He wondered if the Renewer still lived to give his blessing.

"Yes?" the man answered.

"I am eager," Al Zaroor said.

Three words. The man who heard them, not knowing what they meant, would post a

notice on an Internet dating service.
Man seeks Jewish bride.

NINE

Before dawn, Fareed drove Brooke and Anit to the mausoleum of Abbas al-Musawi, the first leader of Hezbollah. The three were silent. The night before, Fareed had asked if Brooke's inquiry related to the missing bomb; Brooke's reply, though noncommittal, had left its shadow in his friend's dark eyes. Anit's insistence on joining them was an unwelcome surprise. She would not say if she was acting on her own; Brooke knew only that she was in grave danger. Consumed by her thoughts, she did not look at him.

The mausoleum was an elaborate shrine of domes and spires, its outline dark against the first thin light. Getting out, Anit stood before the charred shell of a car, itself a shrine. Many years before, an Apache missile fired from an Israeli helicopter had incinerated Musawi, his wife, and his four-year-old son while they drove through the valley. His successor, Hassan Nasrallah, traveled in a caravan of eight land rovers, disembarking under an enormous cloth so that Israel's spy satellites could not detect which vehicle he used. Watching Anit, Brooke tried to imagine her thoughts.

"Let's go," he murmured. Without responding, Anit turned and began walking toward the mausoleum. It was as though she occupied her own space.

Two armed guards awaited them, Hezbollah soldiers. They confiscated Brooke's camera and cell phone, then Anit's and Fareed's phones, and opened the great steel doors so that the three could enter.

Above them a field of tiny spotlights seemed to flicker like candles in the shadows. The mausoleum itself was stone and marble, its ceilings an intricate mosaic of cut glass. Brooke stood beside a display case that held the artifacts of death — Musawi's glasses, his wife's prayer book, their son's charred shoes. At the center of the marble floor was a glass lacework structure through which Brooke could glimpse the tomb of the Shia martyr. Spread before it was a sumptuous carpet on which a lone man prostrated himself in prayer.

Their guard gestured for Brooke and Anit to wait. Silent, they watched the man continue his veneration, his body as still as theirs.

The worshipper stood, tall and slender in a long white robe. As he turned, Brooke saw a bearded man barely older than he, with the thin face of an ascetic or a scholar. He greeted Fareed pleasantly, in Arabic, before the journalist stepped outside. Then he appraised his two visitors with a half smile that did not touch his probing eyes. In perfect English, he said, "I am Hussein Nouri."

His erudition was no surprise — Nouri, Brooke had learned, held a doctorate in political science from the University of Paris. "Adam Chase," Brooke replied. "This is my colleague Laura Reynolds."

Nouri's smile vanished. "I know of you," he told Brooke. "Four days ago, you called on Grand Ayatollah al-Mahdi, delphically warning of events to come." Facing Anit, he said in a sardonic tone, "And you, I understand, are an archaeologist."

Left unspoken was his perception of what else she might be. Nouri's voice was an instrument, Brooke realized, used to convey meaning beyond the words he chose. "As I said," Brooke repeated, "we're colleagues."

Nouri's eyes glinted. "So I am to understand. And now you want my help."

"Yes. In our mutual interests."

"Do we have such interests?" Nouri asked mildly. "In 1982, the Americans came to support the Christians and the Zionist invaders."

"Yes," Brooke said flatly. "And many died."

Nouri crossed his arms. "You are brave to speak of American deaths in such a place. Let alone Jewish deaths." He paused to study Anit before facing Brooke again. "I know nothing about the bombings of your marines or your embassy, or the unfortunate death of your chief spy in Beirut. But those were difficult times. One could say that by coming to a land not theirs, they volunteered to die." His voice rose slightly, its cadence quickening. "Now it is thirty years later, and still you call us terrorists. Do you think we don't belong here? Are you unaware that many thousands of Lebanese have since been killed by the Zionists, your allies? Does it not matter that a plurality of our citizens vote for us in free elections? Or that our only conflict with America occurs in our country, not in yours? And now you, Mr. Chase, come to us not in friendship, but to save the Jews who murder us in our homes."

Brooke paused to choose his words. "I come on behalf of sanity," he replied. "Al

Qaeda would pervert Islam —"

"Do not insult us," Nouri cut in harshly. "We were among the first to condemn the carnage of September 11. We do not commit mass murder against civilians in their own land. That is the work of al Qaeda — and of the Americans and Zionists in Palestine, Pakistan, Iraq, Afghanistan, and Lebanon, our homeland." Again he eyed Anit. "What caused our latest war with the Jews? I ask you. They refused to trade our prisoners for theirs, requiring us to seize a few more hostages to sweeten our proposal. Instead of negotiating, the Zionists bombed our towns and cities and murdered thirteen hundred civilians. The handful of Jews who died here were invaders."

At the corner of his vision, Brooke could see Anit, her face an expressionless mask. "We are Lebanese," Nouri continued, "and we are Shia. We care for our people, and work to make our voices heard in this pantomime of democracy thrust on us by the French. We fight to defend our land, and liberate the borderlands the Zionists have stolen, because our nation's army is too weak." He turned to indicate Musawi's tomb, finishing softly, "We honor our martyrs, but would gladly forgo martyrdom. We wish to live in peace."

"If I'm right," Brooke rejoined, "there will be no peace for anyone. The Shia least of all."

Nouri's lips compressed. "Tell me what you want."

"Osama Bin Laden claims that tomorrow al Qaeda will destroy one of our cities with a stolen Pakistani bomb." Brooke inclined his head toward Anit. "We think Bin Laden lied, and that the bomb is here."

"Here?" Nouri repeated softly.

"In or near the Bekaa, perhaps in the Anti-Lebanon Mountains." Brooke paused, then said bluntly, "We believe that they are using Hezbollah territory as a base. And that they plan to detonate the bomb over Tel Aviv, destroying the city."

Nouri looked from Brooke to Anit. "What evidence do you have?"

"Enough. Rumors of a sensitive shipment through Iraq. The disappearance of a Syrian security officer who helped a truck pass through a checkpoint. Information that the Jefaar clan helped smuggle a mysterious package through the mountains. The presence of a Pakistani nuclear technician. The appearance in this valley of al Qaeda sympathizers from Ayn Al-Hilweh —"

"Yes," Nouri interrupted. "One seems to have been asphyxiated by his own blood, then dumped in a field. It might have been better had someone questioned him first."

For the first time, Anit chose to speak. "Circumstances prevented that," she said coolly. "Now we need your help."

Nouri gave her a brief, chill smile. "What if our help is not forthcoming?"

"Within the next two days, they will try to execute this plan. If they succeed, hundreds of thousands of Israelis will die —"

"And this is my concern?"

"Al Qaeda hopes it will be," Anit said in the same flat tone. "They believe that Israel will retaliate against the enemies they can find. If so, this valley would become a wasteland fit only for cockroaches, where the few Shia still alive will envy their dead."

"So," Nouri responded with a terrible quiet, "you propose that we live to kill Zionists some other time, or they will kill us all before the week is out."

"I propose nothing. But that's what I believe would happen."

Nouri scrutinized her. "Given the Zionists' indiscriminate brutality — which you advance as our reason for helping them — perhaps it would be better if we find this bomb ourselves. I believe the Jews call that a 'deterrent.'"

"No," she said curtly. "They'd call it a

provocation, and assume you'll give the bomb to Iran." She paused, then continued in a tone as cold as his. "I promise you that the Mossad knows where you are — your leaders, your bases, your underground facilities, where you store your rockets. Did you think when you rolled up their agents you found them all? I assure you that's not so. This bomb will be deadly to anyone who possesses it."

Impassive, Nouri stared at her. Only his eyes betrayed anger. "There's no time for this," Brooke told Nouri. "Your men took my camera, from which you can circulate photographs of the Palestinians from Ayn Al-Hilweh. Your network is broad and deep — you have observers who watch for strangers at roadblocks and in every town. Perhaps they've already seen these men, and thought them insignificant. Not so. Any recent sighting could suggest the area where al Qaeda has the bomb."

Nouri's smile was grim. "So this is the extent of your assistance? Then what do we need you for, and why should two enemy spies live another hour? Unless extracting information about your sources in Lebanon takes a little longer."

Anit showed nothing; perhaps she had stopped caring. But Brooke felt the fear in the pit of his stomach. Evenly, he said, "We expect to receive more useful information — our network extends far beyond the Bekaa. In the meanwhile, we can serve to witness your good intentions. By comparison, our deaths would be at most a transient pleasure." Brooke paused, then chose to lie. "So would anything else you do to us. Our superiors value us too greatly."

For a long moment, Nouri studied him. At length, he said, "Do not attempt to leave this valley. If we wish to speak with you further, we will contact Fareed. Now go."

They left in silence, Anit staring straight ahead.

TEN

Brooke and Anit sat in the shade on Fareed's porch, drinking coffee as they looked out at the valley, green and vivid in the bright sun of midmorning. Fareed left them alone; in his mind, Adam Chase had become a dangerous man, Anit perhaps worse. Sentries from Hezbollah watched them from the driveway. Brooke felt time running swiftly.

Anit was pale and silent, as though she had withdrawn an inch beneath the skin. Hezbollah had killed Meir; this morning she had revealed herself to them, destroying years of subterfuge in an hour. All that might come of this was her own death. At length, Brooke said, "I know how difficult this is."

She did not look at him. "We need to stop al Qaeda. Then nothing else will matter."

"Suppose Hezbollah takes the bomb. The Mossad must have a plan."

Anit sipped her coffee, then said in a low voice, "They do. But neither your satellites nor ours can track Hezbollah's search."

"So this 'plan' requires you to be with Hezbollah."

Anit watched the sentries. "There's a GPS on my phone," she answered. "I can call in a strike force — four choppers, thirty or so commandos. They'd land in half an hour."

"Too little," Brooke said bluntly. "And too late. Hezbollah will expect all that."

Anit shrugged. "They gave my phone back."

"Sure. They want the Mossad to know you're still alive. Unless and until they track down the bomb, that serves their purpose. Then, if they like, they can kill us." A sudden thought surfaced. "That may be why they'll take us with them. They'll kill us in a 'firefight,' then blame it on al Qaeda. I'm not sure what to hope for."

Anit faced him. "The survival of Tel Aviv."

And yours, Brooke thought, looking into her face. Once he had imagined a life with her; now he simply prayed for her to live. That their intersection might be fatal to her was too painful, and too obvious, for words.

A phone rang in the house. Fareed appeared on the porch, looking rattled and unshaven. "Nouri wishes to see you," he said.

In his cave, Al Zaroor prayed, his head bowed toward Mecca. *May it please Allah, let us move soon. There are too many uncertainties, our enemies too well armed. They are closing in, unseen, as I await word from the Renewer.*

At length, he stood. The others watched him — the Palestinians, the Iraqis, the Pakistani with haunted eyes. He could no longer conceal the fear that gnawed at him.

His phone buzzed. As the others watched, he removed it from his pocket.

He heard the click of a recording, then the voice he revered above all others, reciting a verse of his own composition:

The devil's light flashes golden in the
    black sky of doom.
Clothed in a shroud of ashes
Our foe vanishes into the past.

Shutting off the phone, Al Zaroor slumped, eyes briefly closing. A shudder of relief ran through him.

Composing himself, he called Salem Rajah. "It is tonight," he said.

"Allahu akbar," the pilot said. "Tell my aunt

575

I love her."

Al Zaroor put the phone away. Then he approached the men who waited, addressing the Pakistani. "It is time to prepare our cargo."

Jawindi bowed his head, as though in awe and fear. Facing the others, Al Zaroor said, "Inside that crate is a nuclear weapon. Tonight, with your help and Allah's blessing, it will destroy the city of Tel Aviv."

All but Asif turned toward the crate, shrinking back a little. Softly, Al Zaroor told him, "It is only dangerous to Jews."

They turned to him again. "The Renewer has spoken," he declaimed. "He has promised our enemies that the clash of civilizations would go on until the Hours. On this day, September 10, the Hours will begin."

Forced to abandon their vehicles, Brooke and Anit rode into the foothills, Fareed at the wheel. The dirt road he followed wound along a ledge, affording views of orchards and fields. Atop a hill dotted with junipers a shepherd, barely more than a boy, herded a flock of sheep. Brooke experienced a moment of disbelief: This bucolic land concealed a terrible weapon, and these hills might themselves become scarred and barren.

At length, they reached a wooded area through which ran a mountain stream. Beneath a grove of trees two men sat at a wooden table eating trout cooked over an open grill. One of them was Hussein Nouri.

Fareed parked in a bare patch of earth. When Brooke and Anit approached the men, Fareed stayed by his car.

Nouri stood. With a courtly air, he gestured toward a hard-looking man dressed in fatigues, with a bulbous nose and a grizzled but neatly trimmed beard. "This is Nahum Khazei," he said in an ironic tone, "Hezbollah's principal military commander in the Bekaa. According to Fareed, you wished to meet him."

Silent, Anit inclined her head. On the table, Brooke saw a map of the valley. Then he heard Fareed's car starting.

"Fareed is no longer necessary," Nouri said pleasantly. "Now you're in our care. Please, sit."

Uneasy, Brooke and Anit complied. Khazei looked at her, an expression of disdain briefly crossing his shrewd peasant's face. Then he touched the map with a stubby finger. "Five days ago, your Palestinians stopped to eat in Shawtarwah. At dusk they drove south, toward Rashaya. Sometime after that, they vanished into the night.

All we found was their car."

Brooke studied the map. "That makes sense. Rashaya is near the mountains, and much closer to Tel Aviv." He looked up at Khazei. "Where would al Qaeda hide the bomb and a handful of men? Also a truck."

Khazei squinted. "Thirty years ago, we trained in these mountains. The men and the bomb could be easy to conceal — there are groves of trees, and many natural caves. But a truck? There are not many caves so large." After a moment, his finger moved. "There's an old aqueduct nearby, dry in summer. They might get a truck in there."

Anit looked not at Khazei, but at the map. "What about an airstrip?"

Khazei stared at her. With a trace of scorn, he said, "You spies have complicated minds. First a truck, now an airfield. Why would al Qaeda make things so difficult?"

Slowly, Anit gazed up at him. "Because of your intelligence network, they won't try to move this bomb through the valley. Nor would they have a truck meet them somewhere, allowing you to follow it. Humor us."

Brooke noted Nouri watching this exchange, eyes glinting with amusement and, perhaps, antipathy for Anit. In a rough voice, Khazei said, "There are no airstrips there, just fields. When I was a boy, the CIA landed planes on one of them, supplying arms for the Christian butchers to kill Muslims."

Palms on the table, Brooke leaned over the map. "What area are we talking about?"

Khazei traced a circle in the hills north of Rashaya. "Here, I would say."

"How many men can you deploy?"

Khazei shrugged. "Enough."

"Then we should go there at once."

Khazei turned to Anit, his front teeth showing in a cynical smile. "Define 'we,' " he said to her. "Do you expect visitors from the entity you call 'Israel'?"

"No."

"Then you won't need your phones."

"If we can't call our superiors," Brooke interjected, "they may get nervous —"

"Let them," Khazei snapped. "If Jews start falling from the sky, you'll both get bullets in the head."

Brooke stared at him. "And if they don't, killing us would be stupid. You won't just have visitors falling from the sky, but bombs."

Khazei flashed the same sardonic smile. "Of course. Dropping bombs is what Zionists do best. Especially on civilians."

Brooke looked from Khazei to Nouri. "Enough of this," he said. "You must be taking us with you for a reason."

"It is as you suggested," Nouri coolly replied. "You've become witnesses to our good faith."

Anit glanced at Brooke. Through the brief current of their eye contact, they shared a common thought — whether at the hands of al Qaeda or Hezbollah, they would die. Then Brooke told Nouri softly, "Whatever else, don't keep the bomb. Not even using it would save you."

Silent, Nouri gave him an enigmatic smile. "Put your cell phones on the table," Khazei ordered.

Brooke complied, then Anit. "Do whatever you need to," Brooke told Khazei. "September 11 comes eight hours from now."

ELEVEN

Within minutes, Brooke, Anit, Khazei, and his lieutenant, Mahmoud Nidal, were headed toward Rashaya in a land rover, followed by two trucks filled with fighters who had seemed to materialize from nowhere. In the privacy of the backseat, Brooke pressed Grey's good luck elephant into Anit's hand. When she looked into his face, asking why, he smiled and murmured, "Keep this. I don't want anything happening to it." Briefly, she touched his hand, then put the elephant in her pocket. There was nothing more to say.

At dusk, they stopped beside a broad, open field at the foot of the mountains, its brown earth dark with shadows cast by the fading sun. Khazei ordered Nidal to turn off the headlights. Glancing over his shoulder, he told Brooke, "This is the place."

"Are there many others like it?"

"None so close to the mountains." He

pointed toward bare rocky hills on which Brooke could discern a dirt road hacked like a scar into the harsh earth. "On that hill are several caves concealed by ledges, one or two large enough to hold a truck. Partway down the hillside there's the abandoned aqueduct that's open at both ends. This place is our best guess."

"How will you search it?"

Khazei glanced at Anit, allowing himself a cold smile. "As this 'archaeologist' well knows, our fighters in the area are equipped with AK-47s, RPGs, night vision goggles, radios, and cell phones. Some are in land cruisers on which machine guns are mounted; others in vans or pickup trucks. When night falls, we'll scour the aqueduct first, then the caves." Khazei scanned the hillside with keen eyes. "We'll find either something or nothing. But the small force you envision can't possibly resist us. Nor," he told Anit curtly, "could a deputation of Jews."

Anit remained silent and composed. Scanning the empty field, Brooke said in Arabic, "What's paramount is to disarm any plane that lands — shoot up the cockpit and gas tank, sheer off the wings with RPGs. A plane is the only means of getting the bomb to Tel Aviv. Wherever they may be, al Qaeda has to meet it."

Khazei gave him a sharp look. "I don't need schooling in the obvious. We'll place some men around the field with rifles and RPGs. But if your scenario is right, tonight is one day early."

"Perhaps not. Killing that Palestinian may have warned them."

"Too bad," Khazei said in the same harsh tone. "Suppose al Qaeda succeeds in loading the bomb on this plane, and one of our RPGs hits it. Will it detonate? If so, better over the Zionists than here."

As Nidal turned to listen, Brooke quickly shook his head. "It's not designed that way. In America, we move these weapons around at will."

Khazei scowled. "But you can't guarantee its safety."

"To a degree, yes. This bomb contains uranium, which puts out very little harmful radiation. Also, it's made to detonate only at a certain elevation. If the plane crashes without reaching that height, or gets blown up in the air, this bomb won't go off. Even a direct hit won't cause total detonation." He paused, looking from Khazei to Nidal. "Still, it's much better not to hit this thing with an RPG. A partial detonation would be more than enough to kill us all."

Khazei gave him a hard look. "If the bomb is on the plane, we'll let it go to Tel Aviv. The Jews can deal with it."

Nidal kept watching Brooke, his thin, bearded face radiating suspicion. "Can al Qaeda bypass this system?" he asked.

Brooke considered his answer. Their technician could, he thought. Instead he replied, "That would be stupid. They want no accidents in Lebanon."

"Nor do we," Khazei said firmly. "Best to seize this bomb on the ground, with the greatest care." Again he faced the hillside. "There's only one road from up there, with branches on both sides of this field. Al Qaeda would have to use it. We'll block the road on either side, then start our search."

Brooke glanced at Anit. Her expression was bleak, as if she were being forced to watch gamblers dicing over the fate of Israel.

"Pray," Khazei said to her. "If this bomb is ready to detonate, al Qaeda could stage a suicide bombing no martyr could imagine."

In the cave, Al Zaroor fired his Luger once, its silencer repressing all sounds but the thud of his bullet striking flesh and bone. He put the Luger in his waistband. Sliding down the side of the cave, the Pakistani gaped at him, brains and blood seeping from the bullet hole in his forehead. The others watched, eyes filled with shock and fear.

Al Zaroor put the Luger back in his waistband. "His work was done," he told them calmly, "the weapon prepared. If captured, he would have betrayed the man who helped us acquire it. I promised him that would never happen." Ignoring the dead man, he pointed to the crate. "Open the top, then load it in the second van —"

His cell phone buzzed. "My flight is delayed," Rajah said quickly. "Tell my aunt I'll try tomorrow."

Al Zaroor smiled in satisfaction. "Pray God she lives."

He shut off the phone, looking around him. Most of the cave was dark; only where they stood was there enough light to illuminate the two vans. Checking his watch, Al Zaroor told the others, "Soon the roads should be clear — the Shia tend not to drive at night. God willing, no one will see us."

"Inshallah," Asif repeated with the softness of a prayer.

Checking his watch, Al Zaroor faced him. "We can take no chances. At ten o'clock, you will drive the first truck alone, turning off your headlights only after you leave the cave. If anyone is out there, it's you I want them to see."

"I understand."

Al Zaroor nodded. "One more time, tell me what you'll do."

Composing his face as he recited, Asif looked and sounded like a student in a madrassa. "A hundred feet down the hillside I'll reach the dirt path. I'll turn right and take it to the paved road, driving fast without lights to draw the suspicion of anyone who may be watching. Then I'll drive north until someone tries to stop me."

"And if they do?"

"I'll report this on my radio." Asif paused, then finished in a determined voice, "Then I'll become a martyr. They'll learn nothing."

Al Zaroor felt a surge of affection. Quickly, he embraced him, then looked into his face. "I know this, brother. On earth or in paradise, you will witness our success."

Standing on the hillside, Brooke and Khazei surveyed its slopes, their forearms resting on a rock. Anit watched from behind them. All they saw was thin moonlight and shadows, the outline of jagged rocks and stubby trees. The silence was complete.

Nearby, Nidal and several fighters in two land cruisers were hidden by massive rocks.

More fighters were stationed at the field, and where both forks of the dirt path reached the paved road running past it. "Where's the aqueduct?" Brooke asked.

Khazei pointed down the slope. "See those two boulders? The aqueduct is just behind that. Our men in land cruisers are driving through it — it's a good place to hide, and it ends at the airfield. If anyone is there, we'll seal it off."

"And if not?"

"Then we'll search the cave," Khazei answered sharply. "With luck, whoever may be there is sleeping, conserving their strength for tomorrow. But I mean to confront them with overwhelming force." His voice became flat. "Better yet, all this is a mirage, and Bin Laden will keep his promise to America. I prefer the valley as it is tonight."

There was nothing for Brooke to say. He was standing on a hillside with a general from Hezbollah, perhaps to no purpose, as Shia fighters searched for a bomb. Maybe Anit was wondering if one of them had killed Meir.

He turned to her. She looked back at him in the moonlight, summoning a faint smile, and moved forward to stand near him. Her footsteps crunched the rocks and dirt.

As Khazei reached for a cell phone, Brooke glanced at his other pocket and saw the bulge of his own cell phone and Anit's. Khazei held the phone to his ear, listening, then gave terse orders. "Search the largest cave. Yasir knows the one." Turning to Brooke, he said, "The aqueduct was empty."

Putting on night goggles, Khazei surveyed the terrain above them.

"What time is it?" Brooke asked.

Khazei eyed his illuminated watch. "A little after ten."

From the hillside above them came a sudden streak of light, vanishing abruptly. "What's that?" Brooke asked swiftly.

Khazei snatched off the goggles, handing them to Brooke. He saw a white van careening down the hillside. Khazei spat orders into his phone. "Go after it."

The van reached the road and turned sharply right. At both ends, land cruisers blocked its path. Accelerating, the van sped toward those in front of it.

"What's he doing?" Anit said tightly.

Brooke heard the crackle of gunfire. From all sides of the van headlights flashed on, a converging circle of attackers. Through the night goggles, Brooke saw Hezbollah fighters jumping out of trucks. In seconds, the van would hit the first land cruiser in its path.

"Suicide," Anit said.

No, Brooke thought suddenly. *Another decoy.*

The van struck its target. There was a violent explosion, then the thunder of an enormous blast echoing through the hillside. The bright orange flame consumed three land cruisers; they shuddered in its glow, then blew into pieces. A fighter burned like a human bonfire before he crumbled to the earth. "Truck bomb," Khazei snapped into his radio. "Get away from there."

Brooke looked toward the cave. The outline of a second truck appeared, its headlights dark. Roughly turning Khazei toward it, Brooke snapped, "This one has the bomb."

Khazei's head jerked toward Nidal. "Let's go," he shouted.

Nidal jumped into his land cruiser.

Running toward it with Anit and Khazei, Brooke said, "We need guns."

"Take them from the back."

Scrambling into the rear seat, Brooke grabbed an AK-47 for Anit, then took another for himself. As they checked their weapons, the land cruiser shot forward, spitting rock and dirt.

They began skidding down the hillside. Suddenly the cruiser lurched, nearly toppling as it threw Anit across Brooke's body. Whipping the steering wheel, Nidal righted the van. Brooke saw the second van reach the dirt road, turning toward the burning wreckage. Suddenly it disappeared.

"The aqueduct," Khazei said tightly.

Reaching the road, Nidal turned on his headlights. He accelerated, then braked abruptly, just past the boulders, veering sharply off the road. Ahead Brooke saw the cement maw of the aqueduct before its black void swallowed them.

Their headlights stabbed the darkness. They had perhaps two feet on either side; Nidal accelerated, his shoulders tense as the concrete walls sped by. Through the windshield Brooke spotted the red taillights of the van. Behind them, the headlights of the second land cruiser appeared. Anit turned to him, naked fear in her eyes. "What if they've mined the tunnel?"

"Speed up," Khazei urged Nidal.

Nidal stomped the gas pedal, the sudden jolt sending a shot of pain up Brooke's spine. The taillights vanished. A circle of black appeared, the end of the aqueduct. Nidal raced for it.

From behind them came a shudder, then

the echo of an explosion reverberating through the tunnel. Turning, Brooke saw the aqueduct collapse on the second land cruiser, sealing off the passage. Glancing in the mirror, Nidal leaned forward, desperate to reach the end. Twenty feet, then ten. As they reached the opening, Brooke heard a second explosion.

The land cruiser shook, breaking free as the aqueduct collapsed. "Praise Allah," Khazei murmured under his breath.

Leaning, Brooke scanned the open field. For an instant, he could not see the van. Then it was caught in a flash of yellow, the lights of a small plane as it glided to earth.

TWELVE

In split seconds, Al Zaroor saw everything — the Cessna landing, two jeeps speeding toward it from the edge of the field, his pursuers escaping the tunnel. Beside him, Walid gripped the steering wheel, driving parallel to the plane as it taxied. Al Zaroor's mind raced.

He picked up the radio, barking at the Iraqis in the rear compartment. "Leave the bomb there. Two jeeps are after the plane."

The van skidded to a stop, rattling over the bumpy ground. "Out," he told Walid, and jumped from the van. The Iraqis scrambled from the rear, grenade launchers at their hips. In the distance, the headlights of the lead cruiser came toward him. The jeeps kept speeding toward the nose of the plane. Pointing at them, Al Zaroor ordered the Iraqis to fire.

Said, Chihab, and Abur fell to their knees, aiming RPGs. Motioning Walid to follow, Al

Zaroor ran to the back of the van.

Through its open doors he saw the dark outline of the bomb. He scrambled in, Walid following. Reaching into the crate, they lifted the steel cylinder, knees buckling with its weight. They carried it to the opening and let it gently drop to earth. Walid closed his eyes at the thud.

The bomb was silver in the moonlight. Sliding out, Al Zaroor heard the sound of an explosion. He saw one jeep in flames, the other speeding toward the plane. As Said launched another grenade at the jeep, a burst of bullets from its machine gun cut down Chihab and Abur.

Rajah leaped from the cockpit. "Kill the others," Al Zaroor told Walid, and knelt alone beside the bomb.

Accelerating, Nidal raced toward the white van. As Khazei snapped orders through the radio, Brooke saw an RPG knock the second jeep on its side. Their headlights caught a man taking the wheel of the van.

Suddenly it was moving. Circling, the van began heading toward them. "Car bomb!" Anit cried out.

Nidal jerked the wheel, turning sharply. The van swerved toward them, its headlights closer. At thirty feet, Brooke knew they could not escape.

Wrenching Anit by the arm, he pushed the door open. For an instant he hesitated, then pulled her with him into the void.

Propelled by the weight of his fall, they tumbled to the earth. Pain shot through Brooke's shoulder. Rolling sideways in the dirt, he saw the van crash into the side of the jeep. For a split second, he saw Nidal's face through the window. Then the orange fireball filled his vision, searing his eyes and skin.

Anit.

Scrambling to his knees, Brooke saw her lying in a bed of grass and dirt. As he crawled toward her, Anit raised her head. In the glow of the flames, he saw a bloody gash on her face. He pulled her upright, stumbling away from the fire. Then they fell to earth again.

Brooke turned toward the wreckage. Nidal curled forward, no longer human, then vanished in the fireball. Framed in orange, Khazei rose from the ground, still gripping his AK-47. Suddenly his head jerked back, its top lifting in the air. Then Brooke saw a lone man with a handgun, his striking face visible in a flash of light.

Al Zaroor.

The pilot was opening the Cessna's cargo

holder. Desperate, Brooke began crawling toward the dead man.

In the light, Al Zaroor spotted the American. *You,* he thought, fighting back the urge to gun him down. There was no time; Adam Chase must not stop him now.

Swiftly, he looked around him. Near the nose of the plane, the surviving Iraqis fired at Hezbollah fighters pinned down near their toppled jeep. Running bent at the knees, Rajah reached Al Zaroor, then lifted the nose of the bomb. Gripping its fins, Al Zaroor said, "Two minutes more."

With a final lunge, Brooke reached Khazei. The fighter's eyes were open, his forehead gone. Grabbing Khazei's rifle, Brooke saw Al Zaroor and the pilot loading the silver cylinder into the cargo hold. As the pilot closed the door, Al Zaroor spun toward Brooke, firing.

Face in the dirt, Brooke heard bullets thud into the earth, another striking the corpse beside him. Blindly, he groped for Khazei's pockets. His fingers touched one cell phone, then another. Brooke shoved them in his shirt pocket and slowly raised his head.

Al Zaroor and the pilot were scrambling into the cockpit. As Brooke reached for

Khazei's rifle, he heard Anit call out for him.

She was kneeling in the grass, her bruised face white in the fiery glow. The plane began to move. From near the ruined jeep, a Hezbollah fighter rose to his knees, aiming an RPG at the cockpit. Brooke swiftly glanced over his shoulder. Then he raised the rifle and fired off two rounds.

The fighter snapped forward, the RPG falling from his hand. Then the plane crushed him beneath its wheels.

In the cockpit beside Rajah, Al Zaroor saw the fighter go down, then felt the thud of the plane running over the man's body.

For an instant, he could not grasp this. His people on the ground were dead — there was no one left to cover his escape. With a sudden terrible finality, he understood.

The American, he thought, and a prayer formed on his lips.

Anit turned to Brooke, stunned. Underhand, he tossed a cell phone to her. As she grasped it, he saw the glint of comprehension in her eyes. She pushed a button and began speaking rapidly in Hebrew.

She paused, listening, then put away the phone. She looked back at Brooke, her voice strained. "It won't reach Tel Aviv. But when one of our pilots shoots it down —"

"No choice," he answered swiftly. "We needed Al Zaroor to take the bomb away from Hezbollah. Pray it falls to earth intact."

The arc of headlights cut him short, coming toward them in the darkness like the eyes of giant insects. Hezbollah, Brooke knew — survivors of the first suicide bomb. He threw the rifle near Khazei's body.

The jeeps stopped beside the wreckage. Emerging, the fighters appeared as dark outlines in the dwindling light.

One walked forward, becoming a compact, bearded man Brooke had not seen before. The man stopped, gazing at the pyre that had consumed Nidal, then at Khazei lying on the ground. Standing, Brooke saw tears in his eyes.

Khazei's body lay between them. "They're all dead," Brooke told the fighter. "The plane escaped."

A flash of anger crossed the man's face, leaving a frightening blankness in his eyes. He raised his rifle, aiming at Brooke. Then he saw Anit behind him.

The rifle moved, as if drawn toward Anit of its own volition. Tightly, Brooke said, "Hussein Nouri guaranteed our safety. Before you do this, ask his consent."

The man froze. He stepped back two paces, the others gathering around him, then took out a cell phone. As he spoke, Brooke turned to Anit.

She gazed into his face. He could read her thoughts. They had achieved what they wanted; their last minutes, if it came to that, would end like this. Neither could find words.

Still gripping his rifle, the man walked toward them. Facing him, Brooke stepped in front of Anit.

The fighter's eyes were cold now, his face grim. In a flat tone, he said, "Nouri offers you a parting gift, a jeep. He suggests that you drive it to Beirut, and that you never come to Lebanon again."

Brooke glanced at Anit. Transfixed, she was staring at the sky. Looking up, he saw an orange flame in the distance, the Cessna exploding, marking the death of Amer Al Zaroor and the failure of his mission. When Brooke turned to her again, Anit's eyes were closed.

"Shalom aleichem," Brooke told the fighter in Arabic. Peace be with you.

THIRTEEN

On the tenth anniversary of September 11, Brooke and Anit ate dinner on an outdoor patio overlooking the Corniche.

As they did, the world absorbed the salvation of Tel Aviv in a barrage of words and images. The Israeli prime minister praised his country's air defenses, and the strike force that had retrieved the bomb and two charred bodies from the wreckage. The American president stressed the close cooperation of the CIA and the Mossad. Ordinary Israelis expressed gratitude and defiance, while Americans returned to their homes, some in tears. Political leaders in both countries proclaimed a great defeat for al Qaeda.

Brooke and Anit were, as they wished, invisible. They had spent the day debriefing their agencies as their governments erased their role. Both were exhausted; both were acutely aware of the date. And yet, despite that and all that had happened to them, they could feel the resonance of what they had achieved — Tel Aviv had been spared a nuclear holocaust, and they were still alive. And so, though spent, they shared lamb, couscous, and a chilled bottle of Chardonnay.

The restaurant, Al Dirwandi, had been a favorite of Brooke's. From their table above the Mediterranean they could see the palm trees, the glittering lights of clubs and hotels, lovers idling along the broad pathway at the water's edge. The night was warm and breezy and, for the moment, safe. Bashir Jameel had stationed his people at the door, a parting gift to Adam Chase on the last evening he would ever spend in Lebanon.

The reddened gash ran across Anit's bruised cheekbone. Touching it absentmindedly, she surveyed the couples all around them — confident men and attractive women, eating and drinking and toasting each other in the afterglow of a historic tragedy averted. At length, she said, "This is surreal, isn't it?"

"Which part?"

"All of it. Being with you. Where we were only hours ago. *Who* we were, and what we did. Half of me is Laura Reynolds, and still in the Bekaa Valley. The other half can barely believe I was there. And now we're sitting here, watching Lebanese try to go about their lives."

Brooke sipped his wine. "For many of these people, tragedy is five feet — or five minutes — away. Denial is their only defense even now. Last night we helped preserve their dream state."

"But what we did and saw never really occurred, did it? We were never in the Bekaa, it seems. The PLO never helped us. And Hezbollah did nothing at all."

Brooke gazed at the wooden elephant Anit had placed between them. "Better for everyone, the argument goes. So this became a triumph for your air defenses, pure and simple. That will save Hezbollah some face, and allow Israelis to sleep a little better. The truth would be too hard, and too complex, to live with."

Anit gave him a guarded look. "That fighter you shot —" she began, then asked, "You thought Hezbollah would take the bomb, didn't you? And then murder the only witnesses — us."

Brooke inhaled. "I don't know. Hussein Nouri let us go. Perhaps we could have trusted him. If so, I killed a man I didn't know, for nothing."

"But you also assured the death of Al Zaroor." Absently, Anit brushed the hair back from her face. "How many others did we kill, or cause to die, and how many lies did we tell? Yet the world keeps on spinning as before. Which is the point of what we do, isn't it."

Brooke gazed at the Mediterranean. "Do you know what makes this even harder to absorb? That I did all that with you — Anit Rahal. And that we're sitting together, ourselves again, trying to make sense of what we've been through."

"Can you?"

"Some of it. No matter what else I accomplish in this job, nothing could match staving off a nuclear 9/11." He paused, trying to find words that captured a still elusive thought. "Then there's something I haven't felt since I saw al Qaeda take down the World Trade Center. The sense that I own my life again, and can do with it what I choose."

She contemplated him across the table. "All I know is that I'm very glad you survived. Beyond that, I feel lost. When I'm not too numb to feel anything." She looked away. "Five years ago, I became someone else. Who am I now, I wonder."

"The person who helped save Tel Aviv.

That no one else knows doesn't make it less so." Brooke hesitated, searching for a way to retrieve the woman he had loved from all that scarred her. Softly, he said, "I know very well what your life has become. But it's not too late to change course. In fact, due to my brilliance, you'll have to."

She tilted her head. "Meaning?"

"That I've completely blown your cover — with Hezbollah, al Qaeda, and the Iranians. As a field agent, you can't be Laura Reynolds, or even Anit Rahal. Your career as a spy is over."

She looked at him steadily. "I've considered that. It's also pretty much true of you, unless you try espionage in China. So where does that leave you?"

To his surprise, Brooke felt his throat constrict, then spoke on impulse. "It's way too soon to answer that, and we're too disoriented to try. But I believe that some things happen for a reason. Ten years ago I lost you. In the last few days I found you again, under the most unimaginable circumstances, and then we saved each other's life. Tonight, looking at you, I remember the life I wanted before."

Her eyes clouded. "We're different now."

"Yes. We know too much. But that shouldn't make it impossible to live much as others do — far less innocent, perhaps, but far happier than we've been."

Anit traced the rim of her wineglass. "What would that even look like, I wonder."

"So many questions, Anit — I'm just making this up as I go. But maybe we could teach in a quieter corner of the world."

She raised her eyebrows. "Teach espionage, you mean?"

"For you, archaeology — after all, Laura Reynolds has a Ph.D. I assume some genius in the Mossad can find a way of transferring her credits to Anit Rahal." He paused, then ventured, "Maybe we can't talk about everything we know. But at least we can say in public what we actually believe — about Lebanon, the Palestinians, and our governments' mistakes. Too many Americans and Israelis like their enemies one-dimensional. You and I know how complicated the world is, and how little slogans have to do with reality."

Anit sipped her wine. "It all sounds very high-minded."

Was there hope for this? Brooke wondered. With an airiness he did not feel, he answered, "Oh, I'm sure we can remember to have fun. But it'll take a little more time to work out all the details. Fortunately, I've booked two first-class tickets to Paris, one in the name of Laura Reynolds. The flight doesn't leave until 2:00 A.M., so you've got the next four hours to decide. You've already got a passport."

For a long time, Anit simply stared at him. "Just leave with you, like that?"

"Just like that. By whatever name, I've never seen a woman more in need of a vacation. Screw the Mossad if they complain. But for you they might all be dead."

"And after Paris?" Anit asked softly. "I'm Israeli, remember? And irreversibly, irretrievably, irrevocably Jewish."

Despite himself, Brooke felt a spark of hope. "Name your terms, Anit. We can split time between countries. Our kids can be Jewish, if you want. I'll even convert, for Christsakes. Just spare me the knife, okay?"

Anit fought to repress a smile and failed. "So Anit Rahal can still do that," Brooke said. "Maybe she can even laugh."

Her smile lingered for a moment, and then her eyes became haunted again. "I don't know yet. She's been in a deep freeze for so long."

Brooke took her hand. "Not for one memorable hour at the Palmyra, a mere three nights ago. I was involved, as you'll recall, and thought we showed a certain promise. We might try it again in Paris."

Anit shook her head in feigned astonishment. "After all this, Brooke Chandler, it's frightening how little you've changed." She filled her glass again, then his. "All right," she told him. "At least we can discuss it."

A shadow crossed his mind, the memory of a friend. Brooke raised his glass to hers. "To Ben," he said, "and to the life he should have lived."

Anit touched his glass, looking into his face as if she never wanted to look away. "To Ben," she answered softly. "Perhaps, this time, you and I should take what we've been given."

AFTERWORD AND ACKNOWLEDGMENTS

The Devil's Light required me to explore several challenging topics, including intelligence, counterterrorism, nuclear proliferation, espionage, the complexities of Lebanon, and the nature of al Qaeda and Hezbollah. This book is also intended to be an authentic account of what is possible in the realm of nuclear terrorism. So I'm all the more indebted to those who helped me. The credit for depth and accuracy is theirs; any errors of fact or interpretation are mine alone.

At the outset, readers should know that I finished my research in June 2009 and the writing in January 2010. In the intervening fifteen months before publication, we had seen extensive reportage on the complex situation in Pakistan, including the Wikileaks disclosures of previously unpublished information. Thus this novel did not incorporate or reflect these journalistic developments or current events, which I noted only by adding a few references in the proofreading process. Instead, the information and analysis in this novel reflected many months of prior research, travel, and interviews, many of them conducted in confidence. As for the story itself, it prefigures rather than reflects information that became public after June 2009. In short, this novel was not, as they say, "ripped from the headlines."

First, I profited from the advice of numerous members of the intelligence and defense communities. For reasons of confidentiality, I'm unable to thank by name several persons still engaged in this work. To coin a phrase, "You know who you are," and therefore know how appreciative I am.

That said, I received extremely helpful advice from past and present members of the CIA: former (then current) deputy director Steve Kappes; former field agent André Le Gallo; George Little and Marie Harf, spokespeople for the agency; Rolf Mowatt-Larssen, former chief of the Counter Terrorism Center; John McLaughlin, former deputy and acting director; and former field agent Martha Sutherland. Thanks also to current director Leon Panetta for his courtesy during my visit. I also read George Tenet's *At the Center of the*

Storm, Tim Weiner's *Legacy of Ashes,* and *Spycraft,* by Robert Wallace and H. Keith Melton.

Other experts helped me think through counterterrorism, and the potential actions of al Qaeda and Hezbollah: Peter Bergen, Dan Byman, my dear friend and former secretary of defense William Cohen, Stephen Flynn, Robert Galucci, Martin Indyk, John Lauder, Brendan Melley, Bilal Saab, Danny Sebright, and Mike Taylor.

I particularly want to mention two former field agents whose advice enabled me to create Brooke Chandler and Amer Al Zaroor, and get the bomb from Pakistan to Lebanon. First, there is Howard Hart. It's impossible to summarize Howard's extraordinary career, but this will impart a sense of it — Howard Hart is the most decorated man in the history of the CIA, and was named by the agency as one of the fifty most important figures in its first fifty years. Not only did Howard give me countless hours of his time, but he allowed me to borrow aspects of his life and persona to create Carter Grey. Though Howard invited me to do my worst, it proved to be impossible. I can only hope that he finds Carter acceptable, and that my description of Grey's redoubt in the Blue Ridge Mountains does some justice to the home graced by Howard and his wife, Jean.

Then there's Bob Baer, the only field agent ever played by George Clooney (*Syriana*). Bob's career over two decades in the field was remarkable and varied. Like Howard, Bob gave generously of his time as we moved a nuclear weapon across the Middle East. In addition, Bob is a fine writer whose sense of narrative and incident enriched the story I was crafting. All in all, his thoughts are woven into the tapestry of my novel.

Finally, Miri Eisen, formerly of military intelligence for the Israeli Defense Force, was tireless in educating me on fieldwork, as well as the possible Israeli perspective on the events portrayed in this novel. I'm grateful beyond words for her advice, patience, and good humor.

A special subset of this work involves the history, operations, and aspirations of al Qaeda, Hezbollah, the Taliban, Lashkar-e-Taiba, and Fatah al-Islam. All the people named above helped me in this area. But I owe special thanks to two former national security advisors, Tony Lake and Sandy Berger, and to Bruce Riedel, widely considered our leading expert on al Qaeda. My understanding was also enriched by reading Bruce Riedel's *The Search for Al Qaeda*.

Critically, I needed help with respect to homeland security and air defenses. Many thanks to General John Campbell, General Maria Owens, and General Bruce Wright, with my special appreciation to General Joe Ralston.

The threats of nuclear proliferation and loose nuclear weapons are the most important, and often least discussed, threats faced by the civilized world. For their expert help in this area, I'm grateful to Dr. Graham Allison, Dr. Matthew Bunn, Charles Curtis, and Scott Miller.

Lebanon is fascinating, beautiful, historic, heartbreaking, and filled with diverse and often wonderful people. My time there was one of the richest experiences of my recent life. Through my friend David Lewis, I was able to meet a number of people who helped me to better understand it. My thanks go to our generous host, Gabriel Abboud; Kassem Aina, head of the PLO at Sabra and Shatilah; Khalid Aref, leader of the PLO in Lebanon; general and former president Michele Aoun; Timur Goksel, formerly of the United Nations; the late grand ayatollah Sayyed Fadlullah, spiritual leader of Shia Islam; Walid Jumblatt, leader of the Druze; Osama Hamdan, spokesman for Hamas; Dr. Cherie Lenzen, public affairs offi-

cer for the American embassy; Ibrahim
Mousawi, spokesman for Hezbollah; journalists Nick Blanford, Ben Gilbert, Nich-
olas Noe, and Hikmat Sharif; and Rawan
Hashem, our guide and translator. I also
profited by reading *Hezbollah* by Hala Jaber,
Hezbollah: A Short History by Augustus Richard Norton, and *A History of Modern Lebanon* by Fawwaz Traboulsi.

Others generously filled in gaps. In addition to Cherie Lenzen, Dr. Joan Breton
Connelly and Dr. Barbara Porter gave me
some of the rudiments of archaeology.
Along with many others, legendary journalist Seymour Hersh helped me assess the
current situation in Pakistan. Eugene Dickey
mapped the route of the bomb on Google
Earth. And our great friends Mitzi Pratt and
Flip Scipio helped me re-create Greenwich
Village.

Naming characters is important. For the
names of Brooke Kenyon Chandler and his
alter ego, Adam Chase, I'm grateful to my
three wonderful sons: Brooke North Patterson, Adam Chandler Patterson, and Chase
Kenyon Patterson.

As always, I received terrific help from my
friend and former editor, John Sterling; my
agent Fred Hill; my assistant and day-to-
day critic, Alison Porter Thomas; my new

editor at Scribner, Colin Harrison; my publisher, Susan Moldow; and my wife, Nancy Clair. Not only did Nancy read each chapter as I wrote it, but she shared my travels to Lebanon, tirelessly helping with research and transcription. All of them helped make this a better book.

Finally, there's David Lewis. Never was a dedication more humbly given or richly deserved. The knowledge that David has gathered as a journalist, news producer, and documentary filmmaker is extraordinary. David introduced me to key experts in counterterrorism, nuclear proliferation, and intelligence. He suggested rich new avenues to explore. And, most remarkably, he organized a trip to Lebanon, including immersion in Beirut and the Bekaa Valley, that for the purpose of this novel was indispensable. Without David's advice and generosity, *The Devil's Light* would not exist.

ABOUT THE AUTHOR

Richard North Patterson is the author of *Degree of Guilt, Protect and Defend, Exile,* and fifteen other bestselling and critically acclaimed novels. Formerly a trial lawyer, he was the SEC liaison to the Watergate special prosecutor and has served on the boards of several Washington advocacy groups. He lives in Martha's Vineyard, Cabo San Lucas, and San Francisco with his wife, Dr. Nancy Clair.